DECEMBER RAIN

Tim Holland

Cactus Mystery Press
an imprint of Blue Fortune Enterprises LLC

For information contact :
Blue Fortune Enterprises, LLC
Cactus Mystery Press
P.O. Box 554
Yorktown, VA 23690
http://blue-fortune.com

Cover design by BFE, LLC

ISBN: 978-1-961548-06-0
First Edition: February 2024

The Novels Of Tim Holland

Featuring Sidney Lake and Tillie James:
The Rising Tide
The Murder Of Amos Dunn
Deception
December Rain

Featuring Tony Carenza:
What the Mirror Doesn't See

Praise for the Sidney Lake series:

"I loved all the interesting people and places. Holland's vivid descriptions make you feel like you're right there in the scene, watching firsthand as the mystery unfolds." Taylor Jones, The Review Team of Jones and Murphy.

"Holland's series is worth a major nationwide publicity barrage. It's THAT good and you'll enjoy it. *Deception* does not require reading the earlier… volumes to be appreciated." Kale on Books.

The Rising Tide

"*The Rising Tide* is both an intriguing and a treatise on human behavior. Holland's character development is superb, creating a host of interesting characters, from down to earth local fishermen—who don't need forensics, only the knowledge of the tides, to know this accident was murder—to charming, if somewhat clueless graduate students, to interfering busybodies eager for any snippet of gossip they can spread to willing ears." Regan Murphy, The Review Team of Jones and Murphy.

"You may want to pick up this really good mystery set in the Lowcountry. I really enjoyed it." Ellen C. Priest – Editor/publisher, Summerville, South Carolina *Journal Scene.*

The Murder of Amos Dunn

"Tim Holland developed *The Murder of Amos Dunn*, set in the Lowcountry of South Carolina, where Gullah, a Creole language, is still spoken. Retired professor Sidney Lake and his academic friend, Hattie Ryan, try to put what little clues there are involving the death of a beloved shopkeeper, Amos Dunn. Sam Cashman, a Gullah-speaking policeman, becomes a detective with the chore of finding the murderer in a no-win situation with his police chief.

This is a great read and my favorite mystery for 2020." Kale on Books.

Deception

"I rate Deception 4 out of 4 stars. The book was an engaging, entertaining, enlightening, and intriguing one. It is one of the best mystery novels I have read. And it truly lived up to its title, *Deception*. I recommend this to book lovers and mature readers, especially those interested in the crime and mystery genre." Ziggy, Official Reviewer for The Online Book Club.

December Rain

"It's (*December Rain*) very good and the history background makes it a standout." Mary Skinner, former director of English program at Oceanside School System, Oceanside, New York.

Praise for Tony Carenza mysteries:

What the Mirror Doesn't See

"*What the Mirror Doesn't See* by Tim Holland is the story of a man trying to do the right thing in a world where that is not always appreciated. Or even helpful to your career. Jim Fairmont and Ed Campbell are concerned that something illegal is going on [in the international department] that might hurt the [reputation and financial stability] of their bank. The two of them begin to investigate, uncovering much more than either of them bargained for, especially when they find out that the bank might use the two of them as fall guys should any bad publicity touch the bank. Holland's background in international banking is clearly evident as the story unfolds, weaving mystery and suspense [full] of excellent character development and a solid plot, to create a tale of high-finance, intrigue, and two honest men who only want to do the right thing, no matter the cost. I found it educational, entertaining, and hard to put down." Regan Murphy, The Review Team of Jones and Murphy.

Acknowledgements

December Rain is a work of fiction. A good number of the characters and events are inspired by historical figures and actual happenings while others are entirely my creation. Apart from the actual historical figures, any resemblance between the fictional characters and actual people, living or dead, is purely coincidental.

December Rain is the fourth novel in the Sidney Lake lowcountry mystery series. While all my novels contain historical elements, this one, beginning in 1718, is the most ambitious. For those who would like to know what I used for resource documentation, I've included the names of the books in a resource list at the end of the book. All the volumes are part of my personal library but can be found in most public libraries and are readily available.

For those who have read any of my previous novels in the Sidney Lake series, as well as the beginning of a new series featuring Tony Carenza, *What The Mirror Doesn't See*, you will note a new publisher for *December Rain*, Blue Fortune Enterprises. I am greatly indebted to Narielle Living and her team at Blue Fortune after the trip, stumble, and bad fall taken by my previous publisher.

December Rain has had a good deal of other help along the way. The Silver Quill Writers critique group (Peter Stipe, Susan Williamson, Elizabeth Brown, Caterina Novelliere, and Bob Archibald) has poured over every page with critical help and encouragement every step of the way. My first full length readers of Mary and Jim Skinner lent their many years of English literature and history teaching to help fine tune many of the critical areas of the novel. Many thanks to them all.

To the many readers of my series who have come up to me at literary events and expressed how much they have enjoyed my novels, I'm sure you're going to love *December Rain*, and I thank you on behalf of Sidney and Tillie.

Tim Holland

Dedication

Dr. Boyd A. Litzinger, Jr.
of St. Bonaventure University whose advice of "
Subject matter, matters" is with me in everything I write.

ONE

1718

The Box

They darkened their light as the small cargo boat known as a *shallop* eased up the Ashley River. The shoreline closed upon them from both sides as the river narrowed. The single sail had come down earlier, and the oars were now extended. Darkness hung all around. The December night air and a cold light rain chilled them. Ignatius Pell sat in the rear of the thirty-foot craft while Thomas Nichols slowly and quietly pulled at the oars.

The two men did not speak, knowing the sound of their voices would travel far in the cold, damp night air.

The rowing had an assist from the incoming tide and helped them travel a good way up the Ashley before the downward flow of fresh water would begin to take over. Pell had made the trip before to reach the market town of Fort Dorchester, where he sold goods captured from commercial vessels.

The boat in which they travelled belonged to the Charles Town merchant, Richard Tookerman, who served as the primary contact for selling some of the valuables Stede Bonnet had liberated from their owners, but Tookerman had his own troubles after having recently been arrested for receiving goods from a variety of questionable sources. Although the charge didn't stick, he thought it best to distance himself from anything to do with Bonnet.

They were halfway up the Ashley when the first words were spoken. "Do you know this man, Joshua Bailey?" Nichols whispered.

"No. I have a good description, but we never met. It's said he has the largest warehouse in Fort Dorchester. He buys direct from Tookerman."

"How will we know him?"

"His slave, Jamaica, will meet us at the wharf."

A short while later, where the river narrowed, Pell whispered, "Extra quiet now. Plantations are being set up along this part of the river. The main houses are set back, but the slave quarters could be nearby. Dawn will be with us in an hour." The rain had stopped, and the moon and stars had begun to appear, enabling him to gauge the hour.

A quarter of an hour went by, and Nichols could feel the flow of water change. The incoming tide had been lost and the fresh-water flow of the Ashley could be felt in full. Pell also noticed the change.

A gust of wind grabbed hold of a flap of the canvas covering their cargo of stolen goods that filled the space behind Nichols. He heard the sound in the quiet darkness and missed his stroke, the right oar making a splash in the water. He stopped rowing. The two men listened. Pell maneuvered the tiller to keep the boat heading up stream against the current. They heard nothing. Saw no light.

"Keep going," Pell said. "Another fifteen minutes or so."

A cloud covered the moon, and Nichols pulled harder in the darkness. His time on the *Royal James* with Stede Bonnet had been his first sailing with a pirate crew. He owed his life to Pell, who swore to the judge and jury Nichols took no part in the attack on Colonel Rhett's forces at Cape Fear and had no experience in pirating.

As the cloud cleared, the moon appeared above them, shining on the floor of the craft and a sparkle reflected from the brass lock of the large chest that sat at Pell's feet. "Any idea what's in that?" Nichols said while indicating the chest with a nod.

"No. We just give it to Bailey. In person."

"Could be gold."

"The chest is from Captain Bonnet not Mister Tookerman. Bonnet never made much gold from pirating that I ever seen. Was with 'im not quite a year. Had money from Barbados when he was a planter. He bought his ship. Didn't steal it like everyone else. Paid all his seamen wages; we didn't share in what he took. Blackbeard and Vane didn't like 'im or trust 'im. Thought he was just playin' at bein' a pirate. Always hidin' away in his quarters readin' books. Angry at somethin' or someone."

Pell moved the tiller to guide the boat into the center of the river. The turns were increasing, and he needed to concentrate to avoid running aground. It had been a cold December rain, the kind that did not melt the snow and ice but made it as hard as glass. In another week or two, the Ashley would stop its flow and freeze to a trickle.

Five more minutes passed. Pell whispered, "It's up ahead. I know that next turn. The wharf is starboard. Go easy now."

Nichols pulled slow but hard, with elongated strokes. Pell peered into the distance. The first glimmer of sunlight would be upon them soon. He wanted the shallop empty by then.

He caught a glimpse of the dock and saw something move. Pell continued to guide the boat with his left hand on the tiller but reached for the knife in his belt with his right. Nichols, seeing Pell's movement, whispered, "Friend or foe?"

"We'll know soon enough. Go easy now."

As the boat came near the dock, a tall Black man came forward. "Mister Pell?"

"Aye. Jamaica?"

"Yes, sir. Mr. Bailey sends his compliments. A line?"

Nichols gave a sigh of relief. Turned in his seat and reached for the mooring line coiled on the floor behind him. As he tossed the rope to Jamaica, he locked eyes with the slave but said nothing.

Jamaica grabbed the line as it came at him and secured the front of the boat to the dock. Pell shifted position and tossed another line as soon as Jamaica was ready.

"Where's Mister Bailey?"

"At the warehouse. He be here on my signal."

"Then you signal 'im. No cargo goes ashore 'till I see 'im."

"Yes, sir." Jamaica turned and quickly walked back and off the wharf. It was a strong, confident walk. Shoulders held back and head held high.

Pell looked after him and took note of the man's demeanor. The dawn light was near, as the outline of the tabby walls of Fort Dorchester began to appear in the distance.

Joshua Bailey waited nearby and watched. Jamaica walked no more than twenty paces on the path toward the Fort when he stopped, and Bailey stepped out from behind the shrubbery. Even wearing a hat, he stood almost a foot shorter than the slave.

Pell eyed Bailey as he came closer, and the light continued to increase. The man at Jamaica's side stood five foot six, heavy set with a full gray beard. It was the description Richard Tookerman had given him. "Good day, Mister Bailey."

"You are Pell?" Bailey challenged.

"Aye."

"And your associate?"

"Thomas Nichols."

Nichols turned to Bailey with a small bow of his head. "Sir."

Bailey wasted no time. "Jamaica, bring the cart down and help them unload." The slave turned and started up the path. Turning back to Pell, the warehouseman narrowed his eyes and lowered his voice as he sternly asked, "You have the box?"

"Right here, sir," Pell replied, looking down at his feet. "And our fee?"

"You'll have it."

TWO

2018

The Palmer Library

Mrs. Cathcart ushered the children into the library as a light rain began to fall. She had five today, a manageable number, especially with a storm approaching. She didn't mind them as they were always a good, well-behaved group. "It looks like we made it just in time," she announced to the three girls and two boys gathered about her.

"My mom said it would rain this afternoon. That's why she made me wear these silly boots," observed eight-year-old Pam Bennett as she took off her coat. Her brother, Carter, two years older, gave her his usual *Oh please* look.

"Your mother was right." Mrs. Cathcart removed her coat as she spoke. "Now, everyone into the reading room."

The routine rarely changed.

The Palmer operated as a small subscription library. Founded in the early 1930s as a private institution—which could control access to the resources it contained—it remained unchanged until the mid-1970s when the county government became obliged to provide services, equally, to all its residents and established the Coastal Rivers County Regional Library. The Palmer and its collection of old books and documents survived by adjusting its mission and becoming a resource of the Historical Society, which took charge of the historically important volumes and maps. The subscription system remained in place but now helped fund the Society's research goals. Adults and children of all socio-economic backgrounds were welcome, although many of the older original members continued to grumble about government overreach.

The rain outside increased as the children headed into the room where they would spend the next few hours doing homework, reading, chatting, laughing, and being their usual inquisitive selves. The Palmer Library did not run an after-school daycare center. However, for library volunteers with children attending the nearby grade school, the library's board encouraged them to have their children spend the afternoon while waiting to be picked up.

Today, they were not there long before the sky darkened even more and rain began to pound against the sides of the building while strong, blustery winds rattled its windows.

The Palmer was housed in an old southern mansion built in 1821. A local attorney had been its owner until the Civil War, when the local Confederate commander and his staff took over. Toward the end of the war, the local Union Army commander then turned it into a hospital. The original library had lost many books, but a large core remained stored in the building's cellar.

The building changed hands many times with a relative of the original owner eventually acquiring it in the 1920s. He subsequently lost his life in World War II but in his will, Colonel Palmer stipulated that upon the death of his wife, their home was to become a library for the Town of Morgan, using what was left of the original book collection as a base.

"Hey Pam, let's go look at the old books in the back room," Carter suggested to his sister. "I'll bet it's spooky in there with all the rain and wind outside."

"Won't scare me."

"Didn't say it would. Come on." He grabbed his sister's hand and they headed for the Historical Documents Room at the back of the building.

Knowing that Mrs. Cathcart might object to their going in unaccompanied, Carter gave a quick look over his shoulder toward the librarian's desk. She wasn't there.

Some of the books on the shelves were more than 200 years old and were protected behind glass doors. Off to one side sat a long wooden reference table with two lamps equally distanced upon it. The lamp closest to the door gave off its light onto the table; the other wasn't lit. On another wall, a pair of wooden doors, closed and locked, provided an exit to the wraparound porch.

Pam looked around the dimly lit room as they entered. "Those books look old and dirty."

"Yeah, but they're supposed to look that way. That's how you know they're old."

Carter led the way as they stepped toward the large table and the eight chairs, four on each side. Another, smaller table with two chairs sat against the wall on the other side of the room. It had some books stacked on it as though someone had been at work there. Next to the double doors to the porch were two small windows, one on each side, which would normally give a small bit of natural light. The storm and the overhang of the porch roof prevented that from happening today, and the only light they had to see by came from the lamp on the large table.

A flash of lightning shot an eerie glow across the room, startling both of them.

"Oh, wow." Pam moved closer to her brother and grabbed the back of his shirt.

Then the thunder roared, and a gust of wind slammed against the windows and porch doors.

Pam whispered, "Maybe we should go back to the other room."

"No, it'll be okay. It's just a storm. Be gone in a bit."

The doors and windows rattled again in the wind.

They were halfway down the length of the table when they heard a voice behind the closed door at the entrance.

Carter grabbed his sister's hand. "Quick, let's hide." He dropped to the floor, pulling Pam down with him. They crawled under the table as the door opened.

"I believe this is where you'll find what you're looking for," said Mrs. Cathcart, as she opened the door and the light from the main room burst into the dimness of the history room.

Lightning flashed again, followed quickly by another blast of thunder.

Two men followed her into the room, and the taller man said, "Getting nasty out there. Guess this place has seen a lot of these storms."

"Oh, yes. The building dates all the way back to 1821."

He looked at the door and the woodwork around it and then at the built-in shelves filled with books. "Built them good back then." He ran his hand along the woodwork as he spoke.

"Now, you said Bailey, didn't you? Joshua Bailey." The librarian looked to her left and walked to the end of the large table. "Yes, this is where they are. Here, let me put this other lamp on for you."

As the room brightened, the two men came fully into it. They both wore business suits and ties.

Carter and Pam were under the center of the table and Carter put his finger to his lips to make sure Pam did not say a word.

More lightning flashed, and the thunder seemed to shake the building this time as it came with a sharp crack.

"That was close," said the shorter of the two men. "How long did you say this place has been here?"

Mrs. Cathcart merely smiled. "A long, long time."

Carter and Pam experienced the sharp *crack* as well and Pam almost let out a scream but Carter squeezed close to her and managed to stifle it.

One of the library volunteers appeared in the doorway and said, "Mrs. Cathcart, there's a call for you up front."

"Oh, I know who that is. Gentlemen, if you'll excuse me. I think you'll find what you are looking for on the second and third shelves here." She pointed to the area. "If you find something of interest and would like to join the library, let me know and I'll have you fill out a membership form at my desk."

"Yes, go ahead," said the tall man. "We'll be just fine."

"If you need me, I'll be at my desk up front," she said as she left the room.

The men waited until they could be sure she was out of sight and hearing before turning to the bookshelves she had indicated.

"Tell me again about Joshua Bailey." The smaller man spoke in a low tone.

"One of the original founders of Morgan. Goes back to before 1700. Had a few plantations between here and Charleston."

"And he had some kind of treasure?"

"Maybe. There's always been a local legend about a treasure box that an old pirate left with him, but nobody's ever been able to prove it."

From under the table, Carter Bennett heard the word *treasure* and immediately perked up. He signaled his sister to be very, very quiet.

The short man continued. "What makes you think there's something here in these books?"

"Because of a guy I do business with. He came across one of Bailey's books with some marks on the inside back cover and said they were part of a map."

"Seriously? We're here looking for a pirate treasure map?" The man shook his head in disbelief.

His companion saw the reaction and retorted, "Actually, I'm looking for a couple of things. You got something better to do in this storm? You're welcome to leave. I can do this by myself."

"No, no. I'm all right. I'll help."

Another quick lightning flash and immediate *crack* of thunder.

"Wow, that definitely hit nearby," the smaller man said.

The lights flickered, and Pam let out a small squeak. Carter put his hand over her mouth.

The man continued, "Better get moving. If we lose the lights, they'll shut the place down. I'll sit at the table, and you grab some books. Take a look at the inside covers, and if you see any markings, put them in a pile here." He placed his left hand on the table. "All the others put here." He specified a spot in front of him with his right hand.

"Is there something specific I should be looking for?"

"Anything you see with the word Bonnet. Also, a small flag drawing. Has a skull on it and a bone and a heart. That book I saw had it in a corner."

As the books were being removed, rain pounded the building, lightning flashed, and thunder clapped.

"Got one," said the man at the shelf.

"Let me see."

Another lightning flash with the thunder coming instantaneously.

The lights went out and the room went dark.

A book hit the floor.

"Shit!" someone said.

The legs of a chair scraped along the wood floor. It fell over with a loud *bang* as the seated man leapt from it.

Pam screamed.

THREE

2018
Pine View Retirement Village

Grace Bennett paced in front of her office window. Her morning had not started well. Another argument at breakfast with Mitchell. She had taken the job of program director at Pine View Retirement Village over Mitchell's objections. Now she had to decide what to do about her children, another distraction.

Mary Louise McBee sat in the right of the two chairs in front of her desk. "Do you think they're telling the truth?"

Grace stopped and looked out the window. Her blonde, shoulder length hair was already mussed from running her fingers through it. Walking to her desk, she turned and looked at Mary Louise. "I don't know. With eight- and ten-year-old's, the answer is always yes and no. They believe what they heard, but is it really what the people said? Mention the word treasure and their ears perk up, but the odds are they didn't hear a lot of what was said before that."

"But Grace, what if they're right? What if there is some sort of treasure at The Palmer Library that someone's planning to steal? Are you going to report it?"

Grace, now standing behind her desk, looked across the room and focused on a print of the Pine View Retirement Village and took a deep breath. "I suppose I have to." She checked her watch. "Mary Louise, I've got a meeting with the director in ten minutes. Nine-thirty. The residents program committee right after that, and the Andersons at ten-thirty. I really don't have time to deal with the police or anyone else this morning."

"You still have time. Call them and see if you can set up a meeting for this afternoon. That way we'll all have a chance to think this through before the police come."

Grace picked up the desk telephone handset and waved it as she spoke. "I could just kill those two." She dialed 9-1-1.

"You can't really blame them."

"Of course I can. Sitting under a table in the library and then not saying anything when those men sat down. What were they thinking?"

"They weren't thinking, Grace. They're children. They're always on the floor. They even sit on the floor in classrooms. I'm sure they never sit on a chair when watching television. Mine never did, and don't forget about that thunderstorm we had yesterday. So dark. I remember...."

A very monotone and rather dull woman's voice answered the phone and Grace held up her hand to Mary Louise as she answered. "I'm sorry to bother you, but I think I should report something my children overheard."

"Is this an emergency?"

"Oh, no, I'm just looking for some advice. It seems a bit silly and I'm not sure it's important." Grace sat down at her desk.

The voice on the phone softened. "Not to worry, we appreciate your calling. Could I have your name please?"

"Grace Bennett."

"And your address?"

"Fifteen Mulligan Court."

Grace answered robotically while thinking, *Why am I doing this? I will absolutely kill those kids this afternoon when I get home.* She continued responding to questions while Mary Louise made faces at her. They had become the best of friends. Mary Louise was the administrative assistant to the executive director of Pine View when Grace came on board as the program director, and there was an instant chemistry between them. Grace finished the interview and ended the call.

"What did they say?" Mary Louise couldn't contain herself and moved to the edge of her chair.

"They're going to have someone stop by this afternoon."

Two hours later, Grace rushed into the reception area outside her office, where an elderly couple sat quietly. "I'm so sorry. I didn't realize you were already here."

The man sitting in the straight-backed chair pulled and twisted his way out of it. "Oh no, no don't get up, I'm Grace Bennett, and you must be the Andersons."

"That's perfectly all right." He stood, took her hand, and formally introduced himself and his wife Gladys. Then, with a look of concern, he asked, "Is there something the matter?"

She was usually very good at keeping her professional face on when in public and Mr. Anderson's seeing through it surprised her.

"A personal matter, I'm afraid. An eight- and ten-year-old sticking their noses, or in this case their ears, where they shouldn't."

He looked puzzled and cocked his head slightly to the side.

"Let's go into the conference room so we can talk a bit." Grace motioned them to a room on the other side of the reception area and spoke as they walked. "I understand you have some concerns. The director asked me to speak with you about them. He's tied up with a conference call to Nashville, but he'll be available this afternoon if you still want to meet with him."

As they moved slowly into the room, Grace stepped to the side and held the door. They were both in their mid-eighties, and Gladys Anderson walked with a cane. As soon as they settled in the chairs of a large round table,

Grace's phone rang.

"Excuse me a moment." She got up from her chair to answer. "Grace Bennett... You're not serious?" Grace turned her back to the Andersons. "He's here now... but he wasn't supposed to come until after lunch... all right." Grace gave an audible sigh. "Can you keep him busy for five minutes? ...Thank you, Jen." She turned back to the Andersons and put down the phone. "Sorry again, this thing with my children seems to be getting out of hand."

"Are they boys or girls?" asked Mrs. Anderson.

"One of each, actually. Carter is ten and Pam is eight."

"Are they in some sort of trouble?"

"Not really. Well, I don't think they are. They overheard something at the Palmer Library yesterday. They shouldn't have been listening, naturally, and I felt I had to report it to the police this morning. The dispatcher said someone would stop by after lunch today, and they've shown up now."

"Oh, my goodness. What did they hear?" Mrs. Anderson had a sincere look of grandmotherly concern on her face.

Grace decided it would be best to give them the reason a policeman had come to Pine View, as his being here would be all over the community by noon. That way, at least someone would have the truth and the usual gossip and speculation might be muted. "They said they heard some men planning to sneak into the Palmer Library to steal something."

"Steal something from the library?"

"I couldn't ignore it when they told me at breakfast this morning, so I called the police when I came to work. He just showed up. If you don't mind, give me about fifteen minutes and I'll be right back with you."

Gladys reached over and touched Jim's arm, "Oh, that's alright. Family always comes first. Besides, we don't have to be anywhere, do we, Jim?"

Jim, who had been about to object, recognized he had been overruled and reluctantly agreed. "Yes, of course. We'll sit here and wait for you."

Grace said, "I'm so sorry. I'll be back as soon as I can."

She rushed out the door. At the reception counter stood a man with dark hair and wearing a business suit. The receptionist, seeing her, said, "Here she is now."

The man turned to Grace. "Mrs. Bennett, I'm Detective Knott of the Morgan Police Department." He extended his hand, which she immediately took.

"Detective, I'm sorry you had to come out like this. I'm sure it's nothing but when they mentioned stealing, I thought I had to do something."

"Don't apologize, ma'am. Is there someplace we could talk quietly?"

A surprised Grace replied, "Sure. My office is right over here." She walked ahead of him.

After entering the room, Knott quietly closed the door behind them. "Hope you don't mind. The news will get around soon enough." He moved over to the chair in front of her desk. "Please, sit down."

Grace, a bit surprised, did as she was told.

"Mrs. Bennett, the reason we're taking the matter so seriously is that there was a break in at the Palmer Library last night after the storm."

A shocked Grace said, "You're not serious."

"Yes, I am. If you could tell me exactly what your children heard, it would be very helpful."

"I... I thought they were making it up. Not really making it up but imagined they heard innocent talk. They said it was a treasure of some sort. Although I can't imagine what treasure could be at Palmer. It's not a very big place, and it's not as though they have some art collection hidden away somewhere. The two of them were sitting under a table in the back room." She could see the look on Detective Knott's face. "Yes, I know. What were they doing under the table? Heaven knows, probably trying to hide from the storm. They were supposed to be reading or something but then two men sat down with some books and began to whisper."

"There were two of them? And your children overheard the men say they planned to steal from the library? Did they say what?"

"That's the fuzzy part. They have different versions. The only thing they seem to agree on is something about *treasure* and a man wearing a hat. Oh, yes, and a flag with a heart on it."

"A heart, hmmm. I can understand why your children's ears perked up—so have mine."

"I'm sure you can see why I didn't take them too seriously when I first heard their story. I mean, why wouldn't the men join the library and borrow the books like everyone else? The membership is only twenty-five dollars a year."

"Understandable though, as the books or documents were in the reference area and cannot be removed, and I'm sure they didn't want to leave their names and addresses. One point of clarification—is there more than one table in the reference room?"

"I believe there are two. I know there's a large table that will sit eight—it's where we have meetings sometimes—and another one against the wall. It's really a desk, and it's opposite the double doors leading outside. The room itself is the farthest one toward the back of the building and also has a small restroom and a utility room attached to it. And your point about registering is well taken. The idea of someone actually stealing from the Palmer is not something we consider, unfortunately. If something of value is there, I'm pretty sure no one involved with the library knows about it."

Grace and Detective Knott continued to go over Pam and Carter's story for another five minutes, after which he left his card and asked her to give him a call if her children remembered anything else.

Mary Louise came barging in within thirty seconds of Detective Knott vacating his chair. "What did he say?"

"Who?"

"The policeman, who else?"

"It looks like the Palmer Library mystery is going to be all over the place anyway. Sit for a minute and I'll tell you about my first ever interrogation by a policeman."

"What Palmer mystery and interrogation?" inquired Haskell Davidson, who stopped at the open door to Grace's office. "Is there a mystery of some sort at Palmer? I'm on the board over there, and I don't know of a mystery."

Oh, boy, just what I need, the boss getting involved, Grace thought. "Let's all sit down for a moment and I'll give you a blow-by-blow account of me and Detective Knott, at least I think that's his name. I have his card here somewhere." She rummaged around her desk as Mary Louise and Haskell took the chairs in front of her. "Ah, here it is, Detective Wilson Knott. Very nice fellow, extremely polite."

"So, what is this about a Palmer mystery?" Haskell shifted to get comfortable in the chair.

Seeing Haskell get comfortable, she realized she wasn't going anywhere. "Mystery may not be the best word but then… maybe? I told Detective Knott everything I know. Mary Louise has heard some of this already, but the crux of everything is that Pam and Carter were under the table in the reference room at the library, and yes, Haskell, it may sound weird but that's where they were. Anyway, they overheard two men apparently planning to steal from the library."

"Okay," said Mary Louise in her usual enthusiastic manner, "tell us what happened with Knott."

Grace began, "Let me go back a bit. First, for your benefit Haskell, as I know you've only been here a short while, Pam and Carter attend school within a short distance of the Palmer Library, and when they don't have after-school activities or the carpool doesn't work out, one or both will go to Palmer and wait for me. I leave here at four, pick up whoever is there, and head for home. Mitchell is a dinner at six person—actually he prefers five forty-five—and expects everyone to be there."

Haskell nodded, indicating he thought it seemed a reasonable expectation for a husband.

Grace went on to relate the story of Pam and Carter under the table during the storm.

Haskell listened quietly and leaned forward in his chair as she finished. "Did they say what they were looking for?"

"That's what Knott asked. The rain was pounding on the roof pretty hard at this point, but Pam said she heard them referring to pages with a heart on them, although Carter said it was a bone, but didn't know what that meant. Carter said it had something to do with the man's hat. It was pretty dark in there, especially with the storm, and Pam became frightened so their attention was diverted some of the time. However, Carter said he specifically remembered one of the men saying that the only way they were going to really study the books would be to steal them from the library. At that point, there was a fierce crack of lightning and thunder, and the lights blinked and went out. The two men quickly put back the books and left the room as Mrs. Cathcart called out to the children. She, of course, found them crawling out from under the table. Then the lights came on and the men were nowhere to be seen."

"You told all of this to Detective Knott?" asked Haskell.

"Yes, and that's when he said apparently someone tried to break into the Palmer Library last night."

"I'd love to know more about this. If you don't mind? I have a meeting over there this afternoon, and I'd like to be aware of what's happening."

"There isn't much more for me to say. I've told you everything."

As Grace spoke, the receptionist came to her still open door, waved to her, and pointed to the reception room. The woman mouthed something, but Grace didn't understand. And then it came to her. "Oh, my God. The Andersons."

FOUR

2018
A Conflict At Dinner

"Anything more on that imaginary robbery at Palmer?" Asking Grace for an update, Mitchell Bennett didn't look up from the local afternoon newspaper he had begun reading at the kitchen table after dinner. She was surprised he even remembered what happened. From the very mention of the library incident when she called him yesterday after her interview with Detective Knott, he downplayed the idea of a robbery and acted completely disinterested, as he usually did when it involved anything remotely having to do with her job. Everything seemed to irritate him lately.

"It's not imaginary. Why do you think it's imaginary? Aside from messing up my whole day, it looks like Carter, Pam, and Mrs. Cathcart are the only ones capable of identifying the men."

Mitchell moved the newspaper away from his face and looked at her accusingly. "You should never have told the police. If they wanted to know something, it's up to them to ask the question. You don't voluntarily present yourself to the police as a witness to anything, unless you know they're looking for information. And you certainly don't put your children in harm's way.

Two kids with overzealous imaginations sitting under the table at Palmer in the middle of a thunderstorm. Grace, you're making something out of nothing. That door in the back of the library couldn't keep the neighborhood cat out. It probably weakened during the storm, and Mrs. Cathcart imagined it was tampered with because of the kid's story."

"You're wrong about that. Mrs. Cathcart didn't know about 'the kids' story' when she reported the attempted break-in, because I hadn't called the police yet. And besides, Detective Knott did call me later this afternoon to see if Carter and Pam remembered anything they hadn't already mentioned. I told him they hadn't."

"And nothing else? It's all a lot of nonsense." He gave the newspaper a shake and put it back in front of him, as he said with a sense of satisfaction that irritated her, "I hope there are a lot more important things for the police to be concerned with than people stealing a worthless book or two."

It wasn't that she wanted their story to be true. Grace didn't want Pam and Carter to be involved with anything criminal, but she would dearly love to prove him wrong. Mitchell had a reputation for claiming to be right about everything, or at least he believed he was.

"I resent your saying we did something wrong here. Pam and Carter were just being normal children. They're curious. They're supposed to be. They heard something exciting. It was an adventure. There's nothing wrong with that."

As she spoke, he continued reading the newspaper and shut her out. His putting something between them had become common lately. He never liked her taking the position at Pine View, and he wouldn't explain why. No matter how often she asked, a response never came. Grace knew Mitchell liked the role of the dominant person in the household. Once she had accused him of trying to recreate his childhood home, with his mother always catering to his father. It was her job. Her only job. This being the twenty-first century, it wasn't going to be Grace's only job.

He finally commented from behind the paper. "This is ridiculous. There has been no robbery. Nothing is missing, and no evidence of anything missing. All you people have too much time on your hands, and you shouldn't be bothering the police. They have bank robbers and murderers to contend with, and you're just costing the taxpayers' money. On Monday the kids misheard something during a frightening thunderstorm. Today, you report a possible theft at the library and dream up all sorts of scenarios. What's everyone going to make up tomorrow?"

Grace's blood pressure rose as she thought, *the children aren't the only ones I would like to strangle sometimes—at the moment, you're a prime candidate.* "That's not true. They're still trying to determine if anything is missing or out of order. They don't have scanners and technical things over there like they have at the county library; they do everything manually. Didn't you say you had to go back to the office for a meeting?"

"No, we made a change. Ladd is meeting with the client by herself."

"That's fine, but I have some work to do so just take your coffee elsewhere while I clean up." There was no point in asking him to help. It wasn't in his genes. She did a slow burn and thought, *I guess that's what comes from marrying a Southern male. Helping around the house is not something they do. Not really true, of course. They're great with cutting grass, painting, building, repairing, and operating complex electrical equipment, unless it's a vacuum cleaner—somehow that completely mystifies them.*

"Here's another good one for you," he said as he picked up the paper again. "Someone's been digging over at Fort Morgan. Maybe you could make something out of that."

"That's the archeological dig they started some time ago."

"No, they say this one's unauthorized."

FIVE

1718

Joshua Bailey

Ignatius Pell and Thomas Nichols sat with Joshua Bailey at a table in his warehouse, where three lanterns cast dancing shards of light through the shadows and across the rough wood plank walls around them. The room's windows were small and provided little assistance in illuminating the table. Jamaica, Bailey's slave and chief warehouse assistant, stood to the side and waited. Having finished unloading the cargo Pell and Nichols brought with them, he now looked to Bailey to signal when to present his findings. Joshua Bailey had not offered any small talk to the men. He didn't know them and had no reason to trust them. They were Bonnet's pirate crewmen and Tookerman's messengers and surely of questionable character. With everyone settled in place, he nodded to Jamaica, who quietly stepped forward from the shadows and placed a piece of paper in front of Bailey containing his count of the silks and linens he unloaded. Picking up the report, he saw Jamaica had written: LINEN 20 SILK 10. He looked up questioningly at his trusted assistant, who understood and nodded a confirmation that the "box" had been secured until Tookerman asked for it. Bailey put the note on the table so it faced the two men. "That the right count?"

Pell took hold of the paper and gave it a close look. While he could not read, he knew his numbers and the bolts of cloth they brought had the letters 'S' and 'L' on them.

"Aye, that's what we brought," confirmed Pell, who also gave Jamaica a stern look. He had heard there were slaves who learned to read and write, but this was the first one he had encountered.

Seeing that all was in order, Bailey relaxed. "Good. Captain Tookerman and I have already agreed on a price now that Bonnet's been hanged. Can't believe they did that to a man of good breeding. Something wrong about the way it was all handled. I intend to make a complaint to the crown." Bailey picked up a pouch beside his chair and removed a small leather bag tied with a piece of thin rope and placed it on the table. There was a clear sound of coins being tossed about inside.

Jamaica stood off to the side and watched the faces of the two seamen, his right hand on the knife in his belt.

Pell's face remained unmoved and wondered how a planter could put such trust in a slave.

Nichols' eyes, however, never left the pouch and the money bag. A small grin began to appear round the corners of his mouth.

Pell spoke in a low, steady voice. "Aye, I have no complaint. But Captain Tookerman asked but one task of me. It must be Spanish silver. Will I open the bag or you?"

"It be yours now. Yer free to open it and see inside."

Pell reached for the bag slowly. Tookerman told him Bailey was an honest man and could be trusted, but Pell lived his life among pirates and, as he took hold of the bag, kept an eye on Jamaica and the knife in the Black man's belt. Pell untied the string, took out two coins, and placed them on the table.

The smile left Nichols' face and a small drop of sweat appeared on his brow.

With slow and deliberate care, Pell picked up one of the coins and held it. He gauged its weight and looked at its markings. He turned it over once and then again. The second coin he merely moved around the table with his finger. He knew what he held. "Good Spanish silver." He also knew the small bag held a great deal more silver than the cargo was worth. He remained quiet.

Bailey did not respond, but he too knew Pell could tell the value of a pouch of silver by its feel rather than its count.

Without thinking, Nichols blurted out, "What about the box?"

Pell and Bailey looked at the young man. Jamaica's posture stiffened. Nichols immediately realized he'd made a mistake.

Pell spoke low and firm. "There be no box."

Nichols' eyes widened. The young seaman became unsettled. He sat back in his chair, nodded in agreement, and said no more.

Bailey stood up and extended his hand to Pell, who took it in a strong grip and said, "Thank you, Mr. Bailey. I'll give Captain Tookerman a good report."

"My regards to him as well. Tell him we'll take good care of his cargo." Bailey stepped back from the table, a smile now on his face seeing Pell understood he was not referring to the silk and linen. "I've told the innkeeper across the way to feed you for your return trip. I might also say the people here are good and trustworthy. If you've room for some cargo and a passenger, you may meet someone at the tavern. He will come to you recommended by me, and he will say so."

"Thank you, Mr. Bailey. I'll tell the captain of your kindness." Pell clearly understood the meaning of Bailey's comments, including the reference to 'cargo,' and would relate them to Tookerman. He also knew his passenger would be there to make sure the bag of silver got to Tookerman.

Nichols remained silent even as Bailey took his hand. He knew something else was going on in front of him but had learned his lesson and would be careful to not speak of it.

SIX

2018

Mrs. Cathcart The Librarian

As Grace entered the library Wednesday afternoon, Mrs. Cathcart looked up from her carefully positioned desk inside the front door. Quite prim and proper as always, with her dark blue, long-sleeved sweater, crisp white blouse, two sets of glasses—one of which always hung around her neck—and her gray hair neatly tied back. Short and a bit on the plump side, with a voice that never seemed to rise above a whisper, she epitomized the image of a librarian who worked in a library that seemed not to have changed since the 1950s.

"Ah, Mrs. Bennett, I knew you'd be in about now. Pam is in the children's room. Riley Hampton and Claudia and Violet Larsen are with her. Told her not to go to the history room this time."

"Thank you. By the way, have you discovered anything missing?"

"Possibly. I originally identified about eight volumes that seemed to be missing, although I found one in the room next door and two others were misfiled on the shelves. I'll have it all sorted out by the end of the day." Mrs. Cathcart said all of this in her soft southern way of speaking, not too fast and not too slow, but displaying a clear concern over the disruption to the decorum in the gentle library world in which she lived. "That detective came back again around noon yesterday to see how I was doing and then left. He said he had to look into some shoplifting problems in a store on Market Street."

"Do you mind if I take a look into the history room?"

"Not at all. No one's there now. The only one they let in was the repairman who inspected the lock on the back door. He admitted it wasn't very good. He's going to get a more modern one for us."

On her way to the reference room, Grace stopped at the children's area to let Pam know she was there. Pam and Violet Larsen were on the floor engaged in a game of some sort. All Grace received was a wave, as she was obviously interrupting. She told her daughter to be ready to leave in five minutes, since they had to stop at a farm stand on the way home.

Grace found the history room unoccupied. She looked around for a few minutes, checked the location where Pam and Carter hid, then left.

In the children's area, Pam looked up at her mother. "I'm ready."

Mrs. Cathcart, carrying books for the adjacent room, appeared behind Pam. She had Detective Knott with her. "Mrs. Bennett, I believe you know Detective Knott."

"Yes. We met yesterday."

Knott stepped forward. "I saw you pull up as I was driving by. I have a couple of questions and a request. Would it be all right if I asked Pam a question or two about the other day? Monday afternoon."

Mrs. Cathcart apologized. "I'll leave you both alone. I have to get ready for the volunteers. They restack the shelves in the evening. I wanted to make sure one of the books I was looking for wasn't among them." She started to move away.

"Before you go, I wanted to ask you about the origin of some of these volumes, but I need to check something with Pam first. Is it okay with you, Mrs. Bennett?"

"Yes, I think so," Grace said, making a note not to tell Mitchell unless Pam blurted it out at dinner.

"Thank you."

"Pam, I was wondering about a comment your brother made when he said the two men mentioned something about a man wearing a hat. Do you remember that?"

Pam looked at Detective Knott and, in a quiet, cautious voice replied, "Yes."

"And you're sure the man used the word *hat*?"

Before answering, she looked at her mother and then to Knott. "Yeah." She paused, looked at her mother again, who gave her a reassuring nod. Pam closed her eyes and visualized her and Carter under the table in the next room. She remembered the flash of lightning, the sound of the thunder and the rain pounding against the windows. She remembered the building shook and jumping at the sudden sound. "I think he said a bonnet, but Carter later said I was wrong and men don't wear bonnets, they wear hats."

"Very true." Knott smiled gently, clearly pleased with the answer. "You were a very brave little girl." He looked up from Pam and said to Grace, "I hope you don't mind my continuing to explore the events of Monday afternoon?"

"No, not at all. Do you have an idea of what this is all about?"

"Let's just say some things are falling into place." He asked Mrs. Cathcart, "What was the significance of those two shelves you pointed out to the men?"

"Why, the Bailey gift. They were books the Bailey family donated to the library when the old Bailey Plantation was sold for development. They weren't particularly unique. They were old, dating to the early 1700s. Not great literary works. They were books on botany, husbandry, farming methods, and the like, common to plantations of the time. They weren't worthy of keeping in the glass-protected shelves. The more valuable and collectable volumes are with the regional library's South Carolina History Room." She shifted her feet as she spoke in an effort to better balance the weight of the books she carried.

Seeing her struggle, Detective Knott suggested, "Why don't you take those books into the next room where you were headed, and I'll catch up with you there."

"Thank you. They are getting a little heavy." Continuing to struggle, she quickly left the room.

"So there *was* a robbery at Palmer?" Grace asked Detective Knott.

"It's possible."

"What did they take?"

He raised his voice so Mrs. Cathcart could hear him. "Mrs. Cathcart has the answer to that question."

The librarian, hearing Knott's comment as she put the books down on a table next to the door, replied with a slight stammer, "I, well, I think so. I still have one more place to check." She came back into the room.

"How many volumes are missing?"

"If I'm correct, it's probably two or three."

"Mom, you said we had to stop at the farm stand on the way home."

"Pam, just a moment. Your father can eat frozen beans for once in his life. A little butter and salt and he'll never know the difference anyway." Grace looked down at Pam and pointed at her. "And don't you dare tell him I said that."

"You might try a little fresh oregano and olive oil, it gives them a nice flavor," Mrs. Cathcart said with a smile. "There really isn't much more to say. As with the other books on the shelf, the missing volumes would have been printed in the late 1600s or early 1700s. I have some others here on the table. The name Joshua Bailey is inscribed inside the front cover. I'm not sure of the subject matter. The last one I checked dealt with farming and fence building. The art of giving value to old books is a very subjective practice, and a rare book dealer would have to be contacted to get an estimate."

"Were they the same size as this one?" Knott held up a volume that was about eight inches by five and an inch thick.

"I can't be absolutely sure, especially about the ones with the pictures. I think it may be somewhat larger."

Knott picked up a much larger book from a nearby table, more coffee table display size. "How about this one?"

"Yes, I'm sure one of them would be that size. Do you really think they could be valuable?"

"Difficult to say. It's not my area of expertise, but there surely has to be some value to them."

"You mean what's in them?" Grace said. "Something more than just an old book?"

Pam had stepped back slightly and stood in front of her mother, who put her hands on her daughter's shoulders.

"Possibly. Most old books achieve a good deal of their value from signatures, notes and messages written in the margins. Do you think that's what we're dealing with here? Some famous person wrote something in the books?"

"I have no idea. It's just an example of why one old book would have value over another."

"Wait till I tell Mitchell about this. He thinks we're imagining everything and making something out of nothing."

"Daddy thinks we're all wasting people's tax money," Pam offered, now more relaxed, having accepted Detective Knott and being more comfortable feeling her mother's touch. "He thinks the police should be chasing bad people who break things, like the people who are digging holes at the Fort."

"Yes, daddy is always worried about taxes." Grace gave Pam a hug and Knott a smile as she continued. "When you own a small business, taxes can make or break you, so Mitchell is pretty focused on the issue. Pam, our little sponge here with ears, overheard us at dinner last night." Grace had also become more comfortable with Knott. She didn't have any experience with the police, and she was surprised how at ease he made her feel. "Mitchell read something about some digging at Colonial Fort Morgan and thought that was a much more serious crime than someone trying to steal a book or two from a library."

"Colonial Fort Morgan?"

Mrs. Cathcart interrupted, "I'm sorry detective, but I really have to get these books sorted. Perhaps we can talk more when we meet later today?"

"Thank you, Mrs. Cathcart. Sure, go ahead."

"Pam and I have to go as well," Grace said with a smile.

Knott smiled in return as he said, "Yes, that's fine. Hmmm." He then addressed Mrs. Cathcart, who had started to walk away. "Colonial Morgan is an interesting place, isn't it? Doesn't it date back to the late 1600s?"

"Yes. It was the original trading town in the Morgan area and flourished through the Revolutionary War. There's an active archeological dig there now."

"Mommy's over there a lot," Pam said. "It's kind of a fun place. I went there with my class, and they gave us a neat tour of the old buildings, but it wasn't as good as Mom's. She knows everyone there."

Knott expressed surprise, "Really?"

Being a bit embarrassed by Pam's enthusiasm, Grace explained, "Actually, it's a regular part of Pine View's activities. I'm the new program director there. We often have outings to the complex, and they use a lot of volunteers at the dig. Several of our residents participate."

"It sounds quite interesting. It's a state facility, so it's not a place we have responsibility for."

"Oh, it's very interesting. It's up Brantley Road across the Combahee River from where all the old plantations are: Wheaton, Tucker, Bailey, Martinson. If you'd be interested, we have a tour scheduled for tomorrow. One of the staff members and I are taking a group of ten over in the morning." She hesitated and then offered, "You're more than welcome to join us." *Now why did I do that? Grace, you asked a detective to go on a tour with you.*

Knott looked at her and smiled. "I may just do that."

SEVEN

2018

Fort Morgan

Grace Bennett stood in an empty parking space directly in front of the Colonial Morgan park office and waited for the mini-bus. There were three cars parked nearby, and she wondered if one of them belonged to Detective Knott. Her reaction to Knott continued to bother her. *Relax Grace*, she scolded herself. *So he's a detective and you've never met one before. And he's tall and handsome.*

"Hello again," Knott said as he exited the door to the park office behind her. He wore a blue suit, white shirt, and blue striped tie. A white handkerchief peeked out from the breast pocket of the jacket. The black shoes were polished to a high shine.

Grace jumped, startled. "I didn't see you. Were you inside? The Pine View mini-bus should be here any minute. Were you with Martin Samuels, the park ranger?"

He smiled at her. "Yes, I had a long talk with him. We compared notes and discussed the two books Mrs. Cathcart confirmed were missing. As she thought, they were provided to the Palmer library as part of a gift by the descendants of Joshua Bailey. Of course, the Bailey family history is well known to Ranger Samuels. He mentioned Joshua Bailey was one of the settlers who came from Massachusetts in 1698 to establish the original market village of Morgan. You probably know a lot of this. Pam said you were an expert."

"In Pam's eyes, maybe. I'm no expert. In trying to put together programs for Pine View, I do a lot of scouting around to find activities for the residents."

"I realize that, but you may have come across something people like Samuels have forgotten about. Tell me what you know, or maybe something that interested you about the Bailey family."

"The old family or the new?"

"Ah, see. He never mentioned the current Bailey's. Let's do the old first and transition up to the current descendants."

Grace calmed down as she focused on answering him. In doing her research for Pine View, she had become interested in the history of the region. Having been born and raised in Arlington, Virginia, just outside of Washington DC, she never really thought of herself as being southern. At least not deep south southern. Washington, DC had been conceived as neutral territory. "From what I've read, the family had multiple plantations across the region. Most are gone now but they extended south from the Dorchester area through parts of what is now Coastal Rivers and Beaufort counties. The family sold off the last of the land to a developer in the 1930s and moved over toward Morgan. I understand there is a golf community in the area called The Bailey Plantation. There doesn't seem to be a connection to the Bailey family, though. However, the Bailey family was part of the original group who founded Morgan College."

"You have been busy. I knew some of that as it relates to the local area but not about the Dorchester location. I'll have to update my notes. Also, the piece about Morgan College, I know some people over there who could fill me in on that part of the family history. Do you know if the college site was originally on one of the Bailey plantations?"

"As I understand it. It was the only major piece that survived in Bailey family hands after the Civil War." She had herself under control now and asked, "So, the books are valuable?"

"That remains to be seen. According to Mrs. Cathcart's records, the books in question dealt with farming methods and techniques and didn't seem to have anything unusual about them. Samuels confirmed her account. Said they were quite common in the late 1600s, especially on large farms."

The bus from Pine View pulled up in front of them and interrupted their conversation. The driver, George, who also served as a tour guide, appeared to be as old as his passengers. He carefully made his way down the steps, greeted Grace, and then helped the occupants down one by one. Most were in their eighties and grasped tightly onto the railing with one hand and extended the other to George, who said, "Well, Grace, our ten-minute ride took a bit longer. They really ought to do something about putting a left turn lane off the main road. You certainly got here quickly, though. Thought I saw you zipping by us on the way over. Who's this handsome young fellah?"

Grace smiled and made the introduction. "George, this is Detective Knott of the Morgan Police Department." As George and Knott exchanged pleasantries, Grace looked at the historic venue around her: the ruins of the original fort, the dirt roads that marked off the perimeter, the historic markers identifying warehouses, taverns, and shops. The open area extended out a hundred yards to where a large stone church stood guard at the far side of the site. Much of the church facade had been restored, and a new roof added. A tent in front served as the headquarters of the archaeological dig team. Knott and George moved slightly off to the side after the bus emptied. Grace became surrounded by the retirement village residents and made sure they moved safely off the gravel roadway. Being mid-morning on a Thursday, the park had few visitors, except a man reading a newspaper at a wooden picnic table in the nearby fenced-in picnic area.

Grace engaged the Pine View residents in idle chit-chat, while keeping Knott in sight. As everyone from the bus lined up in the grass by the side of the road, George came over to her.

"Grace, could I ask you a favor?"

"Sure."

"Would you take everyone to the main historical marker for the town market square and explain the basic layout and where they're standing in relation to the old market? If I'm not back by the time you finish, take them to the grassy area inside the fort."

"Of course. Is something the matter?"

"No. I just have to make a quick visit to the little boy's room. You certainly know as much about the town as I do. I won't be long."

With a smile, she agreed to his request. As she did so, Detective Knott took out his cell phone and answered it.

Grace didn't mind giving a talk about the old Morgan market-town, as it was one of her favorite things to do. Whenever she came to the site, she always envisioned the bustling nature of what was once here. The people came alive for her. Many of the original families who lived and worked at Colonial Morgan still had descendants in the area: Davidson, Izard, Nichols, Baker, Fisher, Osgood.

She gathered the group of three couples and four widowed women. As they made their way to the location of the historical marker for the center of the town, only ten yards in front of them, Grace talked about how the buildings were arranged: the residences, the warehouses, the shops, the fort, and the church. She then explained some of the items that had been found buried throughout the area, but her mind was not completely on the historical subject matter as she kept looking toward the park office.

Finally focusing her attention on the tour group, she thought it best to keep them moving. "George said he would meet us at the fort, so let's take a walk that way. It's a good place to start as it was the first building here. On the other side of it is the river where the original loading docks were located for the shallops, the small cargo boats that serviced the community." Grace began walking slowly as she continued, "The wharf was privately owned by a Richard Baker. Back in the early eighteenth century, there was no such thing as public property. Everything was either owned by individuals or the crown. This was quite an active place. Vessels as large as two-masted ones were common coming up and down the river on the tide. Raw materials and produce were shipped down to Charles Town and finished goods came back up. I'll also show you where the bridge across the Combahee used to be. And mind your step, the pathways tend to be somewhat uneven in places."

When Grace ushered the last of the group inside the tabby walls of the fort, she spotted George making his way across the grass and waited for him.

"Sorry Grace, very interesting stuff, this whole thing with the Palmer library. Looks like you have everything under control here," George said, seeing the tour group members talking among themselves and pointing at the fort. "By the way, Knott asked if you could stop by the office. He has another question or two about what Carter and Pam heard the other day."

"You know about the Palmer? Have they figured it out?"

"I don't know about that. I just heard the detective talking with Ranger Samuels. He said something about being able to answer the question 'why' but it's the 'who' he's having trouble with."

"Fascinating. Well, they're all yours, George. I'll catch up with you later."

Grace took off in a rush and headed across the grass, retracing George's route. What had they found out? She almost tripped over a tree root and decided to slow down a bit. When she entered the building, Ranger Samuels was standing in front of a desk with large scrolls of paper spread across it. Detective Knott was on his phone, pacing in front of a window that overlooked the picnic area. "Hello, Martin, have another good group for you today. George said Detective Knott wanted to see me."

"Yes, he'll be off his phone in a minute. Does look like a good group there. I'll be ready for them by the time they come back from the river." He lowered his voice. "Detective Knott is talking with Mrs. Cathcart. The gentleman in the picnic area had been asking questions about the residents who would have lived here in the early seventeen hundreds."

"Really?"

"Yes. Interesting, isn't it? Nothing like investigating what might be a 300-year-old-crime. Detective Knott has become fascinated with all of it."

"Do they think there really is a treasure?"

"Don't know anything about that. Seems like someone might think so, though."

"Who did the treasure belong to?"

Detective Knott ended his call and walked toward Grace. "We believe it to be a man by the name of Stede Bonnet."

"Bonnet? The man wearing a hat that Carter and Pam heard mentioned? But it wasn't a hat—it was a man called Bonnet? Pam was right."

"Exactly."

"Who was he?"

"A somewhat famous pirate who was hanged in Charleston in 1718."

"A pirate's treasure? You've got to be kidding."

"Wish I was. While speaking with Mrs. Cathcart, our friend in the picnic area over there was good enough to stand up and begin pacing. I had her repeat the description she remembered of both the men who were at the library late Monday afternoon, and I'm pretty sure our friend over there could be one of them. I think I'll take a stroll over that way and pass the time of day with him."

"Are you going to arrest him?"

"At this point, I think a friendly chat is in order."

Knott made his way to the door and as he opened it said, "I would appreciate it if you would both stay inside."

They followed his instruction and headed for the window where Knott previously stood.

Instead of taking the shorter route across the grass to the fenced-in picnic area, Knott walked the ten yards to the parking lot. From there, he strolled down the road at a leisurely pace and arrived at the entry path to where the man now sat at his table. As Knott neared the fence which enclosed the picnic area, he said something to the man, who had been watching the detective approach. The man stood up and warily took a step backward, clearly understanding who came toward him. Knott raised his hand as he began to speak, and the man bolted, running toward the restroom building at the far end of the picnic area outside the fence. Knott took off after him.

Martin and Grace watched as the man went around the left side of the restroom and seemed to head for the heavy brush and woods behind it. Knott was about fifteen yards behind him and again called out, but Grace and Martin couldn't make out what he said.

The man came into view but this time from the back of the building on the right side and headed straight toward the office instead of the woods.

Knott again called out to the man who had disappeared from his view.

"Maybe I can help," Samuels said to Grace as he moved to the entrance doorway and opened it.

The running man saw the movement at the office and changed direction. He now ran down the path that went from the picnic area to the fort ruins and then to the river.

A large black dog ran past the window as Grace watched the chase toward the fort ruins.

"Mickey! Wait!" a large Black woman called out as she ran in pursuit of the dog.

Mickey gave out a couple of loud barks and kept going.

Knott, hearing Mickey bark, realized the man had doubled back. As he came around the corner of the building, Knott spotted the man again and saw Samuels and Grace exit the office. Knott changed course and ran down the path after the man and the dog.

Grace and Ranger Samuels fast-walked to the back of the park office building where they watched the man head for the fort, with Mickey, the Black woman, and Knott in pursuit.

As the man disappeared around the corner of the old fort's tabby wall, Grace exclaimed, "Oh my God, George and the tour are down there."

"Stay here," Martin said as he began to walk hurriedly across the lawn between the fort and the office.

"Stay here? Not on your life!" Grace quickly caught up to the park ranger.

Samuels grabbed Grace's arm and stopped her from following the others. He pulled her in the direction to where she had left the tour at the entrance to the fort. "Come this way," he said, and they both made their way across the grass as quickly as they could.

As the dog closed in on the running man, she let out a couple of more loud barks. The man looked to his right and saw the tour group watching him and decided to switch direction down an intersecting dirt path a few yards ahead that lead to the river. As he reached the junction of the two pathways, he turned his head to look over his shoulder, stubbed his toe on the path, and lost his footing. He fell forward and hit the ground hard, tumbling onto his left shoulder. His face slid across the dirt. Rolling over, he tried to recover.

Detective Knott ran past the woman who called out, "Mickey, wait. Wait!"

Mickey stopped dead in her tracks.

Knott got to the man as he stumbled again while scrambling to get to his feet.

"Stay right there," the detective ordered.

Mickey turned and headed to the woman who called him. The lab's tail wagged playfully all the way.

A few moments later, Grace and Samuels reached the entrance of the fort. A commotion came from the far side of the enclosure, where a path exited through the tabby walls and connected with the paths to the picnic area and the river. Members of the tour group were milling around, with some pointing toward the river and others focusing on something just in front of them.

When Grace and Samuels arrived, the woman and her dog stood in the middle of the group. Down the hill a man lay on the ground, face down, in the middle of the path, his hands behind his back and Knott standing over him. Martin Samuels continued down the path to them. Grace stopped.

"Is everyone okay?" Grace asked the group.

"Yes, but what's going on?" asked one of the women. "All these people running around and then the dog made the man fall…"

"Grace," George said, "I wondered where you were. The detective has him on the ground. It's the one from the picnic area."

"Did you see what happened?"

"It happened quickly. We were coming back from the river and waiting for everyone to catch up when a dog barked and the man ran down the path. Mickey here went halfway after him and gave a few more barks. The man turned to see where the dog was, tripped on something in the path, and landed in a heap. Mickey stopped when Mrs. James called her. She saw us watching everything and came over while Knott pounced on the man. At first some of the people were afraid that Mickey was the problem, but Mrs. James called her again and Mickey stopped. When the two of them came over to us, everyone realized she was part of the solution, not the problem, as you can see."

Mickey continued to revel in the attention from the tour group.

A man Grace didn't recognize limped past her and over to the dog. "So, you've done it again, have you Mrs. Micawber? One of these days you're going to get yourself into real trouble," he admonished Mickey while rubbing her ears and patting her head. He turned to Grace and George and introduced himself. "I'm Professor Sidney Lake. I see you've already met my associate, Mrs. James, and my wayward canine friend, Mickey."

EIGHT

2018
Sidney Lake Is Intrigued

"**S**o, it's solved now?" Grace asked as she and Detective Knott huddled over mid-morning coffee and a snack in the cafeteria at Pine View. They sat across from one another at a table for four in the middle of the room. After the capture and arrest of the man at Fort Morgan yesterday, Knott had promised to keep her up to date on what happened. This is not something he would normally do, but he felt comfortable talking with Grace and enjoyed her company.

"Not really. We have the one man who admits to being in the library during the storm but said he had nothing to do with the break-in and claims to know nothing about it. He did tell us the name of the man he was with. I can't give you his name yet, but I can say he's an independent contractor over in Summerville and probably won't be hard to find. He also said other people were involved but he doesn't know who they are."

"But you know what this is about?" Grace took a sip of her coffee. Knott hadn't touched his yet but had managed to secure a blueberry muffin and began unwrapping it.

"It seems to be about a treasure of some sort that's connected to old books the Bailey family gave to the library. You recall meeting Professor Lake at the Fort? Sometimes he acts as a resource for us, especially with matters relating to the arts and rare books. I asked him to check with some of his former colleagues at the college. He is retired but remains in close contact with everyone at Morgan College. Professor Lake thinks there's more to this than a simple book theft. Apparently, there's some sort of legend about a secret box that was placed in the custody of Joshua Bailey in 1718. Apparently, the box belonged to Stede Bonnet, whose claim to fame is that he wasn't really a pirate. He had a plantation on Barbados, had a mixture of marital and financial problems, got pissed... er... sorry."

"Not a problem." Grace smiled and wondered, *Why do I feel so comfortable with him?*

"He got angry at just about everyone, got himself a ship and went pirating. Lake said Bonnet had a reputation as the 'gentleman pirate' and was mainly an irritant to real pirates like Blackbeard and Vane. Anyway, Bonnet reportedly had a string of successful boardings in the early fall of 1718 along the Virginia and Carolina coast before being captured and imprisoned on what is now Sullivan's Island."

Mary Louise McBee came into the cafeteria and seeing Grace with Knott left some papers on a nearby table while making sure she was seen.

"No one has ever been able to properly verify any of this, as details are sketchy." Knott took a bite out of the muffin and noticed Mary Louise watching them. "Court records indicate Bonnet escaped for several days before being recaptured. During that time, Professor Lake said it was rumored he came up the Ashley River and made a bargain with Bailey about delivering information regarding Edward Teach's secret partnership with another planter. In exchange for the information, Bonnet demanded a payment that would help him secure his freedom. According to some theories, a man by the name of Richard Tookerman was to be the go-between. They have a course at Morgan College that deals with the golden age of piracy. That's where a lot of this information comes from.

"Professor Lake reported that the so-called treasure box has never been found. One of the books at the Palmer Library that belonged to the Bailey family contained a drawing of Bonnet's pirate flag. A rectangle containing a rendering of a heart on the right side and a horizontal bone beneath a skull."

Grace sat back in her chair with a look of complete astonishment and asked the key question, "So, there is a treasure somewhere near Colonial Morgan?"

"Not necessarily." Knott didn't want Grace spreading a rumor that might start a treasure hunt and cautioned her. From the look on Mary Louise's face, he assumed there would be a number of rumors dancing around before the day was out. "Don't get your hopes up. According to Lake and Samuels and what the captured man said, only one of the books they came across had a drawing in it, the others didn't. All the books had marks on them. I guess the man we captured assumed the one with the drawing was the most important, as it indicated something being placed in or near a 'grave', which is why he dug in the old church yard. However, Samuels pointed out that there were a couple of families named 'Graves' living at Morgan in 1718, and without any other pieces to the puzzle, no one will ever find what is hidden there, if anything."

Grace was fascinated by all the information he laid out and never touched her muffin. She just sat watching him and sipping her coffee.

"According to our thief, they were supposed to report whatever they discovered to a third person. However, he became focused on the treasure and decided to make a go for it by himself. He obtained a metal detector and started digging near the old church bell tower. The night the library was broken into, he claimed he was out digging holes at Fort Morgan. He had no idea the church wasn't built until the mid-1700s, well after Bonnet was hanged."

"What about Professor Lake?"

"He's doing additional research, looking for original material in local libraries. The Beaufort Library has a South Carolina Room with a trove of historical material, as do we at the Morgan library. On the other hand, Tillie James is tapping into recordings of oral histories and historical documents both in Morgan and Beaufort. Especially Penn Center on Saint Helena Island."

Grace shifted in her chair, still holding her coffee cup. "I can't believe all this. And all because Pam and Carter were under that table in the room. How do we know all of this?"

"Bonnet is a somewhat mysterious figure even though the whole incident of his capture, escape, and recapture is well documented. The Admiralty Court kept very good records. However, Lake believes something else is going on besides someone looking for buried treasure."

"And the other man or men?"

"Who knows? We don't know the exact number, but Lake believes it's someone in the Charleston area with extensive knowledge of South Carolina colonial history."

Martin Tucker waited impatiently in the dark by the side of the road. With Allan Swift having been arrested at Fort Morgan, he realized how stupid he'd been. *I'm a builder, for Christ's sake. How the fuck did a title search end up in looking for buried treasure? Now I've got the police after me. I told him the treasure tale so he wouldn't know what I was really doing.* He looked around nervously as he awaited the arrival of the special lawyer his attorney had recommended. He wanted professional advice before he marched into police headquarters to give himself up. The entire deal could be in jeopardy. Tucker had invested a lot of time and effort into the project, not to mention money. All he could hope for was that Swift kept quiet. What he didn't understand was why Swift had gone off on his own. And this whole thing about buried treasure, he couldn't believe that a grown, presumably smart, man would spot something that looked like a map drawn on the inside cover of a 300-year-old book and assume it was a treasure map. All they were supposed to be looking for was evidence of who originally owned the property on both sides of Willow Marsh Road. Over the years, it had belonged to several plantations but was always part of the Bailey family until the Civil War, when everything changed. Former slaves had tried to farm it but, as the land had been flooded for growing rice for a hundred years, it had lost its capability to be used for any other form of crop. But Tucker's partner had a plan for it. With the growing migration of retirees coming down from the North, he envisioned a magnificent plantation with deep water access for a marina. Walking and riding trails would weave their way through housing clusters and a magnificent clubhouse complex would dominate the waterfront.

He left his car when he heard a vehicle coming down the road. It had no lights on, which didn't surprise him as he had driven without them when he arrived. A light of any kind along Willow Marsh Road could be seen for miles against the dark of the night.

The car stopped thirty yards from where Martin Tucker parked. It sat quietly. He couldn't see anyone get out of the vehicle, so he began to walk slowly and cautiously along the road toward the car. The engine had been turned off and the inside of the car went dark as he reached it. He still saw no one. "David? Is that you?"

No answer.

Uneasiness crawled up Tucker's spine. "Where the hell are you?"

A faint shadow moved behind him and dirt crunched beneath a footfall. Before Martin had a chance to turn around, he received a massive blow to the back of his head. His knees buckled, and he hit the ground in a heap.

Sidney Lake had become fascinated with the information he uncovered while researching the book thefts from the Palmer Library. His interest went well beyond the books from the old Bailey Plantation that were the focus of his initial review. At first, he pursued a subject he knew something about: pirates. Living in Coastal Rivers County, which contained a group of islands off the city of Morgan called the Pirate Islands, he was well aware of the history of the region and its connection to Edward Teach (Blackbeard). However, Sidney soon learned that much of what he originally knew had been created by Hollywood producers and actors. The fictional swashbuckling characters of movie fame bore little resemblance to historic fact. Unlike the motion pictures, it was not silver and gold pieces that filled the ships the pirates plundered, but the commercial trade cargo that could be turned into silver and gold, and much of that cargo consisted of slaves.

"Want to take a break from all those books?" Tillie had come into the office without Sidney noticing. "Sure looks like they got you cornered."

Books filled his desk, were stacked on the credenza behind him and on the floor, where one even served as a pillow for Mickey.

"Hah, yes, I suppose they do, don't they? This is fascinating material."

Mickey lifted her head and looked toward Tillie as she asked, "How 'bout takin' a break an' comin' for a walk with me and Mickey before lunch? Do that leg of yours some good."

Sidney glanced at the clock sitting on the mantle above the fireplace. "Is it really lunchtime already? My goodness."

"That leg could use some exercise. Doctor said you got to keep it movin'."

"Hmmm. Yes, I'm sure you're right. It's a good time for a break anyway."

"Good. Give me a chance to tell you about what happened last night on The Ridge."

"What?"

Pete Hornig, the Morgan City Chief of Police, was having a quiet Monday morning until he received the call about Martin Tucker being found in the marsh at the edge of The Ridge—Morgan's exclusive residential neighborhood. Any unusual occurrence there always became an immediate priority for him. Detective Sargent Sam Cashman and officer Hampton Butler made it to the scene only a few minutes after the 9-1-1 call came in. It was not uncommon for someone to have seen a log in the tall, dense marsh grass and mistaken it for a person. The first report said there was a body floating in the water, but a neighbor who came to the scene realized Tucker was still alive and not fully in the water. Sam made the call to Chief Hornig as soon as he confirmed Tucker had been attacked. Given the high-profile location, not only did the EMS truck show up almost instantaneously but also the Assistant Coroner, Mary Coffey.

"The first report I received claimed a body had been found," Mary said, surprised to find Martin Tucker alive.

"From the look of him, I'm not sure he will be for long," Sam responded. "Actually, I'm glad you're here. I've got a funny feeling about this. I'm having the entire area secured, and I'd like you to go over everything carefully."

"It's Saturday morning, Sam. People falling off boats on a Saturday night or Sunday after too many beers and only a few caught fish is not uncommon. It's rare for someone to actually drown."

"I'm aware of that, but they also report it. If he was alone, there'd be a missing person report. You didn't get a good look at Tucker yet. He's wearing business slacks and a short-sleeve shirt."

"Ah. Point taken."

A paramedic closed the rear door to the ambulance, ran around to the passenger side, and jumped in. The siren came to life as they made their way across the grassy area and out to the road.

Mary said, "I guess a fishing accident isn't looking like an obvious cause."

"Officially, can't say. Unofficially, very unlikely."

Officer Butler joined them as other officers put up police line tape and held back the growing crowd.

"Whatta ya think, Sam?" asked Butler.

"Tough to tell." Sam looked around the area as he spoke. Marsh grass stood tall and thick at the water's edge. The tide was now out, which contributed to the body's visibility. "Take lots of pictures, Mary. We have none of Tucker lying where he was found as he was still alive, and the EMS team trampled all over the place when they worked on him." He turned to Hamp. "Who made the discovery?"

"Woman walking her dog. Janet Hartnet."

Mary began taking pictures as he spoke.

"Would have passed right by him but she had her dog off-leash and he found him."

Sam stepped away from the scene and surveyed the marsh in front of him. "Did she recognize him?"

"No. Never tried to find out. Just got the dog under control and headed back to the road. When I checked, it looked like a couple of paw prints by the head. Can't tell much else because of all the traffic. Tide's still coming in and that spot's going to be under a foot of water soon." Sam continued to walk away from the water's edge and kept looking at the vegetation nearby. He took out a small notebook and started to draw a pencil sketch of everything, with emphasis on the height of the marsh grass. He then drew some lines indicating the direction of the tidal flow.

Two more police cruisers showed up and then the coroner's SUV and forensic team.

⚜━━━⚜

"Yeah, Miss Hartnet found him," Tillie said.

"Where was he found? You said it was a he, didn't you?" Sidney leaned back in his chair as he spoke and fiddled with his glasses, which he had removed and held in his right hand. He no longer looked as though he was ready for a walk but more like getting settled for a long conversation. Since the last operation on his knee, the pain had been reduced but his mobility hadn't changed. His combined office/library had become his primary location except for his one trip down in the morning and one up at night. Tillie had moved into the spare room on a semi-permanent basis.

"It's a him all right. Found him in the water at the Osgood place. Don't know much else yet. Getting reports from Ester. Workin' across the street today."

"Is she there all day?"

"No, I'm pretty sure she only goes till noon. Got somebody two doors down on River Street, though. Lemme get my schedule. It's upstairs."

Tillie turned to exit the office, but Sidney stopped her. "Tillie, wait a minute. There's something I wanted to mention. Come and sit down." He motioned her to the chair next to his desk.

"Somethin' up?"

"Yes. Something I've been thinking about for a while now."

Tillie looked at Sidney and got a sense that this might be a touchy subject. "Okay, but why don't we walk and talk. That leg still needs exercise."

Sidney decided it might be a good way to handle his problem. "You're right," he said as he got up from his chair, twisting and turning cautiously to protect his knee. They made it onto the front porch with Tillie having the lead controlling Mickey when Sidney blurted out, "I have a proposal for you."

Tillie had a questioning expression. For the first time in a long time, she had no clue as to what he was about to say.

They continued down the four steps.

"I have a problem," Sidney began. "You know I do a lot of my thinking in the office space, and I'm having some difficulty concentrating."

"You want me to stay upstairs to do my work, so I won't bother you?" Tillie was now concerned about where the conversation was going.

"Er… no… actually, just the opposite."

Now Tillie looked really confused.

Seeing the concern on her face, Sidney said, "Let me explain. Do you remember when that FBI agent was shot right in front of me and lay dying on the floor?" He pointed to a spot about eight feet in front of where he now stood, as though it was his office. "Hattie was taken hostage by the stairs?"

"You bet I do."

"That's my problem. I see it too. Every time I close my eyes, I see a body in front of me in a pool of blood. I can't concentrate. It's throwing me off completely."

"You seen a doctor?"

"Yes, I have. And that's what I want to talk to you about. She said it's not unusual and recommended changing things around. Make the room look different. Make it feel different and…"

Tillie immediately jumped in. "Sure, we can do that. I got lots of people that can help. Turn everything around…"

Sidney interrupted, "Yes, I'm sure… but that's not what I'm getting at."

Tillie looked concerned again.

"I want you to move your business down to my office."

"What chew mean?"

"I want you to take over the office." He stopped walking and held up his hand to her. "Now wait. Hear me out. I plan on doing all my work from my library from now on. I don't need two workspaces. Your housekeeping business has been growing steadily. You have, at least by my count, ten people working for you now, and you just started a catering staff service, where you provide people to work parties: waiters, bartenders, valet parkers, drivers, clean-up crews and whatever other people would be needed. You're trying to do all of this from the bedroom upstairs and it makes no sense. I want you to take over the front room."

"But Professor Lake, that don't seem fair. You have to let me pay you to make it fair."

Sidney was ready for the argument. "I've got a proposal for you to make it fair. You take care of the house and me." He held up his hand to her again. "Let me finish. The trade-off is you and or your people do the cleaning and cooking here and get me where I need to go when I need it if I can't drive myself."

"Hell, Professor, I was goin' to do all that stuff anyway."

"I'm sure you were but it would not have been fair. I want you to formally set up your company in my office space. It will be your company headquarters. By the way, I don't know its name."

"Hah, just got it registered. Gullah Island Services, LLC. How's that?"

Sidney broke into a big smile. "That is absolutely perfect."

NINE

1718
Pell's Promise

During the dim light of the mid-December morning, two more vessels arrived at Fort Dorchester. When it was well past noon and the sun had begun to peek through the tree line again, all three vessels were ready to catch the tide and head back down the river. The outward flow of the Ashley River would give them speedy passage through some of the narrow channels. Pell's boat left first, as it was lighter and more maneuverable than the other two. Joshua Bailey's prediction that they would meet someone with goods that needed to be transported down river held true. Now they carried a male passenger and furs in the space where the linens and silks had been housed. The other boats followed at a good distance and carried mostly lumber to be transferred to larger vessels destined for British islands in the Caribbean.

Their newly acquired passenger had stored some of his furs in Bailey's warehouse while awaiting transportation, but the cargo the shallop now carried was not intended to make it all the way to Charles Town. They were advised that their boat would be required to stop and wait at a point three miles above where the Ashley and Cooper rivers met. There they would be intercepted by another vessel. In addition to the warehouse Tookerman owned in Charles Town, he also maintained a small James Island warehouse on the south side of the Ashley. It was well hidden from the spies of Colonel William Rhett, Tookerman's nemesis, and the man who defeated Stede Bonnet in the Battle of Cape Fear. The furs were destined for Spanish traders in violation of the Navigation Acts that England forced upon its colonies, prohibiting colonial traders from dealing with anyone other than an English merchant.

Captain Tookerman, the owner of the shallop, also had his fifty-ton vessel, the *Sea Nymph*, outfitted with eight guns. Unusual for a merchant ship but practical for transporting both legal and illegal goods between the Carolinas and the Bahamas. Because of its armament, the *Sea Nymph* was one of the vessels Robert Johnson, governor of the Province of South Carolina, periodically commandeered for the defense of Charles Town. Colonel William Rhett made use of it when he had been charged with the task of capturing the pirate Charles Vane, who had recently attempted a blockade of the harbor. He needed a fast and well-armed vessel to take on Vane but inadvertently came across Steed Bonnet instead at Cape Fear, which ultimately led to the pirate's capture, trial, and execution.

Colonel Rhett had great disdain for Richard Tookerman, who cast himself as a simple merchant. Rhett even attempted to arrest Tookerman for piracy more than once, only to have the merchant successfully defend his claim insisting the trade he had with the Bahamas was honest and legal, even though it was well known that the Bahamas capital of Nassau was the headquarters for all pirate activity in the region. Nassau had more pirates than settlers and operated as the pirate haven for the entire Caribbean and the Atlantic Coast. Tookerman, sly, crafty, glib, and well versed in the law, successfully defended himself as merely being in the transportation business: moving goods from one English colony to another. He stated he was not aware of the origin of the goods or where they would eventually end up. Tookerman became obsessed with Colonel Rhett's attempts to put him out of business and set himself on a course to do Rhett harm and embarrassment at every opportunity. The constant battling between Rhett and Tookerman reached a peak when Tookerman was accused of burglarizing Rhett's home.

At the arranged meeting place on the Ashley, Thomas Nichols watched as their passenger and his cargo, now stored in the hold of another cargo boat, moved slowly across the river headed for Tookerman's warehouse. "What do you make of all this, Mr. Pell?"

"I make nothing of it. You know nothing. You see nothing. You tell nothing. You stay alive."

"But…"

"But nothing. You could be hanging by the neck as are the other crew of Captain Bonnet. You know nothing. Find yourself another ship to sail on. Join the fight against the Yemassee. Get some land up near the Beaufort settlement. There'll be plenty to have once the Yemassee have been driven off. Get hooked up with Tuscarora Jack Barnwell and his Carolina Scouts. They need good seamen to patrol the inland waters between Beaufort and Saint Augustine. They say he's claimed over 6,000 acres of Yamasee land for himself. Maybe you can get some too."

Thomas Nichols kept looking after the boat that carried away the cargo from Morgan. He had no intention of becoming a settler. It would be the sea for him, but his brother Eli had other dreams. It was land Eli desired and prayed for. He wanted all he could convince God to give him. So Thomas asked Mr. Pell on behalf of his brother, "Where would I find him, Mr. Tookerman?"

"There be a tavern not far from Colonel Rhett's house. Mr. Barnwell's people come in there on their provision trips. Have a small sloop that runs down the coast. I'll show you."

Nichols turned his head away from the receding boat and looked at Pell. He wondered if he should ask. He couldn't resist. "What about the cargo box we gave to Bailey?"

Pell swung around and delivered an explosive backhand to the side of

Nichols' head and roared, "There be no box! There be no cargo!"

The young seaman reeled backwards and fell into the empty cargo area.

Pell stood above him with his knife drawn and spoke in a low, growling voice, his eyes narrowed and fixed on the young man who had a drop of blood beginning to form on his mouth and another on his forehead. "There be no box. By heaven above, if I ever hear a word that you have told other than that, I will cut you into fish bait and hang the rest of you from a yardarm. I'll say no more. But I make you that promise."

TEN

2018

111 Howard Street

Sidney sat at his dinette table in the kitchen and nursed a cup of coffee. He had been looking through the new edition of Brontë Studies when Mickey got up from her usual place by the table and headed for the front door. She didn't bark so Sidney knew it wasn't a stranger on his front porch. Mickey, tail wagging, arrived at the door as Hattie Ryan gave it a brief knock and opened it.

"Sidney, it's me," she called out. There was a time when making herself known with a loud yell as she entered 111 Howard Street would be unusual, but with Sidney having been the subject of two recent murder attempts, his friends all agreed it would be a good idea.

Sidney had been told by the police to keep his door locked, but he refused. No one who knew him was surprised by his reaction. He would not be a prisoner in his own home. Even with the population growth of Morgan, he refused. The charm of Morgan had always been its small-town southern feel, even if there were more people from out-of-state living in and around Coastal Rivers County than the city administrators had planned.

"Back here," he called.

Hattie's first instinct had been to look toward the office to her left as she came in, as that was where Sidney Lake could usually be found.

"Oh, that's right. You're working from the library now. Tillie told me the news. That's awfully nice of you, you know." She closed the door behind her, and she and Mickey made their way to the kitchen.

"News certainly travels fast. I only made the decision yesterday." He put the magazine down. "Well, maybe that's not entirely true." The latter comment, a self-reflective thought, was verbalized in a low tone.

"Ran into Tillie at the hardware store. She said I should come over as she has some news about the man they found in the marsh up at The Ridge."

"Really? She didn't say anything else?"

"No. She decided it would be better not to say anything more in public. Everyone around town seems to know what went on over at Colonial Morgan and that you have become involved." Hattie entered the kitchen. "And Tillie with that network of hers…. You know I was always impressed with her connections, but now with her personal service company in full operation, there isn't a secret in town that's safe. If she tried to say anything in public, everyone in the store would listen in. Mind if I have some of that coffee?" She indicated the quarter full French Press coffee maker on the island.

"No. not at all. I've had more than enough this morning. Got lost in the 'Studies'. Two very interesting articles on Anne Brontë." He held up the journal. "But tell me, what has Tillie discovered?"

Hattie went to the cupboard next to the refrigerator and took out a coffee mug. "She wouldn't say. It looked like she had just checked out and was leaving. Definitely in a hurry to go somewhere, but you know Tillie, always in a rush, never does anything at half speed. Said she would be right over and to wait for her here." The filled cup went into the microwave.

"Very curious, I must say. That whole business over at Colonial Morgan bothers me. I wonder if this is the other man. The one who Grace Bennett's children overheard in the reference room at the library. I think there was more to what went on than what the captured man told the police."

Hattie came over to the table with her cup and sat down. "I thought he didn't really tell them anything."

"According to Sam Cashman, Detective Knott claimed the man didn't know who hired them. Knott is the lead detective on the library investigation."

"I thought it would be Sam?"

Sidney put the journal off to the side. "I did too. But since Detective Knott was the first one on the scene, the Chief believes whoever starts the investigation stays with it. That doesn't mean someone else couldn't get involved. Actually, Colonial Morgan is a state park, and the state police could probably take it over if they wanted to."

"My goodness, how do they keep things straight from one police department to another? Sounds like a lot could fall through the cracks."

"I—" Sidney was interrupted as Tillie came in the back door.

Mickey was the first to greet Tillie, who entered carrying two canvas shopping bags. "Mickey, glad it's you who met me," she said as she walked directly to the kitchen island and placed the bags side by side. "Whew, they sure do pack those bags full. When they give you plastic ones, they put two items in a bag, and you end up with ten bags. Bring your own and they pack 'um so tight you need to hire 'Shaq' to carry them to an' from the car."

Sidney asked, "Er…'Shack,' who's 'Shack?'"

"Basketball player. Big as a mountain. Professor, you have to join the twenty-first century every now an' then."

Sidney looked over his glasses at her.

She responded with, "Yeah, I know. Sorry. Some strange things goin' on."

Hattie stepped into the conversation. "Are you talking about the body they found at The Ridge?"

"Yeah, that's part of it. He ain't dead, by the way."

Sidney asked, "Ah, so they know who the man is?"

"Yeah, they're starting to put some things together, which is worryin' me." As she spoke, Tillie began to empty the bags and Hattie began to help her.

"They connected the man to the book robbery at Palmer Library. The guy who was caught at the Morgan park. The injured man was the other one at the table in the reference room. It's all real curious and secret like. The first guy's name is Alan Swift. He said he didn't know a lot about the other man. The one they found in the marsh. He called him 'Tuck.' Said they didn't go to the library to steal anything. Just doing research for someone else. Never met this third guy but knew he lived in a big house here in Morgan." Tillie stopped. Both Sidney and Hattie stood staring at her. "Okay, yeah, I know all this stuff 'cause I got some people working at police headquarters, City Hall, and the Coroner's Office. They tell me but they don't tell anyone else. 'Cause if they do, they don't work for me anymore."

"Hmmm, that's a bit dangerous, isn't it, Tillie?" questioned Sidney.

"Yeah, that's why I want to talk about security around here."

"That's not what I meant. I was referring to your employees leaking confidential police information. You could lose your contract with the town."

"Police are pretty smart. They know my people are around. If they want somethin' to be private, they go in an office and close the door. That's why I tell 'um to be quiet."

"Ah, I see what you mean. So, what is it about security that concerns you?"

Tillie and Hattie both stopped putting the groceries away and looked at Sidney.

"Professor, that man who was found in the marsh did something stupid that got him knocked on the head," Tillie said. "Whoever he worked for has got lots of money or he wouldn't be livin' in The Ridge. If he's got money, then he's got lots of power around here. Betcha Tuck got hit because he knew who the boss was. And he now knows you're involved. Me too. We got to keep the doors locked."

"You know I think that's giving in." Sidney stopped and looked at Tillie and Hattie. "Am I being pig headed again? Do you really think we're in danger?"

Tillie let out an exasperated breath and shook her head as she looked at

Sidney. "Professor, you got a reputation. We got a reputation. Everyone knows it. How many murders we been involved with? Three, four, maybe five if you add in all the people around the edges. We was at the scene when Detective Knott captured Tuck's partner, and the big boss knows it. He doesn't want it known he's lookin' for some kind of treasure. Which sounds real stupid, if you ask me. Who goes lookin' for pirate treasure these days? You got a better chance of winning the Powerball lottery. There's somethin' else goin on here. Whoever popped Mr. Tuck is an important man and he feels threatened. I think he knows he did somethin' stupid when he hired those two guys to mess around with the library books. Odds are he lives here in Morgan, and he knows us and we know him. Professor, we got to keep the doors locked."

Sidney continued to sit. He made no reply, but he knew she was right. Why did he always do this? Intellectualize everything. Look at problems impersonally, as though it was some sort of exercise. Had he spent too much of his life studying dead people? Authors who died 200 years ago? Or maybe he was incapable of separating the consequences of researching a living person rather that a dead one. If you get something wrong or find out something embarrassing about a person who died more than a hundred years ago, that person isn't going to sue you or retaliate in some way. But a living person—that was a risk that Sidney had not considered. A risk that Tillie was well aware of. A living, breathing risk and not an academic one.

Sidney shifted in his chair and moved his leg into a comfortable position as he looked at the two women standing at the kitchen island. "It never occurred to me," he said. "It seemed like such a benign activity, stealing a book from a library. And as you said, Tillie, who takes searching for pirate treasure seriously?"

"Hmmm, all right, so maybe we should take it seriously. Or, at least, it's time I took it seriously. The doors will stay locked, and we will be on guard." A tone of resolve entered Sidney's voice. "But I will not sit by and wait for something to happen. If this person, what was his name again?"

"Which one?" Hattie said.

"The one who was injured."

"Tuck. Not sure if that refers to his first name or his last." Tillie answered this time.

Sidney reached for the cane that leaned against the wall near his chair. "Good. What else did your contact say about him?"

"Said he thought the police identified him as a builder who lived on James Island. Had an address on Maybank Highway. Not sure though."

Hattie, with a thoughtful expression, sipped her coffee and then directed a question to Tillie. "Now what would a builder called Tuck, who lived all the way over near the Maybank Highway, be doing at The Ridge in the middle of the night?"

Sidney, breaking into a smile, said, "Well, ladies, I think we have some work to do."

Detectives Knott and Cashman walked side by side as they headed down the street toward the City Hall Café. "Appreciate the invitation," Knott said. "You're right about getting the jurisdictional procedure out of the way first before we go too far down the road with this."

"It can be a little complicated at times but at least there's a way to do it."

They stopped at the corner of High and State Streets and waited for a horse and carriage to pass by. They both waved and smiled at passengers in the fringe-adorned tourist vehicle. The passengers waved back and took their picture. "Gotta keep the tourists happy," Knott said with another wave at the people as they switched their focus to the City Hall building behind them. "We may not have as many CCTV cameras around as other cities, but nothing moves in this town without someone taking a picture of it."

"Yeah, and some of those candid pictures ended up putting a few people away."

They quickly crossed the street and walked toward the café. Knott picked up where he left off before the tourists waving interrupted them. "I've had some conversations with the park ranger up at Colonial Morgan. He agreed that since the library break-in took place in town, Swift was all mine. He'll recommend the state police leave that part of everything alone while he works with them to find out more about the supposed treasure and will keep in touch with us directly."

"Good. But now we have another problem. You said Alan Swift ID'd the injured man as Martin Tucker from a picture. How'd you get a picture up so quick?" Sam reached for the door handle of the Café as he spoke.

"Was in the courthouse with Swift for an appearance when Mary Coffey came by. She was headed to the coroner's office downstairs, and we chatted a bit. She showed me the pictures in case I might be able to recognize him. Swift was standin' next to me and blurted out, 'Hey, that's Tuck.' Got so excited he knocked over a trash can in the hallway."

Entering, Sam said, "Hi, Sally, got room for two where we can talk and eat?"

The waitress said, "No problem. No trials today so plenty of room for you in the back corner. Here's a couple of menus, you can find your own way. Got some folks coming in behind you."

"Thanks, Sally." Sam took one of the menus and passed it to Knott as they made their way to the table set for four.

After settling in, Sam got to the heart of the matter. "So the State Park Service is going after the supposed treasure?"

"Yeah, it makes sense. They have access to all sorts of records, right back to the beginning of Charleston."

"And we have the library theft?"

"Yeah, Hornig said I should stay on that one and Alan Swift. Why? You want it?"

"No thanks. I've got an injured man in the hospital to deal with. Although he seems to have a connection to your guy Swift. Chief Hornig doesn't like problems that involve The Ridge. It makes all those people with the million-dollar houses uncomfortable. Soooo… in case Swift and Tucker are connected, how about we both have a chat with Swift?"

Sally came up to the table. "Ready?"

Sam answered, "Club sandwich and iced tea for me."

Knott hesitated and took a quick peek at the menu. "Okay, I'll do the ham and cheese omelet." He gave her the menu with a big smile. "Coffee. Black. It's gonna be a long day." Sally gave him a big smile back.

Sam answered Knott's previous question. "Solution and arrest. ASAP. You take the lead with Swift. He's all yours. I follow."

Knott sat back with a self-satisfied smile on his face. "I know that. Hornig already told me. Knew why you called. Coulda said *it's fine with me* over the phone but I didn't have anyone to have lunch with today, so I thought I'd pull your leg a bit." He laughed.

Sam broke into a big smile. "I knew it too. And this is an official business lunch that you are footing the bill for. Goes on your expenses. So, let's hear what you got from Swift so far."

"Professor Lake, there's somethin' different going on. It's too quiet." Tillie had been in her new office on the phone, planning the staffing of a cocktail party. She stood in the entryway to Professor Lake's new office library in the rear of the house.

Sidney looked up from the keyboard on which he had been tapping away with his two index fingers. "In what way?" He leaned back in his chair and carefully stretched out his right leg.

"Lemme sit down over here for a minute." She crossed over to a comfortable wingback chair near the fireplace. "It's been two whole days since they found the man over at The Ridge. The one connected to the book thefts at the Palmer Library. The folks in The Ridge are complaining like they always do when they think they're being threatened. They're calling City Hall as usual, but there doesn't seem to be anything happening. We're lookin at three now and the newspaper's not sayin' anything since they first reported it. The mayor isn't jumping up and down demanding action, the police are going on about their business, and my people ain't hearing anything."

"Interesting." Sidney absently rubbed his leg. "However, I'm not convinced it's out of the ordinary. It wouldn't surprise me if the theft at the Palmer Library was being considered as a somewhat childish, amateurish attempt at seeking buried pirate treasure and nothing more. I looked into the Bailey family, and they seem like a routine run-of-the-mill plantation owning family of the eighteenth and nineteenth century." He put his hands together across his midsection and began to twiddle his fingers. "I must admit, I did wonder if that theft was the tip of the iceberg and there could be more worth pursuing. Last week, we all believed this was going to be a major worry for us and began thinking about being cautious and careful. But the police seemed to have everything under control. The man didn't die, and there didn't seem to be a continuing threat to the people on The Ridge."

Tillie, now seated, suggested, "This whole idea of there being a pirate's treasure involved coulda thrown us off the track. I mean, people come down here looking for treasure all the time and nobody pays much attention to them. It's kinda like people looking for gold out west. Nobody really takes them serious anymore. There's more gold to be found in Wall Street than in a hole in the ground or sunken ship off the coast. All those ships coming into Charleston were carrying slaves—South Carolina gold—not the silver and gold everyone first thought would line the bottom off the coast."

"Humph, yes." Sidney reached down and carefully moved his knee and straightened in his chair. "Just a thought… you haven't heard anything more about the man they found in the marsh? I saw one item in the paper but nothing more."

"Yeah, that's also kinda strange. He's in a coma but I don't know nothin more. Although, things that happen over in The Ridge don't get a lot of publicity."

"Yes, but you can be certain Sam Cashman and Detective Knott are keeping after everything, and while we may not see much in the newspapers, I'm sure a lot is going on behind the scenes. Keep in mind, the mayor also lives in The

Ridge now. Knowing how he hates anything negative being said about the downtown area, he's probably quietly pestering Chief Hornig." Sidney, now perked up and fully engaged, leaned forward, put his elbows on his desk and folded his hands in front of him one on top of the other.

"You haven't heard anything from your associates around City Hall and the hospital about the man in the marsh?"

"Actually, I haven't asked, and no one's come forward with anything on their own. Too quiet."

The phone on Sidney's desk rang and interrupted them.

"Professor Lake? This is Grace Bennett." Her voice sounded concerned. A bit shaky.

"Hello, Mrs. Bennett. Is something the matter?"

"It's Mitchell, my husband. I'm not sure what to do."

"Is it an emergency?"

Tillie, hearing the comment and seeing Sidney's facial expression change, got out of her chair and came over to the desk.

"I don't know. It could be."

"Is he injured? Hurt in some way? Have you called 911?" Sidney looked up at Tillie, now in front of him.

"That's just it, I don't know." Sidney heard Grace take a deep breath. "I'm sure I must sound crazy, but let me explain."

Sidney held the phone out from his ear slightly so Tillie could hear Grace's side of the conversation.

"Yes, please do," he encouraged.

"He didn't come home last night. It's not that it hasn't happened before. And that's not the only reason I'm calling. It's that silly treasure incident at the library. Last night, he picked up the newspaper from the other day and finally read the description of the man found in the marsh. He believes he knows him. I know you're friendly with the police and I wanted someone to know about this, but I don't want to call them myself. Mitchell refused to call them and would be furious with me if I did. The injured man is a contractor and developer—a very successful one in Dorchester County. He doesn't live on the Maybank Highway on James Island, he lives in Summerville. Mitchell blurted all of this out after dinner last night and then left in a hurry. He said he'd be back later and not to say anything. He never came home."

"You haven't notified the police?"

"No. As I said, Mitchell would be furious with me."

"Do you still have Detective Knotts' phone number?"

"I'm sure I do. It would automatically be in my contacts."

"Don't wait any longer. You've met him. Call him as a friend. Explain to him exactly what you said to me. He can be trusted."

"Yes, I know."

When the call ended, Sidney looked at Tillie. "Did you hear all that?"

"Yeah, I think we ought to call Mister Sam. You or me?"

Sidney thought for a moment. "I think I'd better do it. Sam is following the incident on The Ridge, and I'm sure they've properly identified the injured man. The Bennetts live near The Ridge. This could be a connection he isn't aware of. What I'd like you to do is to start asking questions behind the scenes. Somehow your contacts always know more than they should but don't realize it. I would love to find out what they think is happening."

ELEVEN

2018

Who Is Martin Tucker?

Grace Bennett sat with her iPhone still in her hand. Did she do the right thing to call Sidney Lake? Should she call Detective Knott? She didn't want Mitchell to be angry with her and accuse her of being foolish. Their relationship was on edge recently and she didn't know why. Mitchell seemed to be preoccupied. But she was the same. Pine View was consuming all her time. More than she planned when she took the position. It started out as a way of getting back into the job scene after having Pam and Carter. At first, she worked her duties at Pine View into her schedule but now the tables had turned, and her Pine View schedule had become the priority. Mitchell and the children were something to be worked around her daily routines and responsibilities at the retirement village, not the other way around. She had to make some decisions. Where were her priorities? What would be number one? Should there be only one number one? Could she do both?

"Of course I can, damn it! That's what multi-tasking is all about. That's what they'll all have to learn." She stood up. "Get yourself together, Grace."

She dialed Detective Knott's number.

The operator at Morgan Police Headquarters listened to Grace's concerns. Detective Knott had left instructions not to be disturbed, so the operator offered to have Grace's call switched to another detective but no, Grace wanted to discuss the matter directly with Knott. The operator promised to leave a message for him. Grace hung up and started to pace the kitchen. She was having doubts again. Was she overreacting? Her phone buzzed, indicating a text message. She rushed over to the phone on the kitchen table. The message was from Mitchell.

Sorry I didn't call. Everything ok. On my way. Stay there.

She stood in silence and read the message again.

Now what should she do? Cancel the call to Knott? She considered it but assumed he would call her back. Talking with Detective Knott relaxed her. Besides, having the police involved might be a good way of making sure Mitchell gave her the whole story. He was known to be somewhat creative at times with what he told her. He never lied, just kept key bits of information on the side.

She called Sidney Lake again and updated him. Talking with Professor Lake also had a calming effect. Something about the confident and impartial way he approached a subject.

"I'm certainly glad to hear your husband has not come to any harm." Grace heard a soft *woof*, almost an agreement, and she smiled. That would be Mickey.

"It's all very unsettling. I wish Mitchell had given me the man's name before he rushed off."

"I have a description that Tillie managed to get, and the police have identified him as being a contractor in Dorchester County, which matches with the Summerville address."

Grace picked up the real estate guide she had earlier placed on the kitchen table. Of the five building contractor ads in Dorchester, only one had pictures of people and they all seemed to be satisfied customers standing in front of newly built homes. "I checked Mitchell's real estate guide but unlike real estate company ads, where the pictures of the sales agents seem to be extremely important, no one seems to care what a developer looks like."

"I suppose we'll have to wait and see what your husband says when he returns. I'm glad you called Detective Knott. I have a call to Detective Sargent Cashman, who's a good friend. I wouldn't be surprised if Detectives Knott and Cashman already know a great deal about the injured man." Sidney lowered his voice. "Since your husband seems to be unharmed, let's wait for him to get home. I'm sure there will be a reasonable explanation. Although I'd be very interested to know of his relationship to the injured man."

"I'll definitely call you."

As Sidney ended the call, Mickey made her way out of the office and took a left turn toward the back door. Sidney grabbed his cane and with the other hand on his desk, lifted himself out of the chair and followed Mickey. "Someone there you know, Mickey?" He assumed the person at the door would be Cal Prentice, who had called earlier. Cal had been working on his sermon for Sunday and added some local historical references that he needed to check for accuracy in the South Carolina Room at the Morgan Regional Library. He asked Sidney if he'd like to join him. Sidney jumped at the chance. This would be an opportunity to explore in greater detail the history of the owner of the books that started it all: Joshua Bailey.

While Sidney and Cal Prentice made their way to the library, Grace Bennett received a return phone call from Detective Knott. She started out by feeling embarrassed about bothering him, since Mitchell had texted her that he was on his way home, but Knott didn't look at it that way.

"You're sure he's all right? And it was definitely your husband who texted you?"

"Why… yes. The message said it was from him." She was taken aback. It never occurred to her that it wasn't. "Why do you ask?"

"Just covering all bases. When he didn't come home last night, what was your first reaction?"

"I… I was concerned."

"His not coming home is unusual?"

"Well, yes."

"He's never done this before?"

"Er… no. Well, yes, but he always lets me know."

Detective Knott paused momentarily as he reached across his desk to a printout he had received earlier. "Grace, in the message you left me, I had the feeling there was something else that has you concerned about your husband not coming home last night. Is there something you're not telling me?"

Grace hesitated before responding. "It was the afternoon paper, The Morgan Times, from two days ago. Mitchell hadn't read it at the time but picked it up after dinner. There was a description of the man who had been found in the marsh. Very detailed. Height, weight, clothing, shoes. Mitchell became excited and said he knew who it was. The paper didn't name him. I guess they didn't have a name yet. But Mitchell was sure who it was. Said he knew him and he was a developer who lived over in Summerville. He became agitated and then said he had to go out and not to wait up for him."

"And he didn't identify the man by name?"

"No."

"And the description didn't mean anything to you?"

"No."

Detective Knott gave a deep sigh, as though he was relieved she didn't know the man. "Okay, have you told anyone about what you've told me?"

Grace did not answer immediately, wondering if she would be in trouble of some kind, and then realized she had to answer the question truthfully. "Actually I did."

"Who?" Knott had a piece of paper and a pen at the ready.

"Am I in trouble?"

"Certainly not. No. We're just trying to keep everything under control.

Grace, tell me who else knows."

"You already know who the injured man is, don't you?"

"Ma'am, we know a lot of things we try not to let out into the public until we're ready to do so."

"So, you do know." She took note of the change in his voice.

"Grace, please, who have you spoken to about this?"

Grace paused again. She knew she had to tell him but she didn't want to get Professor Lake into trouble. "Sidney Lake. He won't be in trouble, will he?"

"Certainly not."

"Should I call him and tell him I spoke with you?"

Knott softened his voice. "No, Grace, we'll take care of everything from here but please let me know when your husband gets home. And especially if he doesn't."

"Of course. Yes, I will. Wilson."

Entering the South Carolina Room, Cal Prentice and Sidney Lake set themselves up at different tables. This part of the library stood apart from the main activity of the building. Having a specialized function, it had its own secure entrance where visitors had to identify themselves and sign in on the computer with their identification as they entered and again as they left. The library required a staff member to be present whenever the room was open. This was not the only location in town where historical documents were kept. As with many cities, records were everywhere. There were the official government archives, which now occupied the old city hall building, and the historical society had its headquarters and library in a building that once served as a meeting house for the French Huguenots who came to South Carolina in the first half of the eighteenth century. The Palmer Library reference room was filled with donations from many of the private homes whose residents traced their lineage to the beginnings of Morgan had libraries of their own. The Morgan College library maintained its own historical reference room. The Morgan Regional Library's South Carolina Room's specialty focus was genealogy. Because of this, it held a large collection of old maps and a computerized master database of what they and all the other locations contained in their collections.

"Anything special I can help you with today, Professor Lake?" inquired Etta DeReimer, the room's head librarian.

"Yes. Bailey. Joshua Bailey. Understand he had quite a presence in the early 1700s."

"Joshua Bailey? That name is familiar. Let me do some checking and I'll get right back to y'all." Etta was a no-nonsense person. She had the instinct of a retriever looking for a bird she was sent to find. She would hunt under every bush and bramble until she found what her clients sought.

Cal looked at Sidney with a smile. "Got Julia off on a hunt for you already, I see."

"She's good, isn't she. While she's working the database, I'm going to focus on the maps. They have a separate catalogue of those over here." Sidney pointed to an area to his right, no more than ten feet away from his table. "Where's your focus today, Cal?"

"Slavery. That new museum they're finally getting in Charleston has all of us thinking about the heritage of the region. The organizers are trying to develop as much historical background as possible, and everyone's been asked to help. I'm weaving some of what I learn into an adult Sunday School class I'm starting."

Sidney limped over to the large horizontal map drawers set against the wall as he listened to Cal. This was Sidney's forte: research. He loved digging through old, historic documents. He couldn't wait to start.

TWELVE

1719
Thomas and Eli Nichols

Thomas Nichols, born on the island of Barbados, had a comfortable life for his first eleven years. His father, Jeremiah, served as one of the managers of a sugar plantation on the island, but in 1715, Thomas' world upended. The price of sugar collapsed. The plantation he called home dangled on the edge of bankruptcy. During the previous five years, sugar plantations were created on almost every island in the Caribbean, resulting in an oversupply of the once valuable commodity.

Jeremiah Nichols, responding to reports of new opportunities in the British Colonies north of Spanish Florida, made his way to the Province of South Carolina in early 1716. Thomas, his mother, and Eli, his older brother by three years, followed a few months later, joining Jeremiah on a coastal land grant he had obtained. The grant was in the area north of the recently formed Beaufort settlement on land occupied by the Yemassee for more than a thousand years.

The managers of the Province of South Carolina, anxious to increase the number of white men in the colony, as they had become outnumbered by the growing population of Black slaves, offered generous land grants to Europeans to increase immigration. Jeremiah Nichols obtained his grant in late 1716 but it came with the proviso: if you can keep it. In accepting the grant and moving his family onto land bordering the Combahee River, Jeremiah Nichols found himself caught between the economic and political ambitions of the colony's rulers in Charles Town and the avarice of the settlers that had already moved onto Yemassee lands. Even though enslavement of Native Americans had been rejected by the Spanish as they had been considered Spanish citizens, the English settlers saw them as potential slaves. War with the Yemassee broke out within six months of the family's arrival. Jeremiah was killed in late 1717 during a Yemassee raid before firm title to any land could be secured. The Nichols brothers lost their mother the following year to an incurable infection.

The brothers were now on their own and while Eli, who was seventeen, followed his parent's example and prayed to God daily to be given back the land they lost, Thomas, age fourteen, would have none of it. After a short while trying to find work around Charles Town, he decided to earn his fortune at sea.

At first Thomas tried to sign on with the pirate Charles Vane, who reportedly had made great profits from raids on commercial shipping between Charles Town and the Bahamas. But Vane wanted experienced crewmembers and had no interest in fourteen-year-old Thomas Nichols. Desperate to go to sea, Thomas worked the docks of Charles Town and on shallops along the coast. Finally, he convinced Ignatius Pell, the boatswain of Stede Bonnet's *Royal James*, to employ him. Bonnet had been a wealthy plantation owner in Barbados before becoming disgruntled with the government's response to the sugar crisis. Unlike other Barbados settlers, who left the island to seek new lives in the American colonies, Bonnet took part of his wealth, bought a ship—which he renamed *The Revenge*—hired a crew, and began to plunder commercial shipping in and around the Caribbean Sea. Because of Thomas' Barbados connection and his knowledge of the waters between

Charles Town and the Beaufort settlement, Pell believed he could be a good addition to the crew and assigned the young man to work with the ship's coxswain David Herriot.

Thomas Nichols' only adventure as a pirate ended badly. Shortly after joining Bonnet's crew, Bonnet headed north to Cape Fear.

Charles Vane followed Bonnet to Charles Town and unsuccessfully attempted a blockade of the harbor to hold the merchants hostage to his extortion demands. This act so infuriated the British Governor he authorized the formation of a flotilla under the command of Colonel William Rhett to go after Vane and destroy him.

Rhett thought he had come upon Vane at Cape Fear some days later but was mistaken. He had found Stede Bonnet instead. Bonnet attacked, and the Battle of Cape Fear ensued. Bonnet and all his men were captured, tried in an Admiralty Court at Charles Town, and made an example to all future pirates who would attack in Carolina's waters. Nearly all of Bonnet's crew were sentenced to hang.

Ignatius Pell gave evidence indicating it was really David Herriot, the coxswain of *The Royal James*—formerly *The Revenge*—that controlled the ship, and Bonnet could not be held accountable. Even Colonel William Rhett pled for Bonnet's life, again making the claim he was above the usual *trash* that made up a pirate's crew and must be treated differently. Bonnet was a gentleman who came from a good family and had been well educated. But Pell unexpectedly turned on Bonnet, gave evidence against him, and saved himself from the gallows. He was given the option of saving another seaman and chose fourteen-year-old Thomas Nichols, claiming he took no part in the fighting and was there only to learn the duties of a coxswain.

Thomas Nichols initially felt his future would be with Pell but learned a valuable lesson on the trip to Fort Dorchester. Pell was a hardened man who would take Nichols' life if he believed it useful to do so. Thomas got away from Pell as quickly as possible and became a crew member of a commercial British vessel and planned to leave the American colonies for good.

Before leaving Charles Town, Thomas wanted to do something for his brother, Eli. Eli prayed daily to God to allow him to fulfill his father's dream of owning land and a farm, instead of working for another aristocratic plantation landlord. Thomas looked at the world in a more practical way and sought out the tavern where he knew members of the crew of Tuscarora Jack Barnwell's coastal sloop spent much of their time when in harbor. They had strong and frequent connections with associates of Richard Tookerman. He learned from Pell, as well as Barnwell's crew, of Tookerman's investments in many of the emerging plantations along the Ashley and Cooper Rivers and looked to expand his influence to the Beaufort region.

Barnwell had garnered fame and fortune in support of the settlers who were once again occupying land grants in the area around the Beaufort settlement. His sloop plied the waters along the coast south of Charles Town, a region Eli knew well. But the Yamassee were still there, and no safe land passage existed from Charles Town south to the settlers.

Colonel John Barnwell, known as "Tuscarora Jack" for his role in the Tuscarora War, had been given the task of eliminating all the first peoples from the territory from Charles Town to the Georgia colony. They had been unreliable as slaves and too dangerous to be left in place.

Governor Johnson of the Province of South Carolina received approval to establish townships in all the province lands and to offer the most lucrative land grants possible to white men who would come and claim them. Fifty acres could be had by each man with an additional twenty for each family member, including slaves and servants. Thomas learned of all the important connections that would be necessary for Eli to become a successful plantation owner.

Eli Nichols saw this as God's answer to his prayers and his opportunity to fulfill his father's dream. He knew he could get priority as the current English landholders had also become marginalized by the great numbers of French, Irish, and German immigrants flooding the Carolinas. The colonial English were not happy with the wave of foreign speakers and non-Church of England Christians, but at least they were white.

Eli's first task would be to obtain a land grant of substantial size. He planned for his brother Thomas to also apply for a grant and then combine the lands into a single plantation. Having been a veteran of Jack Barnwell's militia, Eli believed he had the best chance for success, but Thomas objected to the plan as he wanted a life at sea, although he still had the reputation attached to him of being one of Stede Bonnet's crew and the British managers of the province looked at him warily. Eli initially decided to go it alone but eventually joined forces with another of Barnwell's men, William Manley, who had been a coxswain on one of Barnwell's coastal sloops.

Eli and Manley filed grant applications and were not challenged, even though they provided false information to obtain larger blocks of land. Eli claimed to be married with three children, two servants, and three slaves. His grant included just over 200 acres and was located along the Achepoo River. Manley claimed four children and two slaves. His land grant abutted to Nichols'. Some years later, after Manley's death, Eli Nichols acquired Manley's land.

Thomas Nichols' service with Bonnet continued to work against him in the colonies. Frustrated, he gave up and went back to the sea on a commercial vessel headed for England, never to be heard of again.

The lands along the Achepoo became more available, making Eli Nichols' task of retaining his grant much easier. But he did have a problem, one he prayed over daily. To keep his grant, he had to properly validate its terms: he had to find a widow to marry with three children and acquire the required number of slaves. He knew God would help him. Before leaving Charles Town, his brother, Thomas, introduced Eli to Ignatius Pell and learned of the power and importance of Richard Tookerman.

Unable to obtain Ignatius Pell's aid, Eli Nichols decided it would be best to approach Richard Tookerman directly at Three Crows tavern, the primary place of business in the harbor. Tookerman knew his way around Charles Town better than anyone, but Thomas had also warned him that in dealing with Tookerman, there would be a price to pay.

The tavern sat sandwiched between two warehouses along the quay of the Cooper River. Although it was noon, the noise was loud and raucous, akin to the sound expected from a tavern late in the evening. But this was the waterfront, and the days and nights were mostly indistinguishable. The tide drove the day and the night. Not the sun. The workday began as the tide rose and permitted a cargo laden ship to pass easily over the shoals in and around the harbor. By the time the tide had ebbed, the cargo, be it human or cloth, was warehoused and the tavern full.

Nichols approached the barman and caught his attention with, "Is Captain Tookerman about?"

The barman tilted his head and indicated a place to his left. "In the corner. He sits with his back to the wall. Go easy if you approach."

Nichols thanked him. He walked no more than three paces in Tookerman's direction before Tookerman locked eyes on him. A chill went up Eli's spine.

Seeing the young man start to approach the table, at which four others were seated, Tookerman nodded to the man across from him. The man immediately stood and turned around. Before Nichols got to move another two paces, a tall, burly man blocked his way.

"You have business?" It was not so much a question as a challenge. The man was well over six feet and blocked the light coming in through the window to the left of Tookerman. The others at the table continued their conversation with their Captain but were also on alert. They were all well dressed, except the mountain of a man standing in front of Nichols.

"Er... I do. I was told Captain Tookerman could help me." Nichols spoke quietly and respectfully.

"Who are you? Who sends you?"

"Eli Nichols, sir. Er... Mister Pell."

"Ah. Hold your ground." The mountain turned around and caught Tookerman's eye. "He comes from Mister Pell."

"He does, does he? Bring him forward," Tookerman said with eyes narrowed.

The mountain half turned, reached out, and grabbed Nichols by the shoulder. The meaty hand could have lifted him straight up in the air or ripped his arm from its socket. Nichols winced in pain as he came up to the table.

"How do you know Pell?" growled Tookerman.

"We…We… my brother served with him. Coxswain for Captain Bonnet."

"Ah, hope he not be the one saved from the hangman. Bad business. Should have saved Bonnet and thrown him to the fish."

"Don't know. He was with him on your behalf up to Dorchester," said Nichols to show loyalty and participation in a task Tookerman had designed.

The captain was silent. He looked at Nichols. He stroked his chin, as though thinking, *what should I do with him?* Finally, he said, "What do you know of Dorchester?"

Nichols' eyes widened. He remembered his brother, Thomas, telling him about 'The Box' and Pell's reaction to its existence and to never say a word about it in connection with Fort Dorchester. "Nothing. Understand he did the rowing."

Tookerman remained silent again. He looked at Nichols carefully. "Were he paid?"

"Aye, sir."

"So why are you here?"

Nichols looked nervously at the men around the table. "I need help."

"Why in damnation should I help you?"

"I thought… well… Mister Pell. He said you were an important man. You could help me."

"Oh, he did, did he." Tookerman crossed his arms over his chest.

The sun scuttled behind a cloud and Nichols wished he could as well. The room went dark, but Tookerman stared straight at him, his eyes like daggers. "Speak your need."

Eli was taken aback. He wanted to run. He wanted to get away. Sweat trickled down his cheek. "I… need a… wife."

The table went quiet. Tookerman said nothing. The mountain gave him an "are you serious, mate" look and began to get ready to grab the young man and toss him out of the tavern.

Suddenly, Tookerman guffawed. Laughter erupted from the table as all his compatriots joined in.

Tookerman softened and asked, "What in God Almighty do ya need a wife for?"

Nichols let out a huge breath of air. "I have a grant down Beaufort way. It's a good one. I told them I had a wife and three children. I'll need to produce them."

A big smile from Tookerman as he said, "I might help you with the wife, but you'll have to produce the children on your own… as much as I'd like to help you with that as well." He laughed and the table men laughed with him. "Okay. There'll be a sale here in the tavern at noon tomorrow. Be here. Do you want Black or white? We have negras and indents up. You have the silver?"

"Well…."

"Of course you don't. Still okay. There'll be terms, Mister Nichols. Oh, yes. There'll be terms."

THIRTEEN

2018
The South Carolina Room

Sidney Lake sat at a long library table, with maps of coastal South Carolina dating back to the early 1700s spread before him. He was surprised at how small an area the original city of Charleston occupied, and how large the areas were that the early plantation owners claimed for themselves. The Lords Proprietors of the Carolinas—the managers of the King's grant—had no problem declaring the land from Spanish Florida to the Virginia border, as well as the island of Barbados and the islands of the Bahamas, to be within their jurisdiction. This was clearly shown on the maps he had before him, even though the lands marked out for plantations were already occupied by native residents who had been living there for centuries,

"Fascinating, isn't it," commented a young woman who came up alongside Sidney and looked at the maps.

A startled Sidney recovered quickly and replied, "It certainly is. I've read about the history of the area but only from the perspective of a resident, not as a historian. My career has primarily been centered around the nineteenth century, the Victorian Age. I never really looked at the origins of where I live, although it has piqued my interest of late."

"You must be Professor Lake. Mrs. DeReimer told me you were here. I'm Nora Woodman. I work in the library's reference section. I sometime help in this room when Mrs. DeReimer gets tied up with a project."

Sidney smiled. "I'm delighted to meet you. You could probably be of some help if you have the time."

"Actually, Mrs. DeReimer asked me to stop over today as she concentrated on another project."

"I'm afraid I'm tying everyone up. I don't mean to be a bother."

"Not at all, Professor Lake. That's why we're here. How can I help?"

"The Joshua Bailey Plantation. I'm trying to ascertain its original location. I know it was supposed to be up along the Combahee River someplace. I would imagine it should be somewhere near the original site of the colonial market town of Morgan."

"Joshua Bailey. Yes. I'm familiar with him." Nora paused, removed her glasses, took a handkerchief from her pocket, and began to clean the lenses. Sidney noticed the move and saw it as a maneuver he often used when trying to recall something, as he stood before a room full of students.

"By the way, have you ever done any teaching?"

Nora paused in her cleaning and looked questioningly at Sidney. "Why, yes I have. I taught history for a while at Morgan High School."

"I thought so." Sidney nodded at Nora's glasses.

"Ah, caught me. Habit of mine when trying to recall something."

"I understand only too well."

"Yes, I remember now," Nora said as she reached across Sidney and put her finger on the location of the Combahee River. "Joshua Bailey had at least three distinct plantations." She tapped the map with her index finger. "The original one was on the Ashley River. Raised horses and livestock there, I believe. Farther south and east he eventually had one for indigo and another for rice. That last one was not far from here."

"Do you know if any of these maps show the specific locations?" Sidney indicated the other maps lying in front of him.

"I'm sure they do. Also, the library over in Beaufort would have some as well. They set up their South Carolina Room long before we did. As the plantations were bought up and turned into housing developments and golf courses, the original owners donated a lot of what they had to the library. Not all the old books were given to them, but a great many maps were." While Nora talked, she thumbed through the maps on the table and then pulled one out. "Here's one from just east of here. Over toward Edisto. Would probably be rice. I think the indigo one was further inland, over in the direction of Walterboro."

"This is very helpful." Sidney looked at the map of the rice plantation. He then looked up at Nora and said, "Why did you ever leave teaching?"

"I couldn't get the hang of it. I love the history part and doing research but standing up in front of a classroom and going over the same material time and time again… it wasn't for me."

"And the library?"

"Love it." Nora beamed. "Especially in here. Here, history comes alive. It's personal. It's filled with individual and family stories."

Sidney looked at the young woman and recognized he had a valuable resource standing in front of him. "Miss Woodman, I think you're going to be a great help to me."

"I'll certainly try." As Nora replied, a low vibrating buzzer sound interrupted her. She reached for the phone in the case on her belt, glanced at it, and apologized. "I'm sorry Professor Lake, I've been called up to the reference desk. I'll be back in a moment."

"No, no. Go right ahead. I'll be here for a while."

While Nora and Sidney were becoming acquainted, Cal Prentice quietly studied some of the reference books he had chosen. Seeing Nora Woodman step away, he said, "So what do you think of Nora?"

Sidney turned to Cal. "Do you know her?"

"Yes. She's always very helpful. Nice young woman. She's Mrs. Cathcart's niece, you know. The librarian at the Palmer library."

"Really. I have a feeling she's going to be a great help."

Cal stayed behind after Sidney left. His original purpose had been to research some historical events he planned to use in an upcoming sermon, but he had become distracted by the room in which he sat: Morgan Library's South Carolina Room.

Mrs. DeReimer had come back to the room and now sat at her desk as she spoke with Cal. "It's a very interesting topic. Have you ever had your DNA researched?"

"Actually no, I haven't. Ruth has had hers done and is in the process of building a rather large family tree on Ancestry.com. But no, although I think I'll probably do it. Ruth keeps wanting me to. You say you've been researching a great many families lately for people in town as well as other places?"

She removed her glasses and placed them on the papers in front of her. "It's become very popular. And this is a natural place to do that kind of research." She looked around at the shelves nearby filled with books and records dating back hundreds of years. "There's a great deal of information right here. People come from all over the country and say, 'I recently found out an ancestor of mine had a farm in the area, would you have any records about that?' And of course, we do. Local residents have given us copies of land transfer records, marriage records, and all sorts of other legal documents. A portion of the birth and death records have been digitized but a good deal of the more mundane legal and court records can be found here or in the archives at the old city hall building. The county has a Daughters of the American Revolution club. We don't have our own DAR chapter. I don't think we're big enough for that."

"Has Ruth been here to see you?"

"No, she hasn't."

"I have to tell her to get over here." Cal thought for a moment and then said, "She's originally from Pennsylvania. The family goes back a long way. Would you have any resources to help her?"

"Certainly. With all the interest we've been receiving, the library has taken memberships in many of the US and European genealogy search engines. We haven't had too many calls to look at Asian records. The library is also part of the group that is supporting the new African American Museum in Charleston and their genealogy research program. And there's Penn Center over in Beaufort County." She picked up her glasses and took a quick look at the computer screen in front of her.

Cal caught the look and said, "I didn't mean to take up all your time, but I'm definitely going to have Ruth visit."

"It's all right. It's just that the mayor's wife made an appointment to come over in about fifteen minutes. She had her DNA done and found out she's related to a prominent colonial lawyer. Something she knew nothing about."

"Really. This has certainly piqued my interest. Who is it, if I might ask?"

"A fellow named Winslow. John James Winslow, Esquire. He apparently had some connections here in Morgan as well as Charleston."

"Wonderful. I'll bet she's excited. This is all quite interesting and—" He stopped in mid-sentence and shook his head. "I'm sorry. You have things to do and I'm holding you up. Mrs. DeReimer, thank you so much." He started to turn around to leave but made one more comment. "I'm going to get that DNA test done and we'll have a real conversation."

As Dorinda Tooker made her way along the sidewalk, she moved carefully. The walkway contained many perils for a woman of eighty-nine years: large cracks in the concrete, uneven sections where tree roots of tall and ancient oaks had lifted the sidewalk one and two inches above the original surface, and whole sections where the walkway changed from concrete to a dirt path. She used a cane with a grip made of silver, a gift from her granddaughter's husband, the mayor. It represented a peace offering more than a gift. She didn't like Steele Wilcox and often let her feelings be known. The cane, one she admired at the local jewelry store, pleased her, and placed him in her court when it came to her refusal to use a walker. She viewed those ugly metal gadgets, which so many of her contemporaries used, as being a sign of old age, of giving up. She had always been independent and had no intention of stopping now.

Her doctors and family members told her she needed to be careful, act her age, take it easy. Walking around every day on her own could be dangerous. What if she fell? What if she had another heart attack? No. Walking here at The Ridge kept her alive. Walking where her grandfather walked. And his grandfather before him. Walking the ground where they walked, touching the trees they touched, watching the tide come in and out as they did. These were the things that were important to her. For more than 300 years, her family had walked here and so would she.

Her destination could be seen now. A favorite place. Once the location of a fine home that belonged to her fifth great-grandfather, now a small park with a comfortable bench to view the movements of the water and the swaying of the spartina grass. A stone marked the spot where the legendary storm came ashore and washed away the family home.

Finally at her destination, she sat. Tired but happy. This was not a lonely place for her, but one filled with the spirits of her ancestors. Comfortable and content, she envisioned them being here in this same spot.

A voice called out to her, "Mrs. Tooker, I've found it."

Turning, she saw a familiar and friendly face. "Oh, hello, dear."

"The plantation house. I know where it was located. The original location of Marshlands Plantation. Can I take you to it?"

"Oh, my. Are you sure? But of course you are. You've been looking for me for so long. Yes, I would love to see it. All the way back to the 1720s. Yes. To stand in that spot."

"Come on then. I'll take you right to it."

Later in the afternoon, after giving his conversation with Grace Bennett a good deal of thought, Detective Knott decided to call Sam Cashman.

"Very interesting," Sam said. "Can we talk about this later, maybe at HQ? I've got an unidentified body on my hands, and it looks as though she was attacked the same way as Tucker. I've got a pretty good idea who it is but it's too sensitive to make a guess. I need Mary to finish before I move on it."

Knott remained silent.

Sam noted the lack of response and said, "This one wasn't found in the marsh, but Mary Coffey said the head injury looks like the one Martin Tucker received. I'm over in one of the old rice fields about a mile from Palmetto Cove Plantation."

"Really? I don't know what to say. I mean, this whole incident of the stolen books from the Palmer library and the search for buried pirate treasure… it seemed like such a prank. And now we're possibly looking at two people who could have been attacked because of it. What am I missing?" Another pause.

"Wilson, you there?" Sam said, using Detective Knott's first name.

"Yeah. Sorry. I was thinking about Mitchell Bennett having gone missing when he recognized Tucker. I think we need to get together and talk about this. How much have you told Chief Hornig so far?"

"About Tucker? Not much. But he called me right after learning about the second attack. He's in with the mayor right now. I'm going to meet with him as soon as we're finished here."

"I better get over there as well. We could be looking for the same person."

"I agree. Told the chief I'd be there in about twenty minutes."

FOURTEEN

2018
Tucker and Tooker

It was Sidney's habit to walk with Mickey after lunch. The route took them down Market Street and then to the waterfront park. With his damaged leg, he didn't move very fast, which he had no intention of doing. Holding Mickey's leash in his left hand and his walking stick—he would never refer to it as a cane—supporting his right side, they easily made their way along the walkway. This was a peaceful place, another of his thinking locations. Up ahead was a wooden park bench he and Mickey planned to commandeer for a short rest. There was something about looking over moving water that cleared his mind and let thoughts come and go as they pleased. The Morgan River certainly had movement. The incoming and outgoing tide kept the water in constant motion. And then there was the wind, which generated whitecaps that seemed to ignore the tidal push and created a multidirectional effect Sidney found fascinating. For him, it was an allegory for many projects he worked on; the logical push and pull of the tide represented the known facts about a problem and led in the most logical direction while the wind would raise a whitecap making the tide seem as though it was coming in while all the time the water level kept dropping.

He sat down and looked at the water. Mickey took her position next to him and Sidney put his hand gently on the top of her head and gave it a reflexive rub. They both looked at the open expanse in front of them. A gentle breeze blew, and the water lapped against the seawall. Sidney watched and Mickey watched. Five minutes passed. Neither of them moved. Not even Mickey's ever wagging tale stirred.

Suddenly Sidney straightened from his relaxed position. He leaned against the bench as he looked up at a passing snow-white cloud. Mickey stirred and looked at Sidney.

"What if…" Sidney began. "What if the Bonnet treasure has absolutely nothing to do with the Palmer Library theft? What if it's a ruse to cover the real reason for the attack on Mr. Tucker?"

Mickey had a serious look on her face and continued to stare at Sidney.

"What if someone was trying to learn all they could about Bailey and the original land that made up his plantation? What if the original land had become almost worthless when rice production stopped but now could be valuable for real estate development? What if the title to that land is unclear after three hundred years? What if Mitchell Bennett recognized the man because they had discussions about the land? What if Michell Bennett is the third and missing man who had hired the two other men?" Sidney made a move to get up and Mickey became active. Her tail wagged and she looked behind the bench. "You recognize someone?" he asked as he turned to see who was coming toward them.

"When you got Mickey along, there's no way I can sneak up on you," Tillie said as she approached the bench. "Thought you'd be over here. Got some news. Sit down again for a few minutes."

Sidney did as instructed, and Mickey moved in front of Tillie as she sat. "They got another body. This one's dead. Found in the north part of town off the dirt road that goes down to where that old rice plantation was. Word I got is that they may be linkin' it to the guy they found at The Ridge."

"Rice plantation?" Sidney instinctively reached over and grabbed Tillie's wrist. "Wait, I was recently examining some maps at the library and learned that Joshua Bailey owned a rice plantation in the area."

"Really, that would be interesting. Although there's a lot of old rice fields around in the Lowcountry."

An old man walked past them and gave a guarded look in their direction as they talked quietly to one another. The look focused on Sidney's white hand, which appeared to grasping Tillie's Black one rather than holding her wrist.

Tillie spotted the look and said, "I think somebody got the impression we're what they call an item."

Sidney looked up and gave the man a look in return but never moved his hand. He shook his head and continued his train of thought with Tillie. "Yes, I suppose there are a great many old rice plantations around, but what's the chance of there being a connection?"

"A coincidence?" Tillie asked. She did it with a small smile, knowing exactly what Sidney's response would be.

"There is no such a thing as a coincidence," he responded with a firmness born of deep conviction. And then he looked at Tillie's smiling face. "You set me up. Ha, you wicked woman," he said with a laugh.

"You got to be the best straight man I've ever seen. No, there's no coincidence. That Joshua Bailey fella's all over everything. I can't believe we're looking at two people attacked because of a secret buried treasure from over three hundred years ago that probably doesn't even exist."

"You're absolutely right." Sidney stopped and thought for a moment. "I wonder what the police are making of all of this? What do they think is going on? We need to get Ray Morton here from Hilton Head. Ever since he became mixed up with the County Solicitor's Office, he's busier than when he worked for Chief Hornig."

"Yeah, and I don't think Miss Marie is too happy with him being away all the time either," Tillie said as she finally moved her hand and wrist out of Sidney's grip and started to get up. "You talked to that Bennett lady about her husband today. He's an insurance guy, and insurance guys are usually mixed up with real estate guys. And that old rice field where that woman was found is probably worth a lot more than it was ten years ago. Might be interestin' to see who owns it, who'd like to own it, and if it can slip past gov'ment environment people so it can be built on."

Sidney smiled as he put some pieces together. "That treasure being hunted may be a different kind of gold and silver than was first thought. Did your contact have any idea who the second man was? Wait. You said it was a woman. The body of a woman."

"Yeah. He said she looked familiar but couldn't place her."

"Come on Tillie," Sidney said as he got up from the bench. "I need to get to my office and work out a few things. Do you have anything planned for the rest of the day?"

Tillie took Mickey's lead from Sidney as he used both hands to get up from the bench. One held on to the arm while the other leaned on the handle of his walking stick.

"No, I'm good. Whatcha got in mind?"

"Walk with me. We're going to find out what's really happening. I think Mitchell Bennett is up to his neck in something, and he better tell someone what he knows for his own protection."

"Think we should tell Mr. Sam?"

They headed along the same route Sidney and Mickey took to get to the park.

"Not yet," Sidney said. "But I do think it's time for Ray Morton to get involved. I don't care what he's doing for the County Solicitors Office. This is going to be a lot more important."

"Are you sure you want to get in the middle of all this? You're still recovering from the last mess you were in. Both of you." Ray Morton addressed Sidney and Tillie as he spoke. It had been a long day for him shuttling between

Beaufort and Hilton Head. Tomorrow, he had to be in Charleston and all he wanted to do was sit and relax. Sidney, of course, knew that, and had Ray's favorite brand of scotch waiting for his arrival. Tillie's contribution to the meeting was her home-made shortbread cookies. He lived a few doors up the street from Sidney, so it wasn't an arduous journey.

"Ray, there have been two attacks here in the past week," Sidney said, defending his request. He sat in the overstuffed chair with the hassock where he had carefully placed his injured leg.

Ray had also positioned himself in his usual spot, on the sofa next to Sidney's chair, his tall scotch and soda strategically placed next to the plate of shortbread cookies on the coffee table. "Sidney, I'm sure you got your information from Tillie, and Tillie, I'm not going to ask you where you got the details, but I don't see how you can connect the two incidents?"

Tillie answered, "Because Doctor Coffey said so."

"And you know this… never mind. I don't want to know. I've got to talk to Pete Hornig. You say that Sam Cashman's got the lead on this?"

Tillie again responded. "No, sir. Chief Hornig has that new detective he got from Orangeburg as the boss of the treasure stuff. Name is Knott. Mr. Sam's working on the two attacks, though."

"And we're not dealing with some kind of lovers' quarrel? Where Tucker's wife goes off and attacks him and the woman he was fooling around with?"

Sidney chimed in, "I don't believe so. There are too many connections going back to the incident at the Palmer library and Fort Morgan."

Ray paused momentarily as he reached for his drink and one of the cookies before asking, "Bring me up to date on this treasure hunting that's been going on. It sounds a little strange. But then, who knows?"

The conversation Sidney had with Ray Morton was enough to get Ray interested in finding out what he could from his contacts at city hall. The information Tillie obtained from her people, while useful and informative, did not always have a strong factual base. Admittedly, Tillie knew this, as did Sidney, but the information always had an element of believability and Tillie, better than anyone, had the ability to piece through it to find those kernels of truth among the tidbits of gossip and misheard conversations. She also knew the sources of her information and had developed a "reliability" category for each person who passed something on to her.

"I have a name for you," Tillie announced to Sidney, who, having finished dinner, had made himself comfortable in his overstuffed chair in the living room. He brought his laptop with him, a new acquisition. Technology averse wherever possible—he used the desktop in his library primarily as a writing and editing tool rather than a research vehicle—his agreement to obtain a laptop was a great leap for him and he quickly found its convenience addictive.

"What do you mean, a name?"

"The body they found over near the old rice field."

"Ah, yes, the woman. What have you learned?"

Tillie walked into the living room. "Dorinda Tooker."

"Tooker, you say. Hmmm. I know that name. Have you learned any more about her?" Sidney leaned back in his chair and stared up at the ceiling.

"She's an old white lady who used to live in Morgan and now lives in a place for old folks outside of Edisto. Widow. Edisto is out of my territory, but I know some people who know some people. Charlene Mikel comes from there. Family goes back a long time. She'll know something."

Sidney didn't respond and crossed his arms over his chest. He closed his eyes as if trying to visualize something.

Tillie knew the sign and remained quiet as she watched him.

His arms relaxed as he brought his hands together on his chest. The fingers of each hand came together so they lightly touched. He rubbed them against one another. With eyes still closed, he nodded slightly, but Tillie recognized the very subtle movement and quietly waited.

Finally speaking in a low, almost inaudible voice, "I wonder. I wonder."

"You got an idea, Professor? Somthin' comin together?"

Sidney opened his eyes. "Yes. It's a bit of a long shot, but an interesting thought." He turned his head to look directly at her. "Yesterday, I was at the library researching the colonial plantation owner Joshua Bailey about the locations of his plantations and the idea of a map being drawn in some of the books of his that were donated to the Palmer Library. The theft of the Palmer Library books led to the attack on Martin Tucker, about whom we still have little information, especially regarding his connection to Mitchell Bennett. As a result of those books from the seventeenth century being stolen, I did some research on the pirate Stede Bonnet. I thought there might be a clue in some of the historical comments made about him. Bonnet has proven to be a very interesting person, and while there is a great deal of information about him because of the trial that took place in Charleston in 1718, documentation about the origin of his desire to be a pirate is somewhat limited. However, there is a person who has been identified as being an intermediary between Joshua Bailey and Stede Bonnet and his name was Richard Tooker... man. Now—"

Tillie interrupted, "You mean…"

Sidney raised the palm of his hand to her. "Hold on for a moment, Tillie, let me finish. It's my idea. I get to say it first."

Tillie stood quiet but bursting with eagerness to speak.

"As I started to say, this man Tookerman seems to be a link between Bonnet and Bailey. Now, the two people who have been attacked in the past week bear the surnames of Tucker and Tooker, could they have a common ancestor?" Seeing the anxiety on Tillie's face, Sidney said, "You also have a thought or two?"

"You bet. They's lots of Tookers and Tuckers between Charleston and Savannah. Some white and some Black, and you can bet they're all related. Even if none of them want to admit it. But we're talking three hundred years ago. Besides, even if they are, does it mean anything?"

"We don't know. But it certainly would be interesting if they were. I think the easiest place to start would be if Tooker is the murdered woman's maiden or married name."

"So, Wilson, what do you think," Sam asked as the two detectives headed to the police headquarters parking lot after their briefing with Chief Hornig. "Do we have any kind of link between the assault and the murder?"

"I don't think the chief believes they're connected, no matter what Mary Coffey thinks. That's why he's got me on Tucker now and you have Tooker."

"Yeah, I know the chief wants to believe they're separate but Mary seemed pretty sure it was the same weapon."

"Well, whatever it is," Knott stopped walking, "We'll let Mary and the chief work that out. You go your way and I'll go mine. I'm new to Morgan, so it makes sense that I take the case of someone from out of town while you follow Tooker, that one's got City Hall written all over it."

"Yeah. But I think we should compare notes as we move forward. Don't you find the similarities in their names strange?"

"What? Tooker and Tucker? A coincidence. Wouldn't make any difference if it was Simpson and Sampson."

"Okay." Sam started to walk toward his car. "But let's still compare notes. I know somebody who doesn't believe in coincidences and as far as I know, he's never been wrong."

FIFTEEN

1719
The Terms

The meeting with Tookerman did not end well. The words uttered by the warehouseman and merchant, "…there will be terms," would haunt Nichols for the rest of his life. Tookerman had merely looked at the man seated to his right and said, "John, take our new young friend aside and explain our standard terms for what he has asked of us."

Rising immediately from his seat, the man, John Winslow, a lawyer and business confidant of Tookerman, pointed at Nichols and said, "Come with me." He motioned Nichols to the adjoining table where they talked quietly.

Tookerman and Winslow knew the Eli Nichols' type only too well: young, eager, hard-working, uneducated, and God fearing. There were Eli Nicholses all over the Carolinas. It became clear Eli could neither read nor write, and lawyer Winslow's job would be to convince the young man he was in good hands, honest hands, God fearing hands. Eli would sign a contract containing provisions so the land he took from the Yemassee for his own would also be taken from him and end up in the hands of Tookerman and Winslow.

SIXTEEN

2018
Another Victim

Dr. Mary Coffey, the assistant coroner for Coastal Rivers County, and Detective Sam Cashman stood looking at the sheet covering the body of the woman who had been found in the old rice field on the outskirts of Morgan. "She was definitely moved, Sam. She may have been killed in that field, but she was placed in the spot she was found. I can't imagine what a woman in her eighties would be doing out there all by herself. The footing is dangerous for anyone that age."

"You're sure she was killed someplace else and placed where we found her?"

"Makes sense, and I'll tie the time down better before I finish here. Any confirmation on who she is? We couldn't find a purse or any real ID, just that watch she had with the To Dorinda Tooker – DAR inscription."

"Not yet but with that inscription—" Sam's ringing phone interrupted him. He looked at it and raised his palm to Mary. "Hold on a minute. Yes, Dave… Missing person… description fits… he's on his way over… All right, I'll make sure to be here. Is Hornig coming with him? I thought he would. Okay, thanks."

"Who do they think it is?"

"Mayor Wilcox's grandmother-in-law. They reported her missing more than six hours ago. Visiting from Edisto. She's eighty-nine years old. He and Chief Hornig are on their way."

SEVENTEEN

2018
The Enigma Of Stede Bonnet

It took Sidney Lake a full fifteen minutes to walk back to his house on Howard Street. Normally he would drive to the library, but he readily accepted Cal's offer to pick him up. Over the past few days several people had pointed out to him, since his right knee was the problem, manipulating the accelerator pedal would be a potential hazard. He did it successfully last week but came under criticism from everyone around him. His doctor suggested a comfortable walk as good physical therapy. The doctor also suggested losing thirty pounds as the best thing he could do for his knee. The latter advice was duly noted but there it ended.

Mickey greeted him as he came in the rear door to the kitchen and Tillie was not far behind.

"Glad to see you're finally getting used to the ramp. Your leg okay?"

"Yes. I can move rather well when I have to."

Mickey came over to Sidney's side and received a pat on the head.

"How 'bout a cup of tea? Sit at the table and I'll get you one."

"Only if you'll join me."

"I will. Besides, I want to hear what went on at the library."

"All right. If you work on the tea, I'll talk. I have some more ideas." Sidney pulled out the chair nearest him at the kitchen table and plopped down. The chair groaned a bit in protest as his weight hit it full force. Mickey shifted into position at Sidney's side. "There," he said and blew out a deep breath of air. "I'm becoming concerned about Mitchell Bennett. His unusual reaction when he realized Martin Tucker was attacked leads me to believe he's become involved in something he doesn't want revealed."

Tillie had taken a cup and saucer out of the cupboard for Sidney and removed a mug for herself from a stand near the microwave. She didn't look at Sidney when she spoke. "You mean Mr. Bennett could be the missing third man who was behind the search for the treasure?"

"It is a possibility, but I'm sure there's more going on here. Nothing about any of this seems to be simple and straightforward."

She was now at the point of filling the tea kettle with filtered water. Sidney made it clear a few years ago that he wanted nothing to do with unfiltered anything. Tillie learned of his preferences when she tried to give him a cup of tea made from a tea bag and tap water heated in the microwave. "I don't know, Professor. I don't know him, but I do know Miss Bennett, and she seems like a nice lady. Trouble is, a lot of nice ladies have a problem in that they take on not so nice husbands, thinkin he's gonna settle down once they're married and have a family. In the real world, it don't work that way. Now I'm not sayin Mr. Bennett is one of the bad ones. I don't know, but from what you told me about how he reacted to what happened at the Palmer Library, well, I just got to keep him up there with a question mark." She now had the tea pot down and was filling it with hot water to warm it up.

"I'm not sure either, which is why I want Ray to become more involved. The people at City Hall listen to Ray, as does Police Chief Hornig. He's one of them. Ray also listens to what's going on around him. He can tell me if they are pursuing Mitchell Bennett as a possible 'person-of-interest'."

"But what about all this treasure talk? You've been up at the library—what do those people think?"

"It's very interesting. When you look at the actual data and records of what they call 'the Golden Age of Piracy' it's a lot different from what we're fed by Hollywood. A whole generation is being given a cartoon character view of a very serious chapter in the history of not only the United States but also the entire Western hemisphere. Many of the well-known 'Buccaneers', as they were also called, were quietly sanctioned by the governments of England, Spain, and France as long as they plundered an opponent's ships. England, for instance, wanted to disrupt trade between Spain and France, but once a treaty among the countries was established, they pardoned the pirates. Unfortunately, many of the pirates found the life lucrative, and after being pardoned turned themselves on the Colonies. And we're not talking a renegade buccaneer of one ship but someone who controlled a small fleet of ships—possibly five or even as many as ten. And the strangest of all may be this Stede Bonnet person."

By this time, Tillie had the gas full up on the kettle and was spooning loose tea into the warmed teapot. "Why is that? What made him so different?"

"That's what makes him so interesting. He was different. While the other pirates were misfits—for the most part—as they couldn't read or write and were often former general seamen who couldn't handle naval rules and regulations, Bonnet was a well-to-do, educated planter from Barbados who decided to try pirating. While his competitors started out by getting together a band of disaffected men like themselves, then boarding and capturing a ship and turning it into their own, Bonnet bought the vessel that would become his pirate ship. While other pirates operated under a compact whereby the crew elected the captain and everyone shared in the value of the merchandise they captured, Bonnet owned the ship and paid his seamen wages."

"So he kept all the gold and silver for himself. And that's the treasure?"

Sidney stopped and thought for a moment. He was trying to think through the lifestyle Bonnet had developed for himself. A lifestyle dictated by the world in which the man grew up. A world of courtesy and respect for one's peers. A lifestyle other pirates deplored. "I think the key may be the word 'treasure.' To a poor man, treasure may be silver and gold, but what of a well-to-do educated and cultured man, what would 'treasure' be to him?"

The tea kettle started to sing as Tillie expressed some dismay. "But it don't make sense. Just a minute, Professor." She reached over, took the kettle off the burner, and filled the waiting teapot. "Why would a smart man with a plantation want to give it all up to go play pirate?"

"Interesting question. One for which my research has yet to answer. There is a document I would love to get my hands on, a transcript of his trial defense in December 1718 in what was then Charles Town. He carried on for at least a week and some prominent people in the colonies came to his defense because he was a 'gentleman of good family' and not the sort who should be condemned to capital punishment. In fact, there were reports of his being very courteous to those he captured, especially the ship's officers and passengers, even though he relieved them of their cargo and personal wealth."

Tillie poured the tea. "You want milk or cream? We got some cream left over from last night."

"The milk is fine."

"Sorry, Professor, keep going."

"What I started to say was that it's not unusual for someone wealthy and or famous to just 'drop out' as my generation used to call it. Perhaps Mister Stede Bonnet just decided he had had enough and…" Sidney spread his hands apart, palms up, and shrugged. "…dropped out."

"Huh, you mean he was the Patty Hearst of his generation?"

"Exactly! Yes."

"But what about the treasure? Most people when they 'drop out' don't take all their money with them."

"I agree. Which brings me back to my original question of what did Stede Bonnet believe was his most valuable asset?"

EIGHTEEN

2019
Dorinda Tooker

Mayor Steele Wilcox's face lost all its color as he stepped into the hallway of the county morgue. For the first time in his life, he felt comfortable in the company of Police Chief Pete Hornig. Their relationship had always been contentious, but the concern Chief Hornig showed over the death of Olive Wilcox's grandmother impressed him.

Mary Coffey, the assistant coroner, ushered the two men into her office.

Chief Hornig placed a hand on Wilcox's shoulder. "Are you okay, Steele?"

Wilcox answered with a sigh and put his hand up to his mouth.

"Here, take a seat," Mary offered as she moved a chair from the small conference table over to him.

Wilcox sat slowly. He looked up at Hornig as the chief brought another chair over.

"I don't know what to say, Steele. I'm so sorry."

Another sigh from Wilcox and then he said, "Yeah, I just can't believe it. She was eighty-nine years old. How am I going to tell Olive? She loved that woman. I did too. In the last year, they had become even closer. Working on the family history together. It was exciting. We were all excited. Everyone had their DNA done." He looked at the police chief. "God, Pete, are you sure someone killed her?"

Pete Hornig looked at Mary Coffey, who sat in a third chair completing the triangle. She answered. "Yes Mayor, there's no doubt."

Wilcox's voice cracked. "Who the hell would do this?" His anguished gaze switched between Hornig and Mary. "There's no mistake?" Wilcox sat straighter and a touch of anger came into his voice. "I want him caught, Pete. I want to see his face. I want to see him on death row."

"We'll get him. You know we will."

"Get all the help you need." Wilcox, with intense, teary eyes, looked directly at Hornig and then at Mary. "Get it from the county, the state, from anywhere and anyone you need. I mean it, Pete. Don't care what you spend or how you do it." He reached up with both hands and ran his fingers through his hair. Halfway back, he grabbed hold of a fistful and pulled. "Dammit, I can't believe this. An eighty-nine-year-old woman." He released his hair and looked up. "We'll get him, Miss Dory. By God, we'll get him."

The three of them sat talking for another fifteen minutes before Pete Hornig left and drove the mayor home.

Upon arriving, Hornig asked Steele if he wanted him to come in.

The mayor said no. "Just get him, Pete. Get him."

Mary Coffey sat at her desk, reading the file in front of her as Sam Cashman came in. She looked up and motioned him to a chair. "Take a seat, Sam."

"Thanks. Anything new on Miss Tooker?"

Mary leaned back in her chair. "Pete Hornig and the mayor left a little while ago. We didn't get into any specifics. Do you have this one?"

"Yeah."

"They're the same, you know. The iron weapon with a hook at the end. Haven't told anyone officially, yet."

"See that Knott gets a copy when you put the report out."

"I will. It could be a poker for an old fireplace. I'll have more on that later."

"And you're sure she was killed elsewhere."

Mary looked down at the file before answering. "Still doing our analysis. Called the state lab for help but yeah, it sure looks like she was moved."

Chief Hornig immediately put all current investigations on hold. By late afternoon, he had gathered his senior officers together and explained what had happened and the focus he now demanded. "The victim in the rice field murder is Olive Wilcox's grandmother. For those of you who don't know, Olive Wilcox is the mayor's wife. There's also some possibility the rice field murder and the treasure hunter attacked on The Ridge are in some way connected. Wilson Knott will stay focused on The Ridge, although the overall investigation will be handled by Sam Cashman with me looking over his shoulder. I've notified the state I'll be looking for their support on this, and they've already been in touch with Sam. Also, the county solicitor's office is lending us one of their contract investigators, Ray Morton, who used to be my right-hand man here in Morgan. He will report directly to me. The control center will be in this room so we may have to move some desks around. Any questions?"

Detective Patton raised his hand.

The chief looked at him and said, "Yeah."

"Chief, being that Miss Tooker is the mayor's relative, should we do anything different than normal?"

"This may be a small town, but you all know how to behave. Be professional. If you run into something you're not sure of, bring it in here. I'll evaluate it and decide how it should be handled and which resources will deal with it. The 'buck stops with me.' I don't want you making decisions that will jeopardize you in any way. That's my job."

A short pause led to a few chuckles around the room. The chief looked around and focused on Detective Patton in front of him, who had a smile on his face and a raised eyebrow. The chief whispered to him, "What'd I say?"

Then he got it. "Ah, yeah. You know what I mean. I don't want y'all to be criticized for something I told you to do."

"We get it, Chief," Patton said.

"Okay, Sam, set up this place the way you need it. Wilson, come to my office for a minute."

After a few minutes, Sam addressed the group in front of the two plexiglass panels they set up at one end of the room. "The first thing I want is Dorinda Tooker's handbag. According to the mayor, she was last seen walking toward Robins Point Park where she went to watch the tide come in. I want the entire area combed. Including the nearby water. Hamp," referring to Corporal Hampton Butler, "you run that. And get a couple of flat-bottomed boats to poke around offshore." Turning to his left, he said, "Patton, take a few others to the rice field and go over everything again, starting with the main road. I'll need someone to check her house, top to bottom. Canvas the neighborhood to see if anyone has any of those doorbell cameras. We still have a few hours before dark." Addressing the police officer to his right, he said, "Shaun, stay here with me."

Ray had just entered Sidney Lake's living room when he received a call from the county solicitor notifying him of his being loaned to the Morgan Police Department. "Looks like I'm going back to work for Pete Hornig."

Sidney responded from his position in his usual chair. "You don't sound happy about it."

Ray took his usual seat on the sofa. "Mixed emotions. Things change quickly in the world of policing. It's been… what… more than five years since I retired. It's one thing to sit around and chat about a case with old friends, it's something else to be responsible for doing something about it."

"But you're working for the county solicitor now, aren't you? Why is this different?" Sidney knew exactly what Ray meant but he wanted to draw the man out.

As a contract investigator for the solicitor, Ray didn't have to take the assignment. It was one thing to theorize and analyze, do background work, talking with members of other investigative agencies. Looking up old records, roaming around the region in an official capacity and then turning in a report was a long way from chasing down a killer. He didn't carry a weapon anymore; he didn't even own one. He'd had enough of that. And then there was Marie. She spent her whole life worrying about whether he would make it home for dinner in one piece. His time in the Marine Corps was different. After Viet Nam, the world became quiet, predictable, until he retired and became a policeman. Then his new battleground was everywhere and all the time.

"I don't know if I can do this again."

"Ray, I don't think Chief Hornig is looking for you to manage an investigation or even take an active role in any form of policing. I think he's looking for someone to think out loud with. Someone with a fresh approach backed up by years of experience. Did he ask for you?"

"Yes."

"Have you spoken to him yet?"

"No."

"I would suggest you call him. Find out why he wants you and what he expects, and if you don't think it's something you can be comfortable with, talk to Marie. You have the luxury of saying no."

Ray sat back against the pillow of the sofa. He could feel the tension ease as Tillie came in from the kitchen carrying a tray.

"I figured you didn't have lunch, so I fixed a little somethin." She placed the tray on the coffee table in front of him. "Made you a ham and cheese sandwich. Thought you'd like that. An' those cookies, made them this morning."

"Thank you, Tillie. Hold on just a minute, though. I have to make a call." Ray got up from the sofa and took his phone from his jacket pocket. "Excuse me." He walked out onto the porch.

Tillie, seeing the serious look on Ray's face, asked Sidney, "What's goin' on?"

"Chief Hornig called the solicitor and asked for Ray to be temporarily transferred to him."

Tillie thought for a moment and said, "The killin of the Tooker lady, right?"

"Right as usual."

"Yeah, I got a bad feelin about the attack and the killin. Real bad."

"Me too. As we discussed this morning, this could just be the beginning."

Sidney and Tillie talked quietly as Ray made his call. The similarities between the Tucker and Tooker names bothered them both. Morgan was an old southern town with deep roots reaching in the past to a time when most people wrote and spoke phonetically. Census takers and legal documents were written by clerks who spelled what they heard and didn't refer to what someone else may have written before them. Slaves didn't have last names and became identified by the surname of the plantation owner. Most indentured servants didn't read or write.

Ray spent almost ten minutes on the phone and came back into the room with a strange smile on his face.

Sidney immediately asked, "What was that all about?"

Ray didn't reply until he sat down and took hold of part of the sandwich. "Two phone calls. I took your advice. The first to Marie and the second to the chief."

"You hold it right there, Mr. Morton. I got to get us some coffee."

Ray obeyed and took a healthy bite. Tillie came back with a pot of coffee and three mugs before he had a chance to take a second bite.

"Okay, what's goin on?" she said.

Ray sipped his coffee and verbally outlined his phone conversation with Marie. He had emphasized to her how he had the ability to turn the position down and promised he would stay out of harm's way, which allowed Marie to give her approval to take the position with Chief Hornig. Next, he called Chief Hornig to tell him he was on board.

"She did? That easy?" a surprised Sidney observed.

Ray answered with a wry smile, "You were right about most of what you said regarding Pete Hornig's reason for wanting me back on the team, but there was a clincher for me. I also called Marie again and told her why Hornig wanted me in the middle with him. I told her everything, in confidence, of course. She had no problem and I could sense the relief in her voice. She probably heard it in mine, too." Ray stopped and waited for Sidney's reaction, which was immediate.

"Are you going to tell us? Are we not to be privy to this after you've told us everything else?"

"Of course I am. It's the most important part. Pete wants to use me as a conduit to you two." He stopped again, waiting for the reaction.

"Excuse me? Can you explain that please?"

"Look, over the past couple of years, the two of you have pulled his fat out of the fire enough times so he wants your brains in this, but he can't come to you directly. He wants me to do it. The press would have a field day if they knew he was relying on a retired college professor and a Gullah woman who runs a housekeeping service to help solve what is about to become a very high profile, and possibly, multi-murder investigation."

The room became quiet. So much so that it woke Mickey from her spot next to Sidney's chair.

Sidney finally said, "I guess we better get to work."

Sam Cashman had acre after acre combed around the last place Dorinda Tucker had been seen alive, and the area around the old rice field near where her body was discovered. Mary Coffey went over every piece of possible forensic evidence she could find and sent anything questionable off to the lab in Columbia for further evaluation. Wilson Knott worked with the Summerville Police Department to create a profile on Martin Tucker. In conjunction with Dorchester County Sheriff's Department, the local Rotary Club, Contractor's Association, local banks in Summerville and North Charleston, he managed to piece together an interesting picture. He then interviewed Michell and Grace Bennett and lastly, Martin Tucker's family.

Ray Morton was given a desk in the open office area outside Chief Hornig's office. Every piece of information that anyone developed ended up on his desk sooner or later. Ray and the chief talked to one another four to five times a day to review what was happening and usually lunched at the City Hall Café with as many as three other investigators.

Jim Cunningham of the Morgan City Times had regular meetings with Chief Hornig but, by agreement, not much made it to the newspaper. The two incidents were not tied together publicly, so the Savannah and Charleston media outlets never showed much interest.

Every evening, Ray stopped by Sidney's and had a long discussion with Sidney and Tillie, who had their own investigations going. Tillie was developing profiles on the Bennett household and the Tookers in both Morgan and Edisto, which also included Mayor Steele Wilcox. While the police collected their information by going through the front door, Tillie got hers from the back door. Sidney's pursuit went off in a different direction, and he had long conversations with Mrs. DeReimer and Nora Woodman in the South Carolina Room of the library. He also obtained the names of contacts to speak with at the DAR chapter in Charleston.

By the end of the week, the upshot was… nothing. Everyone had plenty of information but not a real clue in sight. Friday came in on a cool breeze and the murder investigation wasn't much warmer. A whole week had slipped away, and they were no closer to a motive than they had been at the start. Not only could they not come up with a reason Martin Tucker and Dorinda Tooker were attacked, but they didn't even have a person-of-interest, much less a suspect on the horizon.

Even more puzzling was the confirmation that the same weapon was used in both killings.

The only person who seemed to be cheerful about the progress being made was Sidney Lake.

NINETEEN

1742
The Battle of Bloody Marsh

More than twenty-two years after Eli Nichols met with the lawyer John Winslow at the tavern on the quay in Charles Town, the memory of the meeting remained vivid and often haunted him. The words uttered by Richard Tookerman, "there will be terms", still rang loud and clear when he recalled that day long ago. A day that changed the direction of his life. Twenty-four hours after signing the agreement proposed by Winslow, Eli acquired the indentured contracts of his now wife, Mary Wilson Nichols, and her three children. Now, sitting at the large wooden table he had crafted with his stepson, Sean, he had an announcement to make. They knew of the agreement he made to acquire the land on which Marshlands now stood, but there were details he had to explain. Details they needed to know before he left them to join with General J. E. Oglethorpe to defend South Carolina against the Spanish, who had their forces headed toward the South Carolina-Georgia border. The attempt by the Scots Regiment and Carolina Troops to dislodge the Spanish from St. Augustine had been a disaster and now the entire Carolina Colony was in jeopardy of being overrun.

He started slowly and spoke in a measured tone. Mary and her two remaining children by her first husband—the youngest having died of the fever ten years ago—and Eli's own two daughters by Mary sat anxiously as they knew this could be their last meal together. It was after supper and two candles glowed, one at each end of the table, giving an ominous feel to the room. Eli Nichols began, "A bit more than twenty years ago, I entered into an arrangement with a man named John Winslow to be able to acquire this land we call home. Winslow was an attorney for Richard Tookerman, the man who provided the funds to start us on this journey God has let us take." He looked up at his wife as she nodded in remembrance of the first day she set eyes on him in the tavern on the quay. "It was also when I bought the indentured contract of your mother." He looked at her children, Kathleen and Sean Wilson, who sat side by side. "And the contracts of you both and your departed brother. Those contracts were destroyed when I took your mother as my wife." He did not look at the other two children at the table, those he fathered with Mary: Alice and Annie Nichols. His two sons by Mary both died before the age of five.

"I leave tomorrow to join the battle to defend us against the Spanish, who would throw us into the sea and take all we have worked for these twenty-odd years." He fixed his gaze on Kathleen and Sean Wilson Nichols. "You are well into your adulthood. Kathleen, you are soon to be married and Sean, you have become a good steward of this land. But there is something you must all know, and it is the terms of an agreement I signed those many years ago."

Mary spoke up, "But Eli, did not Mr. Tookerman die some eighteen years ago? Why should it now matter?"

"He did, yes. But the agreement and my obligation did not die with him. Lawyer Winslow saw to that. To be honest, at the time, I did not know what I signed. I was but a boy." He nodded at Sean. "Younger than you. I knew my numbers. And I knew some letters, but words on a piece of paper written in hand were a mystery to me. Lawyer Winslow explained the terms, but I was so consumed with wanting this land and meeting the terms of the land grant, I barely listened. Most likely I would not have understood his words anyway." Eli lowered his head and shook it from side to side.

Mary reached across the table to her husband and put her hand upon his. "Eli, you have been a good man and father and a fair steward of our property. Is lawyer Winslow still alive to enforce the agreement?"

Eli looked up and placed his hand on top of hers. "No. He's been dead these five years now."

"Well then, God has provided for us. What can be the problem?" she asked with obvious false cheerfulness.

He patted her hand and smiled. "Lawyer John Winslow was a very smart and devious man. I have not mentioned this to you before as it has been my sole responsibility as master of this house and plantation. You have your own responsibilities. Sean knows some of what I will tell you but not all. Let me explain."

Eli reached down and brought up a leather pouch he had earlier positioned beside his chair. He removed a series of worn sheets of paper and placed them on the table. "As you know, I can now read very well," he said with a smile. "I learned with you all as you studied your letters and numbers under the kind hand of the pastor's wife. You were my teachers as she was yours." He picked up the first sheet of paper and shook it in his hand. "Lawyer Winslow told me what was in here that I signed with my mark, but he didn't tell me all of it." Anger entered his voice as he continued, "Yes, I was given the money I needed to acquire the land, the indent contracts, and the Blacks, but there were terms, as Mr. Tookerman so aptly once said. Terms about which I did not know. At that time in my youth, I would not have cared about those terms. But now they haunt me."

Mary had great concern in her voice. "But what are these terms?"

Sean Wilson, now a man soon to be twenty years of age and the de-facto plantation manager, spoke up. "This is why we make payments each season to the office of Lawyer Winslow, even though he be dead?"

"Yes, it is. His eldest son, Ephrem, occupies Lawyer Winslow's position. And we have been faithful to the contract I signed. But let me continue. By the terms of the contract, soon we may no longer own this land."

"No! That can't be. God would not let that happen," Mary exclaimed.

Sean replied with the anger of his youth, "No! This is our land, father. No one will steal it from us." As the dominant male heir in the family, he saw Marshlands Plantation as his rite of family inheritance. "I swear to God, I will not let them. Never! No lawyer will take what we have given our lives to achieve. Three of my brothers and sisters are buried under the Angel Oak."

Eli held up his hand. "Enough. Let me explain. The contract I signed stated that the money I received was to allow me to satisfy the requirements of the land grant regulations so I could acquire this farmof ours.. Your mother, you, your sister and brother, and the Blacks would become my property. The title of the land would be in my name as long as the 'terms' of the settlement were met, but if they were not, title would automatically transfer to Mr. Tookerman and Lawyer Winslow..."

Sean stood. The table shook as he tried to interrupt.

Eli stopped him. "Wait, let me finish."

Sean set his mouth and his eyes glared, but he sat.

"The agreement has a life span of twenty-five years. There be three years left. At its end, Marshlands would be mine free and clear. However, if the terms are not met, the land reverts to Mr. Tookerman seventy-five percent and Lawyer Winslow twenty-five percent. In addition to the seasonal fees I am obligated to pay to Lawyer Winslow, the 'terms' require that should I die before the contract expires, my natural born, legal, male heir could take over the obligations of the contract by paying a one-time amount equal to five times the seasonal fee. The amount is to be paid by the end of the first season after my death. If paid, the agreement would continue to its natural end at which time all obligations would be said to be fulfilled. However, if I should die without a male heir, the one-time fee would increase tenfold and be due and payable at the end of the season of my death or the title to Marshlands will be given to Mister Tookerman and Lawyer Winslow, if living, or their legal heirs if not."

The room was silent for a moment. Finally, Mary said, "Then we're all right. Aren't we? If anything should happen to you, we just continue with Sean as the head of the household and his son to succeed him. Isn't that so?"

Sean answered, "No mother. I am your natural son but not father's. Arthur, who now lives under the Angel Oak, would have been heir. If anything happens to father, this land belongs to the heirs of Mr. Tookerman and Lawyer Winslow. Even if I were father's natural-born son, we do not have the money to pay the amounts that would be required."

"He is right," Eli said. "This is the way the Tookerman and Winslow families have attained their wealth. Unlike many others, we have survived the war with the Yemassee, the great storms of both summer and winter, and the sickness of the swampland. The only possible hope we have is if the child you are carrying is a son. That would at least give you time to acquire funds and negotiate with the Winslow's."

Sean stood up, successfully this time, and addressed his father, "Well, the answer is that you cannot leave us to fight the Spanish in the marsh and swamplands of Georgia. I will go in your place."

"No!" Mary exclaimed. "Neither of you will go."

Eli stood and held up his hands to silence them. "No, I have a possible solution, which I will explain. But first, we must pray for guidance. Come." He stretched out his hands and each of the children and Mary grasped and held tight to the person next to them and formed an unbroken circle.

The prayer Eli uttered was a simple one asking for guidance and protection for the family. But when he finished, Mary had her own request. "And Lord above, please keep Eli safe and well as he leaves us tomorrow to join with the South Carolina troops to protect us from harm. He is a good man and worthy of your help. Amen."

All around the circle they responded with, "Amen."

There was one more task Eli Nichols wanted to complete before he left for

Georgia and the upcoming battle. He dismissed everyone from the room but Mary and Sean.

Seated again at the table with his wife and stepson across from him, Eli began, "There may be an option for us that would enable us to buy the plantation from the heirs of Tookerman and Lawyer Winslow."

"Buy?" Mary asked. "We have no money to buy. Yes, we now live well, but we are by no means people of wealth."

Eli raised his outstretched palm to her. "Mary, hear me out."

Sean, clearly angry over a law that would not let him inherit that which he and his mother should surely have, sat quietly watching the man who raised him as his son.

"Mary, you have heard part of this story I am about to tell but not all. You will remember how Ignatius Pell saved my brother Thomas from the hangman and how it was he who put me on the right path by joining Tuscarora Jack Barnwell to fight the Yemassee."

She nodded.

"There was an errand he participated in with Mr. Pell…." Eli now recounted the story of Thomas' trip up the Ashley River with goods for Joshua Bailey and told them of the box.

Sean perked up. "A treasure box? A treasure box belonging to the pirate Bonnet? And you know where it is?"

"Wait. I know where it could be. But I do know someone who definitely knows where it is, or at least, how to find it."

Mary said anxiously, "And you believe there is enough gold to buy out the agreement now?"

Eli sat back in his chair and thought for a moment. "Of that I cannot be sure. The box was said to be heavy enough."

"Who is this person with the knowledge of its location?" Sean had moved forward in his seat.

"Do you remember when Joshua Bailey's plantation was split up into three separate parts after his death five years ago?"

"Yes, when his heir, Joseph, decided to concentrate on rice and indigo crops. The third, the horse farm near Fort Dorchester, was sold to his daughter's husband," Mary said.

"Two slaves who were part of the horse farm and the warehouses were sold, and I purchased both slaves because I needed help in dealing with the warehousemen in Port Royal."

"Jamie?" asked Sean.

"True. Jamaica, as he was referred to then, was the slave who took the box from Mr. Pell and Thomas at Bailey's warehouse in Fort Dorchester. Thomas suspected even then that Jamaica could read and write, although he disguised it as best he could. A slave who could read and write could be a great danger, but I didn't see it that way. He now helps me as we go to market. He watches the listing of goods and prices put down in the warehouseman's books, which gives me an edge at the market. Over the years, Joshua Bailey spoke highly about him." Eli paused, leaned forward, and whispered, "I ask you to do something for me should I not return."

Mary gasped and put her hand up to her mouth.

"Quiet," he said. "Jamie and I have come to an agreement. He knows where Joshua Bailey placed the box and has created a map of the location. He claims the map is in four parts and is drawn on the inside covers of four of Bailey's books in his office. He has written down the names of three of the books on three sheets of paper. I have obtained two of the pages in exchange for my promise to give him his freedom and to buy the freedom of his two sons and a woman still with the Bailey Plantation. This I have already agreed to with an exchange of land with the Baileys and arranged for the passage of Jamaica's people to Philadelphia. Upon receiving information that they have arrived safely, he is to turn over the other page and be freed and allowed to follow his family north."

Sean, with a fierce look, said, "Why not force him to give them? He's a slave. Why do you bargain with a slave?"

Mary gave her son a shocked look as she turned to him. "Do you not recall that you, your brother, and sister were like slaves? Indents yes, but our indent contracts bought and sold in the marketplace."

"Yes, but—"

"Say no more. God has favored us greatly. Do not anger Him," she instructed her son.

Eli did not interfere but continued speaking. "I intend to keep my bargain with Jamie and have put it in writing. We have both signed it. He has a copy and mine is in my office with other papers."

Mary, with great concern in her voice, asked, "Eli, do you really have to go? Can you not pay to have someone go in your stead?"

"No. I have made many mistakes in my early days and have sworn before God to live an honorable and faithful life. It is the least I can do for all He has permitted me to have. I have much to be thankful for. We all do. I am an officer in the South Carolina regiment and have my obligations which I have sworn to uphold. General Oglethorpe is relying on me, as are the members of the Scots and Carolinas regiment. What kind of a father would I be not to protect his family and friends? No, I will uphold my part of the bargain."

The room was silent again, and the quiet lasted until Sean sheepishly asked, "Does Jamie know what is in the box?"

"The full specifics, no. He was there when old Joshua Bailey first opened it. It was full. The contents were wrapped in oilcloth and the box waterproofed. It was Jamie's understanding that the box was to be held in trust for Stede Bonnet. The Bailey and Bonnet families were close. Both from Barbados. There was a bond of trust between them."

Sean thought for a moment. "So, Jamie did not say how much gold and silver the box contained?"

"Never said he did. What he did say was the contents were of great value to Bonnet, and Bailey saw it as a duty to keep it safe for his friend."

"But was not Bonnet hanged? Why would he keep something safe for a dead man?"

"Bonnet's trial lasted a full month before his hanging. Everyone believed he would be freed. Even his captor, Colonel Rhett, pled for his life. The box was placed in hiding for Bonnet when he was alive. After death, Bailey sent word to Barbados to Bonnet's family. To Jamie's knowledge, the box still lies in its grave."

"Hmm," mused Sean. "So, there is something of value that could get us out from under the thumb of the Tookerman and Winslow families. Something that could secure our futures."

"Agreed."

Mary brought them back to the reality of the immediate threat as she said to her husband, "What we must do now is pray with all our hearts that God protects you and you come back to us from Georgia. We must also ask that the child I carry is the male heir that will keep the Tookermans and Winslows at bay."

The three of them clasped hands and prayed for the future. A future to be placed in jeopardy during the Battle of Bloody Marsh and the beginnings of King George's War. A battle from which Eli Nichols would not return.

TWENTY

2018
Dead End

An entire week had passed since the attack on Martin Tucker and here they were again, Sidney, Tillie, and Ray, in Sidney's living room. Tillie's comment of a few days ago about 'all the Tookers and Tuckers being connected, even if they didn't want to be,' hit a nerve with Sidney.

"The first mistake you are all making," Sidney said from his overstuffed throne in the living room, "is assuming if two people in a small town are attacked with the same weapon, the two people must have known one another. The fact is they probably didn't."

Ray leaned forward from his position on the sofa and rubbed his hands together as though they were filled with soap. "At this point, I'm going to have to agree with you. It's not logical to me though, because even in a random killing, we can always find a connection."

"I didn't say you were wrong with the connection part—and I think you mean pattern more than connection—only I still have to believe in the possibility they could have known of one another. There is definitely a connection. I just don't believe Dorinda Tooker and Martin Tucker knew what it was. I'm also not saying they didn't know their attacker. It's entirely possible they did."

"Now wait a minute, Sidney—you're telling me they knew who attacked them? They went with them voluntarily?"

As Sidney explained his theory, the sky darkened and the wind began to blow. The forecasted afternoon thunderstorm had arrived. In another part of town, a tall, stately Black woman in her mid-sixties, walking with a cane along King Street, looked up at the sky and then quickened her step. She was still a block away from Saint Peter's AME church, where she served as the interim choir director. The street emptied as the rain came down, and she took refuge under a tall oak tree. What started as an afternoon rainstorm suddenly turned into a Lowcountry deluge. Around the country, a rain of this type would be referred to as coming down in buckets or raining cats and dogs but the Lowcountry version would give Noah concern. The woman turned her back to the street and pressed close to the trunk of the tree, protecting her small briefcase by holding it against her breast. Her purse's handles were around the wrist of her left hand and large raindrops bounced off the side of it, making them sound like pebbles rather than water. A car with its lights on and wipers flapping angrily on high speed pulled up to the curb near her. The driver opened the window on the passenger side and called out, "Mrs. Rye, get in. I'll give you a ride the rest of the way."

Mrs. Rye couldn't see who was in the car but as the driver knew her by name, she assumed it was an acquaintance. "Oh, thank you," she called out as she dashed across the eight feet from the tree trunk onto the sidewalk and then the curb. Her head down, she held her purse over her head with her left hand and kept the briefcase pressed to her chest. The driver of the car reached across the seat and opened the door for her. She threw the purse onto the floor of the front seat and swung the door open the rest of the way. Continuing to hold the briefcase containing her music close, she turned her back to the driver and sat down. Swinging her legs and body ninety degrees to get in, she reached out with her right hand and pulled the door shut.

Back at Sidney's, the rain pounded the roof of the front porch. Ray stood as he spoke. "Are you telling me you think you found a connection at the library to the two murdered people?"

Sidney did not reply but had a satisfied look on his face as he peered over his glasses.

"What have you figured out?"

"Genealogy," Sidney finally said.

"What?"

Tillie, who had rushed to close a window in the front of the house, spoke from her office in the front room and spoke louder than normal to compensate for the sound of the rain. "He said 'genealogy.' I've been doin' some of that too. Only different."

"We found the connection this afternoon," Sidney said.

Sam Cashman pulled his car into the parking lot of the AME church and the uniformed police officer, recognizing him, waved him off to the side. The rain continued to fall, but the wind had subsided. Sam rolled down his window and asked, "Is Doctor Coffey here yet?"

"Yeah, they're over by that tree in the back of the lot. The chief's there too."

"Thanks."

The rain made the early evening darker than usual. There were no lights in the parking lot, and large branches and foliage of the two-hundred-year-old tree deepened the shadows of the crime scene outside the range of the flashing blue lights of the police cruisers. Mary Coffey's team, dressed in white protective clothing, was busy setting up lights around the body of a woman lying on the ground. A man carrying a large black bag over his shoulder took pictures as he carefully circled the scene.

Sam made straight for Mary Coffey and started talking as he came forward.

"Mary, don't tell me this is another one."

"Can't say that yet," she answered. "I can say I know who it is. Mrs. Gloria Rye, director of the choir here." She gave a nod toward the church building at the other end of the parking lot. "Blunt force trauma to the head again."

"You act like you know her."

"I do. I belong to the local choral group, The Morgan Chorus."

Sam looked surprised.

Mary caught the look. "Some of us have a life outside of blunt instruments, guns, and ambulances. Yes, I know her… and liked her. Great voice. We did some joint events with her choir. Nice lady."

Chief Hornig came over and acknowledged them, "Mary, Sam, anything to tell me? By the way, who's the cameraman?"

"Forensic photographer from Columbia. We happened to be meeting in my office when the call came in. He was reviewing the pictures I took of The Ridge and rice paddy scenes and giving me suggestions about upgrading my camera equipment. I asked him to come."

Chief Hornig walked up behind Cashman. Peering at the body on the ground, he said, "Please tell me this doesn't have a connection to The Ridge and the rice paddy killings."

"As I said to Sam, it's too soon to make a connection. But with Martin Tucker dying last night…. Once I get her back to the lab, I'll tell you more."

"As much as I hate to say this," the chief glanced sideways at Sam, "I'm almost hoping this one turns out to be a Gullah problem."

"I'd like to chat some more with you and Sam, Chief, but I've got to get back to work." Mary started to turn away, then stopped and addressed the chief. "Don't get your hopes up. Not every Black person in the Lowcountry is Gullah. Besides, as far as I know, she's from Camden, New Jersey. Has a music degree from Temple University in Philadelphia." Mary turned away again and walked over to the body of Gloria Rye.

Sam turned to Chief Hornig and ignored his Gullah comment. "Just got here, Pete. Who found her?"

"One of the members of the church choir," Hornig said. "Shaun Green was the first to arrive and found the body. The man from the choir said he didn't know it was a body. He had called in suspicious behavior after hearing a car pull out loudly and saw what he thought were some bundles on the ground. Shaun was in the area and responded. Everyone's still nervous about the 'Mother Emanuel' killings in Charleston. As they should be. Anyway, you should talk to him. Shaun said the guy didn't see anything, but you know how that goes."

"I'll get his name from Shaun. Let me look around first."

Within an hour after the body of Gloria Rye was discovered, Tillie had a call from one of the members of the AME Church Choir. The caller had her cell phone pressed against her ear as she looked out the window at the flashing lights of police cruisers and an ambulance at the back of the parking lot. They spoke for five minutes. Ten seconds later, she recounted the call to Sidney.

The professor sat in his chair and listened quietly as Tillie spoke. He did not interrupt once. He wanted to hear it all just as the information had been relayed to her. Finally, he said, "Now, tell me everything you know about Gloria Rye. Think about everything you've heard and what you know from your general impressions. Take it slow."

Tillie did. They had been down this road before. She knew his technique. Slow and careful and then repeat. Sidney would ask questions only during the second re-run of information. He took a pencil and his ever-present notebook out of his jacket pocket as she spoke.

"Okay, Tillie, Gloria Rye was not from Morgan, and she was not Gullah. Let's take up both those issues. If she's not from Morgan, where is she from?"

"New Jersey."

"Do you know what city?"

"Hurmph." She looked at him carefully. "I got to sit while we do this." She moved over to the sofa where Ray Morton usually sat. "I think I remember someone telling me she came from Camden. That's across from Philadelphia, right?"

"Yes."

"Okay, that makes sense. She went to college in Philadelphia." She thought for a minute. "Starts with a 'T'. Yeah, I'm pretty sure."

"Temple?"

"That's it, Temple."

"Good. Now, why do you say she's not Gullah?"

"'Cause she comes from New Jersey."

"That's not what I mean. I'm talking about heritage. Just because she wasn't born in the Lowcountry doesn't mean she's not Gullah. Most of the Africans brought to the United States before the American Revolution came into the country through Charleston. They didn't necessarily stay in the Lowcountry, but they did spend time here."

"Yeah, I know that. She wasn't born in the Lowcountry but it don't mean she don't have people who did. A lotta people findin' that out these days."

"Good, let's keep an open mind about this. Now, do you know when she came to Morgan and why?"

Tillie took a deep breath and put her hands together in her lap. "No, but the pastor of Saint Peter's will know. He's the one who hired her to run the choir. I don't know a lot about her. She doesn't live on the islands. Rents a condo here in town. I think it's near the condo place where Miss Hattie lives, and I'll bet Miss Hattie knows her. People in the choirs in town all know one another."

"You're right, Tillie. Professor Ryan would know her." Sidney shifted in his chair and eagerly continued, "She should be in Atlanta by now at that conference she was to attend at Emory. I believe she said there was a reception and dinner this evening. What time is it?"

Tillie looked at her watch. "A few minutes past nine."

"I've got to call her."

TWENTY-ONE

2018
Gloria Rye

The Morgan City Times carried the story of Gloria Rye's murder on the front page, but details were limited to her being attacked in the parking lot of St. Peter's while on her way to choir practice. No connection to the other murders was made.

Behind the scene, police activity was frantic all night. Saturday evenings were active times for the restaurants and bars along Market Street, even in the rain. Church Street being six blocks west of Market, the police activity went unnoticed by most people who were inside and out of the rain. The police picked up a number of people who were acting suspicious, but all were eventually released. Interviews with members of the choir of St. Peters, as well as the neighboring Baptist church, had gone on late into the evening.

A clear bright sky and fresh air carried by a gentle breeze masked the shock and horror of the night before. A night filled with violence and death. The daily newspaper demanded answers from the people of Morgan. Answers that Chief Hornig didn't have but Sidney Lake, after a long conversation with Professor Hattie Ryan the night before, began to develop.

Sidney's late morning walk with Mickey took a half hour and lunch awaited them both as they came in the back door to the kitchen. Sidney saw the table had not been set in the kitchen as would usually be the custom.

Tillie called out, "We're gonna eat in here," referring to the dining room. "I got a feelin we're gonna have company so we might as well make room for it."

The words were hardly out of her mouth when a knock came at the door. Tillie stepped to the side, where she could see down the interior hallway. Mickey didn't bark, which meant the knocker was known to her, so Tillie called out, "Door's open. Come on in."

Ray gently pushed open the front door and peeked around it. Seeing Tillie down the hallway, he said, "Don't you people ever lock doors? Haven't you learned your lesson yet?"

"Yes, we do," Tillie replied. "When I brought in the paper, I saw you down the street rush out of your car at the curb, somethin' you hardly ever do. You always pull in the back like the Professor does. So, I figured something was up and you was comin this way."

"Oh, yeah, I... was. Just had to tell Marie where I'd be." He closed the door behind him and locked it. "How do you do that?"

"What?"

"Know where people are going before they do. Even anticipate what they're going to say."

Sidney called from the dining room, "Ray, don't ask questions the answers to which you may not really want to know."

Tillie smiled as she said, "I set a place for you."

Ray shook his head, rolled his eyes, and mumbled, "You two...."

"Take a seat, have some coffee," Sidney said. "I gave up trying to figure out how she does it a long time ago."

Ray pulled out the chair next to Sidney's right at the head of the table. Tillie's place was across from him on Sidney's left. "We have ourselves a real puzzle. Three murder victims who have absolutely nothing in common, killed with the same weapon. I doubt they ever ran into one another accidentally."

Although Tillie had gone into the kitchen to work on lunch, the shutters that closed off the serving window between the kitchen and the dining room were open and she heard everything they said.

"Sam Cashman talked with the pastor of Saint Peter's last night and came away with a picture of a woman, Gloria Rye, who couldn't possibly have an enemy in the world. She's only been in town for a few months. Took over the choir when the director became ill. Nice lady. Friendly. Well liked. Lives alone. Widow. Volunteers at the food bank. Retired from a bank up in Philadelphia. It doesn't make sense."

Sidney did not respond.

Tillie came into the room carrying a tray and put it down. "Did the pastor tell you why she came to Morgan?"

"Sam said he didn't know. The pastor mentioned that Mrs. Rye said she had always wanted to visit. Didn't explain or give a reason."

"Did Mister Sam say he was comin over later?"

"Yes, he did. How come you don't already know that? You didn't set a place for him." Ray smiled, assuming he had caught Tillie in not knowing something in advance.

"Didn't need to. Dede always gives him a good breakfast at home and they usually have lunch when she's in town, which she is today. Saw her this mornin." A smug look from Tillie as she alluded to Marie Morton's complaints of Ray never seeming to finish a meal when he became involved in an investigation.

Sidney chuckled. Trying to get the better of Tillie was a fool's errand. "Well," he said, addressing Ray who reached for the freshly made coffee Tillie had put in front of him, "tell me what progress has been made and I'll explain what I've been doing."

"What it amounts to is one dead end after another. The Mitchell Bennett connection with Martin Tucker looks like a secret real estate deal they were planning. Bennett's been quietly buying up land in the Four Hole Swamp area. Put some investors together, including Tucker, the actual developer, and was afraid there'd be a ruckus if word got out. Seems there's an Indian tribe been living in there for almost two hundred years. They keep to themselves. Learned to keep a low profile ever since Andrew Jackson tried to kill off all the native Americans east of the Mississippi. Couldn't farm the swamp. No money to be made there like there was in Florida and other places in the South. Wanted to keep everything quiet as they knew the project would be dubbed the new American genocide. Grace Bennet didn't know anything about it and was furious when she found out." Ray paused to reach for the milk for his coffee.

Tillie got her two cents in when Ray stopped. "Yeah, we know all about that. Not surprised someone would go after Four Hole. Look what they done to us on the islands. Bulldozin' Praise Houses and blockin historic designations so they can build more 'Plantations' for the people comin down from the North. Money, land, and greed..." She stopped when she saw the looks on Sidney's and Ray's faces. "Sorry about that. One of my favorite soapbox issues."

"Not a problem," Sidney said. "In fact, I think it's a topic that has to be pursued as it may have some relevance in regard to what has been going on. Land acquisition has always been a major issue here. The people who have it are always trying to obtain more. The people who lost it always believe it's still theirs and want it back, especially if there's a gravesite on it."

"Yeah, there's a lot of old Indian graveyards on the islands that the Gullah won't touch," Tille said, "but the first thing the developers do is bulldoze 'um before they can be officially marked as historic and then claim they didn't know it was there or blame it on the 'dozer' driver. Trouble is, once you dig it up you can't put it back. And the Indians around here have all been killed off or moved out, which is pretty much the same thing. So, there's nobody to complain."

As Sidney reached for the coffee carafe, he added another point for them to consider. "There may not be anyone here to complain, but the stories are told through the generations by the descendants of the survivors. In fact..."

A knock on the door interrupted him. "I'll bet that's Detective Cashman."

Tillie got up and let him in.

While Sam did have a good breakfast and lunch, Tillie still had coffee and biscuits waiting for him when he took his place at the table next to Ray. Sam said the information about the weapon would not be released to the press as Chief Hornig didn't want the three murders publicly connected… yet. They figured they had at least one more day before the press in Charleston and Savannah started to ask questions that would begin to tie everything together.

After a sip of the coffee Tillie put in front of him, Sam continued with his review of the activities of the previous night. "What we're focusing on now is Gloria Rye. Her background, her friends, acquaintances, activities. It's a short list, as she's only been down here a short while. The pastor of St. Peter's and Chief Hornig made a joint call to Mrs. Rye's daughter this morning. She said she and her aunt'd be on the next plane out of Philadelphia and be here this evening. Hopefully, she can add something to the background story."

Sidney had been sitting quietly during the outlines provided by both Ray and Sam but decided it was time for him to speak up. "Those connections you were hoping to find and put together? I have one for you with regard to Martin Tucker and Dorinda Tooker."

TWENTY-TWO

1742
Marshlands Plantation

With the death of Eli Nichols during the Battle of Bloody Marsh, his stepson, Sean, began to develop a plan to save Marshlands Plantation. Once the fate of Eli Nichols became common knowledge, Sean assumed the son of the deceased attorney John Winslow, Ephrem, would be at their front door. Sean's mother, Mary, carried Eli's child, which they hoped would be a male heir and give them at least six months breathing room before the full force of the financial terms of the contract would be due. Sean planned to use the six months to secure the hidden treasure box, the location of which had been provided by the slave, Jaime. However, he needed a contingency plan if his mother were to give birth to a female child, whereby the punitive conditions of the loan would come into play.

The plan would be one of deception. If a female child was born, it would be registered as a male. It sounded simple given children were born in the wilderness of the Carolinas all the time and were simply registered in the nearest Church of England parish. Sean planned to make certain the only non-family members at Marshlands Plantation who would know the difference would be the slave, Helen, who served as the midwife, and the slave, Jamie. It would be Jamie's task to spread the news on market days of the birth of a male son of the late Eli Nichols and his now widow, Mary Wilson Nichols.

The family was convinced that such a plan would never be needed as God would protect them from the evils of the Tookerman and Winslow families. But with the birth of Patricia, all that would change.

The first problem had to do with the baptism of Patricia, who had been registered as Patrick. "How can we do this?" Mary questioned her son, Sean. "You know the Rector always unclothes the child to be baptized. It's part of how they make certain of future claims for ownership of property. It would be a sin to lie about such things."

Sean looked his mother directly in the eye. "We just need to delay the baptism as long as we can. I have already found a male child to be swapped out for Patricia when presented at the church. There will be a male child for him to inspect, baptize, and register as the son of Eli Nichols."

"Sean, Patricia is a girl not a boy. That can't be hidden forever. And I will not risk the eternal damnation of Patricia not being baptized for six months."

"No one will ever get to see Patricia. We will claim her to be Patrick's twin. She will be called sickly and kept hidden from strangers until I have secured the treasure box and paid off the debt. Jamie has given me all the information I need. It will not be six months. Once done, we will raise the male child we have substituted, and he will be called Patrick Nichols, the twin brother of Patricia. The Winslow's and Tookerman's can have their gold, and we will have Marshlands," Sean said with a wry smile.

"But…"

Sean held up his hand to her. "As I said, I have already found the replacement. The child was born a month ago here at Marshlands. We will arrange for the baptism to occur in three months' time, when there will be little difference between a three and four-month-old child. There is some darkness to his skin, but his features are good. I have some darkness to me as well with thanks to your mother and some of her Spanish blood. We can and will do this."

Mary pressed her hands to her abdomen as she expressed her concern, "But what will happen to Patricia?"

"She will be raised as a twin sister and baptized separately. Jamie will tell all of the twin birth on the first subsequent market day. Only then will he leave for Philadelphia."

Mary did not answer. She thought quietly. Given the isolation of Marshlands Plantation, Sean may have found the solution, but it would depend on the silence of the other members of the family and the slaves. Of concern would be the future husband of her daughter from her first marriage, Kathleen Wilson. She didn't worry about the slaves, as no one who mattered ever gave credence to the utterings of a slave, except possibly for Jamie. He was well known in the market as an honorable and trustworthy representative of Eli Nichols and Joshua Bailey before that. Besides, by the terms of the agreement, once he had turned over the books containing the map showing the location of the box, he would be free to join his family already on their way to Philadelphia and not be available for people to question.

TWENTY-THREE

2018
The Connection

Sam leaned slightly forward from his position next to Ray to get a direct view of Sidney as he challenged the Professor's last statement. "What do you mean you have a connection for us? We've interviewed everyone connected with Martin Tucker and Dorinda Tooker and there is no connection. We haven't started on Gloria Rye yet."

"I'm quite sure you have been pursuing every avenue you found." Sidney leaned back in his chair. "The problem, as I see it, is your interviews have only included the living."

Ray and Tillie remained quiet and let Sam ask the obvious questions for them.

"Professor Lake, what in the world are you talking about?"

Sidney leaned forward again. "I thought that would get your attention." Sidney took a deep breath and continued, "I believe that the three murders that have occurred could be just the tip of the iceberg." Sam made a movement indicating he was about to interrupt but Sidney held up his hand. "No, Sam, let me continue." Sam leaned back as Sidney went on, "Over the past week,

I have spent a great deal of time in the company of Mrs. DeReimer at the Library. In some instances, Miss Nora Woodman also joined us. I swore both of them to secrecy, as we were doing genealogical research on our victims.

"During an earlier visit, Mrs. DeReimer confided to me that Olive Wilcox, the granddaughter of Dorinda Tooker—the second of the three victims—had her DNA researched. That seems to be quite popular these days. She found a lineage connection to an attorney by the name of John James Winslow, who lived in Colonial Charleston at the beginning of the eighteenth century, well before the American Revolution."

Ray interrupted. "Sidney, just a clarification. Dorinda Tooker was a DAR member, as we know, which would mean her granddaughter could be as well. So why would she need to do her DNA?"

"Point taken. Dorinda Tooker obtained her membership through family documentation and didn't explore the family history through DNA. She already had all the actual documentation needed to acquire her DAR membership. Olive Wilcox wanted to go back farther and also include other branches of the family tree. She wasn't interested in verifying a connection to the American Revolution, she already had that. No, according to Mrs. DeReimer, she wanted to find out how far back she could go."

"Okay. Got it."

"Now, the service that Olive Wilcox used also took the information they received and populated a family tree going back to the late 1600s. The interesting part here is that the Tooker name is simply a shortened version of the name 'Tookerman.' Specifically, Richard Tookerman, a somewhat notorious individual who consorted with pirates and often served as an outlet for their stolen goods. And one of those pirates was none other than Stede Bonnet." He paused to let the connection sink in.

Ray caught on immediately. "Wait. Bonnet. That's the guy whose treasure Martin Tucker was looking for. So that's the connection?"

Sidney thought for a minute. Leaned forward slightly, placed both elbows on the table, raised his hands and pressed the fingers on both hands against one another and started to tap them.

Everyone around the table waited impatiently for Sidney's answer, except for Mickey, who was used to Sidney's play for the dramatic effect and feigned sleep next to his chair.

"Not entirely," Sidney finally answered. "Yes, there is the connection mentioned but I don't think we should be distracted by it when it comes to the reason for the killings. The treasure seeking is of interest, but my research in the South Carolina Room with regard to Dorinda Tooker also led us to attorney John James Winslow. Winslow's grandfather served as the attorney for Richard Tookerman. According to the records Mrs. DeReimer has uncovered, there were major court cases after the American Revolution where properties of those who supported the British—the loyalists—were expropriated. John James Winslow acquired a great deal of land as a result. Many of the loyalist settled in the Bahamas and continued to fight in the British and American courts for the return of their expropriated property."

"But where does Martin Tucker fit into the Tooker family tree or is his connection the supposed search for the Bonnet treasure?" Sam asked. "And don't tell me you've already found something on Gloria Rye."

"No, nothing on Mrs. Rye. However, the connections with Martin Tucker and Dorinda Tooker are very interesting.

"According to the records, Richard Tookerman's younger brother Charles had a successful importing business and did not support Richard's alleged illegal activities. He subsequently changed his name from Tookerman to Tucker to avoid being confused with his brother. However, the connection to the Winslows is reestablished with one of Charles Tucker's sons, Adam, who read for the law under John James Winslow and joined in the expropriation lawsuits against a number of the Loyalists."

Ray couldn't resist getting into the middle of the explanation. "Sidney, this is all a very nice lesson in American colonial history, but we're looking at three murders in the twenty-first century. Are you trying to tell us someone is running around carrying a three-hundred-year-old grudge over property they believed was stolen from them after the revolution?"

Ray looked at Sam, who merely shook his head slightly and had a small smile on his face. "Sam, do you really think they have something? Are you willing to go to the chief with this?"

Sam put his hand on Ray's shoulder and said, "I don't think the Professor and Tillie are suggesting that at this point." He looked at Sidney and asked, "Are you?"

"No, certainly not. We have more work to do, but I do want you to keep an open mind on what I'm suggesting."

Sam removed his hand from Ray's shoulder. "Ray and I would be very interested in hearing what you have as a specific motive for these killings. We certainly haven't been able to come up with one on our own. I haven't heard anything from Knott either, and he's been all over the place looking for links from the Martin Tucker end. And don't forget, there's also Gloria Rye to consider. If you can find a connection between her and the other two, I think there's a very frustrated chief of police in town who would happily sing your praises from one end of the state to the other."

Ray pushed his chair back and looked to his left. "Sidney, the floor is all yours."

Sidney explained that Mrs. DeReimer had put together a series of genealogical charts over the past week. She had become fascinated by what they were beginning to reveal. The key bit of information she started with was in the file she developed for Olive Wilcox. Originally, she and Mrs. Wilcox had stopped searching when they identified attorney John James Winslow as the owner of a place called Marshlands Plantation. They never pursued the actual location of it since no such place currently existed. Olive Wilcox wasn't interested in places as much as she was the people involved, but Mrs. DeReimer loved finding local historical venues. As a member of the Morgan Historical Society, they were always looking for locations to erect historical signs.

They had found the Tooker and Tucker connection to Richard Tookerman (who died mysteriously in the early 1720s), and Richard's brother Charles, who changed his name to Tucker to escape the nefarious reputation of his brother. Other descendants of Tookerman now called themselves Tooker for the same reason and one of them, Alfred Tooker, had a grandson who married the daughter of John James Winslow, the lawyer who acquired Marshlands Plantation. From this point on, the Tookermans, Tuckers, Tookers and Winslows all fit under the same family tree. According to the records that Dorinda Tooker used to establish her DAR credentials, the Tooker family in post-Colonial Charleston were import and export brokers and maintained their trading business until the Civil War. The Tooker family had a long history of well-respected lawyers, businessmen, and politicians right up to the current day when Olive married Steele Wilcox, the current mayor of Morgan.

The connections to Martin Tucker were found when going through the genealogy records for Olive Wilcox. Martin Tucker's father, George, had his DNA analyzed some time ago and it followed a similar path back to Colonial Charleston. The two linked up in a number of places but the source went back to another son of Richard Tookerman. Their name didn't change to Tucker until sometime after the War of 1812. The family had settled in Georgetown, South Carolina and had a long history of being carpenters and ironmongers. Nora Woodman dug up some of the information through her aunt, Mrs. Cathcart of the Palmer Library. There had been a subscription library in Georgetown, but it closed in the 1970s. A fair amount of documentation was donated to the Palmer, with the balance going to the local library.

As Sidney spoke, his house phone began to ring.

Tillie, on hearing the ring, got up from the table and went to the wall phone in the kitchen.

"All right," Sam said. "You found a connection between Martin Tucker and Dorinda Tooker, but I still don't see it being relevant. From what you describe, they must be thirty-second cousins or something. What we've learned from all our interviews and research, in the twenty-first century not the eighteenth, is they didn't know one another. Also, they had no idea they were related. For heaven's sake, Sidney, for all you know, Chief Hornig could be your great-grandfather's fifteenth cousin. He could have fought on the side of the French at Waterloo while your relatives fought with the English and now he holds you accountable for losing the battle. For that matter, you being from Virginia and I'm from South Carolina, how do you know we're not related? Or Ray here? Or Tillie? You've got to have more than that for us to go on."

Tillie, with the phone to her ear, peeked through the pass-through window from the kitchen and interrupted. "Anyone know where Willow Marsh Road is?"

Ray answered, "Yes. Why?"

Sam looked up and cautiously asked, "Who wants to know?"

"It's Mrs. DeReimer on the phone for you, Professor. She found out where Mrs. Wilcox's ancestor's plantation was. That John James Winslow lawyer fella. Willow Marsh Road is the western boundary of Winslow's Marshlands Plantation."

Sam and Ray looked at one another, and Sam said, "That's where Dorinda Tooker's body was found."

Both Sam and Ray got up and started to leave, but Sidney wasn't finished yet. "Before you rush off, I think you had better listen to what Tillie has learned."

Everyone looked at Tillie, who had returned to the dining room.

"Tillie?" Ray prompted. "You've also found a connection?"

"Sit for a minute."

Both men did.

"Sam, you know how the islands are—not a lot written down but there sure is stories. I spent a good deal of time over at Good Harvest Retirement Home speakin with a ninety-eight-year-old lady by the name of Miriam Tooker. Now we spoke Gullah, which won't help the Professor and Ray, so let me give you all a sense of what she said.

"I've known Miss Miriam for a long time. She used to come to church on Sundays, and when we went off to church school, she would tell us stories of the old days. Miss Miriam was a Story Lady and she could talk forever. She got that from her grandma and her grandma's grandma. So, I asked her how she got the name Tooker.

"She said, 'From the plantation. That's how we all got our names. Family was all slaves. Didn't have no last name. Weren't allowed to. Weren't allowed to talk to God either. Guess they figured if we talked to God, He'd find out what they were doin' to us. As if He didn't know. No, bein' a slave wasn't much fun. But we got along. By me I mean all of us. But you asked about the Tookers, didn't you? And a place called Marshlands?'

"Then I asked her if in the stories she heard if there was anything special about the Marshlands.

"She told me about the big fight. 'They was Tookers and Tuckers and Winslows and Jamaica. He was famous. He beat the system. He got out. Got his freedom and went North. Oh, yeah. Had another lady askin' me about him few weeks back. Nice lady. She asked about Marshlands too. From up North. A singin lady. Heard her sing at the Church in Morgan. Told her about the big fight between the Nichols and the Winslows, an how ole Jamie pulled the wool over their eyes. Ha, shoulda said cotton since we didn't have no wool plantations. Ha, yeah cotton not wool.'

"Tillie shifted in her chair, reached for her glass of water, and took a sip. "Then she told me about the big land fight about the Marshlands Plantation. She said the Nichols owned it but owed money to the Winslow people. When Mister Nichols died, he didn't have a son, only daughters, so the land was supposed to go to the Winslow people. Jamaica gave them a plan. He was smart. Taught himself to read and write but they didn't know it. He told them to change Miss Nichols' newborn daughter from a girl to a boy. There was a Black child just born who could pass—mostly white lookin', a grandson of Jamaica's, and they could say it was the Nichols' child so they could keep the land. Jamaica agreed to keep quiet about it if they give him and his sister and sons freedom. That's what the big fight was about. Those Winslows knew they was cheated but couldn't prove it. Kept fighting till the Revolution, but Jamaica's grandson got the land."

Tillie explained that Miss Miriam talked about a number of other incidents in her Gullah dialect, but they didn't have any bearing on Marshlands Plantation.

Sam spoke first, "Tillie, I've heard a lot of these kind of tales all my life, and while there's truth in all of them, there's no way to be sure where the truth ends and the fiction begins."

"I know it. But you have to admit it sure fits in with an awful lot of what we've been findin' out."

TWENTY-FOUR

1742 – 1750
A Hero Saves Marshlands

In the years after the Spanish were defeated at the Battle of Bloody Marsh, Marshlands Plantation thrived under the management of Sean Wilson. The Yemassee "problem" had been solved, and no one suspected that Patrick Nichols was not the rightful heir of Eli Nichols. The story of the trip to Fort Morgan by Pell and Eli's brother to deliver the mysterious box became just that, a story. A legend which would continue to be handed down from generation to generation: a box of gold and silver hidden somewhere on Joshua Bailey's land.

Not everyone was happy, though. Sean Wilson-Nichols had made a bargain with Ephrem Winslow and convinced him that it would be more lucrative for Sean to continue to manage Marshlands Plantation. Ephrem had no real interest in running the plantation and agreed to waive the agreement demanding the extra seasonal payments. He received great praise for giving honor to the family of the hero Eli Nichols by declaring the debt paid and Eli's natural-born son Patrick, the new owner of Marshlands Plantation. Eli Nichols had become a local hero in the defeat of the Spanish in the Battle of Bloody Marsh and the driving of them back to Florida. Sean Wilson Nichols would be designated the official guardian of Patrick Nichols, who everyone now believed was the heir to Marshlands. Besides, Ephrem had his eye on becoming a judge in the growing Costal Rivers County. It would not sit well with his backers for him to try to dispossess the family of a local hero.

However, John James Winslow, Ephrem's son, had squandered his family's wealth after Ephrem's death in 1750 and seethed with anger over not having inherited the plantation. He began a rumor that Patrick Nichols was not the legitimate heir to Marshlands Plantation and that it truly belonged to him. The tale he told at the taverns in the new market town of Morgan contained elements of deceit and deception by Sean Wilson, but no factual evidence. John James was convinced that the somewhat dark-skinned Patrick Nichols was not the true son of Eli.

TWENTY-FIVE

2018
Searching For Relatives

Sidney and Tillie remained at the table after Sam and Ray left. "Tillie, have many people on the islands had their DNA researched?"

"Not really."

"But did you get the impression that Gloria Rye had hers done before she came down here from Philadelphia?"

"I'm pretty sure she did," Tillie answered as she leaned forward in her seat. "I mentioned it to Mr. Sam before he left, and he said he'd talk with the library people and see what contacts Mrs. Rye had with the South Carolina Room. After church, I talked with some people in the choir, and they said she was lookin for some old connections to the Lowcountry. She learned that her people spent a lot of time as slaves down here. Of course, that could be said of anyone who had family born in the Carolinas before the Civil War."

"Yes, but wouldn't it be interesting to learn there's a Winslow or a Tooker, or perhaps even a Tookerman, lurking in her family tree. If there is, then we have a connection for all three victims, even though they may never have met. Plus, we have the connection to the old rice plantation site, with Dorinda

Tooker's body having been found there."

"Well, okay Professor, but we still don't know why they was killed."

"True. I'm also wondering if someone ought to be taking another look at the real estate development plan that Mitchell Bennett and Martin Tucker had been trying to keep quiet. I don't think it was the one dealing with the Four Hole Swamp area, since people seem to know about that one."

Ray Morton took the seat in front of Chief Hornig's desk. It was a comfortable place for him. Their relationship had always been a close one and, while each had their own particular way of approaching problems, they respected one another's desire to do the job right, regardless of political or personal pressures. Chief Hornig, although not having the concerns of running for office every four years as did the county sheriff—the position of Chief of Police being appointed by the mayor—was well aware of the political environment around him. Ray, on the other hand, having the luxury of having been an employee, always approached city politics with a touch of disdain, believing that politics and policing shouldn't be mixed.

"Pete, you talk to the mayor. We're going to need access to the genealogical information that Olive Wilcox developed, as well as whatever family history material Dorinda Tooker had. We both know there'll be resistance from Mayor Wilcox. If there's a skeleton in the family closet… you know how he is. He looks at everything through the prism of the next election."

Pete had a quizzical look on his face. "You found something that might involve him?"

"No, not yet, anyway, but Sidney has come up with something that, on the face of it, seems a bit off the wall. But he's managed to suggest a connection between two of the three victims. A connection we never considered."

"Why am I not surprised?"

"Yeah, well, listen to this." Ray went on to explain the genealogical connections and added what Tillie learned.

"Are you serious? You mean there may be someone out there holding a three-hundred-year-old grudge? Are you sure about this?"

"Pete, I've been down this road with Sidney and Tillie before. So have you. I think we should take this seriously. Besides, we don't have anything else."

"What about the land deal?"

"It's still on the table even though Knott hasn't been able to put anything together yet. We'll let him keep trying."

"So, what do you want from me?"

"I want you to convince the mayor that he should have his wife give Sam full access to her genealogy account. I don't think we want to go to court to do this. Sam wants to work with Mrs. DeReimer at the library in going through the records to see if they can find some links that'll be useful."

Chief Hornig sat back in his chair and took a deep breath. Jousting with Mayor Wilcox never turned out well. The two men clearly didn't like one another, and both knew the less they tangled, the better they could do their jobs. "You want me to convince the mayor to allow Sam to go on a fishing expedition into the Wilcox and Tooker families that could go back 300 years? Even if he did tell us to pull out all the stops, given his general paranoia, he's going to immediately assume his family tree is full of hidden horse thieves and crooks who, if come to light, could hurt his ambition to live in the governor's mansion someday."

Ray smiled. "Aw, Chief, you're good at this. You know how to handle him. Besides, didn't he tell you, specifically, to do everything possible to find who killed his grandmother-in-law?"

Pete sat quietly for a moment, giving Ray a look that said, *And we're supposed to be friends?* He rubbed his chin with his right hand and asked, "Are you sure this is necessary?"

"I know this sounds like a bit of a reach, but I think Sidney may be right, and someone's out there with psychological problems trying to right a wrong that happened a long time ago. Something that's been handed down through the generations and made this person believe they have to become some kind of avenging angel on the descendants of the wrongdoers."

"Sidney believes we're looking at a serial killer, doesn't he?"

"He never mentioned those words but, yeah, only it's a targeted one. There's nothing random about what's going on, and if we don't move quickly, we're going to have more bodies showing up on our doorstep."

Mrs. DeReimer left the South Carolina Room just before Sam arrived. Nora Woodman now sat in her place.

"You just missed her, but she'll be right back. Can I help you with anything?"

Sam looked at Nora and tried to decide if he should mention the purpose of his visit. Sidney had not mentioned Nora's name, so Sam decided to play it cautious for the time being. "I'm not sure. Mrs. DeReimer was doing some research for Sidney Lake, and I need to talk to her about it."

"Oh, yes. I helped them with part of that. She'll be back in a few minutes. There's a folder here on her desk someplace." Nora stood and began to move some papers around. "Have a seat, Detective. I worked with them on researching some of the older records in the library and also sent out requests to Charleston with regard to an attorney by the name of John James Winslow." She continued to rummage around, and Sam took the seat he was offered. "I also put in a request for information on an Ian W. Nichols, a Revolutionary War officer. I received the information back on Mr. Winslow, but we didn't receive anything for Lt. Nichols yet."

"That does fit in with some of the names that've been mentioned.'

Nora looked up. "Oh, here's Mrs. DeReimer."

"Detective Cashman, how nice to see you. I see Nora has been taking good care of you." Nora stood up and Mrs. DeReimer moved behind the desk and replaced Nora in the chair. She could tell some of her files and papers had been moved, something she told Nora, and everyone else, never to do.

"Yes, she has. I stopped in because I need to go over some of the material you've been covering with Professor Lake. Is there someplace we could talk quietly?"

Nora, taking the hint, said, "I'll let you two do what you have to. I'll be at the reference desk if you need me."

"Thank you, Miss Woodman," Sam replied.

Nora left.

"Mrs. DeReimer, I need to see what you've developed while working with Professor Lake. I understand you have access to the genealogy trees of a number of people in town, including Olive Wilcox."

"Yes, but, as I mentioned to Professor Lake, I don't feel comfortable allowing someone else to view the files without authorization. I could possibly answer a specific question though."

"I understand. I expect Mrs. Wilcox provide authorization for that shortly. When I have it, I'd like to sit down with you and review the data." Sam shifted his chair so it was closer to the desk. "What I'll also need is your expertise in navigating the different databases and copying some of the material, as well as getting a listing of sources for the most relevant documents."

"I could certainly do that… as long as everything is authorized."

"Don't worry. It will be. I'm also looking for other links to the same ancestor. In this case, John James Winslow and possibly a Richard Tookerman. To be perfectly honest, we're not entirely sure what we're looking for, but Professor Lake feels certain he'll know it when he sees it."

Mrs. DeReimer didn't answer right away. Her concern was to ensure she didn't reveal something she shouldn't. "Yes, that's the same route I've been taking with Professor Lake. Only he's been doing some research on his own and would provide me with specific questions about people during the colonial period in Charleston and Beaufort."

After everyone left, Sidney went to his library. He needed a quiet place to review the information he'd accumulated. When he did literary research for his own benefit and enjoyment, he liked being slow, meticulous, and precise. The world would not come to an end if he didn't complete a task by the end of the day. But this was different. People were dying. He needed something to confirm he was moving in the right direction.

As she did with Sam, Mrs. DeReimer advised Sidney he could not give him direct access to the genealogy records of Olive Wilcox or Dorinda Tooker without written approval. Dorinda Tooker was dead, but as Olive Wilcox was Dorinda's granddaughter, she could provide the authority needed. The practice he had been following of coming up with specific questions for Mrs. DeReimer to investigate irritated him because it all seemed too slow and cumbersome, and an irritated Sidney Lake was a very unhappy Sidney Lake. Following legal procedures could get someone else killed. Over the years, it hadn't been unusual for the professor to push ahead with a research project over the objections of others. When he was at Morgan College, he often used a little bombastic yelling and screaming now and again to get the funding he needed for his department. It had become part of his public image: the irascible, obnoxious, uncompromising professor. In the recent past, he had tried the technique with the police chief only to realize the legal world of policing was an exclusive club to which he could never be a member. So, he needed to learn and obey the rules. The likelihood of the Wilcox family providing access for him, a private citizen, to root around in their confidential family records would never happen, so it was up to Detective Sargent Sam Cashman and Ray Morton to get it for him.

He opened the loose-leaf binder he had created for the project. It now had three sections, one for each victim. As he began thumbing through the pages, Tillie and Mickey came back from their short walk.

"Tillie, can you come in here for a minute?"

"Sure, Professor," she answered from the kitchen, where she returned Mickey's leash to its hook near the back door.

Mickey arrived in the office first, but Tillie was not far behind.

"Let's talk a bit," he said, leaning back in his chair. "Didn't you say that Mrs. Rye had her DNA analyzed?"

"That's what one of her people in the choir said."

"And that was one of the main reasons she came to Morgan?"

"Yes. She became interested in learning all she could about her family. Her sister and her daughter should be in town a little later today. I'm sure they have lots of questions. They plan to take her body back to Philadelphia along with whatever is in her condo."

"We have to meet with them. All three of these people were killed with the same weapon, and that old rice plantation is mixed up in everything. I'm convinced there has to be a family connection and it may involve what you found out from your contact at the retirement home. What did she say the slave's name was who played a trick on someone to get his freedom?"

"Jamaica. Jamie, she called him."

"And on what plantation was he a slave?"

"She mentioned a couple of names, but I can find out for sure this afternoon."

They both went silent when they heard the sirens.

TWENTY-SIX

2018
Cooking Up A Solution

Sidney needed to sort out some things. However, his usual procedure of analyzing a problem while cooking did not go well with his injured knee. Hobbling around the kitchen while explaining to Mickey what puzzled him no longer presented itself as a viable method of analysis. Sometimes he could do it with Tillie present, but it didn't work as well. Mickey was an alter ego, an avatar to bounce ideas off of without being contradicted. Besides, Tillie had left for a meeting on Deer Island, after they learned the sirens they heard earlier were for a traffic accident, so he and Mickey had the place to themselves. But how could he do his review and analysis in a different way and get the result he desired?

Sidney stood in front of the kitchen window and looked into the backyard and the garden. "That's it, Mickey. The green house and potting shed. I can sit there and work on repotting some of my cuttings. Yes, that will work just fine. What do you say?"

Mickey was non-committal except for a slight wag of her tail, which Sidney took as a yes, despite her glance at the bed she had in a corner of the kitchen.

"Good girl. The shed it is."

He brought Mickey's lead with him but never put it on her as she always roamed around the backyard on her own. Sidney hobbled into the shed and cleaned off a workspace made from an old desk he had strategically placed by the doorway.

"I think this will work out just fine for us. What do you think, Mickey?" Sidney looked down at his side and realized Mickey wasn't there. He lspotted Mickey lying in the doorway where she could keep an eye on Sidney and still catch the warm December sunshine. "Why am I not surprised?"

Sidney sat down and moved a pot in front of him. It contained six hibiscus cuttings taken two months earlier. All had rooted and were ready to be moved into individual pots. As he worked, he began his analysis. "All right. What do we have? Three murders. One is a middle-aged real estate developer. A second is an eighty-nine-year-old woman and the third is a retired banker from Philadelphia, who recently moved to Morgan. The only provable connection among the three is the weapon that killed them: a fireplace poker.

"Thus far, we have not uncovered any direct link to indicate they ever met or even knew one another. The real estate developer, Martin Tucker, didn't live in Morgan but did have business connections here with Mitchell Bennett, who owns a real estate and insurance company. The second victim, Dorinda Tooker, lived in an independent living facility over in Edisto but quite frequently visited her daughter-in-law who lived in The Ridge neighborhood, in the house Mrs. Tooker once owned. Now the third victim, Gloria Rye, lived in a condominium in Morgan but she was new to the area. There is no reason why any of these three people would be associated with one another in any way. Also, the first two victims were white and the third Black. One victim was male and two were female."

Sidney managed to get one of the cuttings out of its nursery pot and into a slightly larger one and filled it with fresh compost. He looked behind him at Mickey, who immediately raised her head to indicate she was listening to his every word, which, of course, she wasn't. He continued talking as he took on the task of the second cutting.

"Now, in working with Mrs. DeReimer at the library, we found a connection whereby all three, directly or indirectly, had their DNA analyzed. So, that gives us three people murdered in Morgan with the same weapon, all three of whom appeared in DNA searches, although not all three had a DNA search executed on their behalf. We found a link between Martin Tucker and Dorinda Tooker in that they have a common ancestor in Richard Tookerman, a merchant and warehouseman originally from Barbados who plied his rather nefarious trade in Charleston between 1700 and 1721. The Tooker and Tucker names are derivatives of Tookerman. There is also another name that pops up, which is Winslow. This one is also connected to Tookerman and apparently, there was a marriage between the Tookerman and Winslow families from which both Dorinda Tooker and Martin Tucker are descended. This gives us an ancestral connection going back about 300 years for two of our three victims."

He held up the newly repotted hibiscus for Mickey to see. "Looks pretty good, doesn't it?"

Mickey again lifted her head to see what Sidney was holding and then, unimpressed, put it back down.

"Okay, so you are unimpressed. I can deal with that. Time for the next one."

Sidney turned his back to Mickey and continued working and talking through the answers to the questions which arose from the specific inquiries he had been making to Mrs. DeReimer. "I think the interesting news may be contained in the Ancestry search Gloria Rye had done. Now, the question seems to be, where does a Black woman from Philadelphia interact with the Tookers and Tuckers of Charleston in the early 1700s? I have a pretty good idea. Olive Wilcox's Ancestry files gave us the connection back to Tookerman and Martin Tucker's brother, who also had his DNA done, which is where we found the connection with Martin and both the Tookermans and Winslows. However, I think we need to get our hands on the family history files and records Dorinda Tooker had that related to her DAR application and certification. My understanding is she had original documents going back to the early 1700s and at least one of them mentions a place called Marshlands Plantation and a person called Eli Nichols. There are also some references to the Bailey Plantation. Now both Marshlands and Bailey Plantations no longer exist although the descendants of the Bailey line are still around Morgan, which is how the books that were stolen from the Palmer Library came to be donated. It's also interesting that Dorinda Tooker's body was found on what is believed to be a rice field that may be part of Marshlands. Martin Tucker had been one of the people involved in the bogus search for a treasure belonging to the pirate Stede Bonnet, but who owned Marshlands Plantation, and why is that important? If this all sounds confusing, Mickey, it most certainly is. If only I could get direct access to all these records instead of dancing around with a bunch of questions to Mrs. DeReimer."

The third hibiscus cutting—a bit unkempt and ragged compared to the first two—had now been repotted. Sidney took another look over his shoulder to see if Mickey was still there, which she was, but no longer feigning listening as she gently snored. Sidney smiled.

"Glad to see I'm not disturbing your nap. You're supposed to be helping me, you know. Oh, well, I suppose you are. As far as the murders are concerned, I think Gloria Rye may be the key. We don't know a lot about her. Mrs. DeReimer said Mrs. Rye had been in to see her and asked if she could help with some of the information obtained about her relatives. She said she had her DNA done but never got a chance to review the findings with Mrs. DeReimer. Tillie has to arrange a meeting with Gloria Rye's sister and get access to their Ancestry data."

A fourth pot was done but, before continuing, Sidney sat back in a chair and closed his eyes.

No more than a minute passed before Tillie returned. She could see Mickey lying in the doorway to the shed and knew where to find Sidney. Upon Tillie's reaching the entrance, Mickey raised her head but did not move otherwise.

"You two sure look like you're workin' hard. One dozin' by the door and the other asleep at his desk."

Sidney did not move as he said, "I have not been sleeping. To the contrary, I have been analyzing the situation in which we currently find ourselves."

"I sure hope so. I stopped in at Good Harvest to see Miss Miriam again and saw the headline in the Post and Courier. 'Marshland Murders Stump Police' it said. Boy, that ain't gonna make Chief Hornig happy."

"Oh, my. I should say not." Sidney turned in his chair to face Tillie, who stood inside the shed, having successfully maneuvered around Mickey. "He's managed to keep the lid on everything so far by not admitting there is a connection among the three." Sidney shifted his leg to get into a more comfortable position. "I've just been going over everything with Mickey. Ray and I have to get together on some things. That headline is going to have a rather large impact going forward. It's one thing to have Jim Cunningham of The Times roaming around police headquarters but once the reporters from the Charleston, Columbia and Savannah papers get their noses in everything, life is going to become greatly complicated."

"Yeah, I can see that."

"The chief has to firm up the connections between the three victims, so the local residents don't feel we have a random killer on the loose. Any more news from Mrs. Tooker?"

"Yeah, but it's not clear. She said something about someone named Nichols who was in the Revolution War. Something important that happened up north someplace. Wasn't too clear today. That kinda happens with Miss Tooker sometimes. Kinda happens with a lot of us when we get older. Names and events just pop in and out and can't always remember why somethin' is important and why it might not be."

"I can't argue with that. All I know is that something happened a long time ago—around 300 years—that has disturbed someone here in Morgan so much that it led him or her to seek revenge for it. Revenge on people who have no knowledge of the event. While the murders are connected and targeted, there's no way anyone in the Morgan area will be safe until we know what that connection is. But then, who knows, everyone in town who can trace their Lowcountry history back 300 years could all be connected and, very possibly, vulnerable."

"So, what're we gonna do?"

Sidney stretched his bad leg out straight and then cradled his right foot across the left. "Keep after Mrs. Miriam Tooker if you can. See if she knows anyone who could add to the information she has already given you. At the same time, I think it would be a good idea for you and one of the members of St. Peter's AME church choir to visit with Mrs. Rye's sister. Find out about that DNA test she had and what she learned that brought her to Morgan. I think that's going to be a big piece of the pie. I'm not sure how seriously Chief Hornig is looking into my 300-year-old revenge and retribution theory. I know both Sam and Ray are giving it strong consideration, but the chief has to deal with Mayor Wilcox. For my part, I want a look at Dorinda Tooker's family files. I'm convinced something's in there that will shed light on both the Marshlands Plantation and Bailey family connections. Lastly, Ray and Sam have to get to the bottom of this Stede Bonnet mystery. That's what started everything, and no one is paying attention to it."

"Yeah. You're right about that. And how about this Mitchell Bennett person? He and the real estate deal he was workin' on with the Martin Tucker fella seemed to have been left in the middle of nowhere." Tillie moved over to where Mickey still made believe she was asleep. "There's got to be a lot going on there."

"As I understand it, Detective Knott has been given that task. It would be interesting to see how Tucker and Bennett fit together. That Miss Bennett seems like a nice lady, but I don't like her husband. A bit shifty for me."

The business of policing is no longer solely about protecting people and capturing the law breakers, it's now about technology, which is everywhere. For the police to do their job effectively, it must be used and understood.

Unfortunately, training and standards are a local responsibility, which is totally driven by city, county, and state budgets. Chief of Police Pete Hornig was only too aware of the limitations of his department, and while the resources of the county and state were always at his disposal, no one wanted to ask for their help unless it was absolutely necessary. The mayor of Morgan, Steele Wilcox, had bigger political ambitions and believed asking for outside help would reflect negatively on his current job performance.

"You're sure we need to do this?" Mayor Wilcox asked of his police chief as they sat across from each other in the mayor's office conversation area. Always the politician with an eye to perception being more important than reality, Steele Wilcox did not have chairs in front of his desk. Meetings of importance were reserved for conference rooms, while individual conversations were held in a more relaxed setting.

"Yes, sir. We really do. You know I wouldn't ask for something like this if it wasn't necessary, but if we're going to get these murders solved, we need all the information possible at our disposal. Accessing your wife's DNA information is key to understanding the relationships among all the different players. If we have to bring the state into this, the first thing they're going to do is get a subpoena for the information, and then it won't be under your control. The state will bring in someone to dig through the databases and suddenly you and your wife's family will be in the public domain. The newspapers would just love to explore your family history. Somehow I don't think you want that."

The mayor stood up from the high-backed armchair he had been sitting in, turned his back to Chief Hornig, and walked over to the main window of his office, which was flanked by the city and state flags. The front steps to the city hall building were below him and in the distance, part of the Morgan River was visible. "This is still a small town, Pete. Growing, but still a bunch of local neighborhoods with a Main Street. Do we have the expertise to do the kind of database searching you think we're going to need? We won't have to bring in experts from the state?" He turned and faced the chief again.

"Absolutely. Mrs. DeReimer at the South Carolina Room is really good at this. Has all sorts of certifications. The library has been lending her to other locations to teach genealogy investigations. She also understands the confidentiality issues. We'll keep everything we do on a need-to-know basis, and with any luck, we'll have this mess under control. The press will be kept at arms-length."

Mayor Wilcox stood quietly for a few moments, looking at the plaques, certificates, and photos featuring him on the wall surrounding the sitting area. "All right, but you've got to keep me informed. I don't anticipate you'll find anything embarrassing that I can't handle. I just need to know it before certain other people do."

He meant his political rivals, and Chief Hornig knew only too well who they were. "Don't worry. My people have been cautioned. We may not be Columbia, but we know the rules. I'll see that you get regular progress reports. With any luck, we'll have it wrapped up in a couple of days."

The mayor looked over at his desk and focused on the corner where, earlier, he had placed a folded copy of *The Post and Courier.* "You've seen the Post this morning?"

"Yes. Although I try not to let a newspaper headline influence my schedule, this time I may just have to. If I don't have something before the next edition, I know I'm going to hear from Columbia."

"You're not the only one. There's an election coming up and everyone running for office is going to be on the phone to me for an update so they can stay ahead of the news."

Chief Hornig started to get up from his chair as he said, "Steele, if you would give Mrs. DeReimer the go ahead to give us her full cooperation, I promise you as soon as I have something put together, I'll be in here with it."

Having made the prediction to have everything under control in a few days, Chief Hornig called Detective Sam Cashman within ten seconds of leaving the mayor's office and simply said, "My office. Fifteen minutes."

TWENTY-SEVEN
1755
The French and Indian War

The world changed for John James Winslow one afternoon in 1755. War had broken out with the French over control of all the land beyond the Appalachian Mountains. A member of the South Carolina troop who fought with Colonel Washington at the fork of the Ohio River told of being entertained by a traveler he met up north with the story of a Black former male slave from South Carolina called James Bailey. A slave that received his freedom, along with a female called Helen, for playing a trick on a bunch of lawyers in Charleston and passing a light-skinned child of a slave and the manager of the plantation as the rightful heir of that same large plantation not far from Morgan in the Beaufort District. The storyteller claimed the slave now lived free in Trenton, New Jersey, and had become prosperous as the owner of a warehouse and operator of a ferry across the Delaware River to Pennsylvania.

"Who told this tale?" demanded John James as he leapt to his feet and grabbed the arm of the man sitting next to him in the tavern.

The startled traveler tried to get out of John James' grip and pulled away.

"What's it to you? He was just a planter from Virginia."

"That plantation is rightly mine. Stolen from me. You've got to tell me what you know."

The man looked at the hate-filled face of John James and again tried to free himself of the madman whose grip on the frightened man only tightened.

"All right. I'll tell you what I know, but it is surely filtered through many a telling."

John James' grip loosened, and he signaled the man to be seated. The two other men at the table, who were shocked at the violent reaction of John James and had started to leave, decided to stay and hear the story as well.

"I heard the tale from the man from Virginia who claimed to have heard it from another who had been at Fort Necessary with Colonel Washington in fifty-four. The tale interested me, as I too had been with Mackay's South Carolina Independents. We held our positions while Washington's troops scattered as best they could in the downpour of rain and mud and blood. The man and two of his compatriots escaped in the madness and confusion and headed east to the safety of Philadelphia. I listened as the tale spoke the truth of Fort Necessary and not the lies of Washington and Mackay in their reports to Governor Dinwiddie in Williamsburg."

John James implored the speaker to get to the story of deception. "But what of the Black man's story?"

"I'll tell you it all or I'll tell you none."

"Ah, then tell it."

The man nodded. "Two of the three men made it back to Philadelphia and a few years later, the man who told the story was crossing the ferry to Trenton with me when it broke loose and stranded us on the Pennsylvania side. Being late in the day, we two and the ferryman waited till daybreak to reset the lines and cross the river. The ferryman, a freed slave from Virginia, was the one who confirmed the deception tale. His employer was another freed man named James Bailey, he said, and although he believed the Black man's name to be false, the story he thought was true. It told of striking an agreement with the plantation owner when his wife could not produce a male heir. Without which the plantation would become the property of some lawyer's kin in Charleston."

"Ah hah," exclaimed John James.

The speaker paused and gave him a look before continuing. "In order to satisfy the need for a male heir, the slave James Bailey offered his own newborn light-skinned grandchild to be substituted for the female child. The agreement would be freedom for himself, his two sons, and a woman if they were successful in the deception. And they were."

"Did he identify the plantation?"

"No, but there was an added inducement James Bailey offered, which was the location of a great treasure believed to be buried nearby."

"The Bailey box!" John James exclaimed. "I must know where to find this slave, James Bailey." He grabbed the speaker's wrist.

"Unhand me," the man said, now in complete control of the situation. "That is your business. I have no idea if the tale be true or not and have no interest in it. I listened to it only because it described a lawyer being tricked instead of being the one doing the tricking. An event I am most in favor with. If you believe the tale to be true, then it be up to you to pursue it. For me, I have more important tasks in front of me and nothing more to tell."

TWENTY-EIGHT

2018
The Search For A Motive

Mrs. DeReimer felt a little uncomfortable. The police coming in and out of the South Carolina Room had unnerved her. Living in a world of books and research, she drifted through each day with a sense of calm accomplishment. People came in looking for help, and she provided it. She felt good about what she did and with each task completed took pleasure in having helped someone learn about the history of the town and how it related to them. The police had changed all that.

Helping Professor Sidney Lake and his friend the Reverend Prentice locate a historical fact or two they could use in a presentation or a sermon thrilled her. She became interested in the topic with the same enthusiasm they did. But the police, well, that was a different matter. They were secretive. They made her promise not to tell anyone what they were doing. They instructed her not to speak with other members of the staff. Now, when having lunch with a co-worker, she had to be on guard. She didn't like that. The friendly banter over lunch or in the office made working in the library the friendly place it had always been. Talking about an unusual request from a patron or exchanging commentary about the strange actions of someone roaming through the shelves was known to generate a chuckle or two. And then there were the accidentally observed clandestine meetings between library patrons, who huddled in a quiet corner of a room and were more interested in one another than anything they could possibly find on the shelves. Everyone among the library staff had some form of gossip to relate about the local townspeople. But now… all this secrecy. She didn't want to be involved in a murder investigation, no matter how interesting it seemed to be.

Then came the phone call from Mayor Wilcox.

"Mrs. DeReimer, I have a favor to ask of you but first, I want to thank you on behalf of Olive and myself for all the help you have been giving us with her family search activity. Olive has been so impressed with your knowledge of the town's history, and you have made her very happy with all the work you've done on her behalf. You can be assured the attention you have shown her has not gone unnoticed." This was classic Steele Wilcox. The politeness, the courtesy, the words of caring and appreciation—all political finesse, of course, but they were instinctive and well-honed during his long training and tenure as Morgan's major funeral director.

The initial nervousness Mrs. DeReimer felt upon hearing the mayor's voice dissipated with each platitude he sent her way.

"Why thank you, Mayor. That's very kind of you to say. I always try to be helpful in any way I can."

"Yes, I know, and I'm afraid I'm going to have to take advantage of that wonderful support you have always given the library and the town."

"Is there something special I can help you with?" Her nervousness returned.

"Yes, there is. My mother-in-law died recently at the hands of an unknown person, and we believe there may be a clue to his identity somewhere in the family search material you have been helping Mrs. Wilcox with. Now, I know you have been diligent in your protection of the information you uncovered, and I applaud you for that, but the wonderful expertise you have in genealogy and Morgan history is valuable for another reason."

She knew what was coming but let him continue.

"Mrs. DeReimer, we need your help. I would appreciate it if you would work closely with Chief Hornig of the Morgan Police Department in every way you can. Both Olive and I told Chief Hornig they can have access to any information you uncovered in our family search material. I have also authorized Chief Hornig to officially employ you as a police department consultant to help them understand the ins and outs of the databases you use. That way, any additional expenses will be covered if you run into some extra fees somewhere. And don't worry, I'll clear everything with the library director. So, can we count on your help?"

"Of course… most certainly. Yes. Detective Cashman was just here. He left rather quickly but said he would return shortly." She started to get herself under control as she continued. "I hope I haven't caused any problem in my caution about answering Detective Cashman's questions."

"No," the mayor assured her. "You acted exactly as you should have. In fact, you acted as I would hope any citizen of our town would in protecting the privacy of personal information. Police Chief Hornig has been very impressed by your actions and your ability to understand the need for confidentially in such matters."

"Thank you, Mayor. I will be happy to help in any way I can."

The call ended with a few more platitudes from Mayor Wilcox and additional assurances from Mrs. DeReimer that she would not discuss the matter with others.

When she finally put the phone back in its cradle, she looked up and saw Mrs. Cathcart of the Palmer Library standing in the doorway and wondered how long she had been there.

"Saw you were busy on the phone, and I didn't want to interrupt you," Mrs. Cathcart explained. "I came by to see my niece, Nora, and thought I'd stop in. Nora's wandering around the library someplace. We're going out to lunch. Would you like to join us?"

As she spoke, Nora Woodman came up behind her aunt and tapped her on the shoulder. "Right behind you, Auntie. Had to go upstairs for a minute." She then looked at Mrs. DeReimer and said, "Yes, Mrs. DeReimer, why don't you join us?"

"I… um… err… no, I can't. I have that detective coming back again." *Oh, my. Should I have said that?*

"The detective? I'll bet it's that handsome Black one," Nora said. "Maybe we could get *him* to join us."

"Oh…well…I'm not sure when he'll be here. He said he'd be right back."

"He was here earlier? I didn't see him."

"A short time ago. He had to leave. Received a phone call."

Nora continued, "I didn't hear a phone."

"No, you wouldn't. I'm sure it was on silent ring or whatever they call it. I didn't hear it either. You wouldn't hear it up at the reference desk anyway."

"That's true. What are you helping him with?"

"I… I really don't know. He said he would be back."

"Isn't he the one that's the friend of the professor from Morgan College who was involved in catching the man who stole the books from the Palmer Library?" Mrs. Cathcart said. "I'm sure he's the one. We only have one Black detective, I believe."

"Professor Lake?" Nora said. "He's been in here too? Is he involved in solving the murders in town?"

"I'm sure I don't know. He's often in the library. In fact," Mrs. DeReimer thought of a way to change the subject, since she had been, technically, feeding him information about the Wilcox family, "he was here the other day with Reverend Prentice from Bay View Presbyterian. Professor Lake was helping him with his theological research. You saw them that day, didn't you, Nora?"

"Ah, now that you mention it. Yes, I did. They were working on something together, I think. Oh, well. Auntie, I guess we can't convince her to leave her post and join us for lunch. Maybe another time."

Mrs. DeReimer saw her opportunity to make a graceful exit. "That would be nice. Yes, maybe next week. I'm sure to be tied up in the early part of the week, but maybe after Wednesday."

"We'll make a point of it. The three of us," Nora replied.

The conversation ended, and Mrs. DeReimer gave a sigh of relief as the door to the South Carolina Room closed behind Nora and Mrs. Cathcart.

Her chance to regroup didn't last long, though. Curiosity got the best of her and she signed into Olive Wilcox's Ancestry file.

TWENTY-NINE

2018

Putting Some Pieces Together

Ray had taken his usual seat on the sofa in Sidney Lake's living room. Being just before noon, they were both sipping leftover morning coffee instead of Sidney's sherry and Ray's scotch that were their usual discussion drinks. The friendship between the two neighbors had grown over the years. Ray could be rough and tumble in his street-smart way but always straightforward and honest. Sidney's personality matched Ray's, but his was a carefully orchestrated rough and tumble and the straightforward part often had some unexpected turns.

"Sidney, why do the last seventy-five years interest you?"

"It's the Tucker connection. It appears Martin Tucker's grandfather came to South Carolina after the Second World War and started the family construction business."

"But I thought the family can be traced to Morgan and Charleston?"

"It can but I don't think he knew that. Which is what makes it interesting. It was Martin Tucker's brother who had his DNA researched which showed the family emigrating back to England after the Civil War. The connection to the Winslow's and Tookerman's was undoubtedly lost in the moves."

Ray leaned back in his chair and looked past Sidney toward a painting of a praise house on the wall behind the professor. "This has got to be the strangest can of worms I've ever seen. Why can't we just have an old-fashioned murder? One guy gets mad at another over something stupid and they take shots at one another. Or maybe a love affair. Nice, simple, easy to understand motives."

Tillie's voice answered Ray from her desk in the front room across the hall. She sat in a corner and couldn't be seen from the living room. "'Cause if it was that simple, Professor Lake wouldn't be interested."

Sidney laughed. "She's right. In fact, no one would be interested."

Tillie stood up and peeked around the corner. "And if we didn't have this DNA stuff someone *would* think it was real simple. The wrong person would be arrested and the real one would never be connected to any of it."

"But isn't that the problem?" Ray answered. "Even with the DNA connection, we still don't have a motive. Not even a hint of one. Do we?'

"Don't we?" Sidney said. "I'm not so sure. Just because we now have the ability to track someone's lineage using chemical testing, that doesn't mean hate crimes have not been happening and many are unsolved."

"So, you're convinced this is a hate crime?"

"Yes, I am. But with a variation. A long festering hate crime that's really about revenge and retribution. One that has been building for centuries."

Ray reacted immediately. "Now that's one of the scariest things I've ever heard. Someone who's so full of hate he'd be willing to take out a whole family from a genocide perspective. There could be thousands of people connected over 300 years. Sidney, do you think that's what we're looking at?"

Before Sidney could answer, Tillie continued vehemently, "Mr. Ray, don't forget that Dylan Ruff guy. That man shot all those people in Mother Emanuel while they was prayin'. All he saw was Black people. All he wanted to do is kill Black people. It didn't matter if there was two people or two hundred people. Hate ain't got no bounds. A couple hundred years don't make no difference."

Sidney paused before answering, letting Tillie's observation stand alone. "A variation… possibly. There's something that deals specifically with Morgan here. This is where the hate and mistrust began. This is where it has been reactivated. Someone has become incensed at something that happened recently. Something that mirrors what happened 300 years ago and the same family is involved again. Yes, revenge and retribution. Hate, yes, but a more focused and targeted hate than the kind that infected Mr. Ruff."

"But what about Miss Rye bein Black, how's she fit in? She just came down from Philly."

"Tillie, you're right about hate but it doesn't only live along Black and white racial lines, which is why I believe her DNA is critical to what is happening. I truly believe there is a link we don't know about—"

Tillie's ringing phone interrupted the conversation. She looked at her phone that had been in her pocket and said, "Oh, I know who this is. Speak o' the devil." She answered the call. "Mrs. McCann, this is Tillie James. Glad you called… Oh, that's good… Yeah, we can meet anytime…Sure. Where… Library is good for me… Okay, one o'clock… Yes, the South Carolina Room… I'll call Mrs. DeReimer… Lookin forward to it." She disconnected and said, "That was Florence McCann, Gloria Rye's sister. She wants to meet."

"Well now," Sidney began with a satisfied lilt to his voice. "The missing connections may be revealed. I wonder how far back Gloria Rye's DNA will take us?"

"Given my conversations with Pete, they better take us back to this lawyer, John James Winslow. He seems to be a key figure in everything."

"Ray, I think you're on the right track. According to Mrs. DeReimer, her research has shown that Richard Tookerman may have been an unscrupulous man of his time, but he died only a few years after Stede Bonnet's hanging. It appears the Winslow family line holds the clue to what has set our murderer on the course he now pursues."

THIRTY

2018
Florence McCann

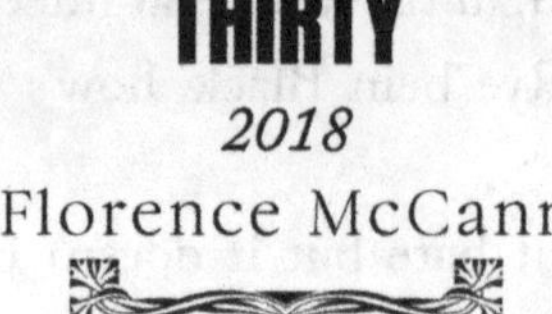

As Tillie approached the Morgan Regional Library for her one o'clock appointment with Florence McCann, she was surprised to see two police cars parked at the entrance and a policeman monitoring the front door. Ahead of schedule, she had planned to meet with Mrs. DeReimer first so she could tell her about her conversations with Miriam Tooker at the nursing home. Family oral histories, while once the only connection to the past for most rural communities, were beginning to disappear, and Mrs. DeReimer, along with many historical societies, didn't want that to happen.

Recognizing Officer Green standing by the front door, she went right up to him. "Library closed?"

"Oh, hi, Tillie. No, just the South Carolina Room."

"What's goin on? Mrs. DeReimer ain't hurt, is she?"

"No, somebody messed up the place a bit. We're trying to see if they took ething."

ally. That'd be the second time a library's been messed up in town."

re right. That's why we're going over everything carefully."

Tillie paused and shook her head. She peered at the front double doors and asked, "Is Mrs. DeReimer here? Got an appointment with her this afternoon."

Officer Green nodded. "Pretty sure she is. Want me to check for you?"

"Yeah, if you would. Is it okay to go in?"

Green made a move toward the door and answered her over his shoulder. "Should be. I'm pretty sure she's in the South Carolina Room. Let me tell her you're here. I think we're mostly done." He reached for the door then looked back at Tillie with a smile on his face and asked, "Say Tillie, you remember when I was watching over Professor Lake's place in my car down the street, those biscuits you brought me, did you make them home made?"

"Course I did. Never make any other kind."

"They were the best biscuits I ever had. Told my wife, Caroline, about them. Think you could let me have the recipe?"

With a big smile, Tillie answered, "Sure. Tell you what. You get me in to see Mrs. DeReimer so we can keep our appointment and then come by the house this afternoon and I'll have it for you."

"You got yourself a deal."

The moment Officer Green went into the library, Tillie took out her phone and dialed Sidney Lake. "Professor, did you know somebody did something to the South Carolina Room today?"

"Again?"

"No, not that library, the one downtown."

Sidney remained silent for a moment and asked, "The South Carolina Room, right?"

"You got it. You thinkin what I'm thinkin?"

"Yes, I believe I am. Are you able to have your meeting with Mrs. DeReimer and Mrs. McCann?"

"Think so. Officer Green is runnin interference for me. Those biscuits of mine work every time."

"Biscuits?"

"Never mind. I want to give Florence McCann a call and warn her about what's goin on before I get to Mrs. DeReimer."

"All right, keep in touch once you learn what happened. I'll talk with Ray Morton and see what he knows. However you have to do it, keep that meeting with Florence McCann."

"I will."

Officer Green came out and called Tillie to the entrance door. "Sam Cashman and a couple of people from Dr. Coffey's group are in the South Carolina Room, but he said you and Mrs. DeReimer can get together if you meet in the Children's Story Room. That area isn't impacted by anything."

"Thanks, that's great. And there's another lady comin'. A Mrs. McCann. Should be here in about twenty minutes."

"No problem. I'll let her know where to find you. I think Sam wants to talk to you, so don't leave without talking with him."

"I'll make sure of it." As she made her way to the door she added, "And you come by the Professor's around three and I'll have that recipe for you."

Green, with a big smile, said, "Oh, I won't forget."

Once inside, Tillie made a quick phone call to Florence McCann to let her know what to expect when she got to the library. She peeked at the South Carolina Room as she passed. The glass-paned door was closed, and she could see Detective Cashman in discussion with two people she didn't recognize. They didn't look up, and she proceeded to the Children's Story Room and Mrs. DeReimer.

The Children's Story Room was a place in miniature; small chairs and tables randomly placed around the room. As Tillie came through the door, she was immediately followed by Mrs. DeReimer carrying two adult-sized chairs from another room.

"Let me help you with that." Tillie held the door open, and Mrs. DeReimer passed one of the chairs to her.

"Thank you. When Detective Cashman said we would have to meet in here, I realized we would have a problem. There's only one adult-size chair in this room on a regular basis. Since Mrs. McCann is joining us, I took these from the reference area."

As they walked together to where the other adult chair sat, Tillie asked, "What happened here?"

"Goodness. My room is a mess. Well, it's not really my room." Mrs. DeReimer positioned her chair directly across from the one already in place. "I spend so much time in the South Carolina Room, it's as though it was part of my home. Just put that here so we'll be in a sort of circle. Is Mrs. McCann still coming?"

Tillie put down her chair as instructed. "Yes, I phoned her and told her not to worry about the policeman out front. He's expectin' her. I told officer Green about our meeting, and he'll make sure she gets to the right place."

"Ah, very good."

"So, what happened?"

"I don't know. When I came in after being called unexpectedly, someone had been into the South Carolina Room and left it a mess."

"Is anything missing?"

"I don't know. Detective Cashman said he'd need me to do an inspection, or something to that effect, after they were finished. Although I did notice the microfiche drawers were open. I always make sure everything is tidied up when I have to leave the room unattended. This is all very strange."

Tillie looked at her watch and said, "I think Mrs. McCann will be here in a few minutes. What can I tell you about the Good Harvest Retirement Home?"

"You know I've been working with the historical society on obtaining oral histories from some of the older residents of Morgan, and they're very interesting. However, I've observed a major gap in their data collection: all the histories were from white families."

Tillie smiled.

Mrs. DeReimer saw the look on Tillie's face and said, "You're not surprised?"

"No, not in the least. The Gullah have been here for almost 400 years, and you'd think we just arrived the other day. I'll bet you don't have too many

Black people in that historic society."

"No… erm… no, now that you mention it, there's no one involved in the oral history project."

"Well, let me just say thank you, Mrs. DeReimer. In all the history and heritage stuff they do around Morgan, you gotta be the first person who ever thought of making the Gullah a part of it."

"I guess we're going to have to change that, aren't we? It's Tillie, isn't it?"

"Yes, Ma'am."

"Well, I'm Etta, and…" she held out her hand, which Tillie took eagerly, "I think it's time we changed some things."

"I'm for that. Step one is for you and me to visit Good Harvest and let me introduce you to everyone."

A knock came at the entrance to the room. Tillie and Mrs. DeReimer looked up to see a tall, slim Black woman wearing a dark blue pants suit with a white blouse.

"Am I in the right place? I'm looking for a Mrs. Tillie James."

"You must be Mrs. Florence McCann," said Tillie.

"Yes, I am."

"And I'm Etta DeReimer. I'm with the library and manage the South Carolina Room." She extended her hand to Florence. "I'm so sorry about what happened to your sister. I enjoyed working with her so much."

"Yes, she mentioned you." Florence looked back over her shoulder. "What's going on here? Police cars outside and a guard on the door."

"We may have had a robbery. The South Carolina Room is in great disarray."

"My goodness. I've never heard of someone trying to rob a library. Was anyone injured?"

Etta DeReimer motioned her to one of the chairs she had arranged for their meeting. "No. I found the South Carolina Room all disrupted."

"Miss McCann," Tillie began as they moved across the room, "there've been some strange things happenin' around here over the past few weeks. And I don't just mean the attack on your sister, Lord bless her. Nobody seems to have an idea about what's happening or why. Police is in the dark. Only one who is getting his arms around anything is the Professor."

"The professor?" Florence asked as she removed the shoulder bag she carried and placed it next to the chair Etta had assigned to her.

"Professor Lake. I'd like you to meet him. He used to teach at the college. Now he writes books about other writers, mainly English ones. We talk a lot, and he has some good ideas about what's been goin' on in Morgan. Police ask him to help sometimes when they got a puzzle that doesn't look right."

"Yes, I think I'd like to meet him. I still have no idea why someone would want to kill my sister, Gloria." She sat down and the others followed her lead. "She had been so enthusiastic about coming to Morgan. After her husband died, she became interested in our family history. She always watched that PBS show about finding your roots. She didn't know it would be possible to trace the Bailey name all the way back to before the American Revolution."

"She was able to do that?" Etta DeReimer asked. "I know she had her DNA done but I had no idea she was that successful. We were going to meet and review the findings, but we never had the opportunity."

"Oh, yes. We knew the family were slaves, as so many were, and there were all the family stories. We didn't know what was true and what were just tales."

"Tillie here knows all about family stories and tales. We were speaking before you arrived."

"Yeah, we were. I've been out at the Good Harvest Retirement Home speakin- to lots of people. There's a story lady there. Don't know how much you know about Gullah, but we been together for more than 400 years, and people kept the stories alive by rememberin and repeatin them. Couldn't do it any other way. Weren't allowed to. So, Professor Lake and me decided there may be a story that connects what's been going on."

Looking confused, Florence asked, "I don't understand. I thought Gloria was the victim of a mugging of some type? The police haven't told me anything else."

"Well, Mrs. McCann…"

"Please, call me Florence."

Tillie smiled. "Okay, Florence. Let me tell you what's been happenin'." Tillie explained the three murders and the theory about how, while all three of the victims did not know one another, they were connected by their DNA that reached back at least 300 years. "They found firm links between Dorinda Tooker and Martin Tucker and are convinced there is a link to Gloria Rye as well."

Etta said, "Your sister and I had some phone conversations over the past month, and she and I planned to get together to analyze what she had discovered from her DNA. Might be even more important now if we can find a match with the DNA of the other victims."

"But we're talking hundreds of years."

"Exactly," Tillie said. "It sounds not too believable, but I think Professor Lake is on to somethin', especially after I had a long talk with Miss Miriam at the retirement home. She's the story lady. She told me a story about a man from the old Bailey Plantation…"

"Bailey? That's our name, Bailey." Florence said. "Our grandfather was Thomas Bailey."

Silence.

Tillie reached over and touched Florence McCann's shoulder as she recommended, "If I could make a suggestion, I think you really need to meet with Professor Lake."

"I'd be happy to but what does the Bailey name have to do with anything?"

"Two plantations keep popping up regardin' what's been goin' on over at the Marshlands Plantation. If you've got a connection to the Bailey Plantation, we got some diggin to do. You know your sister asked Etta if she could help with her Ancestry search; did she also give you access to her information?"

"Yes. She did."

"Would you be willing to let Etta look at it while we go visit the Professor?"

"Yes, if you think it would help."

"It would. Everyone's trying to find the connection between your sister and the other two people who were killed."

Etta DeReimer, after giving it some serious thought while Tillie was speaking, felt she had to let both Tillie and Florence McCann know that her position in doing family research had changed. "There's something I have to mention," Etta began, "because I'm in the middle of everything as a result of my position with the library and the South Carolina Room, the Mayor has asked me to serve as a special consultant to the police department. I'll be doing extensive research into the family histories of the other victims, Martin Tucker and Dorinda Tooker and, if I add Gloria Rye to my activities, I'll be obliged to let them know what I've learned. If you think this would be a problem, please let me know."

Florence McCann didn't answer immediately.

"I don't know," she finally said. "I don't know how much I want to get involved. I would like them to catch whoever killed my sister, but will it make me a target as well?"

"Tell you what," offered Tillie, "how about you and me we go and talk with Professor Lake. He's pretty even headed with this sort of thing. We only live a few streets away. You can always give Etta a call later and tell her what you want to do."

Etta reached into her pocket and pulled out one of her business cards. "Here is my direct number for the South Carolina Room. Let me know what you want me to do. I'll be here all day trying to figure out what might have been stolen and cleaning up the mess."

"Tillie, I think you're right. I need to talk with someone before I do anything. I'd like to walk over to Professor Lake's with you before I get too involved."

Tillie stood up and they followed her lead.

Etta walked Tillie and Florence to the door, but as she passed the entrance to the South Carolina Room, Detective Cashman waved her over.

"I'll leave you two here. Detective Cashman needs to speak with me. Florence, I'm delighted to have the chance to meet you. I'll wait for your call."

Goodbyes completed, she went into the South Carolina Room.

"Mrs. DeReimer, hope I didn't disrupt your meeting."

"No, we were finished for now. Is there something I can help you with?"

"The fingerprint people are done so if you can start working on the inventory we need, I'd appreciate it."

"I can't imagine what they were looking for. Although, I suppose some of the books and maps in here could be quite valuable. Is there any particular place you'd like me to start?"

"As you say, the rare books and maps might be good place to start. Who was that you and Tillie were talking with?"

"Florence McCann. Gloria Rye's sister. Came back to close up her sister's condo. I had been helping Mrs. Rye with some questions she had about the history of the Morgan region."

"Really?"

"That's what brought her to Morgan. Although Mrs. Rye's from Philadelphia, she found out she had roots here and came to explore her family history and decided to stay. Her sister never knew what the connections were as she wasn't interested in the subject, but now she is."

"Do you have her number?"

"No, but I'm sure Tillie does."

"Good. I'll get it from her. Oh, another matter. Do you know who has keys to the South Carolina Room and also the library?"

"Not entirely. I do, of course. There should be a list at the Reference Desk."

"Are they secured in any way?"

"Not really. There's a box in a cabinet behind the main desk at the inquiry station. Everyone knows where it is. I don't know if the box is locked, I know the cabinet isn't."

"Hmmm. Okay, thanks. Let me know if you discover something's missing. I'll be in the reference area."

THIRTY-ONE

1780

Nichols versus Bailey

On the twentieth of December, General Washington began to assemble the resources needed for the attack on Trenton and the three Hessian regiments quartered there. Washington would have 6,000 troops under his command and at least twenty small artillery pieces. The attack would be three pronged and was set for the twenty-fifth of December. Washington would cross the Delaware River nine miles above Trenton in the region of McKonkey's ferry. At the same time, there would be two other crossings, one just below Trenton and another below that. Everything was to occur simultaneously. The plan was a good one except for the December rain, sleet, and snow.

There were ferry crossings all along the Delaware River near Trenton, but they would soon be closing as the river was near freezing. The British forces were patiently waiting for the ice to solidify, which would permit them to cross and make their march on Philadelphia. Washington feared the American forces would wait too long, for if the Delaware froze before he could attack, there would be no stopping the British.

The colonial forces had to move immediately in order to maintain the element of surprise. The Hessian troops of Rahl, Lossberg, and Knyphanses knew exactly what was across the Delaware but were convinced Washington was no match for them and did not see his army as an offensive threat. Christmas Day had been planned as a holiday for the Hessians and all the British forces within range of Trenton.

On December twenty-fourth, the main contingent of the Philadelphia Militia, commanded by Colonel Griffin, moved toward the bank of the Delaware River, where the boats to move 600 men across were staged. Their primary objective was to cut off the retreat of the Hessians as well as any attempt to support them from the south. They had estimated it would take three hours to move all the men and equipment to the other side of the river. This would be Lieutenant Ian Wilson Nichols' task, aided by the ferryman who had agreed to help them with their wagons and light artillery.

Three wagons filled with supplies and provisions were lined up along the road as Lieutenant Nichols, wearing a greatcoat and scarf made from an old blanket, slowly walked to the ferryman's hut along with three of the Philadelphia volunteers. The wind howled, and the rain and sleet pounded him. He kept his head down but the cold penetrated everywhere.

He called out, "Ferryman, it's time to load the wagons."

No one answered. He turned to the musket man next to him and whispered, "See if anyone is in there. One of us has to get across and warn the Hessians. It's only four hours to sunset."

The militia man went to the hut and pounded on the door once again and opened it. A fire warmed the small, empty building and indicated the ferryman was nearby. "He's not here, Sir."

"Just as well. One of us has got to get this ferry across the river. Can you handle the lines?"

"Aye, Sir. Have done it before. I'll get across and then cut the lines, disabling it while I get to Trenton."

Outside, on the far side of the hut, Caleb Bailey listened quietly. When he learned the name of the officer in charge of the ferry bore the name

Nichols, he became cautious. His grandfather, James Bailey, often told the story of how he gained his freedom from the Nichols family and a place called Marshlands Plantation. He warned they were a devious lot, especially Sean Wilson Nichols, the manager of the plantation. Caleb was sure the Lieutenant Nichols standing at the hut was a direct descendant of the Sean Wilson Nichols he had been warned about. And now he knew him to be a spy for the British as well. But what should he do? What would his grandfather Jamie have advised him?

Caleb stayed put. He would neither help nor hinder. His grandfather often said, "Remember, the English brought slavery to this land, but the Colonials perfected it." Caleb had heard there were movements afoot in England to bring slavery to an end as there were in the colonies, and the American Revolution had put forth principals of freedom for all men. But Caleb also knew that in the South, where so many of the leaders of the independence movement were slave holders, they did not believe the negro was a man and could prove it by passages from the bible. He could not believe that the leaders of the Virginia and Carolina colonies would be willing to free their slaves and face economic ruin for a noble principle. No, Caleb would wait and watch.

As Lieutenant Nichols and the militia soldier prepared the ferry to launch, they kept a careful eye on the cold and angry Delaware River. The masses of floating ice looked as though they were getting larger.

"Are you sure you can handle this?" Nichols asked.

"Yes, Sir. I'm from these parts. The Delaware is always angry at Christmas. I guess they don't have this weather where you're from, Sir."

"No, not that I've ever known. Our rivers are friendly in the Carolinas." A blast of wind filled with sleet and snow slammed against the Lieutenant, and he had to hold on to the tow rope to keep from being blown into the river.

"I'll be all right, Sir. Old James Bailey builds a good ferry."

Nichols reset his footing and looked at the soldier. "Who did you say?"

"James Bailey. He built the ferry and his family the warehouses on the Jersey side. He doesn't anymore. Old Jamie died some ten years ago. Son runs everything now. Him and his sons." Another blast of snow and ice. "Arragh. It's bone chillin' that wind."

"I'll help with the lines." Nichols moved into position. "Tell me one thing. Do you know where Bailey's from?"

The ferry began to move.

"The Carolinas."

Holding on to his hat in the wind, Lieutenant Nichols called to the soldier, "The son who runs the ferry, his name."

A large block of ice hit the ferry and rocked it as the soldier replied, "His grandson, Caleb. Caleb Bailey."

As the ferry disappeared into the storm, Nichols looked after it a final time as the wind and driving sleet pushed him toward the hut. He said to himself, "Caleb, eh? Caleb Bailey, you and I shall have a talk."

The ferryman heard it all from his place of cover. He knew Lieutenant Nichols was someone to avoid. But what would he have against a man he never met?

Caleb Bailey watched Lieutenant Nichols make his way to the road where the carts waited. The Lieutenant would tell Colonel Griffin the ferry was gone, and they would have to do their best to get everything they needed across the raging Delaware in the five boats now available to them. It would not be possible to move 600 men and supplies across the river and be able to keep the schedule that had been set. Their only hope would be to find the wayward ferry somewhere on the Eastern shore of the river.

Sundown came and while Washington managed to get his 1,200 troops and cannon across the river nine miles above Trenton, the raging waters of the Delaware, filled with larger and larger ice flows, delayed them for hours. The status of the second prong of the attack under Colonel Ewing was unknown, as communication became impossible in the driving sleet and snow. Their task had been to come in one mile below Trenton and take the pressure off Washington's column by capturing the bridge over the Assunpink and thereby forcing the Hessians to surrender. The third crossing was well behind schedule as it was to occur at the ferry where Lieutenant Nichols had interrupted the river craft. Here Colonel Griffin's Philadelphia militia was to cross below Bordentown and cut off any reinforcements coming from the south to support the Hessians.

All of Washington's divisions were to be in place on the Eastern shore of the Delaware, in position and ready to attack simultaneously at dawn, on Christmas Day. By three in the morning, Washington's forces had finally made it to the east side of the Delaware but had yet to begin their march toward Trenton. The sun would soon be up and with a nine-mile march ahead of them, they had lost the element of surprise. Ewing's forces never made it across the raging ice-filled river. While Colonel Griffin managed to get his troops across, they found themselves trying to accomplish their own mission as well as Ewing's.

Lieutenant Nichols stayed behind with a small force to secure the now functioning ferry to protect an escape route if it was needed. However, he had another agenda: find Caleb Bailey.

The Nichols family had become aware of the story told to John James Winslow detailing how Sean Wilson Nichols had fooled the authorities and substituted a child that was not legitimate as the natural-born son of Eli Nichols. Winslow had put their ownership of Marshlands Plantation in jeopardy. Lieutenant Nichols would get even.

Caleb Bailey watched the colonial forces cross the river. The missing ferry caused a delay, but it was the river and the ice that was the problem. Boat after boat had to return to the Western shore and start over. They persisted. The landings on the other shore were erratic, as many of the boats were driven downstream and away from the designated assembly point. With boats returning empty to be filled with new militia, boats not making it across, the ferry taking two and three times longer than it normally would to make a crossing, Lieutenant Nichols was too busy to search for Caleb, but the desire to do so never left him. Caleb, on the other hand, stayed nearby. He wanted to keep Nichols in sight. His grandfather had drilled into him, as he did with all his offspring, a fear of being dragged back into slavery. Yes, they were free, but what did that matter if an influential Carolina planter claimed your freedom papers were not true.

Caleb made a mistake. He had been up all night watching. At five in the morning, all became quiet. The troops and supplies were on the other side. He was a hundred yards from his hut. His warm comfortable hut. He watched carefully. Everyone was gone. He was alone. His feet and hands were frozen. Even his breath felt cold. He made his way to the hut. There was a window in the rear facing the river so the ferryman could watch for the ferry. He made his way around to the back and peeked into the warm and cozy room. It was empty. Not looking around, he entered in a rush.

Caleb stood in front of the fire a full five minutes, warming himself, and never heard the door behind him open.

"Caleb Bailey. So, you are here."

Caleb jumped at the sound of Lieutenant Nichols, who stood in the doorway blocking his exit.

Nichols spoke in a low, firm tone. "Your family betrayed our trust. You may have thought you could hide and get away with it. A bargain was made that you have broken."

A shiver ran through Caleb, his back now to the fire. "Sir, I have no idea who you are or what you speak of."

"Ha. You know. Oh, you know. Jamaica… Jamie will have told you. Your freedom and that of all your relations is forfeit. You are mine, Bailey. Oh, yes, you are mine." A smile grew upon Lieutenant Nichols' face as he spoke. He took a step forward and began to draw his sword.

"You're mad! I'm a freeman. Born across the river. I have never been in the Carolinas." He could feel the heat of the fire behind him as his heel touched the andiron.

Lieutenant Nichols drew his sword and took a step forward. "How did you know I spoke of the Carolinas, of Morgan, and my home of Marshlands Plantation? A place under siege by the radical Winslows and Tookermans who seek its fortunes. Under siege because of Bailey treachery."

Caleb reached behind him with his right hand, searching… and then he felt it. The poker. He grabbed it, and in a firm, quick motion swung it at Nichols.

The Lieutenant tried to deflect the blow, but the attack was too unexpected and fast. His left arm came up in defense. The poker hit his wrist and broke it while continuing to the side of his head as he tried to turn away. He dropped the sword and yelled in pain as he fell to the floor. Caleb placed his left foot on the blade of the fallen sword and delivered a second blow to the top of Nichols' head, killing him instantly.

Nichols' scream was heard by two militia men who were coming down the road to the ferry landing. They ran to the hut and found Caleb kneeling over the body.

Caleb Bailey saved his life by telling the story of Lieutenant Nichols' deception about moving the ferry to the Eastern shore of the Delaware to delay the crossing. He also told them he heard Nichols telling a militia man to scuttle the ferry and then head for Trenton to warn the Hessians of the pending attack.

Colonel Griffin heard of Caleb Bailey's story and then of the capture of one of his militiamen among the ranks of more than 1,000 Hessian troops captured by General Washington. The man had admitted being a spy under orders from Lieutenant Nichols. The incident was recorded in the records of the raid on Trenton. The spy was one of three Loyalists found among the ranks of Washington's forces. All three were hung.

Bailey was freed but the record of Lieutenant Nichols' treason against the American forces would be used by the family of John James Winslow to their advantage when the war ended.

THIRTY-TWO

2018
A Campaign Of Hate

Florence McCann could understand why her sister liked the town of Morgan, South Carolina—it was manageable. Living in Philadelphia, the feeling of not being in control of your surroundings attached itself to almost everything. Morgan contained one characteristic that made it different: its size. It only took an afternoon walk around downtown to know where to find everything and everyone. The library, City Hall, museum, hospital, college, the mayor, police chief, school board, and city council members were all visible. Accessible. Gloria Rye loved it. But her sister, Florence, was completely different. Gloria was trusting, friendly, outgoing. Florence trusted no one. Friendships did not come easy to her. She looked at everyone with a suspicious eye.

As she and Tillie walked from the library to Sidney's house on Howard Street, she peppered Tillie with questions.

"Why is this Professor Lake interested in helping? What is he getting out of this?"

Tillie understood the question, as she had asked it herself a few years ago. She had also taken measure of Florence and understood where she was coming from. So, she answered her directly, "I was waitin' for that." She smiled as they walked. "He can't help it. Let me explain a little. Professor Lake spent most of his life in books. Mostly readin' and studying the writers and people in the books. He lived in a simple world. One in which the good people always win and the bad get what they deserve. He believes in right from wrong and has trouble with places in the middle. He sees the world around him in the same way. Had a reputation as a hard nose. Then his wife got sick and died. It wasn't supposed to happen. She was a good person. In his world, bad things didn't happen to good people. It was around that time I met him and went to work for him.

"You're a big city person an you know what the real world looks like. This is a small town, what they call a 'bubble.' It looks peaceful, but it ain't. Lot of the people here live by different rules than the rest of us. They stick with their own kind. I worked for a lot of 'um. Still do. Morgan has a bad history, but no one wants to talk about it. The Professor woke up after his wife died. Began to look around, and things he took for granted didn't seem to make sense. Especially after he retired from the college. Wasn't just race. It was the old versus the new. The outsider versus the insider. Professor Lake found himself outside the 'bubble' and seeing things for the first time. He started to challenge the system. When he saw something that didn't look right, he said so. Looks into things on his own. Has a couple of good friends. One is a retired policeman; another is a college lady friend. He's also close to the pastor of the local Presbyterian church. They look at things different and ain't afraid to speak up."

"How did you get mixed up in all of this?"

Tillie stopped as they reached a corner. "I like to speak up too."

"Well, tell me something. Why does your Professor Lake think my sister was murdered?"

"Hate. Pure and simple. But not race hate. At least not that we've been able to figure out. He called it revenge and retribution for past wrongs."

They came to another street corner and waited for two cars to pass before moving on.

"I have to admit, Florence, this whole situation is a real puzzle. We got three dead people and they're as different as you could imagine. One Black and two white. One real old, one sorta old, and one not so old. Dorinda Tooker was eighty-nine. Your sister was in her sixties, I'm guessin."

"Just turned sixty-four," Florence said.

"And then this Tucker fella. They say he was in his mid-forties. One was from Morgan, one from Philadelphia, and one from Summerville. Police are looking for connections, but they're scratchin' their heads on this one."

"But Professor Lake thinks he has something." Florence stopped in the middle of the sidewalk.

"That's why I want you to talk to him. Apparently, the only connection seems to be that they were all killed in the same way." Tillie specifically omitted the fact they were also killed with the same weapon: the poker. That information had not been released to the public yet. "They found a connection in the DNA of Dorinda Tooker and Martin Tucker that goes back a couple of hundred years, and when we learned that your sister, Gloria, was asking Mrs. DeReimer at the library to help with her ancestry searching, Professor Lake figured she was connected to the other two, but we don't know how. Then, a little while ago, you mentioned your grandfather was a Bailey and it clicked. The Baileys had a big plantation here some three hundred years ago. I got a feeling that's our third link,"

"Really."

They started walking again. Howard Street and Sidney Lake were a block and a half away.

<hr>

After Sidney received the call from Tillie, he immediately got out of his chair, grabbed his cane, and began to walk from room to room. Mickey, at first, thought she and Sidney would be going for a walk and followed him, but it soon became evident that wasn't the case. Sidney was on his thinking circuit. He went from the living room to the front hall and then made a right turn and walked down the hallway to the kitchen. Mickey went back to Sidney's chair and waited for him to return. Sidney slowly continued into the kitchen, made a turn around the island, went back out of the kitchen and into the dining room and then over to his starting point at his chair in the living room. Sidney completed three full trips before stopping at his chair. "Yes, yes, yes," he said. "It's starting to fit."

He sat in his chair, reached for his phone, and called Ray. "Ray, can you come over in the next fifteen minutes or so? I'm expecting Tillie and Florence McCann. That's Gloria Rye's sister."

"Sure. What's going on?"

"I think we may have found the missing link to Gloria Rye's murder."

"Be right there."

Ray, living only two doors away from Sidney, came down his front steps as Tillie and Florence rounded the corner ahead of him. He made it to Sidney's walkway before them and decided to wait.

"Mr. Morton, this is Florence McCann."

They greeted one another and Florence asked, "Are you with the police?"

"Yes and no. I'm retired but have been doing contract investigations for the county solicitor's office, and they loaned me to the Morgan Police Department."

The three of them walked up the front steps to Sidney's porch and Tillie opened the door. Florence took a step back when she saw the big black dog come running over to them.

"Oh, don't mind Mickey, she won't hurt you. Be the best friend you have in town by the time you leave."

Florence looked at Mickey and said, "Strange dogs and I don't get along. Nothing personal. Been bitten a couple of times back home, so I like to keep my distance."

"Mickey, come here," Sidney called from his chair. "Come in, everyone." Sidney started to get up from his chair and reached for his cane.

Florence, seeing him reach, said, "Don't get up. You must be Professor Lake; I'm Florence McCann." She walked toward Sidney as he sat back down. Mickey moved to her position next to the chair and lay down in her usual place.

As they shook hands, Sidney said, "I'm very pleased to meet you, Mrs. McCann. I'm so sorry about what happened to your sister. You have my sincere condolences."

"Thank you, Professor Lake. Tillie has told me quite a bit about you."

"Please, take a seat." He motioned her to the sofa beside his chair. Ray moved a straight-back chair near the fireplace and placed it opposite the coffee table as Tillie joined Florence on the sofa. Tillie brought Ray up-to-date on the conversation that occurred in the Children's Story Room.

Sidney asked Ray, "Have you heard any more about the break-in at the library?"

"No. Sam said he had some ideas. They're still trying to figure it out."

"Hrumph, very interesting." He directed his attention to Florence. "Tillie tells me that you may be connected to the Bailey Plantation in some way."

"I don't really know. My grandfather was a Bailey, and my sister Gloria told us she believed we used to live in South Carolina. She was the one doing all the family research. I never really paid attention to it. She found some old documents and papers our mother kept. Gloria came to Morgan because the town was mentioned in some of those documents."

"I see," said Sidney. "Did she bring them with her to Morgan?"

"I believe she did. Some of the old ones she put into a safe deposit box in a bank in Philadelphia, but she said she made copies. Everything is in two boxes that are still in the condo. My niece, Gloria's daughter, wants to ship everything back to Philly. She had to get back to work in Jersey, so I promised I'd finish the job."

"Interesting," Sidney said. "Would it be all right if I took a look at those documents with you before they are sent back to Philadelphia?"

Florence thought for a minute and then, with a shrug, said, "I don't see why not. If it will help find Gloria's killer."

Ray interrupted. "I think you might talk with Sam, Sidney; he would probably want to be there with you."

Florence looked at Ray. "Who is Sam?"

Sidney answered, "He's the police detective assigned to the case."

"You saw him this morning at the library," Tillie reminded her.

"Not the one at the entrance door."

"No, Mr. Sam was the one in the South Carolina Room. The one who wanted to see Etta after we finished talking. The tall Black man in the suit."

"Okay, now I know who you're talking about."

"Who is Etta?" asked Sidney.

"Mrs. DeReimer. The library lady."

"I see. I never knew her first name. You must be getting on well with her."

"I'm gonna take her to Golden Harvest and have her meet Miss Miriam, so she can talk to her about a project she's working on. I told her part of the story Miss Miriam told me about Jamie, the slave that put one over on that plantation owner."

"Jamie?" Florence asked. "Like James?"

"I think so."

"My grandfather was James Bailey. The name James has always been given to a son. I don't know the story behind it. Gloria said it's a famous name and it originates from down here. It's one of the reasons she moved here."

Sidney and Ray sat quietly watching the interchange between Florence and Tillie. They realized a breakthrough may have been found. Neither wanted to interrupt, as they also didn't want to give anything away. Not all the information the authorities found had been made public. Ray knew all of it and had even held some data back from Sidney, although he knew he would eventually make it available. Sidney also knew this and did not press Ray for answers. Ray knew Tillie to be a safe confidant, but he didn't know Florence McCann. Sidney and Ray viewed the meeting as one of gathering information, not revealing it.

They continued to ask Florence questions. Questions she mostly couldn't answer. Like many people, family history was not a great interest. She had a career and a very busy social life. Regular trips to the New York theater district with a group of co-workers. Then there was the Philadelphia Symphony, where she had season tickets. Spending time rummaging through old family documents and listening to family stories did not interest her. Her sister Gloria made up for Florence's lack of interest.

Florence McCann continued to outline her life in and around Philadelphia, and it became quite evident to those assembled in Sidney's living room that she did not like being in Morgan, South Carolina—or anywhere outside the Northeast corridor. After rambling on for a few minutes, she suddenly stopped and said, "Oh." She reached down for her bag at the side of the sofa, hurriedly picked it up and searched inside, frantic. "Ah, it's still here."

"Is something the matter?" asked Tillie.

"The envelope. I put it in my purse and forgot all about it. It came for Gloria. I was in a rush going out, so I just stuffed it in my bag and never looked at it." The bag sat on her lap as she reached in and pulled out a large, folded-over manila envelope. "Here it is."

"Who's it from?" asked Ray.

Florence unfolded the envelope and looked at the return address. "Division of Records, Archive Department, City of Charleston."

Ray leaned forward in his chair. "Might be a good idea to take a look. See if it might have anything to do with why she was killed."

Florence gingerly opened the envelope and took out the contents—ten sheets of paper that were copies of original handwritten records from a large book of some kind and a cover letter. She read the letter silently and then said, "The papers are copies from the official records book of 1783. The letter states it records a judgement in favor of John James Winslow, Esquire, whereby his claim for ownership of Marshlands Plantation is affirmed based upon statements of the former slave Jamaica, formerly of the Marshlands Plantation and the Bailey Plantation. The expropriation of the property was authorized due to the owner of the property, Lieutenant Eli Nichols, having been determined to be a British spy during the Battle of Trenton and executed by Caleb Bailey, a ferryman. The enclosed documents show that Marshlands Plantation, in accordance with a loan document provided by John James Winslow, Esquire, was divided between the Tooker and Winslow families as the heirs of Richard Tookerman and John Winslow, Esquire. The original documents related to the treason judgement against Eli Nichols are contained in the official records of the War Department in Washington, DC. Wow."

"Could I see those papers?" Sidney asked. "Ray, you might want to get copies of everything for Chief Hornig. If you don't mind, Mrs. McCann?"

"No, not at all," she said, passing the papers to Sidney.

While Sidney read over the cover letter, Ray got up, took the copies of the original documents from Sidney, and went into Tillie's office to use the copier.

While Sidney read and Ray copied, Florence asked Tillie, "I don't understand what all this is about. This has to do with the Revolutionary War, like 250 years ago?"

"That's the puzzle. The three people who've been killed didn't know one another, but it looks like their ancestors did and didn't get along. I know it's a stretch, but every time we come up with somethin', it keeps pointing back hundreds of years."

"I can't believe this," said an exasperated Florence. "I know people laugh about maybe you really don't want to know who your ancestors were, as you're more likely to find a horse thief than a king, but I never heard of someone getting killed because of it. And who is this Jamaica person?"

"Interestingly enough, I think I know."

Hearing Tillie's last comment while reading the text of the photocopies, Sidney asked, "You do? You know how he fits in?"

"Yeah, I think I do. Miss Miriam, the story lady at Golden Harvest that I told you about, related a famous story about a slave who tricked a plantation owner into givin' him and his family their freedom. The plantation owner was trying to cheat some lawyer and the slave came up with a plan to do it. I think she referred to him as Jaimie."

"Yes, Tillie," said a satisfied sounding Sidney, "I think you've found the key person for us. Jamie would be Jamaica, originally of the Bailey Plantation and would have carried the name Jamie Bailey as he headed north to freedom. And, according to the letter, a Caleb Bailey was the ferryman who killed Lieutenant Nichols, the Loyalist spy, who was the owner of Marshlands Plantation. Yes, Tillie, I think we've uncovered a most consequential man."

Sam Cashman's comment to Chief Hornig about Gloria Rye's direct connection to the Bailey and Marshlands Plantations more than 300 years ago had members of the Morgan Police Department wondering how many more people there could be in Coastal Rivers County with a similar ancestry. The other question being asked had to do with motivation. Yes, the connection was there, but what event in 2018 triggered someone to seek out descendants who were involved with the contested ownership of Marshlands Plantation in 1783? Before the day ended, Detective Sam Cashman and Police Chief Hornig were in the South Carolina Room of the Morgan Library peering over Etta DeReimer's shoulder while she searched the ancestry files of Gloria Rye. They were looking not only for links to current families that might be harboring a grudge but also potential victims of what they were beginning to believe was a revenge campaign.

THIRTY-THREE

2018
The Links Confirmed

An hour later, Sidney, Tillie, and Gloria Rye's sister, Florence McCann, were back around the dining room table at Sidney's where a different search was underway. Florence had retrieved from Gloria's condo the box of material and records she had brought from Philadelphia, as well as the new material she obtained since arriving in Morgan. Sidney wanted to understand the origins of the proposed dispute and work forward from there. Having spent so much of his career researching literary and historic events of the nineteenth century, he had a perspective on the timeframe of the mid-eighteenth century that the others did not. For him, it seemed like current events.

Ray had left earlier to meet with Detective Knott, who'd been exploring the relationship between Mitchell Bennett and the late Martin Tucker. Ray had a feeling the covert nature of the real estate transaction in which they were involved could be a major factor connecting the murders.

Sidney sat back in his chair and addressed Florence. "Your sister has certainly gathered an amazing amount of information. The fact that your family has been in the Philadelphia and Southern New Jersey region since before the French and Indian War, my goodness, the history of the Bailey family is the history of the United States."

"Gloria was like that. Tenacious. She was vice president and manager of the domestic credit department at the bank and spent her whole career going through files and records. While researching the sale of a warehouse to a real estate developer in New Jersey, she discovered the warehouse had once been owned by our great, great, grandfather, and it was a business handed down through the family for a hundred years. It was then she decided to find out the whole story."

"Now that's an interesting piece of information as well. What do the records you have tell us about the warehouse business?"

Florence shuffled through some papers in front of her, moved them aside, and then pulled closer the Bankers Box that had been staring at her from the middle of the table. She thumbed through some files inside and pulled out a thick one. "Gloria was more precise in her record keeping than I am. As a CPA, I'm verifying numbers and have to keep the supporting documentation in order. As a credit analyst at the bank, she'd take the numbers provided by a CPA and then add her research, validating the actual ownership on the property supporting the loan, including its age, history, and any filings against it." She pulled a group of papers from the file. "I think this is what we're looking for. Let's see…" Florence spread sets of papers out in front of her. "Here it is." She picked up one with five sheets attached to it. "The building she researched was owned by Arthur James Bailey in 1893. It was originally purchased by Steven James Bailey in 1835. Steven Bailey sold a smaller warehouse and ferry service across the Delaware River and bought a new, larger warehouse. The original ferry service had warehouses on each side of the Delaware. That business had been run by Caleb Bailey from 1770 and was originally registered to a James Bailey, who in Gloria's notes was Caleb's grandfather."

"Well, that certainly ties things together."

"She has a lot of papers in here referring to other Bailey family members who owned businesses formed after 1893, with the proceeds of the warehouse sale."

Tillie leaned forward and looked at the papers. "You mean you've been able to track your family all the way back to before the American Revolution?"

"Sure looks like it," said Florence.

Tillie sat back in her chair and smiled and laughed as she exclaimed, "Florence, girl… you're DAR! You even got a hero in the family, that Caleb fella who caught that English spy. I got to shake your hand." And she reached across the table as the two of them laughed.

Sidney had a big smile on his face as he said, "Well, I'm proud to be in such distinguished company."

More laughter and then Tillie's face turned serious. "We gotta just hope it ain't the reason Miss Gloria got killed."

"Oh, my God," Florence said. "I hadn't thought of that."

"Don't worry, you'll be protected," said Sidney. "Ray will see to it. However, right now we need to take a step back and start putting all these pieces together. Tillie, if we take what your Miss Miriam of the Golden Harvest Retirement Home said about a slave who achieved freedom for his family with a bit of trickery, we might be able to connect him directly to James Bailey. Freeing a slave was a legal process, and the Colonial British were meticulous about recording all activities relating to colonial property, which the slaves were. So, where would we look for such records?"

"Professor Lake, as I said, my sister was comprehensive in her historical and legal research when she was at the bank. She managed to get all that information from the Charleston archives, and while I was looking for those property transfer records, I noticed a bunch of other letters in one of the file folders." Florence reached into the box and pulled out another file folder. "There are letters here to Charleston, Columbia, Washington, DC, and London." She scanned the letters as she spoke. "I can see right off that, in some of them, she's asking the same questions we are. Some of the letters are dated only a month ago, but the rest are much older. I think we ought to divide up everything in this box among us and see what she was looking for, what she received an answer to, and what's still outstanding."

"An excellent idea," said Sidney. "A very excellent idea indeed."

Ray and Detective Knott sat across from one another in a small conference room in police headquarters. File folders and individual sheets of paper were spread out on the table.

"Ray, I managed to get a description of the original location of the Bailey Plantation from a sale of a portion of it to investors thirty-five years ago." He shifted some pages across the table so Ray could see them. "From what I can tell, there was not just one Bailey Plantation but at least three. One was here in Morgan, another was on the Ashley River northwest of Charleston, and a third was due west of there. The portion the investors got, they sold to a development company with plans to create a Sun City type of community, but it never took off. The whole deal collapsed. The land Tucker and Bennett were trying to acquire was not only that piece but also another one, which used to be part of the old colonial rice fields where Dorinda Tooker was found. An area we now believe was part of Marshlands Plantation."

"Really? So, do we have a connection to the murders?"

Knott sat back away from the table and looked directly at Ray. "Yes and no. Martin Tucker and Mitchell Bennett were trying to secretly acquire some property that seems to have a connection to the people murdered— including Tucker. However, I think it may be a stretch to assume the land deal was the motive. I know you said there seems to be a connection to the Bailey Plantation as far as Gloria Rye is concerned, but I'm not seeing a place for Dorinda Tooker in the mix."

"Hmmmm. I see your point, but I still think we need to consider this as the possible primary motive. So far, it's all we have. Do you have anything else on the land deal? From what you can tell, are Tooker and Bennett the only people involved?"

Knott looked through some of the folders on the table and then pulled out two of them. He opened both folders and placed them on the table in front of him. "I've come up with two LLCs formed for the purpose of acquiring the land. One shows Bennett as the principal, and the other Tucker. Bank accounts were set up for both in different banks. What I need to do is get a look at the transaction records to see where the funds came from to support the capital investments in the LLCs. That's my task for tomorrow."

Ray asked, "Can we get some help on the other side of the transaction? Who actually owns the property? We know Dorinda Tooker's body was found on land believed to be part of the original Marshlands Plantation, and part of the old Bailey Plantation is right next to it. Nobody's thought about either of those properties since that deal fell apart forty years ago. Who owned them then and who owns them now?"

"I'll have to check. Recent records are maintained in the assessor's office and are all digitized but earlier ones are on microfiche. I'm not sure what the cut-off date is and where they're stored. More research for tomorrow."

Both men were quiet. Ray focused his thoughts on Sidney's belief in a 300-year-old hate crime of some sort. Ray had initially dismissed it, but he was having second thoughts knowing Sidney and Tillie usually ended up being right. Although, not always in exactly the way they first thought. Could there be something in those old historic records they all missed or maybe just hadn't found yet?

Detective Knott was thinking about the amount of legwork facing him and how to approach it. He could have the assessor's office do the searching and he could also get the office of the Secretary of State to do additional research about the LLCs set up by Bennett and Tucker, as well as other people in their firms. He decided it might be a good idea to go back to Mitchell Bennett and Martin Tucker's business partners and ask specific questions based on what he and Ray had learned. Something else occurred to him. "Ray, remember how this all started? The treasure hunt. We kind of dismissed it when the second murder happened. Someone should go back and have a long chat with Swift. That third man was never identified. It could be the missing piece."

"Damn it. You're right. Here we're running around trying to find a solution to a supposed 300-year-old crime, and we may have lost sight of something a little simpler: greed. What if this is all about finding that box?"

Etta DeReimer was exhausted. Staring for hours at her computer screen while Detective Cashman pieced together bits and pieces of information. Her back hurt and her neck was stiff.

"Detective Cashman, can we take a break? For that matter, could we call it a day?"

Sam looked up from his seat at the table next to her desk. "I'm sorry." He checked his watch. "Yes, of course. I'd lost track of the time. Chief Hornig left us more than an hour ago. I became so involved in what you were printing out I…. Well, you've done great work for us. I have more material here than I expected. Yes, let's call it a day."

"Thank you. Oh, and something occurred to me a little while ago and I forgot to mention it. You probably need to talk with Mrs. Cathcart over at the Palmer Library. I seem to remember Mrs. Wilcox telling me that Mrs. Dorinda Tooker used material from over there when she applied to the DAR more than sixty years ago. The Palmer's been around a lot longer than the Morgan library. Most libraries used to be private or subscription back then. We have some of the old records from there in our cross-reference index but not all of them. Palmer still uses those three-by-five index cards, which are more interesting for research as they have notations written all over them. I've actually seen some records that have four and five cards stapled together. They never throw anything away."

Sam looked shocked. "Good point. With all our emphasis on DNA and digital searching, well…. Hmmm. Do you have a list of private subscription libraries in the region like the Palmer?"

"Actually, we do. I can print it out for you."

"I wasn't involved with the investigation of the theft at the Palmer Library, that was another detective, but I remember from the reports I read, the books in question were donated many years ago by heirs of the Bailey Plantation. Are you aware of any old families similar to the Baileys who might still have family libraries?"

"I could come up with a list for you of donations we received over the years. People are always donating material to us that they found and believed to be… old. Books and maps that are not really valuable as collectables. Most families either keep the good ones or sell them off. But yes, I have a list of those as well."

Rather than leaving as Mrs. DeReimer had hoped, she and Sam stayed for almost another hour as they went through the various lists. Mrs. DeReimer also gave Sam a rundown on the backgrounds of the families who had made donations. Material not relating to South Carolina was kept elsewhere in the library, but the online database clearly indicated where they could be found: the reference department.

By the time Sam left, he felt energized. More and more, he began to believe that Sidney Lake was on the right track, and the secret to everything would be found in all those old records. It would be a matter of time before they came across a link. However, time was not on their side. Chief Hornig had to come up with an answer to the three murders and action needed to be taken. Someone had to be charged with something. Despite Morgan being a small town, the local authorities were expected to solve big crimes. The deadline for getting the job done, before the state moved in, stared Chief Hornig and Mayor Wilcox in the face. They needed to come up with something and quickly.

THIRTY-FOUR

1783

Expropriation

The war for American independence may have ended but another raged on. In the market town of Morgan, South Carolina, the new war was not fought by American soldier against British soldier, with musket and cannon, but by patriot neighbor against loyalist neighbor, with lawyers and court decrees. This was John James Winslow's opportunity to finally obtain the prize he had long sought.

His argument had not changed over the years. He claimed Marshlands Plantation was his by law and had been stolen from his family through the deceit of Sean Wilson and Patrick Nichols. Repeatedly, John James had told the story of Eli Nichols not having a natural-born son and failed to pay the sums outlined in the loan agreement between Richard Tookerman and Eli Nichols, drawn up by his father, John Winslow, and thereby making the rightful owners of Marshlands Plantation the Tookerman and Winslow families.

John James Winslow stood before the court, raising his hand high and firmly clutching the original loan agreement as he pleaded his case. His face was red with anger and his two sons stood by his side, physically supporting him. "There should be no dispute here," he argued. "It is clear that the Tory, Patrick Nichols, is not the natural heir of Eli Nichols but the unnatural product of an alliance between Sean Wilson and a slave on Marshlands Plantation. A slave who obtained her freedom by this deception and left the Carolinas for Pennsylvania. It is also a well-known fact Patrick Nichols fought with the British auxiliaries at Stono River and Lieutenant Ian Wilson Nichols served as a spy for the British at the Battle of Trenton. Having done so, the Nichols clan lost whatever rights they may have had to be a landowner in South Carolina." He became unsteady on his feet as he yelled and waved the document above his head. "I have legal claim to the land!" Spittle came down the side of his mouth. His sons held him tight to keep him from falling.

The petition by John James Winslow, now an old man of seventy-five, whose plantation had been burned to the ground by the British, succeeded. He would finally have the holy grail he so long sought. Marshlands would be his.

Believing the British would be successful in suppressing the patriot revolt, the Nichols family had joined the Tory auxiliaries, a mixture of Loyalists, indentured servants, and slaves, who provided the British with much needed knowledge of the Lowcountry waterways. That knowledge was the key to the British success in securing Port Royal Island, much of the Beaufort district, and the neighboring region containing the market town of Morgan.

Sean Wilson Nichols escaped to Nassau with his entire family and took their slaves with them, as had so many others. The war ended in 1783, and the Loyalists were given land grants in the Bahamas as reward for their service to the crown in the American Revolution.

Patrick Nichols had been taught from birth to fear the Winslow family. Sean Wilson Nichols, whose indentured servant mother, Mary Wilson, had married Eli Nichols, filled Patrick (who Sean had passed off as the natural-born son of his deceased stepfather) with stories of hate and fear of lawyer John Winslow and his son John James. "You must never trust them. Avoid them whenever you can, for they are sworn to destroy us. They and their accomplices of the Tookerman clan attempted to deceive our father Eli and steal not only our land but also the treasure still hidden on the Bailey Plantation. The fortune that lies buried there will someday be yours. Be patient. The books containing the location of Captain Bonnet's box should still be in old Joshua Bailey's library."

Sean and Patrick drilled into their children and siblings the story of how Eli Nichols had been duped by the Winslow and Tookerman families and how someday the opportunity to return to Morgan, South Carolina would present itself. "Never forget, Marshlands Plantation is your heritage. You must get it back. If you are not successful, your children and your children's children eventually will be. We have truth and honor on our side."

On one of the occasions when Sean told the story, Patrick interrupted him with a question Sean did not want to hear. "But Uncle, Aunt Kathleen told me there is another who knows the full story. A man named Jamie who left Marshlands shortly after I was born."

"That man is of no consequence. He is a slave. He is not believable, and no court will listen to anything he says. You are the rightful heir to Marshlands. You are the son of Eli Nichols. Lawyer Winslow was a thief as was Tookerman. The lawful court in Charles Town denied them their claim."

"But that was a British court. The American court gave our land to John James Winslow?"

"Nothing changes. The land is ours. The land is yours. Never forget! You must get it back!"

They did not forget. The story of the Winslow and Tookerman treachery against the Nichols family was passed on. Hope sprang up during the War of 1812, as the children of Patrick Nichols watched from the Bahamas. More hope arose as the American Civil War boiled across the waters to the northwest of Nassau. The story continued to create hate against the Winslow and Tookerman families. A hate that blotted out reason. A hate that would not be cooled by time.

THIRTY-FIVE

2018
A Secret Investor

The lights were still on at police headquarters when Sam arrived the following morning. Not that he expected the building to be dark, but this early on a Tuesday morning at the City Hall complex, very few people were expected to be in the building. Multiple cars were in the parking lot and lights were on all over. Obviously, something had happened.

Sam Cashman's wife, Dede, became concerned about him the previous evening. He had forgotten to call her to let her know he would be late. It was an agreement they had. Sam had become so involved with the material he and Mrs. DeReimer had uncovered he lost track of the time. Dede finally called him at six-fifteen.

Police work had changed over the past few years, especially during the latter part of the Obama administration. A few months earlier, he had attended a meeting in Charleston where the county sheriff shared his concern about the growing threat of white supremacist organizations and armed militia group training camps appearing in the region. Black policemen had a particularly difficult tightrope to walk, often being a target of all sides.

Detectives Sam Cashman and Wilson Knott sat at a small conference room table across from Ryan Packer, a lawyer from the Coastal Rivers County Commerce Department.

Sam leaned forward as he asked the critical question, "So, you're saying, Mr. Packer, the land where Dorinda Tucker was found is actually part of the original Marshlands Plantation that was established by a land grant dating from the early 1700s?"

"I'm not the one saying it. What I'm confirming is the current ownership of the property. The fact that it's part of an old land grant plantation has been determined by Mrs. DeReimer."

"Yes, I understand that, but the land is definitely owned by this company called MPBP, LLC, correct?"

"Yes."

"And who own it?"

"Martin Tucker, on behalf of three other LLCs. Where is Mrs. DeReimer, by the way?"

"She's in a meeting with the mayor and police chief. She should be here as soon as they're finished."

"Good. I know she's done some research in the county archives with regard to another piece of property she thought I should see. Something to do with the actual historical ownership." Ryan sat back in his chair and took a handkerchief out of his pocket to clean his glasses.

Detective Knott asked, "Who owns that LLC?"

Ryan leaned forward again and picked up a sheet of paper. "The person who filed the original application is Martin Tucker, on behalf of the same investment LLCs that control MPBP, LLC. One of those is Tucker Development LLC, which is owned by Martin Tucker. The other two I don't know. One is MB Sales LLC, and the other is SAR Heritage LLC. Each of these LLCs could have multiple partners."

"Holy shit," said Sam.

"Welcome to the world of real estate development." Ryan leaned back in his chair.

Knott reached over and took the sheet of paper Ryan had been holding. "Wait a minute, I've seen that name before. MB Sales."

"Really?"

"Really, Sam. I was in Mitchell Bennett's office at his house talking with his wife when he went missing and I saw a framed certificate on his wall with the name MB Sales."

"Ah, a piece of the puzzle falls into place." Sam then addressed Ryan. "How quickly can you get us information on SAR Heritage?"

"I don't have access to the files of the Commerce Department from here but give me a few hours at a computer in my office and I should be able to run it down."

"Okay. Go to it. Wilson, can you find out from Bennett about his relationship with Tucker and MB Sales involvement with Marshlands Plantation?"

"Sure, let me give his office a call right now." He looked at his watch. "It's a bit early. He may not be there, but I'm sure someone is. Take me only a few minutes to get to Market Street." They talked for a few more minutes before the meeting broke up. Sam sat alone in the room and wrote notes to himself, mostly questions he needed to have answered. He checked the clock on the far wall. Knott went out to his desk and made a few phone calls.

THIRTY-SIX

2018
The Marshlands Plantation Connection

Sidney and Tillie agreed to meet with Ray and his wife Marie at the City Hall Café for lunch. However, it turned out Marie had a conflict with another luncheon at her church and couldn't come. The get-together had become a weekly routine for the four of them. It originally began almost a year before Sidney's wife died, which was more than three years ago.

Ray arrived first and secured a table in a corner. Tillie arrived before Sidney, as she had a two block shorter walk to the Café than Sidney did. "Good morning, Mr. Ray." Ray looked up from the Charleston paper he'd found at the table and returned the greeting. "Good morning. Although I guess it should be good afternoon since it's almost twelve-thirty. Pull up a seat." Tillie took the chair directly opposite Ray, as this would leave the two remaining chairs empty and put Sidney between them. Ray placed the newspaper on one of the empty seats and said, "Just checking to see if Charleston had anything to say about our sudden death problem."

Tillie took out her napkin and utensils from the roll-up set on the table. "Did they?"

"Not that I could find. I suppose there's good and bad in that. Good that it's not front and center scaring the public and bad in that we haven't come up with something for them to write about." Ray looked up and said, "Here's Sidney." They watched as Sidney tried to find them, and Ray waved at him. He waited until the exiting people made their way along the aisle between tables before he made his way to the table. "I have to be careful with this cane," he said. "It's easy to get it caught on a chair in these tight quarters." Sidney took the open chair to Tillie's right. As he dropped into the chair, it squeaked and groaned under him but held. He let out a rush of air. "That walk seems to be getting longer and longer. Have you ordered yet?"

"No," said Tillie. "I just got here myself."

Ray didn't answer. He held his menu up in the air and waved it at the waitress, who came over and took their order. The conversation among the three of them covered the weather, the crowd in the restaurant, a few observations about some of the people nearby, and finally settled on the matter at hand, just as the food began to arrive.

Sidney asked Ray, "What can you tell us about where your friends in the police department are at this juncture?"

"Making progress on all fronts. Forensics has determined that Martin Tucker was not attacked where he was found. Based on an analysis of his clothes, they believe he could have been knocked out and left for dead somewhere near where the body of Dorinda Tooker was found. There's a possibility that when he came to, he struggled to escape by moving farther out into the adjacent water and marsh grass. We figured he was just too tired and hurt to fight the tide, and it probably moved him to where he was found. Made a last-ditch effort to get out of the water and it was too much for him."

Sidney interrupted, "So both Martin Tucker and Dorinda Tooker were intended to be found in the same vicinity?"

"That's the general thinking at this point."

"And the location has to do with where the original place Marshlands Plantation was believed to be?"

"That's the theory. Mrs. DeReimer has come up with an old map showing the plantation, but it's hand drawn and the accuracy is suspect. They're looking through the archives with her now to see if we can get a legal description of when it changed hands. There are also some old family documents Dorinda Tooker had referencing an ancestor who owned the property."

"What about Miss Gloria? She was found in the AME church parking lot. If the other two were supposed to be found on the old plantation, why wasn't she?"

"Good question," Ray said. "Mary Coffee and the forensic people said the body was moved or someone tried to move her after she was killed. Remember one of the choir members looked out the window and saw a car back in the dark area of the parking lot? We think the killer had planned to move her but was afraid to be seen, so he just left her there."

"Hmmmm." Sidney leaned back in his chair and looked at the ceiling fan blades turning slowly above his head. "So, it would appear I was on the right track when I mentioned Marshlands Plantation playing a key role in everything." He returned his gaze toward Ray and then Tillie.

"Sure seems like it," offered Tillie.

Sidney continued, "When it comes to motivation, have they decided to give serious consideration to my theory of multi-generation hate indoctrination?"

"Let's just say it's one avenue they're pursuing."

"And the other…?"

"A real estate transaction." Ray leaned forward and began to speak in a lower voice. "Wilson Knott and Sam Cashman plan to have a chat with Alan Swift. He was the one you caught at Fort Morgan searching for buried treasure."

"Oh, yes. Actually, it was Mickey who did the catching… or made it happen."

"Yes, but let me tell you what we found out about that buried treasure hunt."

THIRTY-SEVEN

2018
The Warning

Detective Knott peeked into the conference room where Sam continued to write notes on his pad and said, "Sam, the Chief and Mrs. D are delayed, how about we pay a visit to Swift and see if we can clear up a few things before they get here?"

"Sounds good. Give me a couple of minutes."

They went together in Knott's car to Swift's place. He had recently moved out of town to a nearby1960s development that showed its age. The background information on him indicated he separated from his wife two months ago. Apparently, he and a woman who worked for a building supply company had a relationship his wife didn't appreciate.

The drive to Swift's place was quick. Alan Swift acted surprised when he opened the door to Detectives Knott and Cashman. He assumed he would be left alone when the judge granted him bail. He admitted to being embarrassed at his stupidity in thinking there was a buried treasure someplace in Colonial Fort Morgan. "Knott. Cashman. Now what have I done?"

"We need your help with a few things," Sam said. "A couple of questions have come up that you may have the answers to. Mind if we come in?"

Swift hesitated at first, but then stepped back and ushered the two detectives into the sparsely decorated living room. As Sam gave the place a quick once over, Swift said, "The wife and I separated a few months back. Moved in about three weeks ago. She and the kids are still up at Emerald Shores."

"We know," said Knott.

"Yeah, I guess you would. Can I get you a cup of coffee or something? I just made a fresh pot." The tremor in his voice revealed his nervousness.

"Thanks. We're fine," Sam answered.

"Well, have a seat." He motioned them toward the sofa and two chairs in front of them.

Cashman and Knott took the two chairs and Swift the sofa, putting him between the two detectives.

"Alan," began Sam, "I know you told us about finding the drawings in the books at the Palmer Library, and how you just lost it and became obsessed with finding Bonnet's treasure, but what about Tucker? You said you never saw him after the theft at the library. Did he show any interest in the treasure?"

"Well, like I said, we never talked about it. I made some quick drawings of what was in the binding and stuck the papers in my pocket. I'm not sure Tucker saw me do it."

"What was he doing at that time?" continued Sam.

"I don't know. He just kept looking at the books. Thumbing through them. I remember him getting up from the table and going back to the bookshelf and looking at some other books just before the lights went out, and the kid under the table screamed. We dropped everything and ran."

Knott kept looking around the room as Sam continued the questioning. "And that was the last time you saw him. You didn't come back later in the evening and steal the books?"

"As I told the judge, no, I didn't."

"Okay. Tell me, have you ever partnered with Tucker in any of his real estate projects? Invested with him over the years?"

Swift remained quiet for a moment, and then said, "Yeah, when something looked good and I had the money."

"Is he the only one you did this with?"

"Well, no. We all did it."

"Who's we?"

"Other developers. Real estate people. Sometimes a hedge fund would come up with some money. We weren't Donald Trump or somebody. We're small scale. Somebody has a good idea for a development, they need money and shop around. That's the real estate development business."

"Did you recently invest in one of Tucker's projects?"

Swift paused again before answering. "Yeah, but what does that have to do with anything?"

"Maybe nothing. Do you know an outfit by the name of MB Sales?"

"Bennett? Sure."

"Is he one of Tucker's investors?"

"Has been." Swift looked concerned. "What's this all about?"

"Alan, take it easy, there's nothing to get upset about," Knott said. "We're just trying to understand how Martin Tucker did business. Did you ever hear of an LLC by the name of SAR Heritage?"

"SAR. That's a new one, I think."

"Nothing comes to mind?"

"A lot of people just use their initials when they set something up."

"Can you think of anyone with the initials SAR who has been involved with Tucker?"

"Let me think on that for a moment."

Swift looked off in the distance and started running some names through a mental Rolodex. Lips moving slightly, he began to stroke his chin. "Only thing that comes to mind is Skinny's Always Ready."

"Excuse me," said Knott. "Skinny's Always Ready? What is that?"

Alan Swift got a little smile on his face and moved his hand from his chin to the back of his neck. "There's this guy who comes around every now and then. A tall skinny guy. I don't really know him. He's not a builder or developer but he's always looking for a deal to invest in. He's actually a front guy for a bunch of investors. He's kind of a mystery since Tucker didn't know who they were either but Skinny was all ready to put up some money. Tucker knew his real name, but the rest of us just referred to him as Skinny's always ready. He was a nervous kind of guy, and we never really understood why Tucker put up with him. I guess he figured Skinny's money was just as green as everyone else's."

"You'd know him if you saw him again?" Knott asked.

"Oh, sure."

"This new project that Tucker was involved with," Sam said. "The one that would involve the old rice field area and also part of the old Bailey Plantation—do you know if this Skinny guy had a piece of it?"

"Can't say. I know I didn't. He was hanging around a lot lately, though."

After a short discussion about how Martin Tucker went looking for investors for his developments, the two detectives decided they had enough information to expand their search envelope and left.

As they walked back to Knott's car, he said, "Sam, let me drop you off at PHQ. I want to go to Bennett's office and see if he's there. Never got a call back from him."

"That's fine. I've got to get together with the Mayor and Mrs. DeReimer. She should be finished with Ryan by now."

Officer Hampton Butler had the assignment of watching over Florence McCann. He did his best to stay out of her way and be as invisible as possible. When she left for a meeting with the undertaker who was making the arrangements to ship Gloria's body back to Philadelphia, he drove a reasonable distance behind her in his own car and parked in the same parking lot an aisle away. He wore comfortable street clothes instead of his uniform.

While Florence met with the funeral director, Hamp went over and chatted with the police officer assigned to handle the traffic for an upcoming funeral. He didn't see the person watching his every move from the black sedan parked across the street. Once Hamp became deeply engrossed in conversation with the other police officer, the sedan left and headed in the direction of Gloria's residence.

Arriving near the condo, the driver parked the sedan a half a block away and walked back to the building. Parking garages were in the rear of the building, which contained four units, two upstairs and two down. Gloria's unit was downstairs on the left as you entered the building. The driver of the sedan, without hesitation, walked directly down the driveway to the rear of the unit, went up to the back door, and slipped an envelope underneath it. The driver immediately left but instead of walking back to the sedan, went completely around the block in the opposite direction.

At the City Hall café, the conversation rambled on, with most of the talking being done by Tillie and Ray. Sidney listened carefully and took in the theories they bounced around. They were finishing their coffee when Sam came in looking for them. After Detective Knott had left him at police headquarters, he checked his watch and knew Sidney, Tillie, and Ray would still be at lunch. A short while earlier, he received a message that Mayor Wilcox and Chief Hornig had gone to lunch and rescheduled their meeting with him for two o'clock.

"Mind if I sit in for a few minutes," he said, surprising his friends.

"Sam, not at all," said Ray. "Grab a chair."

Sam removed the newspaper from the chair and placed it on the neighboring table. "Ray, I have something to bounce off you." He sat down.

"Did you and Knott come up with anything after seeing Alan Swift?"

"Possibly. We confirmed Mitchell Bennett is one of the investors in the development Martin Tucker was putting together at the old Marshlands and Bailey Plantation sites."

"Interesting," Ray said.

"Very. Knott is over at Bennett's real estate office on Market Street in the hope of catching him. He's got some explaining to do. Apparently, there is another major investor using an LLC called SAR Heritage, and Ryan is checking the Secretary of State and Commerce Department's databases for information on it. Also, there's a character called Skinny, who may also have something to do with it."

Tillie spoke up, "Skinny? He a tall skinny man, kinda nervous, hangs around City Hall?"

"Could be," said Sam. All eyes now turned to Tillie.

"Might be nothin' but last week when CJ was cleanin' outside the mayor's office, he said there was a tall skinny man inside. Might not mean anything but the mayor was kinda unhappy him bein' there and rushed him outta sight. CJ tried to get a look at 'um when he brought a box in for the mayor's secretary. Couldn't though. Mayor had 'um tucked away in the back. Man seemed nervous and the mayor said somethin' about he was supposed to stay away. Never heard any more about it. I can check with CJ an see if he heard anything else?"

"Do that," said Ray. He then looked at Sam and said, "You don't think the mayor could be mixed up in all this, do you?"

"At this point, I have no idea. Although, seeing it was the mayor's mother-in-law who was killed, I'd be surprised. Sidney, you've been quiet. What do you think?"

Sidney had been unusually quiet. They all focused his way.

"Hmmm." Sidney shifted in his chair. He gave Sam, Ray, and Tillie separate looks and said, "Sorry, I've been trying to put a great number of pieces together. That material Gloria accumulated before she was murdered made for very interesting reading. She had gathered information on not just her own relative, James Bailey, but a man named Eli Nichols as well. He was the original owner of Marshlands Plantation. There's also a Sean Nichols involved. She traced the Nichols family's attempt to get Marshlands Plantation back from the people who the Nichols claimed stole it from them. The information covers the hundred years from 1718 right through the War of 1812. There were also letters she had sent to both Columbia and Washington with regard to the Civil War, but she hadn't received an answer yet."

Sidney paused and looked directly at Sam. He then continued. "I'm beginning to believe you're correct in believing a real estate transaction is the trigger point for everything. However, the answer to who the perpetrator of the murders may be is probably in those genealogy records. I definitely believe the final clues are there."

Sidney proceeded to outline what he knew of the stories he'd learned from personal letters and Caleb Bailey's diary about the Nichols family, Stede Bonnet, Jamaica and Tookerman. "Eli Nichols was the brother of Thomas Nichols, one of the seamen who was not hanged with Stede Bonnet and the rest of his crew. Thomas Nichols told his brother Eli of a trip he made to Colonial Fort Dorchester to deliver a box to Joshua Bailey for safe keeping. The box belonged to Stede Bonnet and was put into the care of a trusted slave by the name of Jamaica at the Bailey warehouse.

"Thomas Nichols went back to the sea and was never heard from again. Eli decided to apply for a land grant in the Morgan area, but he needed funding. In order to obtain the largest grant possible, he also needed a family. Thomas Nichols, before he left, recommended Eli go to Richard Tookerman, who Thomas knew to be somewhat unscrupulous but might provide both the money and the family for a price. According to the records, Tookerman and his attorney, John Winslow, drew up an agreement Eli Nichols readily signed, although he didn't know how to read or write.

"The family Eli Nichols acquired was an indentured servant by the name of Mary Wilson and her three children, the oldest of whom was a male by the name of Sean. Eli and Mary were subsequently married."

Sidney stopped as he noticed that Tillie, Ray, and Sam were practically in a trance listening to him. Ray finally said, "Well, don't stop now."

Sidney smiled and continued, "Shortly after Eli and Mary were married, Joshua Bailey died and a portion of the Bailey Plantation around Morgan was sold. Eli Nichols obtained a part of it. He also acquired four slaves as part of the purchase, one of whom was Jamaica, now also referred to as Jamie.

"The Nichols family began a period of prosperity and stability until 1743 when Eli Nichols was killed during the Battle of Bloody Marsh, which stopped the Spanish advance through Georgia and into South Carolina. And it is at this point information developed by Tillie comes into play. Her contact at the Golden Harvest Retirement Home recounted a famous tale of a slave who tricked a planter into giving him and his family freedom by providing him with a male heir that was needed to keep a local plantation from falling into the hands of a lawyer. The lawyer claimed it belonged to him when the patriarch of the family died without a male heir. I'm quite certain the slave in question was Jamaica, Jamie, who when obtaining his freedom adopted the surname Bailey and is the ancestor of Gloria Rye and her sister Florence McCann. Also, the lawyer who claimed ownership of the plantation, I believe to be Marshlands, was John James Winslow, who is the ancestor of both Dorinda Tooker and Martin Tucker. John James Winslow was the son of the deceased John Winslow, the lawyer for Richard Tookerman, who crafted the original loan agreement signed by Eli Nichols."

Sidney stopped again as Sam asked, "And all this is documented in the papers Gloria Rye had?"

"Not entirely. Some of it comes from the documents Olive Wilcox developed from her ancestry searches. Remember, she is the daughter of Dorinda Tooker and a direct line back to John James Winslow. Also, we have a direct line back to John James Winslow by way of Martin Tucker, our first victim."

"So, this is the beginning of the bad blood around Marshlands Plantation?" Sam asked.

Sidney hedged his answer a bit. "It would seem so but there is more when we look at the documents Gloria obtained about the expropriation of the plantation after the Revolutionary War because the Nichols family were Loyalists. Mrs. Rye, before her murder, made an inquiry about the basis for the expropriation decision, the answer of which has yet to be received. There is also an inquiry outstanding regarding the Civil War. What we're missing is information about the Nichols family and their descendants."

"Perhaps something will show up when we get more information about the attempt to develop the lands that once encompassed the original Marshlands and Bailey Plantations," Ray said. "Sam, did you get any more information about the people who invested in the project?"

As Ray updated everyone on the conversation Wilson Knott and he had with Alan Swift, Hampton Butler had just finished following Florence McCann home after her visit with the funeral director. He waited outside while she drove into the driveway alongside the condo and put her car into the garage. Once it was clear she was safely inside and she gave him a wave from the front window, he went down the street to park in a location where he could keep the front door of the condo in view. After a few minutes, she opened the door and came out of the house in a run toward his car. He spotted her immediately, left his car, and rushed toward her. She waved an envelope at him as she approached.

"Inside," she gasped. "Inside."

She stopped in front of him, and before he took the envelope from her, he put on a pair of gloves so he wouldn't contaminate anything. He opened the envelope and took a folded sheet of paper out. It read,

LEAVE OR STAY FOREVER

Sam's phone buzzed. With the conversation stopped, Tillie took the opportunity to call CJ and left a message.

The ID on Sam's phone read Hampton Butler, "Yeah, Hamp."

"Heading for HQ with McCann. She found a threatening note when she came home."

"Okay, I'll be right there."

As Sam got up from the table, he looked at Sidney and said, "Mrs. McCann just received a threatening note. Sidney, I sure hope you find a link to that

Nichols family soon. We can't afford to lose any more people."

Tillie gave an audible sigh as Sam headed for the door. "Professor, this is terrible. How we gonna find this Nichols person?"

"Tillie, the problem is just like Mrs. McCann. She doesn't carry the Bailey name any more just as the person we're looking for undoubtedly doesn't carry the Nichols surname. It could be anyone."

"Sidney, the historical story you just recounted, where did the Nichols family go when the Loyalists were kicked out of South Carolina?" Ray asked. "Would there be a record of where they went?"

Sidney leaned back in his chair and thought for a moment. "The general historical records for the period indicated a good many families took their belongings and slaves and headed to the Bahamas; perhaps that's where the Nichols went. The British government at the time offered the former colonists land grants and compensation if they resettled in the Bahamas. Knowing how meticulous the British bureaucracy has always been, if the Nichols family applied for a grant and compensation there'd be a record. So, here's what I recommend we do. I will pursue the Bahamas connection. Ray, I need you to use all the connections you can find to learn where the records of land sales regarding Marshlands Plantation are kept. We need specific information about the confiscation of the property after the Revolutionary War and also what happed to it after the Civil War. Tillie, you talk with CJ about that 'Skinny' person, but I also need you to go back to the land ownership shifts that occurred after the Civil War with regard to the Gullah population. As you know, there are a lot of stories out there based on fact that never made it into the history books. You might want to check with the people at Penn Center over in Beaufort. Maybe they can lead us to a Gullah historian who can parse the fact and fiction for us."

"I can do that."

"Ray, it might be a good idea if you mentioned this 'Skinny' person to Chief Hornig and see if he might know who it is. I know Chief Hornig is not a fan of the mayor, and I have to assume he would be interested in any unusual people the mayor might be involved with."

"Good possibility. This is the first time I've seen them being nice to one another about a police matter. Mayor Wilcox is always pushing Hornig for an immediate solution. Then again, it could be that since Wilcox's family is directly involved, he's putting politics aside and willing to work with the police chief for once in his life. But he probably doesn't want to rock the boat and bring more attention to himself than necessary. His usual approach is to look out for his own interest first, especially if there's an election coming up next year, which there is. I'll bet Hornig is the one who's most surprised. Yeah, let me talk with him." Ray got up from his chair and said, "Sidney, take care of the tab and I'll get it next week."

Sidney nodded in agreement.

"Tillie," said Ray, "be careful as you go nosing around. There's a dangerous person out there. Don't take any chances." Ray left the café.

With only Sidney and Tillie at the table, Tillie started to get up, but Sidney stopped her when he put his hand across the table and grabbed her wrist. "Sit down for just a minute." Sidney motioned her to move to the chair next to him.

Tillie sat as instructed.

"I want to reinforce what Ray just said. I know you think of yourself as being independent and more than capable of taking care of yourself, but he's right. This is different." He then reached out with both hands and gently enveloped hers. "You're very important to me, Tillie. I don't want anything to happen to you. Please call Sam, Ray, or me if anything goes wrong. Will you promise me that?"

Tillie looked at Sidney and saw the concern in his eyes.

Detective Cashman and officers Shawn Green and Hampton Butler stood in Florence McCann's condo, originally her murdered sister's place.

"I checked with the immediate neighbors across the street," Green said. "No one saw anything. They were either all out or having lunch at the time."

"Same on this side of the street except for the woman across the driveway," Hamp said as he looked at his notes. "Older woman. Doesn't go out much. A bit of a news junkie. Watched the morning and lunchtime news shows. Anyway, she thinks she saw someone go down the alley to the back door. Said she got up to refill her coffee in the kitchen. These units here are identical and you can look right across to her kitchen."

They all looked across the driveway to the other building, assessing the obvious line of sight. They couldn't see into the kitchen across the way, but you could definitely see out clearly.

Hamp continued, "When she looked up, she saw someone come down the driveway. At first, she thought it was Gloria, as that's how she usually came in. Didn't use the front door. She then remembered Mrs. Rye was dead and it must have been her sister. Didn't have a clear view as she was filling her coffee cup. Said the woman just went up to the back door and then turned around and left the way she came."

"She said it was a woman?" Sam asked.

"I pressed her on it, and she said she thought so. Had slacks and a lightweight jacket on. Wore a cap. Couldn't see her face."

"Was she Black or white?"

"That's the confusing part. She thought it was the Rye woman because that's who she expected to see, and Gloria was Black. But when I pushed her on the person's color, she admitted she never saw the woman's face."

"So, maybe it wasn't a Black woman," Sam said. "She was seeing what she expected to see. How is she sure it was a woman? Couldn't she be making the same assumption since the woman who lived there liked to go in through the back door?"

"I couldn't knock down the woman description. She seemed pretty sure of that. Said she was built like a woman and walked like one. Walked like Gloria Rye."

Sam thought for a moment and then said, "A woman. Interesting. That would put a whole new spin on everything."

Mayor Steele Wilcox had an ambitious streak. His original profession had kept him in the public eye, with the Wilcox Funeral Home being advertised continually. Most of the white population's residents eventually passed through its doors to pay their last respects to a friend or relative. It was a family business begun by his grandfather, continued by his father, and passed on to him. When his father died, he became the center of attention in Morgan; visible in his own right rather than being "the son of the owner". But Steele never really liked the business. He wanted to do more. Wanted to be a success in his own right, but where? Where could he branch out and continue making use of his current skills with dead bodies? His wife, Olivia, had the answer—politics. And what would be the logical first rung of the ladder? The elected position of county coroner, of course.

Although the coroner didn't need to have a medical degree, a candidate needed to have paramedic skills and pass the state exams that would involve extensive medical knowledge. A good deal of the qualifications would be covered by the courses he took to become an undertaker, but he also had to pass all the state exams for a paramedic. So, for two years before he decided to run for county coroner, he acquired all the education the state had to offer and finally received his paramedic certification.

Not long after his election as coroner, Steele experienced the aphrodisiac of power. In order for the policing organizations of the county to declare a death suspicious—especially when the death had not been observed by an independent authority—he had to give them the authorization to do so by holding an inquest indicating whatever were the unusual circumstances surrounding the death. People in authority needed his approval to do their jobs. An immediate sense of importance surrounded him, and he enjoyed the feeling. The enjoyment Coroner Wilcox felt became apparent to many in government, especially the Morgan Chief of Police, Pete Hornig.

Although Pete Hornig and Steele Wilcox had known one another for many years and occasionally socialized at community events, they did not move in the same social circles.

Hornig's upbringing centered around military posts as both child and adult. He came from a military family and dutifully followed his father and grandfather into the service. He served in a number of military police units during his more than twenty-five-year career before coming to Coastal Rivers County and accepting a position with the County Sheriff's Office.

Steele Wilcox followed a different path. Born in South Carolina, he had a narrower view of the world. Being a third-generation funeral director, he felt himself to be more servant than leader. Always consoling others and accommodating the bereaved family's wishes, no matter how strange, did not make him comfortable, regardless of the money he made.

No, Steele Wilcox did not see himself as someone else's servant, and Pete Hornig picked up on the trait. He knew it well, as he had to deal with such egos during his entire career in the military.

A small plaque Steele kept in the center drawer of his desk at home expressed his true feelings. It read:

It's better to rule than to serve.

He also learned politics and power had to do with money, as it was the primary fuel of power. He acquired access to a fair amount when he married Olivia, whose family had substantial property interests in the region. The subsequent selling of the family undertaking business to a national chain provided him with significant resources in his own name.

When Chief Hornig and Sam Cashman came to the mayor's office just after two o'clock on Sunday afternoon, Steele Wilcox's antennae were quick to pick up on some warnings that drifted his way.

"A woman?" questioned Wilcox. "Isn't that unusual? I mean, I don't think I've ever heard of a woman as a mass murderer. Besides, what woman would want to kill my mother-in-law? We need to tread carefully here."

"I suppose there have been female mass murderers," said Hornig. "But I agree, it wouldn't be very common. Some psychologists would have a field day working on that one."

"Yes, I can see that. Is tracking down the person more difficult if the murderer is a woman?"

Sam was about to respond but Chief Hornig said, "It's bad enough as it is. All I know, Mayor, is that we don't have a lot of time to keep working on this on our own. If word gets out that another person has been threatened, the state will be all over us."

Mayor Wilcox leaned back in his chair as he said, "As you know, I don't want that to happen. Have you any persons of interest? Any suspects that you're focusing on?"

Chief Hornig let out a long breath of air before he replied. "We've had a few but nobody who made any sense. We're still stymied over a motive. Three murders unconnected by any real evidence other than the weapon. And even that's questionable unless we can find it. Sam here, Ray Morton and Sidney Lake have come up with a theory—which I must admit I thought was quite a reach at first—that is starting to look more reasonable. It has to do with a place called Marshlands Plantation, and it may be part of the answer of who would want to harm your mother-in-law."

Sam carefully watched the mayor to see if he reacted to the Marshlands Plantation name. He did. It wasn't a big reaction, but it was there, and Sam spotted it.

"Marshlands Plantation." Mayor Wilcox tried to act as though the name was vaguely familiar as he feigned deep thought trying to recall it. "I think I've heard of that. Can't remember in what context. I'm pretty sure the place doesn't exist anymore."

Sam decided to enter the conversation. "It goes back quite a way. Back to the 1700s."

"Ah," said the mayor, seeing a way to innocently confirm knowledge of Marshlands. "All this research of my mother-in-law's genealogy information and the Tooker family history. Didn't Mrs. DeReimer mention it this morning, Chief?"

"Yes, I believe she did."

Mayor Wilcox leaned forward as he became more engaged. "But we're talking 300 years ago. It was mentioned in those documents Miss Dorinda had in her family history files, wasn't it?"

Hornig answered, "Yes, it was. Sam, tell us what Sidney and you have been piecing together."

Mayor Wilcox now focused on the detective.

Sam began, "As you know, it was by looking into your wife's ancestry records, as well as Dorinda Tooker's, that we found the connection between the first two victims, Martin Tucker and Dorinda Tooker. They both connected through a colonial attorney named John James Winslow. Winslow acquired Marshlands Plantation in a lawsuit against the original owners, the Nichols family. Nichols was indebted to Winslow and defaulted on a loan agreement. However, we have now learned this is also how Gloria Rye, the third victim, is connected to the first two."

Mayor Wilcox seemed genuinely surprised. "Really?"

"Yes. We learned that her ancestor, a James Bailey, had been a slave at Marshlands Plantation and may have participated in a deception to keep

John James Winslow from obtaining Marshlands Plantation. I won't go into the full details, but we also believe the slave's grandson had something to do with having Nichols declared a traitor and British spy during the American Revolution, resulting in the expropriation of Marshlands Plantation on behalf of Winslow. We don't have all the information on this but expect it shortly, as Gloria Rye, before her death, had requested it."

Chief Hornig turned to him. "I didn't know any of this. When did this come to light?"

Sam apologized, "Sorry Chief, Sidney Lake has been following the Gloria Rye connections, with Tillie James' help, and I just heard this a short while ago."

"Are you saying we finally have a motive and a suspect?" Chief Hornig asked.

Sam cautiously answered, "It still may be a stretch, but we think there's a descendant of the Nichols family in town who has completely lost his or her mind and is seeking revenge for what he or she believes was a miscarriage of justice after the American Revolution. Apparently, there may also have been some actions taken after the Civil War that are also involved and, more recently, something has happened that pushed the person or persons over the edge."

"And it could be a woman?" asked Chief Hornig.

"That possibility came up this morning based on Shaun Green's interview with one of Gloria Rye's neighbors. We're following up on that as we speak."

"We *are* making progress," the mayor said. "Excellent."

As the meeting continued in the mayor's office, Detective Knott waited for Mitchell Bennett in his real estate office on Market Street. Bennett had called the office to let them know he would be in after lunch. As he waited, Knott spent his time talking with the two agents. One was there to meet with a client to look at properties and the other had floor duty for the day. He took the opportunity to ask about the local real estate market with a specific emphasis on their take on speculation about possible new developments in the planning stage. He also dropped the names of Marshlands and Bailey Plantations, which elicited an immediate response from both of them. It seems that rumors had begun about a possible large development in the old rice fields. The problem being faced had to do with historic and environmental considerations. Attempts to develop the area had been tried before and usually fell apart over land title difficulties and the need to fill in the old rice fields. Neither of the agents could clearly identify the specific locations of the plantations but knew that the rice fields must have been part of one or the other—if not both. There were a couple of farms in the area that predated the environmental regulations regarding wetlands, and they seemed sure nothing could be developed in the area without acquiring both properties.

Armed with this new information, Knott waited impatiently for Mitchell Bennett while the two agents responded to phone calls. A few moments later, Bennett came in the back door of the building, spotted the detective in the waiting area up front, and signaled to one of the agents, who made her way to him. He asked her if she knew what Detective Knott wanted and she explained his interest in local property development. Bennett considered leaving before Knott spotted him but realized such an action might be considered suspicious, not only to Detective Knott but also his two agents. So, gathering himself in preparation for the meeting he kept out of sight and began putting together some answers to questions be believed Knott would ask. Once comfortable with how he would handle the meeting, he headed for the reception area.

"Detective Knott, nice to see you again," Bennett said as he came forward. "Thinking about a move?"

Knott put down the magazine he had been browsing through and came forward as he said, "Came in from the parking lot, I see. Mrs. Bennett and the children on their way home?"

"Yes, Carter and Pam can't wait to hit the backyard. Too nice a day to be stuck indoors."

"Yes it is. I don't think I could handle another move, though. I've still got boxes from my last move stored in the garage. I think the general thinking is that you should never get rid of some of them as the moment you do, you'll find out you'll need them again."

A laugh from Bennett and then, "So, how can I help you? Come into the office." Bennett motioned Knott to follow him down the center aisle.

Inside Bennett's office, Knott was directed to a seating arrangement of three armchairs off to the side of the desk.

"How about some coffee? Tea? Water?"

"Actually, water would be good."

Bennett went over to a small refrigerator against the side wall and removed two bottles and came back to the awaiting chairs. "Here you go. Have a seat."

They both sat down and opened their waters.

"So, what can I do for you?"

"Doing some research on some of the property near the old rice fields north of town. I understand you have an interest in it through one of your companies, MB Sales, LLC."

Mitchell Bennett's face went white. This was not one of the questions he expected. He had no answers.

After lunch, Sidney and Tillie walked back to Sidney's. They didn't speak except for questions Tillie raised about Sidney's knee. His limp seemed more exaggerated to her and, from the occasional wince she heard, the pain had become worse. Stubborn as usual, he brushed off her questions and concerns. He had other issues on his mind.

They walked along quietly for another block when Sidney stopped. He had the kind of look on his face that a person would get who just realized he had missed something that should have been obvious to him. He looked at Tillie and said, "As soon as we get back to the house, I have to make some phone calls to the Bahamas. While I'm doing that, I need you to do something very basic. Go to the phone book, both the paper one and online, and search the name 'Nichols.' Then call Hattie and ask her to check with her church friends in the Episcopal Church and ask them to search their records going back fifty to a hundred years for members with the Nichols and Winslow names. Also, burial records. I'll do the same with Reverend Prentice at Bay View Presbyterian. Then I'm going to need you to go back to the Golden Harvest Retirement Home and see who might have heard a family history tale of a relative who worked at Marshlands Plantation around the time of the Civil War. We've spent most of our time working from the twenty-first century back to the eighteenth rather than doing it the other way."

"But Professor, isn't that the way this genealogy stuff is done?"

"Yes, because you know the person in the twenty-first century. If you don't know the person and want to find out who the current day relatives of, say, Tuscarora Jack Barnwell, you have to start with Barnwell."

"I get it. That's why you got to call the Bahamas. Wouldn't all the government buildings there be closed? Today's Sunday."

"Yes, but not Professor Leeseman. An old friend. I just remembered he taught Colonial American history at USC Beaufort and moved to Nassau five years ago. If the Nichols family left a paper trail from here to Nassau and then back here again, he'd know how to find it."

A normal, quiet Wednesday afternoon in Morgan became a hyper-workday for the City Hall complex. Sam marshalled every officer he could to gather information about the mysterious note deliverer. Every person in every house up and down the street where Florence McCann stayed had been interviewed—with no additional success. Only the next-door neighbor had seen someone. They had no corroboration. Mary Coffey and her forensic team found nothing at the condo. No footprints, no fingerprints could be found. Since the driveway and the rear steps were concrete, the lack of evidence didn't surprise anyone. Their best hope, the envelope, and the note inside, revealed nothing. The envelope lacked an address. The simple message inside being hand-printed might be useful at a later date, but there were no other marks on it. No fingerprints, no smudges, just clearly printed letters, very precisely done. Not a squiggle or a blot anywhere. The writer used a ballpoint pen. A neat and orderly person, Mary Coffey concluded. "If only there had been a security camera on one of the buildings," she had mentioned to Sam. Except for the note, they would appear to be back to square one, but… not entirely.

As Sam left police headquarters later in the afternoon and headed for Sidney's, he had become convinced the Bennett/Tucker real estate deal was at the heart of everything.

THIRTY-NINE
1789 – 1866
The Escape

The Nichols family and their slaves abandoned Marshlands Plantation within two months after the Revolutionary War ended and emigrated to the Bahamas. They had been offered safety for defending the British crown and land grants to re-establish their lives. But when the United Kingdom passed the Slave Trade Act of 1807, they knew their way of life would never be as it once was. However, when British troops burned the city of Washington during the War of 1812, the new patriarch of the family, Liam W. Nichols, gathered his wife and offspring around him every evening and prayed to God England would take back the American colonies. With England back in control, he hoped they would be able to return to South Carolina, take back Marshlands Plantation, and resume some form of the life the family once knew. When Liam learned of the signing of the Treaty of Ghent in 1814 by the United States of America and the United Kingdom of Great Britain and Ireland, all his hopes were dashed. Britain ended slavery in 1833 by means of *The Slavery Ablution Act*, which also provided extensive compensation to slave owners in the Bahamas. Following the example of other former colonial slaveholders, the Nichols family sold all they had and emigrated to Halifax, Nova Scotia.

Liam Nichols was the son of Lieutenant Ian Nichols who had been killed by Caleb Bailey during the battle of Trenton. Caleb discovered Nichols to be a British spy bent on scuttling General George Washington's Christmas Day surprise attack and ultimate victory over the Hessians. It seemed that every time the Nichols family tried to get back on their feet, there was a descendent of the Winslow, Tookerman, or Bailey family standing in their way.

It was now 1866. The Civil War had ended and Liam, now an old man in his late seventies, decided to make the trip to Morgan, South Carolina, to take back Marshlands Plantation, which he understood had been abandoned. His son Simon and grandson Angus accompanied him. The arduous trip began by ship from Halifax to New York and continued by carriage to Philadelphia, where Liam demanded they stop, as he wanted to visit the place where his father, Lieutenant Ian Nichols, died. He always referred to the death of his father as a murder at the hands of the lying, cheating grandson of the slave, James Bailey. The event had been drilled into his son and grandson along with the conviction the Bailey's were bad blood who needed to be stamped out.

Upon arriving at the ferry crossing where Caleb Bailey killed Lieutenant Nichols with a poker from the fireplace of a ferryman's shack, there now stood a historic marker. It claimed that on this spot a courageous ferryman by the name of Caleb Bailey saved the attack on Trenton by General George Washington's troops, which had crossed the Delaware River ten miles north of the spot. It went on to read that Bailey discovered the plan being executed by the British spy, Ian Nichols, and killed him, thus foiling the attempt to disrupt the crossing of the Delaware by Colonial troops. Liam Nichols became enraged as he read the marker. He collapsed, holding his chest. As he lay in the arms of his son, with his grandson kneeling nearby, he looked up at the three-story warehouse that stood across the way from the historic marker. A large sign hung between the second and third floors: BAILEY and SONS – GENERAL WAREHOUSE.

Liam Nichols raised his fist and shook it at the building as a curse crossed his lips and a tremor consumed him. His body then arched as he gasped, "Stop them, Simon. Stop all of them." And he was gone. Simon clutched his dead father to his chest, looked to the heavens and gave his oath, "I will, Father. I will do all I can to stop them, and Angus will stop them, and his son will stop them until Marshlands Plantation will again be ours."

FORTY

2018
The Bahamas Connection

Since retiring, Sidney's alarm clock had become Mickey who, like most animals, lived by the sun's arrival and departure and not an artificial determination of when each day should begin. The Bahamas and the East coast of the United States share the same time zone, although the sun appeared above the horizon a little later in Morgan than in Nassau. However, on this cloudy Thursday morning the sun decided to sleep in, as did the professor.

Sidney mistook the ring of the house phone on his bedside table as the sound of his alarm clock and managed to knock the phone to the floor in an attempt to silence it. The noise also disturbed Mickey, who immediately leapt from the overstuffed armchair where she slept next to Sidney's bed.

"I'm so sorry, Sidney," said Professor George Leeseman after Sidney apologized for dropping the phone. "I had forgotten you retired. Didn't mean to call this early but the message you left yesterday sounded intriguing. When did you become a detective?"

"Hah, it was a natural extension of more than thirty years of investigating literary figures."

"I suppose that's true for both of us. Although, I must admit your inquiry certainly caught my attention. A murder with origins in the 1700s. Three murders, in fact. Wow! How I can help you?"

Sidney explained what had been happening in Morgan over the past few weeks, with particular emphasis on the genealogical aspects.

"Fascinating," said George. "We've been doing a good deal of research here on the historical aspects of the slave trade and its impact on the Bahamas. I had studied it from the US viewpoint as you know but looking at it from here opened up a truly global picture. And the Marshlands Plantation name rings a bell for me. About five years ago, I had a graduate student do a thesis on property expropriation in South Carolina after the War for Independence. I remember it because of the court case she uncovered involving the place and people you inquired about, Marshlands and the Nichols family."

"That sounds very interesting indeed."

"You've really got me hooked, Sidney. The University and the Government of the Bahamas is working on a project to digitize all the old records from the colonial period. We're a bit behind in the technology. Don't have the money to throw at a project the way the US does, so I don't know how far they've progressed. You certainly have my curiosity index up. I know what I'm going to be doing for most of today."

"That would be a great help, George."

"You ought to think about coming down here. You're retired now. I've found this to be a terrific experience. Your kind of expertise would be a great asset to us."

"Hmmm. I'll have to think about that. It might be a good idea to get away from everything up here for a while when this is all over. Been a long time since I've been in the Bahamas. I'll give that some serious thought."

"Do that. In the meantime, I'll get to work on this right away and give you a call the moment I have something."

"Thanks, George. I'll give your suggestion about a visit some serious thought."

After disconnecting, Sidney spoke to Mickey. "I think this is going to be a very interesting day. I'll bet Tillie is way ahead of us. Knowing her, I'm sure breakfast is already made, and she left for the islands already." He gave the clock a quick look. "All right, we better get moving. It's too early for Ray to be at the archive building but I'll bet he's online with the database both here and in Charleston. A quick walk and some breakfast. Sound good?"

Mickey agreed completely and curled up outside the bathroom door as Sidney got ready.

＊＊＊

Sidney's early start to the day had some company around town. As Sam rushed through breakfast, he kept thinking about the Martin Tucker, Mitchell Bennett real estate connection and the mystery skinny man. He had mentioned it to Dede when he came home Sunday evening. He used Dede as his sounding board whenever he had a puzzle to solve, as she looked at his police problems from a different perspective.

Tillie had an uneasy night as well, as her head had been filled late Tuesday with the stories she'd heard over the past few days. Stories of slavery, fear, brutality, death, and sadness. Some of the people she spoke with broke into tears as they recounted family histories that came across as current events and not old stories of long-ago horrors. Other interviewees were angry and lashed out, seeing the white supremacist activities of recent years as a continuing extension of the brutal treatment of their relatives more than a hundred and seventy-five years ago.

Ray's breakfast musings envisioned the potential battle brewing among his friend Police Chief Hornig, Mayor Steele Wilcox, and the State Law Enforcement Division in Columbia. They needed a breakthrough, and they needed it quickly. He knew Sidney would like him to work on the Marshland Plantation historical records, but the real estate deal kept bothering him. His gut told him it sat at the heart of everything. *Skinny. Skinny. Somebody at City Hall has got to know who this guy is.* Ray recalled that Tillie mentioned the mayor's office and the comments made by CJ. *Secretaries know everything,* he thought, *and I'll bet she knows exactly who Skinny is.*

Sidney's morning walk with Mickey proved to be brief, not just because he wanted to get to back to work on Gloria Rye's historical records, but also it began to rain as they made their way along Howard Street. He had anticipated the rain and brought an umbrella. Mickey, although a Labrador Retriever, a well-known water dog, loved the water but not the rain. She took care of business quickly, and they made the turn for home a mere three quarters of a block away. The sun would normally have come up around seven, but the clouds were heavy and dark and it seemed more like evening than daybreak. He placed the closed umbrella against a tree by the curb as he bent over to clean up after Mickey and had the uncomfortable feeling someone was watching him. As he straightened and retrieved the umbrella, the rain began to fall in earnest. He opened the umbrella and looked around. A few cars were parked along the street, but he could see no one on the sidewalk. It also didn't help that his field of vision had become impaired by the now open umbrella and the act of switching Mickey's lead from one hand to another while steadying himself with his cane.

"We'd better get back quickly, Mickey," he said as lightning flashed in the distance.

Quick movement by an overweight man with a cane, an open umbrella, and a dog wanting to get out of the rain in a thunderstorm, was more of an aspiration than an achievable fact, they both started to get wet as a strong downpour began. Being distracted by the weather conditions didn't relieve Sidney's uncomfortable feeling of being watched and, even with his head down and his umbrella buffeted by wind and rain, he tried to look around him. Lights came on in some of the houses along his route, and people peered out their windows as the sky continued to darken and thunder rumbled. The people who watched as he and Mickey moved along the sidewalk were not the watchers he was concerned about. He had felt this feeling before and knew he needed to get back to the safety of his house. A hand grabbed his shoulder. His eyes widened, and a shiver went down his spine.

"Sidney, let me help."

He recognized the voice. Ray stood before him, wearing a yellow slicker.

Ray took Mickey's lead and grabbed the umbrella, which they both hunched under. As they moved down the walkway to Ray's front porch, Sidney turned. A dark sedan pulled away from the curb.

"That came on awfully quick," Ray said as they reached the porch. Mickey shook the water off her back as Ray did the same to the umbrella. "Spotted you from my office upstairs."

The rain whooshed down in a torrent while a vicious burst of wind swept across the porch and knocked over a small table next to a loveseat. "Why don't you two come on in until it eases a bit? I have a fresh pot of coffee on." Ray opened the door. "We can chat for a few minutes. Marie's at an early morning church meeting."

As they went through the front doorway Ray added, "Let me take that." He reached over and took the waste bag Sidney still carried. "Come on back to the kitchen."

Ray led the way and disposed of the bag in a receptacle out the back door. The layout of the house, although similar to Sidney's two doors away, had a much brighter and cheerier feel to it. The kitchen remodel a year ago gave it a modern, fresh appearance.

"Did you see that car out front?" Sidney asked as he took a seat at the dinette table.

"Car? Which car?"

"The one that pulled away as we came in."

"I don't recall."

"Hmmm."

Ray had his back to Sidney as he filled two coffee mugs. "What about it?"

"I don't know. It could be nothing. We appreciate you rescuing us. That's a nasty storm out there this morning."

Ray turned and brought the mugs to the table and sat down. "Where's

Tillie? Thought you wouldn't have sent her out on a morning like this."

Lightning flashed, followed by a strong clap of thunder that shook the house. The lights blinked.

"Wow, that was close," Ray said.

They both looked toward the back door as the rain pounded even harder and water poured off the overhang of the porch. They remained silent as they watched.

"What's this about the car?"

"I had a feeling I was being watched."

"I was watching. Probably a lot of people up and down the street were as well. You know how this neighborhood is. Full of retirees looking out of their windows. Watch everything. Make good witnesses," Ray observed.

"No, I don't mean that kind of watching. I think you might call it surveillance. Targeted. Focused."

"Really?" Ray peered questioningly across the table at Sidney. "Not a casual look at someone caught in a sudden downpour?"

Sidney replied thoughtfully, "No. I don't think so. This was different. This was someone who was caught watching another person and wanted to get away to avoid an explanation or possibly be identified. Whoever it was turned away quickly. The person wore a hat with a long brim, like a baseball cap."

"Man or woman?"

"I couldn't tell. The rain was coming down quite heavy at that point and I had the umbrella and my cane to manipulate."

"The car?"

"A dark sedan. I had no time to observe the license plate. Actually, it's only now, sitting here, that I feel certain I had been under observation."

Ray's phone rang. He checked the name of the caller.

"Hold on a minute, Sidney, I have to take this." He put the phone up to his ear and said, "Ryan, you have something for me? Good. It didn't take long.... SAR Heritage had how many investors?... I guess that's not unusual for this kind of real estate deal... Find anything interesting? .... The filing? .... You're not serious. … And he's not listed as a partner? …. The Chief is going to love this. Thanks Ryan. I owe you one."

The call ended and Ray got up from the table. "Gotta go, Sidney. That was Ryan Packer. Chief Hornig is going to love this. The person who is the principal of SAR Heritage LLC is none other than the mayor's mother-in-law, the late Dorinda Tooker."

"The mayor's mother-in-law. Is the mayor listed as a partner?"

"Not according to the filing. Just throw the latch when you and Mickey leave."

FORTY-ONE

2018
A Slave's Story

Tillie stood at the window of the Golden Harvest Retirement Home and watched the heavy rain pound the cars in the parking lot. Her meeting with Miss Miriam didn't reveal anything new but the nurse attending her was Anitra Sheldon, the daughter of a good friend and neighbor.

"Glad I'm not out in that," observed Anitra as she came up behind Tillie. "This one came up awful fast. Unusual to get hit by a surprise storm in the morning. The pop-ups you expect in the afternoon."

Tillie turned to the nurse and said, "You're right about that. Weather seems to be doin' strange things lately."

"I'm sorry Miss Miriam couldn't help you more this morning. She has days when some things come to her and then other times they don't. I wasn't here when you spoke with her the last time, and I was interested in that you were talking about Marshlands Plantation."

"Do you know about Marshlands?" Tillie asked.

"A bit. Heard about it from my mother and grandmother. That story she told you about the slave who tricked the plantation owner, that came from my grandmother."

"Girl, we got to talk. You got time to sit and chat?"

Anitra looked at her watch. "Yeah, I'm not due anyplace for another ten minutes."

"Good. Let's sit for a bit."

Tillie and Anitra moved over to where a table and four chairs sat in front of a side window that looked over the walkway up to the front door. They were alone in the visitor area.

"Was someone in your family connected to Marshlands Plantation?" asked Tillie.

"That's the story. My grandmother used to talk about it. As I understand, her grandmother had been a slave there before the Civil War. I guess she heard it from *her* grandmother. My mother knows more about it than I do. Some people have been trying to get her to write it all down. I think she has been, but I don't live at home anymore. Share an apartment with two nurses the other side of the Deer Island bridge. Been sharing with people ever since nursing school. My mother said someone from the AME church in Morgan came to see her. I don't know her name. My mother said something about her being in the choir. She said she wasn't from here but moved from up north a little while ago. Her name had something to do with bread."

"Mrs. Rye?"

Anitra perked up. "Yeah, that's it. Mrs. Rye. Funny name. You need to go talk to my mother."

"You know, I'm gonna do just that. She at home today?"

"Thursday. Let me think." Anitra sat back in her chair. "Thursday, I'm almost sure she's at the church's Good Neighbor Store today. It's out by Coffin Landing."

"I know where it is," said Tillie. "You have her number? I think your mother and I need to have a good conversation about Marshlands."

Coffin Landing stood as a testament and a reminder of a world that once was. Named for the coffins waiting for burial that lined the wharf during the Civil War, its wooden timbers were now a home for shrimp boats waiting the tide. Tillie knew the area well. Her father, grandfather, and great-grandfather fished these waters and now she had come here to do fishing of a different sort.

"Let morning star greet you on yo' prayin' groun'," said Ester as Tillie rushed through the front door of the store. Tillie had her head lowered and covered by her purse, which she had placed in a plastic shopping bag for protection before she left her car. Lightning flashed and thunder rolled as she wiped her feet on the mat inside the doorway.

"Oh, my," answered Tillie, "I haven't heard that one lately." She looked up and shook some of the rain off.

"Hah, Tillie. We've been getting a lot of tourists and visitors stopping by lately, and I started using it to prime the pump on Gullah."

"It's good to hear, but you're not going to find too many mornin' stars out in this rain. It just won't quit today."

"Prayin' groun' gonna be safe today though," Ester said with a smile. "Anybody who sneaks out into the woods to pray today ought to have their head examined. Although our forefathers would probably have taken advantage of it to do just that. Only way you could get to pray without being whipped."

Tillie closed the door behind her. "Did Anitra call after I left you the message I was comin'?"

"Yeah, I have some pictures over here that show what the area looked like in 1865." Another flash of lightning lit up the parking lot and the waters of the Morgan River beyond. Ester looked past Tillie to the rain pouring off the front porch of the Good Neighbor store. The rain kept coming in waves, A pounding accompanied by wind that pushed it into every quarter. The covered porch offered no safety as the deluge came from every direction at once.

"Yes, I've seen some of these." Tillie glanced over the photos Ester had placed on the sales counter. She sat the bag with her purse on the floor at the end of the counter.

Ester continued to look out the window at the rain. It had stopped for a short while just before Tillie arrived but then everything broke loose again.

Tillie continued examining the pictures. "Given the dreary mess that's outside now, it doesn't look much different."

Ester, a tall, thin woman about Tillie's age, wore a cheerful, flowered print dress. "Yeah, I got all dressed up to come here today and you're the first person to come in." She smoothed out her dress and continued. "I always like to look nice when I work. A lot of what's here were family treasures that had been in homes for generations. But you know all this. You used to work here sometimes before you got so busy."

"I keep tellin' myself I'm gonna get over here again. Guess I should slow down a bit. You're right though."

"Sometimes, when I'm alone on a day like this, I walk around and touch the tables and chairs and I can feel the presence of the people who for generations sat while they laughed and cried and prayed for better days.

"Tillie, I know you heard about the story of the slave who got his freedom with a bit of trickery. I told it to Mrs. Rye when she visited, but I'll bet you don't know what happened after the war."

"I'm not sure what you mean."

"Why don't we sit over here for a bit." Ester stepped away from the counter and over to a round table with four chairs. "I'm not expecting anyone to come shopping in this storm. I've got fresh coffee on too. Let me get us some."

"That'd be just fine. The rain is making it a bit chilly."

Once settled at the table with hot coffee and a few biscuits, Tillie asked, "So, what's this about the Civil War?"

"My grandmother, bless her soul, said the family had been all set to begin a new life after the war. The life we're finally beginning to see one hundred and sixty years later. They were slaves on Marshland, I'll bet you didn't know that."

"No, I didn't."

"They had just settled into farming a part of the land they were told they could claim as their own, as it had been declared abandoned property. They didn't have the whole place. It was being divided up into a bunch of separate farms. Now, as I heard it, some people came down from Canada and said the land was theirs, as their family were the original owners and they wanted it back. They demanded it back and threatened to have them driven off of it, as was happening in other places. My people resisted and claimed the government gave them the land. They argued a bit and then the Canadian people offered to buy it. Seeing what was happening around them, the family decided it would probably be safer to take the money and set up here on Deer Island. This was in sixty-six or sixty-seven, when the Union troops were leaving, and a lot of white people were trying to set up the plantations again. Stories were all around about land grabbing and killings and beatings everywhere. So, as my grandmother explained it, her mother told her that the family had already decided to head for Deer Island even before the Canadian people came and put money on the table. It could have been five cents, and they would have taken it."

"She didn't remember the name of those Canadian people, did she?"

Ester looked up past Tillie and dreamily watched the rain come down. "I'm not sure. I don't know why but something about Christmas just popped into my mind."

"Something religious?"

"No. Something more Santa Claus like."

"Santa Claus?"

Ester was frustrated at not being able to remember.

Tillie tried to help. "How about reindeer names, like Dancer and Donner and Vixen?"

"No." Ester shook her head as though trying to get the scrambled thoughts into the right order. She stopped. Looked right at Tillie and said, "Saint Nicholas. That's it, Saint Nicholas, or something like it."

"Saint Nicholas? Nicholas." Now it was Tillies turn to wrack her brain. "Wait a minute. Professor Lake mentioned this morning the name of a Mr.

Nichols. I'll bet that's them. And they were from Canada?"

"That's the way the story goes." Ester stopped again and then said, "But it wasn't the whole story."

"What happened?"

"What usually happened. After the Nichols people left, a band of riders showed up and, according to great grandma, they chased everybody off the land. But before they did, one of the riders shoved a paper in front of them and demanded the oldest male make his mark on it. One of the other riders said, 'That's a lawyer for ya.' All the Gullah took off and didn't look back. The ones that survived the raid headed for Deer Island. No one knew the lawyer man's name and didn't care. Everybody just wanted to stay alive and get away."

Tillie had her hand up to her mouth as she listened. "Yeah, the killin' time. Trouble is, it's still going on. But tell me, did she know any of the people on horseback?"

"No, they all looked alike. She did say they were from out of area. Most likely came down from Columbia than over from Charleston. At least the Canadian ones offered money along with the threats."

"And the riders didn't have any connection to the Canadians?"

"That I don't know. It seemed to me, the way I heard the story, it was two different events, but you never can tell."

"What I find interesting is there was a lawyer with the group. He probably went and registered it as a legal transfer of property. And that means there's a record with the lawyer's name on it. A lawyer from Columbia."

FORTY-TWO

2018
The Police Chief Versus The Mayor

The storm eased for a short while but began to pound away again as Sidney and Mickey made their way to Sidney's front porch. Although only two doors down from Ray's, they still managed to get soaking wet, and the umbrella turned inside out.

"How're you doing, Mickey?" he said as he tried to right the umbrella and Mickey shook the excess water off her back. A blast of wind and rain hit them. "Let's get inside and out of harm's way."

Sidney always kept a few towels in the utility closet under the stairs for just such occasions. Before dealing with his wet clothes, he took one of the towels and began wiping down Mickey. Before he finished, the house phone rang. He answered it at the desk in his office next to the kitchen, removing his jacket as he limped along. Mickey headed for the kitchen.

"Hello… George, you certainly moved quickly. Can you hold on a minute? I got caught in one of our legendary Lowcountry downpours and I need to get my wet shoes off." George Leeseman continued to speak as Sidney sat at his desk and removed his wet shoes and socks. The phone, placed in the center of the desk, enabled Sidney to continue to hear George's comments.

"You don't say… Yes, I'm sure you do get the same kind of weather we do here in the Lowcountry. It probably makes you feel right at home…. Yes, I know the politics are a lot nicer there than here, but it hasn't always been that way, which, by the way, leads me to the big question. Have you found some colonial records on the Nichols family?"

Thursday morning had become a hubbub of activity on many levels. While Tillie drove to Coffin Landing and a meeting with Anitra's mother, Ray headed for police headquarters and a meeting with Chief Hornig. Sam had an agenda of his own and a meeting scheduled with Mrs. DeReimer at the library to go over some early records she had found when searching the archives in Charleston. Sidney sat at his desk and wrote note after note while George Leeseman in the Bahamas read him document after document he had printed out from his search of Bahamian colonial records. Three of the four locations had something in common: they were all on the move. Sidney remained in his office and pored over the notes he'd made and waited for emails from Leeseman, who promised to scan everything and send them to him.

Meanwhile, a dark sedan remained parked a block away, where the driver tried to decide about approaching Sidney Lake.

The meeting between Ray Morton and Chief Pete Hornig became animated when Hornig slammed his hand on the desk. The sound reverberated beyond his office and was noted by his secretary and the two police officers she had been speaking with. All three stopped what they were doing. Hornig's secretary rolled her eyes and the two officers decided they could finish the conversation later and quietly took their exit.

"What the fuck!" Hornig's hand hit the desk again. "You mean to tell me Steele's mother-in-law was the principal in the real estate deal we think is at the heart of all this? Including her murder. And Steele doesn't tell us. What the hell is he playing at?"

Ray, doing his best to moderate the tone, said, "Pete, we still have to give him the benefit of the doubt."

"Are you kidding me? Steele is the most calculating person I've ever met. He may seem like a dumbass now and again, but I guarantee there's a plan in there someplace. It may not be a long-range one, he doesn't have the brainpower for that, but if he has an objective, he'll manage to get to it somehow."

"I'm not disagreeing with you. The question is, do the two activities go together? Was her murder related to the real estate deal? He doesn't know we're looking at the deal being the centerpiece of everything, so if he knew about her involvement, he could be looking at it as two non-related events."

Chief Hornig sat down and leaned back in his chair. Calming himself, he continued in a more moderate voice. "All right. Let's see if we can look at this objectively. I admit I have a blind spot with the mayor, and I can't let it get in the way of being clearheaded about everything. But our mayor, Mr. Steele Wilcox, is a devious son-of-a-bitch. I'll bet Dorinda Tooker didn't even know her name was on those papers. I'll bet she was a front for him."

Ray said thoughtfully, "Pete, that's an interesting approach. That would make sense."

"What?"

"Dorinda Tooker as a front for him. It's like a crook putting his wife's name on property he doesn't want flagged as something he has an interest in. His hands are clean. Say, as mayor, it would be inappropriate for him to be involved in ruling on a rezoning application where he has an interest. Does that sound like Wilcox?"

"Damn right it does. Probably learned it from John Gotti, like they say Trump did. But why the hell would he want to kill his mother-in-law?" Hornig stopped and looked at Ray, who raised his eyebrows and had a half-smile on his face. "Okay, so everybody wants to kill their mother-in-law now and again, but nobody ever does it. And then there's this guy Tucker. Why kill him? And the woman from Philadelphia—where the hell does she fit into the real estate deal?"

"No answers… yet. But at least we have the right questions for a change. This place, Marshlands Plantation, is at the center of everything. We need to focus on the current day and get every bit of information we can on this deal."

Hornig tapped his fingers on the desk. "Right," he said as he stood up from his chair. "We have Knott going after Bennett, Cashman's going through the archives trying to get a handle of the past ownership of the place. What's Sidney Lake up to?"

"He's coming at it from the other end. He's tracing the Nichols family. He's more convinced than ever that *that's* the key to everything. Someone in town is a distant family relative who's taking revenge on the descendants of a John James Winslow. He's the one with the direct connection to Dorinda Tooker and Martin Tucker. And Tillie has found a connection between our third victim, Gloria Rye, and the Nichols family."

Hornig raised his arms up in a stretch, clasped his hands together over his head and, linked, dropped them onto the top of his head. "Damn, something's got to come together here… and soon." He unlinked his fingers and let his arms drop. "All I know is the mayor and I are about to have a very interesting chat, but I have a couple of phone calls to make first."

"Fine, I'll get after Knott and see where he is with his end. Will it be a few minutes before you confront Wilcox?" Ray asked while getting up.

"Yeah."

"Good, I need to wander over there and have a chat with the mayor's secretary before I track down Knott."

Sidney took over his dining room table to lay out the papers he'd been receiving from Leeseman in Nassau. He hadn't expected quite the volume that sat before him: he had counted ten emails with three to five attachments each. Not being a super expert with electronic devices, the opening of each email and related attachments proved to be a slow and methodical process. After seeing what the first two emails contained, he decided to prioritize his action based upon the subject of each email. Leeseman did not send them in a specific order but did categorize them by date as much as possible.

As Sidney arranged the material, the phone rang.

"Sidney. Leeseman here. How's it coming?"

"My goodness, George, you certainly work fast. How did you find all this material so quickly?"

"As I mentioned, we're trying to digitize all our historical documents and it seems the colonial period has received the most attention. There's a lot of work going on in that area at present, and I enlisted the help of some of the people doing the work. The information you provided really spurred them on when they found out you were looking into a series of murders with a potential 300-year-old motive—well, there was no holding them back. In fact, one of the researchers is a graduate student at the university and is mulling over changing the subject of his thesis. By the way, I remembered the name of the student at USC Beaufort who did the work on Marshlands Plantation. Her name is Sommer, Janet Sommer. She lives in Walterboro, South Carolina. Or at least she did then. The Alumni Office at USCB should have a record of her."

Sidney scribbled down the name as he said, "George, you've done heroic work here."

"Now you have to do me a favor. You have to let me know what happens. You have us all fascinated by this project. In fact, we're still at it. One of our researchers has been on the phone to St. Mary's College in Halifax, Nova Scotia, to follow up on the Nichols clan up there. You'll see from some of the documents, they sold what they had here after slavery became forbidden in 1833."

"Oh, don't you worry. After this is all over, you may find me on your doorstep to tell you the whole story in person."

Once the phone call ended, Sidney needed to let Mickey out the back door to take care of business. While waiting, he refilled his coffee cup and stared out the kitchen window, mentally reviewing some of the subject titles in the emails. Suddenly, he jumped. "Wilson!" His head jerked up as he repeated, "Wilson! Is it possible?" He grabbed his cane and headed for the back door. He opened it and yelled, "Mickey, hurry up."

Back at the table, he looked through the material he had printed out and found the heading "Wilson Family". Attached to it, he found a document attesting to the marriage of Eli Nichols and Mary Wilson. It listed her children, one of whom was named Sean. Next, he went back to the computer and found a subject relating to the British spy Lieutenant Ian Wilson Nichols. He opened one of the attachments and found the mention of Ian Wilson Nichols' capture and killing by Caleb Bailey.

"Oh, my God." Sidney exhaled. "Oh my God. Detective R. Wilson Knott. Could it be you?"

Sidney stood near the end of his dining room table and looked at what he had assembled. Papers were placed in small groups of two to five sheets according to topic. There were five categories. He had placed them in a line down the center of the table in easy reach of the people who would soon arrive: Ray, Sam, and Tillie. Sidney had spent his lunch hour making phone calls and organizing the material. He arranged the seating with him and Tillie on one side and Ray and Sam on the other.

Mickey barked at the sound of a knock at the front door. Ray opened it as Mickey came toward him with her tail wagging.

"I thought I told you to keep this door locked."

"You did," answered Sidney, "but I decided to leave it open because of the storm so you could get inside quicker."

"Okay. We'll let it pass this time." Ray wiped his feet on the inside doormat. Mickey loped over to greet him and received a pat on the head in return.

"Come on in," instructed Sidney. "Were you able to reach Sam?"

"Yeah. He should be along in a few minutes."

"Tillie's driving over from Deer Island and could be a little late."

Ray looked over the dining room table and said, "Looks like you've been busy. Where did you get all this stuff?"

Another knock at the door and Mickey quickly responded to it. Sam peeked in.

"Come in, Detective. We're here in the dining room."

After briefly exchanging greetings, Sidney responded to Ray's earlier question. "The papers on the table are a mixture of material obtained by the late Gloria Rye, Mrs. DeReimer, and George Leeseman. Professor Leeseman is a friend and colleague who is now with the University of the Bahamas but had been with the University of South Carolina Beaufort. He is a historian who specializes in the Colonial Period of North America. I know you haven't fully bought into my theory of a multi-generational hate crime, but Professor Leeseman has come up with historical information I believe we can't ignore."

Sam said, "At this point, I'm open to just about anything. When I was with Mrs. DeReimer at the library earlier, she came up with some interesting post-Colonial Period material from the Charleston archives. I know this isn't the direction that Chief Hornig wants to go in. He's gone all-in on the real estate stuff and is convinced the mayor has something to do with all of it."

"Mayor Wilcox?" Sidney asked. "Let's sit down and see where we are with all the different parts of these murders. Tillie will be here in a few minutes. I think she had a few pieces that may fit in with your recent research." He pointed to the papers in the folder Sam placed on the table. Sidney then positioned Ray and Sam in the two chairs he had carefully determined would be the best places for them to sit.

Ray pulled his chair out and spoke first, sounding urgent. "Something came up this morning you need to know—Dorinda Tooker is listed as the principal of SAR Heritage, LLC, and the full name of the mysterious 'Skinny' is B. Ahern Cutliff. I cornered Mayor Wilcox's secretary this morning. The Cutliff family has been in real estate in Charleston for generations. Made their money by owning hunting camps on what is now Kiawah Island before it became a fancy resort location. The chief blew his stack when he found out about Wilcox's mother-in-law being the principal organizer of SAR Heritage. He and Hornig are having an interesting private conversation at the moment."

"So, Wilcox was aware of what was going on with the real estate deal involving Martin Tucker and Mitchell Bennett?" Sam asked.

"I don't see how he couldn't be. What has the chief all riled up is that we've been running around trying to find connections among the victims and the mayor already knew about a connection between two of them that doesn't go back three hundred years." Ray looked across at Sidney and then continued, "I can't believe he thought he could get away with it."

"I don't understand why the mayor didn't say something," Sidney said, now also seated.

Ray looked across the table and replied, "Money and politics. If I'm right, I'll bet that property we believe to be the site of the old Marshlands Plantation is going to need some rezoning approvals and environmental waivers. If the mayor can deny any involvement or knowledge of the project, he can support the waivers publicly."

"Does he?" asked Sam.

"Not sure yet, but I can't believe he doesn't."

"Before you go on, I have something to add to the theory." Sam took some papers from the folder in front of him. "You'll never guess who owned Marshlands after the Civil War—a Tucker family in Columbia. Mrs. DeReimer came up with a land transfer document dating to 1867. Then, in the 1880s, a portion of the land was sold to Arnold Tooker and I'll put even money on that being Dorinda Tooker's father or grandfather."

Sidney asked, "But wouldn't Tooker be her married name?'

"No. After the first two husbands died, she reverted to her maiden name. Mrs. DeReimer came up with that when she did Olive Wilcox's family history."

"What about Knott?" asked Ray. "Wasn't he looking into the real estate part of all this? Has he come up with anything?"

"Ah, that's something…" Sidney began but Mickey got up from her position next to his chair and took off at a run to the kitchen and the back door. "I think Tillie just arrived."

It took no time for Tillie to come in the back door and join them at the table. "Sorry to be late. At last it looks like it's startin' to clear."

"Take the seat next to me," Sidney instructed as he tapped the table in front of the chair.

As Tillie got settled, Sidney continued where he left off. "Ray, you just mentioned Detective Knott, and I have some questions for both of you. How well do you know Detective Knott?"

"He's been with us for about six months," Sam said. "Was previously up in Orangeburg. I've worked pretty close with him on a number of robberies and theft investigations. He's thorough. Handles himself well. Professional. There haven't been any complaints against him."

"Why did he leave Orangeburg?"

"Oh, yeah, Professor, when I said there were no complaints against him, I meant here in Morgan. Knott got himself in trouble with another police officer in Orangeburg. Female. Made a few unwelcome passes—maybe more than a few. She filed a formal complaint and it got nasty. The police chief up there decided to make an example of him and asked, or demanded, he find himself a new home. He has a good policing record, and from working with him I think he's a good detective. He just has to learn to keep his fly zipped as well as his mouth. Oh, sorry Tillie."

Tillie smiled.

"I don't really know him," said Ray. "Is he originally from Orangeburg?"

"No. He comes from Columbia. Left there after his divorce. Playin' around again. Been okay since he's been with us. Why the interest in Knott, Professor?"

Sidney reached for the papers nearest to him in the center of the table and picked a sheet with his own handwriting on it. "If I understand correctly,

Detective Knot's full name is R. Wilson Knott. The common practice in the south is to use the middle name to give respect to an ancestor of note. Do you have any ideas who the Wilson was in Detective Knott's background?"

"No idea," answered Sam. "Didn't give it any thought. As you say, it's a pretty common way of naming children. Take Steele Wilcox, for instance."

"Consider the following," Sidney said. "The original owner of Marshlands Plantation, Eli Nichols, married an indentured servant widow by the name of Mary Wilson, who came to him with three children, one of whom was named Sean Wilson. While he took the name of his new father, he kept the Wilson name and became known as Sean Wilson Nichols. Sean's youngest son, Lieutenant Ian Wilson Nichols, was killed by Caleb Bailey. Bailey, during the American Revolution, discovered that Ian Nichols was a spy for the British. Caleb Bailey is also an ancestor of Gloria Rye, our third victim. The report of Ian Nichols being a spy for the British tagged the Wilson Nichols family at Marshlands Plantation as loyalists during the war. This resulted in their lands being expropriated and the Wilson Nicholses escaping to the Bahamas. I have an email from Professor Leeseman stating that he has obtained a copy of the Wilson Nichols original immigration application as refugees escaping the Americans in South Carolina after having their property, Marshlands Plantation, expropriated because they were loyalists to the Crown."

"Are you saying Knott could be our killer?" asked Sam.

"What I'm saying is Detective R. Wilson Knott needs to be questioned about his family connections. Everyone's looking for suspects, and we may have one right in front of us."

"Shit!" In disgust, Sam closed the folder in front of him and sat up straight. "First Ray fingers Wilcox as a suspect and now you come up with Knott. Is Chief Hornig next? How about the mayor's wife, can we put her in the mix as well?" He leaned back in his chair and folded his arms only to immediately unfold them and leaned forward. "All right then, do your papers." He waved his hand at the documents on the table. "Tell us how we go from the Bahamas to Columbia, South Carolina?"

"No, but they do get us from the Bahamas back to the mainland of North America."

"What?'

"Sam, the second group of papers in front of you are documents showing that after slavery was forbidden by the United Kingdom in 1833, the Wilson Nichols family sold off all they had in the Bahamas and migrated to Canada."

At hearing the word "Canada,"Tillie looked over at Sidney as he continued.

"When the slaves in the Bahamas were emancipated by the Crown, it also provided compensation to the slave owners for their loss of property."

"Hah," remarked Tillie. "That sounds about right. Anybody ever think about giving compensation to the slaves for their two hundred years and more of free labor? Sorry Professor, couldn't not comment on the obvious. At least to me."

"Point acknowledged and duly noted. Also worthy of exploration as an argument put forth for the Civil War." He then turned back to the matter at hand. "According to the documentation, the Wilson Nichols family took the government payment, added it to the land sale proceeds, and left the country for Halifax, Nova Scotia. What's not here is information about them when they arrived in Halifax. But it's coming. Professor Leeseman has already been in contact with St. Mary's University in Halifax, where they have documented extensive research and can supply the immigration documents on the Wilson Nichols family and their connection to the province."

"Wait a minute, Professor,"Tillie interrupted. "I just come back from a visit with a lady who volunteers at the Good Neighbor Store at Coffin Landing, and she told me a story of her family having a farm on what was Marshlands Plantation after the Civil War. Her family history tells of being driven off the farmland, given to them by the US Government in Washington, by a bunch or raiders, but also of some Canadians that claimed ownership of Marshlands as they were the original founders of the plantation. Are we gettin some dots connected, finally?"

"Yeah," Ray said. "I think we are."

Sidney took a deep breath. "I have another important piece of information from Professor Leeseman. When he taught at USCB before he left for the Bahamas, he had a student present a master's thesis on Marshlands Plantation's historical origins and the court cases that surrounded it. He provided me with the author's name. That's in the other group of papers."

As Sidney couldn't reach far enough down the table, Sam stood up and pulled the pile to him.

"I think it's on the second sheet."

Sam read the paper with Sidney's notes. "I think this is it. Janet Sommer. Walterboro."

"That's the one. The Alumni Association Office at USCB should have a record of her and, hopefully, a current address. Professor Leeseman said it was a couple of years before he went to the Bahamas. That would make it about ten years ago."

"Ten years?" Tillie asked as she calculated the date.

"I think we have our work cut out for us this afternoon. This has been very helpful, Sidney." Ray then said to Sam, "How about if you have a chat with Knott and check with USCB for some addresses and background. I'll talk with Chief Hornig and call my contacts in Orangeburg and Columbia."

Tillie spoke up, "And I'll have another chat with a certain nurse over at Golden Harvest. She mentioned something that didn't seem important at the time…"

Sam's radio crackled. "Nine-one-one just had an emergency call from the Palmer library."

FORTY-THREE

1866

The Return

Simon and his son Angus buried Liam Nichols in the churchyard of the nearby Anglican Church. They stood by the grave and swore again to fulfill their promise.

After posting a letter to his mother, Simon and Angus boarded a coach to Philadelphia. They would make Liam's dream come true. Nothing would deter them. A train would take them from Philadelphia to Washington and then to Richmond, where they would wait for another train to take them to Charleston. Delays were frequent due to reconstruction; the infrastructure was far from being repaired. Once in Charleston, they obtained passage on a coastal trade vessel for the trip to Morgan, arriving as their great grandfather Eli did a hundred and twenty-five years before them. Simon and Angus reflected on the significance of their arrival in the now bustling port town of Morgan, South Carolina.

"This is providence," Simon said to his son. "We are destined to make the family proud. The Nichols family will once again be masters of Marshlands Plantation. I'm sure of it. Everything will be set right. It is God's will."

The inn where they were to stay stood at the corner of Howard and Castle Streets, two streets away from the wharf and the Morgan ferry terminal. The ferry served as the principal transportation hub connecting the islands through which the Morgan River flowed to the sea.

The inns and boarding houses were full of out-of-towners. This was not the Morgan they expected. Black and white mixed everywhere, with the Union Army keeping the peace, a tenuous one at best. The newfound freedom of the slaves was an ominous dance that no one seemed comfortable with. Simon and Angus also noticed a great many of the white people were like them—outsiders. As had happened before, many of the lands had been expropriated by the new government. The government that ruled from Washington this time, not Richmond or Columbia.

Simon's first task would be to locate the plantation. He had the directions his father carried, which were the original ones provided by his grandfather, Patrick Nichols. They indicated a very tiny market village with a single dock and the best route to the plantation being by water. Landmarks were trees and Indian pathways. His father, Liam, had the map memorized and rarely referred to it as his grandfather often drilled other landmarks and details into him over the years, but now, finally being in Morgan, he realized it bore no resemblance to what he imagined.

Standing in the lobby of the inn on Howard Street, Simon decided to get some help. "Excuse me, Sir, could you provide me with directions to Marshlands Plantation?" he inquired of the man standing behind the check-in counter.

"Seems to be a popular place today."

"Really?"

"Bunch of places going up for sale this week. Must be one of um."

Angus spoke up. "We're new here. Not sure how the buyin' works."

Simon gave his son a look that said, *Quiet. I'll handle this.* He then explained to the clerk, "That's not true. Family lived here a while back. Thought we might see if we could get back a piece of the old homestead. Family fought with Barnwell back before the war."

"Hah," said the clerk in a disdainful manner, "Another loyalist tryin' to sneak back in, hah,"

"Well…I…er."

Another man at the counter next to Simon answered for him, "That's no fair attitude to take. Where you from, gentlemen?"

"Why, er, Canada," said Simon.

"There you go," the man said to the clerk. "He's a better choice than a Yankee or one of them new rich negras tryin' to take over the place."

The clerk thought for a moment, then agreed. "I guess you're right. Even got a negro over in Beaufort says he's gonna run for the Congress. Heard his name is Smalls or something. Can't have that. We'll put a stop to him, though. Once the Yankees go home and take the army with them, we'll get things back the way God intended."

The stranger said, "Just have to be patient is all. Yes, it'll all come together as it should." He looked at Simon and placed a hand on his shoulder. "I know Marshlands. Lemme tell you how to get there."

Simon wrote down the directions and said to the stranger, "I appreciate your help."

"Just want to be fair. You come in on the Charleston boat this mornin?"

"Yes, I'm Simon Nichols and this is my son Angus."

The stranger looked up at the clock on the wall behind the counter. "Good to meet you. Look, I got to get myself over to the Town Hall for a meeting. Good luck to you both." The man turned and headed for the door.

Speaking again to the counter man, "We have to be off, too. Someplace we can get some horses nearby?"

"Stables are behind the inn. Tell them you're stayin' with us and they'll take good care of you."

"Thank you." They began to turn away but stopped as Simon said to the clerk, "Never did get the man's name."

"That's Silas Tucker. Used to be pretty important around here. Or at least the family was. They was all Tookermans."

Simon's head snapped up and looked fiercely at the clerk. "Tookerman? But you said he was Tucker."

"Changed the name around Revolutionary War times when the family got into lawyerin.' Tookermans didn't have too good a reputation, so lots of um changed the name to Tucker or Tooker. Do their lawyerin' up in Columbia now. Plan to be part of the new government once they get the Yankees out. Yankees don't want to be here. Tired of fighting just like everybody else. Wanna get home. Figure once they're gone, we'll get things back to normal again. What you want with Marshlands?"

"Family. As I said, it's where we all started when we first came from England." Simon felt it was best not to bring up that the original Nichols was Eli, brother to Thomas, who stood trial for piracy as one of Stede Bonnet's seamen.

"Good luck to you. We need farmers to get everything back to normal. The right kind of farmers. Property's been broken up all over the place by the speculators. Might even find yourselves bidding against one of um or even some slaves."

Simon paused. "Now that would be very interesting. Very interesting." He then turned to Angus and said quietly, "We should make our way to Marshlands without delay."

"Father, wouldn't it be better to go to town hall first to know what's happening and how we can make an offer on the land? We don't know what's for sale and what's not."

The clerk, overhearing, suggested, "Your boy's got the right idea. Lotta speculation going on. Property's been sold two and three times in a week. Negra's been grabbing what's on the islands, and we'll let um have that. The land along the rivers going inland is the dirt with the value."

When Simon and Angus left the inn, they were surprised to see so many men on Castle Street. Town Hall stood at the end of Castle. With all the traffic that came out of the stables behind the Inn and the people going in and out of Town Hall, the street seemed full. These were not Morgan farmers who come to town for the market. They wore long black coats and tall hats, had white shirts and black ties, and carried folders of papers. These were the speculators from the north and elsewhere they had heard about. Morgan came out of the war relatively unscathed, as did most of the Lowcountry. The nearby town of Beaufort had been taken early by the Union and controlled much of the area between Charleston and Savannah. After taking Savannah, Sherman made a feint toward Beaufort and Charleston and then headed northwest toward Columbia, the state capital. The Union generals, like Sherman and Grant, knew the only way to kill a snake was to cut off its head. So, Morgan and the other towns between Savannah and Charleston were spared the scorched earth tactics used by Sherman in his march from Atlanta to the sea. The farms and market towns kept their records and history intact.

"The innkeeper was right, father. These men seem to be buying and selling right here on the street. Look, there's the man we met at the inn who was so helpful."

Simon looked in the direction Angus pointed and saw Silas Tucker turn his eyes away from them and whisper to the man alongside him.

"We must be careful. I don't believe that man Tucker is our friend. We must get to the town hall. I have a bad feeling."

Oddly enough, once inside the town hall building, the crowd disappeared; there were only a few men standing around. Simon and Angus were directed to a room off the main hall. Inside, a counter ran along the rear with two men answering questions and a Union soldier standing by the entranceway. They approached the counter and a clerk asked, "How can I help you two gentlemen?"

Simon answered, "We are travelers whose family were once homesteaders before the Revolution. They were the owners of Marshlands Plantation."

"Marshlands, yes. Just up-river. Lot of interest up that way recently. Thinkin about buyin' a piece of Marshlands?"

Simon answered, "We understand all or portions of the original land might be for sale. My father's dream has always been to return to Morgan and Marshlands, and we thought this might be a good time."

The clerk looked the two men up and down. "Good time? Yes, could be. Lot of change going on. Lot of confusion, too. Union army took control of all abandoned property. Marshlands was one. Rules are all set by Washington right now, but that will change once Columbia is in control again. Right now, abandoned farmland is being given to the slaves living on it. And it's up to them to keep it. Lot of folks just waiting for the Army to leave. Gonna be some bad time coming."

"So how do we go about acquiring Marshlands?"

The clerk shook his head. "You young folk, always think everything is easy. Parts of Marshlands been bought and sold a number of times already."

"What are we to do?" asked Angus. "We've come a long distance and my grandfather died along the way."

The clerk gave them a long look again. He saw two men trying to achieve a family dream. These were not speculators and land dealers out to steal what they could, these were farmers wanting to build a new life. These were the kind of people Morgan needed.

"Personally, I think the best way to go about getting the land you want is to talk to the negras living there now. See if they'll sell you some of what they got. They don't know what to do with it anyway. If they're smart, they'll sell out like a lot of others did. Once the Yankees leave and the new government in Columbia starts to write the rules, all the land that's any good is gonna be taken away from them. Lawyer fella from Columbia just registered a big piece of the property next to Marshlands, the southern part of the Bailey Plantation."

Simon said, "Would that be a tall man, black hat, heavy, clean shaven?"

"That's him. Lawyer from Columbia. Do you know him?"

"Met earlier today at the inn down the street. Offered some help."

"Son, watch you self. You ain't gonna get no help from Silas Tucker. No sir." The clerk glanced around the room anxiously as he spoke. "Lawyers all over the place. Don't care about the islands so much, but around Morgan there's farms and plantations that'll be goin' full time again once the Yankees are out. They're like vultures sitting in the trees waiting for something to die. Sometimes they go after stuff that ain't dead yet and just help them along."

Simon said nothing, but Angus expressed concern. "What should we be doing?"

The clerk leaned across the desk and whispered, "Get yourselves out to Marshlands, find some negras to deal with. Be tough. Tell um this is your family land from before the war. Tell um to git off it. Don't offer um nothin. Bring your guns and keep them at the ready. Tell um if they're not gone in twenty-four hours, you'll come back with a bunch from town to drive um off."

Simon said, "What about the Army? Won't they come after us?"

"They want to go home. Long as there ain't no killing, you should be okay. If there is, hide the bodies or dump them in the river. Your word against a dead Black man. You want to get your land back then you got to fight for it. You not being a Confederate, you can probably get away with it."

Angus was speechless, but not Simon, who took hold of his son's shoulder and turned him around as he said, "Think of what your grandfather would have done. He swore to God and prayed for Him to show us the way to get back the land. Now He's showing us the way. Angus, we got no time to lose. This is how we can do it. This will make father proud." He then addressed the clerk, "Once we chase the negros away, how do we claim ownership?"

"You come back here and I'll show you what to do?"

Simon extended his hand to the clerk. "Thank you, sir. What are you called?"

"Nat. Nat Jenkins."

They shook hands.

"We'll be back," said Simon.

The father and son had no sooner closed the door behind them when a door opened near where the clerk stood.

"How'd it go?" said the newcomer, a rough-looking short man with a full beard and a pistol at his waist.

"That was easy. Tell Mr. Tucker to come by when he's ready."

"Good."

No other words were said as the newcomer moved to the front of the counter, took a small leather pouch from his pocket, and placed it in front of him. The clerk picked it up and stuffed it in his jacket in one easy, well-practiced movement that would go unnoticed by the Union soldier, who had conveniently turned his back to look out a nearby window. The clerk did not check the contents of the pouch but knew by its weight the agreed to amount was in it.

The newcomer left to notify Silas Tucker, Esqire, of the transaction being completed and followed the Nichols to the livery stable where they obtained horses for their ride to Marshlands Plantation.

Three hours later, Silas Tucker appeared at the clerk's counter with documentation showing he had acquired one third of what was known as Marshlands Plantation from the slaves to whom it was awarded. The transaction was properly recorded. Later the same afternoon, Simon and Angus Nichols were brought to the Army hospital in Morgan. They had been found by the side of the road severely beaten and robbed. Luckily, they did not take all their funds with them for the purchase of the land but kept most of it in the safe at the Inn. Upon learning of the purchase of much of Marshlands by Silas Tucker, they took the interisland trade ship to Charleston where Simon decided to remain while his son Angus booked passage to New York and then on to Halifax.

FORTY-FOUR

2018
More Trouble At The Palmer Library

Mrs. Cathcart sat at her desk near the front door of the Palmer Library reviewing the past due list of books, when Mrs. Evans came by.

"You wanted to see me?"

Mrs. Cathcart looked up. "Yes. We finished cataloguing the new donations for the reference room. Could you put them in order on the shelves? You may have to move some of the books around to make room for them."

"I just love that room; it's so full of history."

"The books are on the table behind me. It's not too much, is it? Take the cart if you need it."

"It won't be a problem. It's the best way for me to learn my way around."

"Good. I'll be here if you need anything."

Mrs. Evans gathered a few of the large volumes in her arms and walked to the historic books and documents room. Seeing the door closed, she placed the books on a nearby table. As she turned to open the door, she heard something hit it from the other side. Keeping still and listening carefully, she then heard a scraping sound and a clatter, as though a chair had been knocked over. Twisting the doorknob and pulling, Mrs. Evans couldn't move it. She rattled the doorknob and gave it a firmer pull. It still wouldn't move. Assuming it was stuck, not unusual for an old building like the Palmer, she gave it an even stronger pull. Hearing sounds coming from inside, she called out, "Hello, is someone there? The door seems to be stuck."

All sounds from inside ceased.

"Hello," she called out again.

Seeing another volunteer in the children's room nearby, she called to him, "Mr. Nadler, could you help me? The door seems to be stuck and there may be someone inside."

Jimmy Nadler, a tall, lanky man in his mid-eighties, wearing a brown sport coat, white shirt, and tie answered, "Certainly, Mrs. Evans. It does that on damp days sometimes."

Moving quickly, he came to the door and tugged on the doorknob. It wouldn't move. He gave it another pull and observed, "I think it's locked."

"Really? I think someone's in there. They must have locked it from the other side. I wonder if they're hurt? I thought I heard a chair go over."

"I'm sure Mrs. Cathcart has another key. I'll stay here, Mrs. Evans. Why don't you go and get the key from her?"

Off she went and immediately returned with Mrs. Cathcart leading the way. Jimmy Nadler continued to listen at the door for any signs of movement.

"This is most unusual," said Mrs. Cathcart. "Mr. Nadler, are you sure it's locked? And someone is inside?"

"Yes, I peeked through the keyhole and the view is blocked by a key. I can push it out of the way with another key so we can open it."

She handed him the key she carried but as he took hold of the doorknob, there was a loud click. The door swung open violently and hit Mr. Nadler in the head. He fell back into Mrs. Cathcart who, in turn, fell against Mrs. Evans, who completely lost her footing and fell backwards with her arms up in the air. She yelled and twisted her torso to try to break her fall, only to hit her head on the end of a table as she went down.

Sam took stock of the scene around the Palmer Library as he stepped out of his car: two police cruisers with their lights flashing, a police officer speaking with a small group of people near the front door, and three small groups of people out by the curb speaking among themselves. Curious bystanders stood on the sidewalk, trying to figure out what was happening. He carefully noted everyone and watched their movements. He had no idea what happened inside but there was always the possibility the perpetrators chose to mix with the crowd outside and watch the chaos they created.

Officer Shaun Green stopped him at the door. "Hamp's inside and there's an EMS truck out back. Two more uniforms down the street looking for suspects and witnesses."

"Someone hurt?"

"Elderly woman. A library volunteer. Knocked down and hit her head on a table."

"We'll talk later." Sam entered the building.

The Palmer Library, being in a converted Victorian home, had been restructured to accommodate the bookshelves and reading areas, but it still retained its original layout and character. Sam found Hampton Butler sitting at a table to his right talking with Mrs. Cathcart. In the room to his left another uniformed officer interviewed three women at a large table. He walked over to Hamp and the librarian.

Hamp looked up as the detective approached. "Sam, you know Mrs. Cathcart, don't you?"

"Yes, we're old friends." He leaned forward and said softly, "How are you? Are you all right?"

"Yes, I think so. I never envisioned being a librarian could be so dangerous. This is the second time in less than two weeks. What could they be looking for? You don't think there's still a treasure here someplace?"

Sam ignored the questions and asked, "Can you tell me what happened?"

"I'm not sure. Mrs. Evans would know more. She took a terrible fall. My goodness, blood was everywhere. They say that's what happens when you injure your head. The poor woman. She's a volunteer. Only been with us a few weeks. I pray she'll be all right."

Sam recognized the short-clipped sentences of panic and trauma and placed his hand on her shoulder. "It looks like she's in good hands."

"Yes, the EMS people have been nice. So helpful."

"Had she been in the reference room with whoever did this?" He squatted in front of her so she wouldn't have to twist in her chair to see him.

"Why no, that's just it. Someone apparently came in the back door and then locked the door to the rest of the library. I can't imagine where they obtained the key. Although I suppose almost any old key would open these antique locks. Mrs. Evans tried to enter and found the door closed. At first she thought it was stuck. That happens sometimes when we have a heavy rain like we did today. I went down there with a spare key in case it was locked instead of being stuck. Mr. Nadler, he's another volunteer, said Mrs. Evans thought someone was in the room and could be injured. He tried to look through the keyhole but couldn't see anything because the other key was in the lock. This has all been so distressing."

"Yes, you're right. It is. Stay here with Officer Butler. I want to check the room and then I'll come back and we'll talk more."

Sam stepped away from the table and spoke quietly with Hamp. "Have the EMS people talked with her?"

"Yeah, she's okay. Just a little shook up."

Sam scanned the back of the building and the children's room. "No kids in there today?"

"No. Too early. Start to show up after three."

"Dr. Coffey been notified?'

"Yes. On her way."

Sam was puzzled. "What about the locked door? Why?"

"Old door. Old lock. The kind that takes an old-fashioned long key. All the internal doors in the building have them. Part of the charm, I guess.

Not intended as part of the building security system. Only the doors to the outside have latch key locks and deadbolts. Could have just walked in from out here and locked the door behind him."

"Yeah, I remember that from last time. No one saw who was inside?"

"One of the other volunteers, James Nadler, was also involved. Said he didn't see anyone go in. Didn't recall seeing anyone nearby. He called inside but no one responded. Thought maybe someone fell and was injured or something."

"Good. I'm going to look around." Sam pulled latex gloves from his jacket pocket and headed for the old book room.

On the other side of town, Sidney spoke quietly with Ray for a few minutes longer after the meeting in his dining room broke up. Sam had already left because of the 911 call to the Palmer Library. Tillie went to her office, where she sat trying to remember the conversation she had with Nurse Anitra at Golden Harvest.arvestHarvest

Once Ray left, Sidney said, "Tillie, I'll be in my office. I have to speak with Professor Leeseman in the Bahamas."

"Okay," Tillie replied in an offhanded way, as she wrote in a notebook, *Let's see, she's got to be about 30 years old so, 10 years ago she'd be 20, which means she'd be in nursing school. Most likely the Sommers woman would be a year or two older cause she was in graduate school.* She spoke out loud to herself, "Tillie, you got to call her and find out." She picked up her phone.

Back inside the Palmer library reference room, Sam stood, looking at the mess: chairs were turned over, books were on the floor, papers were scattered about, there were gouges on the large table and some of the books still on the shelves were clearly damaged. *Someone's very unhappy. Looking for something and not finding it. Frustrated. Angry. In a rage.*

Sam's phone rang. "Yeah, Hamp."

"Sam, they have a lead on the person who did the damage. Someone running full out and heading toward Church Street was spotted by a neighbor. I'm on the way. Want to come?"

"Be right there."

As Sam turned and left the room, he spotted Mary Coffey and one of her team at the front desk with Mrs. Cathcart. He called out to her, "Mary, have to go. Haven't touched anything. Be back as soon as I can."

Sidney sat at his desk and looked over his notes. He had just finished a conversation with a Canadian history professor at St. Mary's University in Nova Scotia. The name and number had been provided by Professor Leeseman, who thought it best Sidney talk directly with her. He learned how the whole Wilson-Nichols family had immigrated to Halifax. The University had obtained copies of letters written by Simon Wilson-Nichols to his brother Angus. They outlined a failed attempt to regain Marshlands Plantation due to the duplicity of an attorney by the name of Silas Tucker. The letters were written from Columbia, South Carolina,

where Simon then resided. Apparently, attorney Silas Tucker also lived and had offices there. Simon had decided to stay in Columbia and not return to Canada. He made it clear it would be his life's mission to bring vengeance upon lawyer Silas Tucker.

Sidney sat back in his chair as his printer spit out copies of the letters from Simon Wilson-Nichols. The University agreed to provide them when they learned they could be needed in an ongoing police investigation of three murders. They also agreed to continue to pursue other historical material that could be relevant to the background of the Wilson-Nichols family, as well as a current address of the family living outside the town of Sackville, Nova Scotia.

Sidney decided to check on Tillie to see what she had found but as he headed for the doorway, Tillie rushed in.

"Professor, wait till you hear this."

FORTY-FIVE

2018
A Link Discovered

The excitement in Tillie's voice not only attracted Sidney's attention but also woke Mickey from a sound sleep. The three met in the middle of the living room.

"You beat me to it," Sidney said. "I also found something of interest. Let's hear what you have and then I'll add mine."

"Okay. Let's go to the dining room table."

Tillie placed the papers she carried on the table and sat down. "Professor, you remember Nurse Anitra Banks mentioned something that jogged my memory? It was when you talked about that Miss Sommer who did the report for Professor Leeseman. Well, Anitra shared an apartment with two other college students ten years ago. That matched up with Miss Sommer's comment of sharing an apartment with some other college students around the time she was doing that report on Marshlands Plantation. I couldn't resist, so I called Anitra to see if she could tell me who she shared the apartment with. She shared with Miss Sommer. They spent the whole school year together until Anitra graduated and moved back to Deer Island."

"And the name of the third person?"

"That's the interesting part. Nora Woodman."

"Nora Woodman? The librarian at Morgan Regional Library?"

"That's the one. Unless there's someone around the same age with the same name."

Sidney sat down, stunned. "She's been right in front of us the whole time." A thought popped into his head. "Tillie, Nora Woodman is also the niece of Mrs. Cathcart at the Palmer Library. I have to call USCB. Can you get me my phone? I left it on my desk in the office."

She got up immediately. "You gonna get Miss Sommer's phone number and address?"

"Yes. I want to firm up the information before I call Sam."

Unfortunately, the alumni association wouldn't release Sommer's personal information to Sidney, but they did offer to call her and give her his phone number so she could call him if she wanted to.

Fifteen minutes later, Sidney and Tillie pulled up in front of the Palmer Library.

Police cars were still in evidence, but the onlookers were gone. Also, both Hampton Butler and Shaun Green had moved on to other assignments.

As they entered the library, Mrs. Cathcart again occupied her desk near the front door.

"Professor Lake and Tillie, you heard about what happened here earlier?"

"Yes," replied Sidney. "We wondered if any serious damage had been done. I understand someone was hurt."

She waved at them to come and sit by her desk as she began telling the story of the stuck door again. Sidney asked, "I understand some books and furniture were damaged?"

"Whoever it was had some type of stick or something and scraped the table and used it on books on the shelves. They made a terrible mess."

"Were the Bailey books targeted?"

"I don't know. I hadn't really thought about it. You mean it could be the same people who were here before? I thought they caught them."

"Possibly not. Have the police finished in the reference area?"

"I'm not sure."

Sidney looked toward the location of the room. "I'd love to take a look if you don't mind?"

Tillie, who had remained quiet until now, asked, "Mrs. Cathcart, do you got a lot of librarians in your family?"

Surprised, she answered, "Why… I don't think so."

"I was wondering. I thought you had a relative over at the regional library."

"Ah, you must mean Nora."

As they spoke, Sidney drifted toward the history room.

"Yeah, that's her," said Tillie.

"Nora's my husband's niece. Well, I guess it is all family in a way. But no, not in my own family."

"Her name was also Cathcart?"

"No, she's my husband's sister's daughter. His name is Henry W. Woodman."

"I get it. And the family is from Columbia?"

"The Woodmans are. My family are all Aherns. From the Beaufort area."

As Tillie gently probed Mrs. Cathcart's family connections, Sidney ambled toward the history reading room. Although no policeman guarded the door, yellow police tape stretched across the open doorway.

Upon arriving, he peeked into the now empty room. A few minutes later, Tillie came up alongside him.

"I wonder, Tillie. Why return a second time? Mmmm, maybe it's not a second time. There were two people here the first time books were stolen from the room and one of those people, Martin Tucker, is now dead and the other was caught by the police. There was always a suggestion of another person. Mr. Swift told the police he didn't know the identity of the third person, and he managed to convince them he told the truth. So, who did this? What were they looking for? Could it be we are back to the original bogus story of a treasure map hidden in one of Joshua Bailey's books the family donated to the library? It all seemed rather fanciful at the time."

Sidney looked at the long table in the main part of the room and saw the gouge in the center. "That was rage. Anger. Frustration." Chairs were overturned, books were on the floor, and papers scattered about. "Whatever the person was looking for, he or she didn't find it. In the books we recovered, there were drawings on the inside back covers that might have been a map, but no one could figure it out. None of the landmarks made sense. So, we discounted them. Could we be wrong? What have we missed? What information does the murderer have that we don't? Everything centers on the rightful ownership of Marshlands Plantation."

Sidney stepped back from the doorway and looked up to see Mrs. Cathcart speaking with another library staff member. He mulled over everything he knew, brow furrowed.

"Professor, you think you got it figured out, don't you?"

Sidney again went over to the police tape and peeked around the doorway so he could have another look at the damage done to the room. "Tillie, this is serious rage. Someone completely out of control. Could it be Nora Woodman? Could someone be that angry about an incident occurring more than three hundred years ago?" He stepped away from the door and said nothing, thinking. Finally, he continued, "Although I imagine it might not be so unusual if you consider the Irish kicking the British out after almost eight hundred years, the Spanish doing the same to the Moors, and the Jews taking over Palestine and recreating Israel. But I think what we have here is something very personal. Could a descendant of the Nichols family, who has been drilled into believing the time has come to get back at the Tookerman and Winslow families for having cheated Eli Nichols, be responsible for all that has happened? Actually, it does seem somewhat unrealistic, but the indoctrination of children can be very, very effective. Of course…."

A uniformed police officer rushed over to them. "Professor, Tillie, I just heard there's some kind of incident at Florence McCann's place. Thought you might want to know since you folks have become friends."

Turning to Sidney, Tillie said, "Think we ought to go see what's happening?"

"Absolutely."

The officer assigned to keep watch over Florence McCann's condominium had been sitting quietly in an unmarked police car parked across the street and two doors down from the condo's entrance when he heard someone yell.

"Help! Stop him!"

Hearing the scream, he looked toward the building he was assigned to watch. He saw no one but caught motion to his right. A woman, waving her hands in the air furiously, stood in her doorway. He grabbed his radio. "Unit 17 to dispatch. Call for help. Investigating."

"Tippy! Tippy! Stop," she yelled as a small white dog ran down the three front steps of the single-family home, right past a brown uniformed, startled UPS delivery woman. The officer took up the chase, as did the UPS driver, much to the delight of the escaping dog.

"He's just a puppy. He'll get run over."

"I'll chase him back your way," the officer hollered.

Nora Woodman moved slowly down the driveway between the two condominium buildings as the chase for the wayward puppy focused everyone's attention on the opposite side of the street. The last time she made this walk she'd hurried, knowing Florence McCann wasn't home. Then, Nora had a note to deliver—a warning. This time she wanted a confrontation. She felt compelled to say something and wanted the element of surprise on her side. The bushes at the front of the building had been her hiding place for fifteen minutes and the delay made her nervous, fidgety, anxious. But this was her chance.

As the noise in the street became louder, she saw motion in the first-floor unit of the building opposite the driveway. The nosey neighbor would be heading for her front window. Nora, wearing a dark blue baseball cap without an insignia and a sweatshirt with a hood, hunched over as she assumed Florence McCann, in the unit above her, would be heading in the same direction to see what caused the disturbance outside. In her right hand she gripped a fireplace poker with a hook on the end and a small pistol was concealed in her sweatshirt pouch. As the buildings on this side of the street were all raised four steps, by crouching she could easily get past the windows that lined the driveway without being seen.

By the time she reached Florence's back door, the elusive, happy puppy had been safely corralled and now wiggled excitedly in the arms of his owner.

The rear door of the condominium being locked, Nora pressed her back against the building to keep from being seen.

Inside, Florence had been watching the drama unfold across the street. With a smile at the happy conclusion of events, she opened the door and stepped out onto the small porch area. Florence was not the only one, as a group of neighbors also stood watching the conclusion of the hunt for the wayward puppy.

After exchanging waves with neighbors across the street, she returned to her unit, carefully closing and double locking the front door.

Florence breathed a sigh of relief as she made her way to the kitchen to make a cup of tea. "At least it wasn't about me." The airline boarding pass she had printed out earlier sat on the table. "I'm outta here the first thing tomorrow morning."

A knock at the back door stopped her.

I'll bet that's old Mrs. Etheridge from across the way wanting to talk about the excitement out front.

"Be right there. You can join me for a cup of tea." She turned on the burner where the tea kettle sat at the ready and went into the laundry area to open the rear door. As soon as she unlocked it, a push from the other side slammed the door into her, making her stumble sideways.

By the time the officer on Florence McCann's protection detail got back to his car, the dispatcher had already checked the location of the nearest unit. Hampton Butler arrived just after the puppy was leashed and placed on the ground, and its owner was conversing with neighbors about how relieved she was. The UPS driver had returned to her truck and retrieved a small dog biscuit for Tippy and was in the process of rejoining the group.

Hamp pulled up next to the other cruiser and asked, "Everything okay?"

"Yeah. Just called the all-clear in."

"Everything okay down the street?"

"Yeah. Quiet. Understand she's leaving town tomorrow."

"Smart."

They talked for a few minutes when Tillie and Sidney drove up. Seeing the two officers standing casually, Tillie assumed whatever happened wasn't serious and said so to Sidney. Hamp gave Tillie a wave, indicating everything was okay. She parked almost in front of the McCann condominium but across the street from it.

"Sidney, have you ever met Florence?"

"Yes, you brought her over the other day after your meeting at the library."

"You're right. She's leaving town tomorrow. Any reason we shouldn't tell her our suspicions about Nora?"

Sidney thought for a moment and then answered, "I'm… not sure. It's still premature. That should come from the police."

"Yeah, you're right. Lemme clear our making a visit here with Mister Hamp."

Tillie got out first and left Sidney to do his usual struggling routine of exiting the car by himself. By the time he was ready to cross the street, Tillie had received another okay from Officer Butler.

"No problem," she announced. "She's at home so let's just knock on the door."

While crossing the street, Sidney thought he saw someone at the window of the McCann condominium. He couldn't be sure as the blinds were down, but the slats were in the half open position, which made it difficult to see inside. The building sat back fifteen feet from the sidewalk with a line of five-foot high bushes stretching across the front from the four entry steps.

Tillie went up the steps first and rang the bell. As Sidney reached the front door, he noticed the slats of the blinds were now closed.

"Nobody's answering," she said. "Hamp said she's home. Maybe she's upstairs or in the kitchen."

She rang the bell again. Still no answer.

Sidney said, "I thought I saw someone at the window before." He indicated the large living room window to the left of the door.

Tillie looked at the window. "How? The blinds is closed."

"They were open before. Be a pest and ring again. I'm sure someone is inside… and I have an uncomfortable feeling."

Inside, Florence stood in the entry hall with her back to the door. Nora, armed with the poker in her right hand and the small pistol in her left, stood in front of her.

Nervously, Florence said, "They know I'm in here. The police are just down the street."

"I know… all right, tell them you don't want to see them."

"I can't do that. Tillie and I have become friends."

Nora was in a quandary. Her original plan had been to give Florence a good scare and let her know how she felt about the Baileys, Winslows, and Tookermans. But now, she couldn't let her go free, especially with the police outside. Nora felt angry and cheated. *They've got to know why. They've got to know I'm rendering justice.* It then occurred to her that Sidney Lake and Tillie James would be the perfect audience. *They will tell the story.*

"All right, let them in," Nora said. "I'll tell you how. Open the door and get them to the sofa over there." She pointed with the poker to the living room area to the right of the front door. "I'll be behind the door. I want you all seated. And there'll be no trouble, or I swear I'll use the gun on the three of you."

As Florence began to open the door, Sam drove past the condo to where Hampton Butler was now conversing with the owner of the wayward puppy. He never looked toward the McCann residence as he went by. Upon stopping,

Sam rolled down his window. "Hamp, everything under control?"

"Yes sir, the escapee has been caught and is now under firm control." The puppy's happy owner held Tippy in the air so his firmly attached leash could be seen by the relieved crowd. "He'll be going into his crate for a brief period of punishment. He'll be eligible for parole in about fifteen minutes."

Sam refocused on Hamp as the assembled neighbors began discussing the possibility of having a backyard barbeque and trial. "How's everything across the street?"

"Nothing out of the ordinary. Professor Lake and Tillie just went over to say hello."

"Maybe I should check—" Sam's phone interrupted him. "Ray, how can I help you?… You have Wilson with you now?… What did he say?… I'm not surprised. He may have some personal problems but Knott's a good detective. How about I come over right now?… Good, see you in five minutes." The call ended. "Gotta go, Hamp. I'll try to stop in across the street later."

Sidney and Tillie had no sooner entered the condominium when the concealed Nora slammed the door behind them. They jumped and turned, shocked at staring down the barrel of Nora Woodman's pistol.

"Both of you. Sit on the sofa. You, Florence. In the chair over there."

Tillie balked and started to speak but Nora shut her down. "No. I'm talking and you three are going to listen. Now sit!" She waved the gun and poker at them.

Everyone followed the instructions. Florence looked particularly frightened. Her voice shook as she asked, "Who are you? What do you want? I don't even know you."

"But I know you. You're a Bailey. You come from the lying, devious blood line of Jamaica James Bailey. You're not a Winslow or a Tookerman but you're just as bad, if not worse."

"I…I don't know what you're talking about. This is crazy."

Sidney intervened, "But I do, Nora. I know the whole story, probably better than you do, now."

Florence looked at him, surprised.

Nora snarled, "No you don't. No one knows it better than I do—I've lived it. Lived it for over two hundred years. Every day and night the story was told to me. And that Jamaica fella, he was as slick as they come. If it wasn't for him…"

"Now, Nora." Sidney kept his voice calm and evenly modulated. "You can't blame a slave who wanted to be free. For his family to be safe. No, I think that part of the story needs correction. Now for Richard Tookerman and his lawyer John Winslow…,"

Nora looked shocked as Sidney mentioned the hated names.

"You may have a case. They took advantage of Eli Nichols, didn't they?"

"Yes. Yes." She focused on Sidney now. "They stole Marshlands from us. Them and their legal agreements. Winslow was the worst. He made me sign an agreement I didn't understand. It wasn't my fault. I couldn't read."

She began speaking differently, taking on the persona of someone else, Eli Nichols.

"They knew that. They intended to cheat me from the beginning, but I wasn't going to let them. I would outlive them, and no one would know what the agreement said about the need for a male heir."

Sidney decided to play along, "But Lawyer Winslow's son John James knew, didn't he? You thought you were in the clear when you went off to fight the Spanish invaders at Bloody Marsh. If you didn't survive, you expected ownership to go to your wife, Mary Wilson, who would pass it on to her son Sean as he had taken the name Sean Wilson Nichols."

Nora looked at Sidney as though she had an ally and eased her grip on both the poker and the gun, lowering them slightly. Tillie saw the slight movement and shifted, ready to pounce at the first opportunity, but Nora tightened her grip again as she lashed out with, "But it didn't happen! My Eli died a hero at Bloody Marsh. A hero! My Eli!"

Tears glistened in her eyes. Nora had now become Mary Wilson Nichols.

"A hero! And they cheated us, his family. We should have gone to the

Governor and pleaded our case as I wanted to but no, that Jamaica, he had my Sean's ear. He conceived a plan of deception to save Marshlands from John James Winslow and get his freedom in the bargain. They passed off a white-looking child of one of the slaves as the male heir, Patrick Nichols. He was supposed to be my and Eli's son, born when Eli was fighting in Georgia. Everything would have been fine if Jamaica, that sneaky nigger, who changed his name to James Bailey when he and his family got to New Jersey, hadn't bragged to some passing South Carolinians about what he did to get his freedom. John James Winslow found out and filed suit, but we beat him back. He swore he would get Marshlands from us, one way or another."

"And they did, didn't they?" Sidney continued to speak softly. "You were loyalists during the Revolution and Marshlands became expropriated property."

Nora's face twisted with rage as she backhanded a lamp with the poker on a side table next to Florence McCann.

"Ahhhh!" Florence cried as pieces whizzed past her face and the lampshade flew across the room.

"That was a secret. Nobody knew. Nobody needed to know." Spittle flew from Nora's mouth. Her knuckles whitened as she squeezed the handle of the poker and shook it at Sidney.

Tillie tried to deflect the anger away from Sidney. "If it was a secret, how'd they find out?" As she spoke, she shifted closer to Sidney and moved her feet slightly, ready to launch herself at Nora if any attempt was made to use the poker against Sidney.

Nora pointed the poker toward Florence and said, "It was Bailey again. Proud of what he did. The lie he made us live. He passed his bad blood onto his grandson Caleb, the ferryman at Trenton. He killed our Ian. Claimed he admitted to being a spy for the British. He would never have done that! Yes, he was loyal as we all were, but he knew what would happen to us and Marshlands if he helped the British."

Sidney could not figure out who she was speaking for at this point.

Tillie tried to deflect her attention again to keep her talking and not acting.

"So what happened?"

In a low, angry tone, Nora said, "John James Wilson found out and immediately demanded we be thrown out of the colonies. He wanted Marshland, and this time the court gave it to him." Her jaw set as she relived their escape from South Carolina with only the clothes on their backs and whatever their slaves could carry.

"But you were safe in the Bahamas," offered Sidney.

"Yes," Nora softened. "The British were good to us. They rewarded our loyalty and gave us land to start over. Patrick had a son, Liam, who took charge. But this was an alien land. We had only one mission in life: to get Marshlands back."

"Did you succeed?" Tillie realized her mistake in asking as Nora's face again darkened.

"It was in our grasp. My father and I bought the land after the Civil War. But again, we were cheated. The land was stolen from us by Lawyer Tucker. We were both robbed and left for dead at his hands." Nora's anger reached a boiling point as she raised the poker up and took a swipe at a lamp that sat on the table between Sidney and Florence McCann. The base shattered, the shade and upper part of the lamp went flying into Florence, who screamed and began to cry.

Sidney made a move to help her, and Nora brought the poker down on the arm of the sofa next to him. It hit with a loud thump and tore into the fabric.

"Stay where you are!"

Sidney had no idea who he was dealing with now. The persona of Mary Wilson Nichols had been replaced, but by whom?

Tillie tried to defuse Nora's anger. "But that was happening to everyone back then. We had the land given to us and we lost it too."

Sidney, believing Tillie had just put herself in Nora's line of fire, tried to switch the attention back to him. "That's when you all were in Canada. Is that where Mary Wilson Nichols died?"

Nora, furious again, raised the poker to swing at Sidney.

Tillie reacted instinctively and threw her body onto Sidney to protect him. Nora became even angrier at the move and paused slightly before starting to bring her arm down. Sidney had started to raise his arms and ended up enveloping Tillie in them as the blow deflected off his forearm and caught her on the back of her right shoulder, where it tore into the jacket she wore. The hook of the poker ripped through it and caught in the fabric. Sidney grabbed it and knocked Nora off balance. Her left hand jerked. The pistol fired, breaking a front window pane, and tires screeched on the street. Nora freed the poker from Sidney's grip, swung it around, and pointed it at Florence, who had managed to get half out of her chair.

"Back down!"

She then focused on Tillie and Sidney. Nora was shocked at Tillie's reaction. "Why did you protect him?"

"Because he's my friend."

Nora heard shouting outside and didn't respond to Tillie but began to back toward the kitchen.

<hr>

Detective Sam Cashman's car screeched as he slammed on the brakes in front of the condominium. He didn't hear the glass break in Florence's window, but he did hear the gunshot and the bullet ricocheted off the hood of his car.

"What the…"

Instinct and training took over as he slammed on the brakes and threw his car into reverse. He assumed the bullet had been intended for him and the shooter would be tracking him in the forward direction.

By the time he made it to Hamp's position, Hamp had already contacted the dispatcher. "Shots fired."

The phrase initiated an instantaneous response with a call to nearby units to proceed to Hampton Butler's location.

Hamp drew his weapon, crouched behind his cruiser, and yelled to the still assembled neighbors to take cover.

Sam rolled out of his vehicle and squatted next to Hamp. "Someone took a shot at me."

"From which direction?"

"Left side. Didn't see anyone."

"That's the McCann condo."

Sam looked at Hamp. "Shit. Sidney and Tillie are in there. You're sure McCann is in there?"

"Didn't see anyone come out."

"Did you see anyone else go in?"

"Not from the front."

As they spoke, the radios from both cars crackled with instructions. Other neighbors opened their front doors to see what caused the disturbance. Hamp popped the trunk on his vehicle open, reached in, and pulled out a bullhorn. "Everybody take cover and stay inside," he issued before turning to Sam. "Told her not to use the back door. Keep it locked. We don't have coverage there."

Sam went partially back into his car and retrieved binoculars. He looked at the front of the McCann condo and spotted the broken window. "Looks like the shot came through the window from the inside. Blinds are closed but look damaged."

Sirens screamed in the distance.

Referring to the soon-to-arrive support, Sam said, "Give them an update on what's happening. I'm going to try to get closer."

"Wait! The front door is opening."

They looked out from their protected positions. Hamp said, "Is that a white flag?"

Sam focused his binoculars on the doorway. "White handkerchief on a stick of sorts." He lowered the binoculars and yelled, "Keep your hands in sight and come out onto the grass."

Tillie yelled as she came out, "She went out the back."

"Call it in," Sam barked. "Get that street covered."

Florence stepped in front of Tillie and came out first with her hands in the air. Next came Tillie holding Sidney's hand. Tillie continued to hold their white flag up with her other hand while Sidney limped on his cane.

Sam called out, "How many were there?"

"Just one. Nora Woodman. She's gone. "

Sam and Hamp both stood from their positions.

Hamp took off at a run and said, "I'll check the back."

Some people started to come out from their front doors and Sam yelled, "Please. Stay inside." He then moved quickly but cautiously toward the three hostages now standing on the front lawn of the condo while Hamp sprinted down the driveway between the buildings.

"Professor, is everybody okay?"

"Yes, Nora left after her gun went off accidentally and the window broke."

Sam moved closer but kept his gun out until he could verify Sidney's assurance.

Sidney shook his head. "She's a very sick woman, Sam. Very sick."

"I'll say," added Tillie.

"Sick?" Florence said in a shaky voice. "She's just plain crazy."

"Walk over to Officer Butler's cruiser. I want to have a look inside. You three okay?"

Sidney replied, "Yes."

Sam nodded and cautiously went up the four steps to the front door, crouching slightly and with his hand on his weapon. Before entering, he called in to headquarters and explained the situation.

As Sidney, Tillie, and Florence made their way down the street, police cars with lights flashing appeared at both ends of the block and closed it off.

After losing Nora, Hamp joined Sam. They went inside and cleared the condo, verifying nobody was there.

By the time he got back to where the three hostages waited, the street had filled with police. He first spoke with two uniformed officers who while Hampton went back to his vehicle. More police vehicles and personnel began to search the surrounding streets. There was no sign of Nora Woodman.

Sam said, "Professor, why don't you get off that bad leg of yours and sit on the edge of the front seat of the cruiser while we talk. We have an ambulance coming. I want them to look at your arm and Tillie's shoulder."

They gathered around Sidney.

Pete Hornig showed up just as Sidney and Tillie began to tell their stories to Sam. "Nora Woodman. I never would have guessed that. Talk about having something come out of left field." Hornig took off his hat and rubbed his head as he spoke.

"It was coming together, though," offered Sidney. "Over the past two days, we found enough links to make her the center of attention."

"This morning, Ray and Detective Knott put some pieces together in my office as well. Now, if we can figure out where she is."

Sidney answered, "I know where she is."

Everyone looked at him and asked together, "Where?'

"Marshlands Plantation."

FORTY-SIX

2018
Nora Woodman

Nora clambered over the back fence of the condominium property and ran to her car. She pulled away from the curb within minutes of Sam getting back to Hampton's police cruiser.

She had to get away.

She had to get to her safe place.

She had to go home.

She went straight to Marshlands Plantation.

She whipped the steering wheel to the left and parked near a grove of trees just off the dirt road that went down to the old rice fields. It was there she had attacked Martin Tucker after railing against him as being part of the Tookerman family tree and learning of the changes he presented to the town planning board. Changes designed to steal Marshlands again from her family.

In the other direction, where the road was more visible and where the indigo once grew, she had left the body of Dorinda Tooker, who had declared herself a proud member of both the Winslow and Tookerman families.

Her plan had been to place the body of Gloria Rye where she now stood, as she believed this place to be where the original slave quarters were. A place where all members of Jamaica's family belonged, back into slavery.

Off to the left stood another grove of trees. It contained the original footings of the house Eli Nichols built almost three hundred years ago. Martin Tucker had promised her she could have all three locations for the home he would build for her. Marshlands Plantation would finally be in Nichols family hands. The million-dollar inheritance received from her grandfather, which she gave to Martin Tucker as an investment in SAR Heritage LLC, would guarantee it.

Nora sat on the grass under a tree, the poker in her lap and the pistol in her right hand.

A soft December rain began to fall and mixed with the late afternoon fog drifting in from the nearby waters of the Lowcountry as she stared at the place where the Marshlands Plantation house once stood.

While the police continued to search for Nora Woodman, Tillie and Sidney headed for Marshlands Plantation. Sam had become so involved in coordinating the search effort with Chief Hornig, it didn't register, and he dismissed them with a wave of his hand. Sidney, uncomfortable about going on their own and worried about the condition of Tillie's shoulder, called Ray at police headquarters, explained what had happened and their plan to go to Marshlands. Ray objected but knew they would go anyway, so he told them not to do anything until he arrived with Detective Knott.

Tillie drove slowly along the dirt road. The intermittent setting of the windshield wipers occasionally made a soft sweeping sound. They searched for Nora's car and spoke little as they made their way through the fog and mist toward the site of the old plantation. Seeing Tillie occasionally wince in pain as she drove, he asked about her shoulder and she merely said, "It's nothin'. Just a little stiff is all."

Sidney cautioned, "Let's stop. If she is here, I don't want her to see us before Ray arrives." Peering through the growing darkness, Sidney spotted a grouping of palmettos under trees to his right. "How about over there?"

Tillie eased the car off the road and drove slowly to the spot Sidney suggested. "Now what?" she asked.

"I'll call Ray and tell him where we are."

A short distance down the road, Nora continued to sit under her tree… dreaming. She envisioned the old plantation as it must have been. Mary Wilson-Nichols sat on the front porch holding one of her children on her lap. A female slave swept the porch at the far end. Eli Nichols looked at more slaves working in the rice field. A young man on horseback, Sean Wilson-Nichols, Mary's son, rode toward the house. For Nora, the idealized scene brought a smile to her face. But then it darkened as a tall male slave, Jamaica, Jamie, who would become known as James Bailey, came around the side of the house and walked toward the oncoming rider. A female slave carrying a baby in her arms walked with Jamaica. Nora set her jaw and tightened her grip on the pistol.

Less than fifty yards away in the fog, Sidney and Tillie stood by the car and waited for Ray. Sidney spoke quietly. "Tell me something, Tillie. Why are you so certain I'm right and Nora is here?"

"I seen it before. We had a man near where I live who worked on the tomato farms and became so obsessed with his slave ancestors that he believed he was the… whatcha call it… reincarnation of three or four of them. He'd be working in the fields when he'd start having conversations with himself. Only it wasn't just himself, it was the three people inside him. He would disappear sometimes, but his daughter always knew where to find him. In the woods near where they lived. She said he claimed it was the praying ground of his ancestors. A safe place the plantation owner didn't know about. It was *their* safe place, and it became his. I figure you're right, and Marshlands Plantation is Nora's safe place. This is where she would come. Now if she's not crazy in the head and she committed those murders on purpose because of some sort of grudge she had against those people, then I'm wrong and she won't be here. But I got a feeling I'm right."

Sidney looked at her for a moment and said, "I'm sure you are right. How's that shoulder?"

Tillie shook her shoulders and scrunched up her face a bit. "It's okay. Didn't break the skin. Ruined a good jacket, though. Probably going to have a bruise. Glad you made a grab at the poker. Didn't hurt your hand, did you, Professor?"

"Now, Tillie. I thought we agreed you would call me Sidney when we're alone. And no, my hand's just fine."

"Oh, yeah. Sorry Profess…. Hah. Old habits." She gave a quiet laugh. "Tough to break."

Sidney stepped forward and put his arm around her. "If we're going to be partners," he said, "we need to be on a first name basis."

"Yeah, I know." She lifted her head and whispered, "I hear something."

Sidney looked about. "Coming from in front of us or behind?"

"Behind."

"I imagine that's Ray. I'm sure we didn't get here before Nora."

They stood by the car and looked down the road. A car without lights came slowly through the fog toward them. It was Ray, with Detective Knott sitting next to him.

<hr>

Nora didn't hear Ray's car, but she felt uncomfortable and got up from her seat under the large live oak tree and looked toward the road. The light, misting rain and fog obscured her view and, although she neither heard nor saw anyone, she decided to move her car to the grove of trees where she believed the original plantation house once stood.

Ray, spotting Sidney and Tillie standing under a nearby tree, quietly drove across the soft grass and parked behind them.

Careful to not make a noise when exiting his car, Ray whispered when he reached Sidney's. "I asked Wilson to come along, as he's done a lot of research on Marshlands Plantation while investigating SAR Heritage and Mitchell Bennett."

Wilson added, "And no, I'm not related to the Wilson-Nichols of Marshlands. My mother is Mary Wilson. She was born in Castleisland, County Kerry and came to the United States after the Second World War. Although with all that's been going on, I can understand why the name might send up some red flags."

Sidney smiled as he said, "I'm glad you understand."

Ray, seeing the issue solved, got to the point. "Update us on what's going on."

Sidney went through the entire string of events and gave specific emphasis on Nora's rambling in three voices.

"Wow. I would never have guessed any of this. She always seemed so nice. Very helpful in the library. I guess we now know why she was so helpful. Tillie, you really think she's here? I checked with Sam a few minutes ago, and she definitely left the area around the condo."

"Yes, I do, Mr. Ray. Do you know where the main house would be? I believe that's where she'd be."

Wilson replied, "I brought a couple of maps with me that we put together based on what Mitchell Bennett told us about the development they planned to build in here. It was originally approved for three-to-five-acre homesites with a recreation of the Plantation layout. That all changed recently, by the way; Martin Tucker, our first victim, put in a request for the lot sizes to be dropped down to a half-acre, and condos and townhouses would be added. Also, they weren't going to recreate the historic original site of the plantation but were going to make that area into a clubhouse, pool, and tennis court and put up a plaque mentioning the Marshlands Plantation."

Ray added, "Not unusual for developments around here. Get the initial approval according to the rules, then get it changed so they can put more saleable units in and make a killing. City Council objects at first but then starts drooling at the new tax revenue potential."

"Let's see those maps," Sidney said. "If Nora is here, I wonder how close she is?"

Nora left her car where she parked it and walked to the site of the original plantation house. The fog hovered above her and the mist fell on her face. It felt good, as Nora believed she now experienced what her ancestors felt, the raw nature of the place. Being so absorbed by her surroundings and having moved farther from where she parked, she didn't hear the sound of the car doors closing and whispering voices a quarter of a mile behind her.

Sidney, Tillie, Ray, and Knott drove cautiously through the fog. Ray's car led the way, with Knott in the passenger seat holding the map.

"From what I can tell, the slave quarters would be up here on our right somewhere. The original house would have been another eighth of a mile beyond that on the left. There's no road to these places, just some tree groupings. Looks like there should be some very old live oak trees around the sites. They're probably three to four hundred years old. Visibility's getting worse in this fog. Being back on standard time isn't helping us."

Ray slowed his car to a crawl. "I think I see a car up ahead. I think we should stop. Turn your radio on low and let Sam know we may have found her. Tell him to approach slow and quiet."

Tillie followed Ray's example and stopped behind them. "They must see something, Prof…. Damn, I ain't never gonna get this right. Sidney. There, I said it."

Sidney smiled broadly and chuckled quietly in the passenger seat. "Thank you." He looked to his left and asked, "Can you see anything?"

"No. This weather is makin' it tough to see too far."

"Looks like they're getting out. Detective Knott is on his radio so they must see something."

Tillie noticed how quietly Ray and Knott closed the doors to their car, so she did the same. Sidney, having trouble exiting, took longer and when he tried to follow everyone's example, he slipped on the wet grass, lost his footing, and in an attempt to keep from falling, reached for the door handle, missed it, and caused the door to slam shut. Everyone jumped at the noise.

Nora heard it too. She looked back in the direction she came from. She couldn't see anyone in the now thick fog and receding light.

She removed the pistol from the pouch of her sweatshirt, took aim and fired at where she believed the slave Jamaica would be.

The bullet hit a tree ten yards to the left of Ray and he and Knott dropped to the ground, but both registered the location of the flash in the distance. Tillie also took cover and saw the flash, but Sidney just stood by the car door. He heard the sound and flinched a bit. Sidney had never been shot at, ever. Dropping to his knees never occurred to him, especially as he just tried to save himself from a fall.

"Get back in the car," Tillie whispered to him.

Ray and Knott moved behind their car, where Tillie joined them. All three were now in the space between the rear bumper of one car and the front bumper of the other, crouching slightly.

Ray whispered, "Everybody okay?"

Tillie and Knott nodded. Sidney stood behind the open car door, using it as cover.

"Professor's okay," Tillie whispered.

Knott texted Sam: *Shots fired.* He then said to Ray, "What now?"

"You see the flash?"

Knott answered, "Yeah."

"Based on your map, where would that be?"

"Between the slave quarters and the house."

Tillie couldn't resist. "She's goin' home. Like the professor said."

Ray answered, "You're right, as usual."

Sidney, with the door still open, asked, "What are you going to do?"

Ray answered in a low voice, "Stay here until help comes. She can't see any better than we can. It's late afternoon and will be completely dark soon. We just keep quiet. She has no idea who we are or even if we're really here."

Sidney shifted from foot to foot, considering what Ray said. "Let me talk with her."

Tillie shook her head. "Oh, no. That lady's crazy. I know you want to help but she doesn't even know who she is, and she certainly won't know who you are. And if she does, she might shoot you anyway."

Both Knott and Ray looked at Sidney in disbelief.

"I understand that, Tillie. The woman needs help. In a few minutes, sirens and flashing lights will be all over this place. I'm sure she'll panic, and the police will respond with full force."

"As they should," Knott said. "Professor Lake, Nora Woodman killed three people, and a few minutes ago she was prepared to kill four more. You included. We can't take the chance she'll get away and attempt to kill someone else."

Sidney stepped away from the car and his friends and yelled out to Nora, "Mrs. Nichols. Mrs. Mary Wilson Nichols. Are you there? This is Professor Sidney Lake. I have good news about Marshlands Plantation."

Silence.

Sidney whispered over his shoulder as Tillie, Ray, and Knott looked at him in dismay. "I have to give it a chance."

Silence.

Then came, "Professor Lake. What news do you have for me?"

"The developers are reverting to the original plan for the recreation of Marshlands Plantation. Everything will be as it should. We have a map to show you where everything will be. Can we talk?"

Silence from the mist.

In the distance, a police siren could be heard.

Nora answered, "Are you sure? The family's been waiting a long time."

Sidney whispered to Ray, "Confirm what I said."

Ray shook his head but agreed. "This is Ray Morton of the county solicitor's office. I have the map with me that Professor Lake mentioned. If you just come with us, I'm sure we can get everything straightened out."

Ray tapped Knott on the shoulder and indicated for him to go around to the right side of the car they were behind. He then whispered, "I think I see her.

Off to the left near some trees. The fog is starting to lift. You two get behind the right side of your car," he said to Tillie and Sidney. Looking carefully at Nora as she came into view he said, "I'm over here by the car. There's no need for the gun." Ray could make out she held something in her right hand. "We just need to talk. We're going to need your advice on some things."

Nora moved forward. "Is Professor Lake still with you?"

Sidney answered, "Yes, I'm here. Marshlands will finally be recognized as yours."

She moved closer, holding the poker in her left hand. Her right hand was stuffed in her sweatshirt pouch. The brim of her cap concealed her eyes as she watched her step on the uneven ground.

Detective Knott moved carefully around the front of the car, staying as low as possible in his crouch. *Just a little bit closer, Nora, just a little bit closer.*

A touch of light peeked through in the western sky.

Sirens drew closer, and Nora stopped. She looked up at the cars protecting Ray, Sidney, and Tillie and then to her right where the sirens wailed.

"Over here, Mrs. Nichols," encouraged Sidney, peeking over the top of the car.

Nora stood no more than ten yards from Sidney but only six or seven from where Detective Knott hid.

The sirens became louder and a flash of red and blue burst out of the wooded area a half mile down the road. It caught her eye, and she turned toward it, her back to Knott.

Knott made his move and ran at her.

Tillie had a rock in her hand and threw it at Nora.

Nora heard Knott coming and started to pull the gun out as she turned but saw the rock coming at her. Confused, she ducked. The gun discharged. The bullet hit her in the ankle as Knott slammed her with a blind-sided tackle, which lifted her into the air and drove her to the ground.

FORTY-SEVEN

2018
Questions Answered

Ray pulled up a chair to the large umbrella-shaded table outside the City Hall Café. Being a typical early December day in the Lowcountry, the midday sun at sixty degrees felt warm and comfortable. He sat down and waved to Sam, who came out the door from the main part of the restaurant. Tillie, Sidney, and Mickey arrived shortly thereafter by the walkway from the sidewalk.

"Back to normal finally?" asked Ray.

"Pretty much," Sam said. "That woman sure ripped this town apart. I can't imagine one generation of a family continuing to indoctrinate the next and having it go on for 300 years."

Sidney, now at the table, couldn't resist. "Human beings seem to be very susceptible to such indoctrination. Religion, warfare, political ideology, they all prey upon our innate desires to obtain the unattainable while we hold on to the dream of achieving it. I've asked Mrs. DeReimer from the library to joins us. She has additional information she thought would be of interest."

"What about Hattie Ryan? Is she coming?"

"No. She had a previous engagement with our appraiser friend, Burke Mansfield."

"Oh," commented Tillie with a smile and a raised eyebrow.

The waiter arrived to take orders. Ray ignored Sidney's indoctrination comment, as he wanted to ask the question he was dying to get answered. "What happened to the treasure? The thing that started all this."

"We found it," said Sam. "Why don't we wait for Mrs. DeReimer—here she is."

Sidney started to stand, only to have the librarian wave at him to stay in place. Tillie grabbed his arm to keep him there. Mrs. DeReimer took the open chair next to Sam.

"We're just ordering. What'll you have? Sidney's buying so don't be bashful," a smiling Ray suggested. Chuckles made their way around the table.

After ordering, Mrs. DeReimer directed a question to both Ray and Sam, "Now that this nightmare is over, what will happen to Nora? In some ways, I feel quite sorry for her. She too could be considered a victim, couldn't she?"

Sam looked first at Ray, who simply said, "The floor is all yours, Detective."

Taking a deep breath and clearing his throat, Sam began. "First, Mayor Wilcox resigned last night. Although he never officially lied to the police, his withholding information made our task more difficult than it should have been. His attorney is trying to work out some sort of deal to keep formal charges from being filed against him for obstruction. It has become clear that Tucker's reneging on the agreement to make a mini–Marshlands Plantation for Nora Woodman put her over the edge. From her perspective, the consortium of a Tookerman, a Winslow, and a Bailey had done it to the Nichols family again. Woodman's in psychiatric care at the moment. I wouldn't be surprised if she never gets to trial."

Sidney had an unanswered question. "Have the police figured out who the third man was? He seemed to be the instigator of the treasure theory."

"We have some people we're looking to as the possible third person behind the library search, which originally had nothing to do with any treasure. Mitchell Bennett believed there was an accurate description of the boundaries of the local Bailey Plantation contained in the books at the Palmer but claims there was no intention to steal them. That was Tucker's idea. Swift claimed Skinny told him about the treasure. We can't prove Bennett was our third man, but it's still a possibility."

Tillie added, "As I see it, that Miss Woodman seems to have missed an important fact. Her own blood relative was the cause of everything."

Ray's head popped up. "Who?"

"That Liam fella who made them promise to get even and take back Marshland's was actually the son of Patrick Nichols, who wasn't a Nichols at all. Remember Patrick was the son of a slave mother who the oral histories claim was Jamaica's daughter and probably the Sean Wilson guy was the father. That all makes Nora Woodman a Bailey and a Wilson. She ain't got no Nichols blood."

Sidney had a mischievous smile as he picked up his coffee cup.

A few minutes later, with the food and drinks out of the way, Sam followed up on the original question and said to Mrs. DeReimer., "Ray asked about the treasure box and I told him you found it for us."

"Yes and no. I merely provided the historical accuracy as to where it would be, if it existed. Everyone kept looking for it on the old Bailey plantation outside of Morgan, not far from Colonial Fort Morgan. It couldn't possibly be there, as the plantation did not exist until the Yemassee people had been eliminated, and that didn't occur until well after the pirate Stede Bonnet and his crew were hanged in old Charles Town. The Bailey family had three plantations with the one here in Morgan being the last established. Everyone should have been looking at Fort Dorchester where Joshua Bailey had a warehouse in support of his plantation on the Ashley River. Both Stede Bonnet and Joshua Bailey were born on the island of Barbados, as many of the early settlers here were, and there may have been a family connection."

"I'm not surprised at that, as so many of the early settlers came to the Carolinas from the British colonies in the Caribbean," Sidney said. "I received quite an education from Dr. Leeseman over the past few days."

Sam leaned forward. "But how did you know the box could be found at the location of the original Bailey warehouse?"

Mrs. DeReimer shifted her chair to become more comfortable. "That information was provided by the documentation the late Gloria Rye had discovered about her ancestor, the original slave Jamaica. He taught himself to write. Something he was very proud of, although he tried to keep it a secret. It was a skill I'm sure gave Joshua Bailey great concern but later endorsed seeing its value in running the warehouse. Bonnet's box had been given to Jamaica to bury. He made a note of the location, which Mrs. Rye found in an old trunk. Apparently, she didn't know its significance."

"What was the treasure?" Ray asked. "Was it still intact? How did the box and its contents remain viable after being in the ground all these years?"

"Oh, that's an easy one. In the South Carolina Room, we have many old books and manuscripts that came through being buried a long time, as well as contents of boxes that survived sunken ships. At the time they were referred to as 'library boxes'. They were airtight and waterproof. Specially treated oil cloth kept the air and water out and was a wonderful preservative. No person of wealth coming to the colonies by boat would consider packing anything of value in anything other than a library box. We have such boxes in the archives. I also believe there are a few on display at the local museum."

"I bet I know what the actual treasure was," said Sidney.

"Gold and silver coins, right? That's what pirate treasure is all about."

"Ray, you watch too much television. I would be very surprised if it didn't contain books."

"Books, Sidney? Books? We're talking about a pirate. I'm sure the slave Jamaica was far more literate than any pirate of his day."

Sidney paused for effect momentarily before he said, "Yes, that is true, except for one particular pirate named Stede Bonnet. He was an abnormal one. Well known to be a very learned aristocratic pirate nicknamed the 'gentleman pirate' by his friends and enemies. One who enjoyed the turning of a page and intellectual pursuits as well as the fingering of gold and silver. What do you say, Mrs. DeReimer?"

With a gentle smile on her face, she reached down and brought her handbag up to her lap. "You're absolutely right, Professor. I brought a list of the contents with me." She removed a sheet of paper and read:

"The treasure:

Don Quixote by Miguel de Cervantes Saavedra

Paradise Lost by John Milton

Areopagitica by John Milton

The Pilgrim's Progress by John Bunyan

Dr. Faustus by Christopher Marlowe

Pensées by Blaise Pascal

Discourse on Method and Meditations on First Philosophy by René Descartes

John Donne's Poetry by John Donne

Ethics by Baruch Spinoza

Dialogue Concerning the Two Chief World Systems by Galileo Galilei

Two Treatises of Government by John Locke

A Letter Concerning Toleration by John Locke

Bartholomew Fair by Ben Johnson

Every Man in his Humor by Ben Johnson

The New Atlantis by Francis Bacon

"Keep in mind, these are all current editions of the time. First printings, if you will. I'm sure they're worth a great deal more than the total of any gold and silver coins you might have thought would be in the box."

After a few minutes of trying to put a dollar amount on the books, Ray looked at Sidney. "Now that you're back to boring retirement, what's next?"

Before answering, Sidney gave Mickey, lying beside his chair, a pat on the head and then a nod to Tillie. "First, Tillie has finally convinced me to follow doctor's orders, including a couple of specialists at the Medical University of South Carolina, and get my right leg fixed. Then, as part of the recoateration and rehabilitation, Mickey, Tillie, and I are heading to the Bahamas."

THE END

Resource List

Brodie, Fawn M., Thomas Jefferson – An Intimate History, W.W Norton & Co

Chernow, Ron, Washington, A life, The Penguin Press

Eastman, Carolyn, Douglas R Burgess, John R. Coakley, The Golden Age of Piracy, University of Georgia Press

Edgar, Walter, South Carolina – A History, Univ, of South Carolina Press

Ellis, Joseph H., American Creation, Alfred A. Knoph

Foote, Shelby, Stars in their Courses-Gettysburg, Modern Library

Foote, Shelby, The Civil War, Random House

Irving, Washington, Life of George Washington, Sleepy Hollow Restorations

Larson, Edward J., A Magnificent Catastrophe, Simon & Schuster

Lemann, Nicholas, Redemption, Ferrar, Straus and Giroux

McCullough, David, 1776, Simon & Schuster

McCullough, Davis, John Adams, Simon & Schuster

Meacham, Jon, American Lion, Random House

Meacham, Jon, Thomas Jefferson – the Art of Power, Random House

Mitchell, Broadus, Alexandr Hamilton – A Concise Biography

Roberts, Cokie, Founding Mothers, Harper Collins

Rowland, Lawrence S., Alexander Moore, George C. Rogers, Jr., The History of Beaufort County, South Carolina, Volume 1, 1514-1861

Rutland, Robert A., James Madison – The Founding Father, Macmillan

Shepard, Jack, The Adams Chronicles, Little, Brown & Company

Wright, Esmond, Franklin of Philadelphia, Harvard University Press.

Other resources:
The 1619 Project, The New York Times

Tim Holland is the author of four Sidney Lake Lowcountry Mysteries, including *The Rising Tide, The Murder of Amos Dunn, Deception,* and *December Rain*. In addition, he authored *What the Mirror Doesn't See*, a mystery set in the world of banking. He is a director of the Williamsburg Book Festival, a past director of Chesapeake Bay Writers, a member of Mystery Writers of America, and The Brontë Society of Haworth, England. He has received Keating and Golden Nib awards for his short fiction. Over the years, his freelance articles have appeared in a wide variety of newspapers and magazines, and he also wrote book reviews and literary criticism for Recorder Publishing's eight newspapers in New Jersey (while working in New York in the world of global trade finance). He has given speeches and presentations in 12 countries and 22 states and served as president of the lifelong learning program at the University of South Carolina Beaufort, where he also taught a course on the Brontë sisters. Visit him at www.tim-holland.com.